D1732469

J.W. DURRAH

JACOB THE JEW IN PURSUIT OF THE

ASIAN BLOOD MERCHANTS

BOOK ONE
of a Jacob the Jew Trilogy

REVISED AND ABRIDGED

ISBN: 978-1-09836-116-7

CONTENTS

DEDICATIONS

This book is dedicated to my mother
Bennie Mae (Johnson) Durrah
Who, at times of peril, I always feel
Is there protecting me.
Thank you, Mama.
I love you.

ACKNOWLEDGMENTS

I thank my grandmother, Elizabeth B. Jefferson, my friends, and neighbors in Winston Salem, North Carolina. Also, I thank the indigenous people of Taiwan, Japan, Singapore, and Korea, whom I was privileged to meet and be invited into their homes, where I enjoyed their and their families' wonderful hospitality.

I also offer a very special acknowledgment and "thank you" to Mother Riley of 2811-13 Eighth Avenue in New York City. We young boys feared you and your powers, but what you prognosticated for me oh-those-many years ago has indeed become true; and I thank you for the knowledge you gave me that day in your very, very special room of white.

CHAPTER 1

THE CAVES OF NO RETURN

Things were fine for years, but then many tourists and local citizens began to disappear. At first it was attributed to careless cave exploring, but when bodies were found mutilated and more than half-eaten, superstitious village folk all painted causes of absolute terror: rumors of half human, transitory creatures who roam the caves and whom the spelunkers disturbed in the midst of it devouring a female explorer. The hysterical rescue team member who interrupted the creature's meal said he has never seen such a horrible looking entity in his life and that it chased him to within fifty yards of the cave' entrance. All in all, twenty five bodies were recovered—well, almost recovered. Several of the bodies were unidentifiable due to their being so little of the corpse left. It did not take long for superstitious townsfolk to name the site: "The caves of no return," and for the next twenty years the caves continued to be a pariah for all who knew of their eerie past.

Jiao could hardly believe his good fortune of being told of the cave, Jiao was hardly able to believe his fortune in finding such an area as this that was also bathed in such a perfect silence; it all seemed to him to be something well beyond a thing remarkable, rather he considered it all to be bordering, he thought, perhaps on a matter most miraculous. And he certainly had no difficulty in finding the series of caves and one there, the sign left absolutely no doubt as to it being the right location:

ENTRY STRICTLY FORBIDDEN
Prosecution rigorously enforced.
The Ministry of The Interior

Once inside the cave, Jiao stealthily moved deep into and through the dark caverns that snaked out into at least twenty different paths that splayed out leading to many entrances to a great number of caves.

He ventured a short way into one cave after another but not all the way inside. But then, after returning to the huge entrance of the cave he had first Jiao noticed what appeared to be a separation in one of the solid rock walls. Peering through the slit, he could see that on the other side of the wall there was some light source and he pushed and squeezed through the slight space until he was on the other side of the wall and standing in a large room; the light he had seen was coming from the luminous walls of the cave itself.

The very special thing about this part of the bowels of this mountainous edifice of forlorn, gaping mouths was that this particular cave, this particular room that was well hidden within the maze of forsaken interiors. Jiao knew at that he could continue trudging relentlessly through corridor after corridor seeking the perfect area to convert into a holy room for his continuing practice of sorcery but none was ever going to be more perfect that the one he was standing in.

He walked about the area, examining the almost pristine space he just found; Jiao shone his flashlight up at the ceiling and saw there were no bats roosting, the walls and ground were smooth, not water soaked or gravelly; they were even, no bugs or snakes scurrying about their surfaces.

There were no bats fussing with one another using their rubbery wings to slap about as they squeal noisily positioning themselves for space. There were no snakes or rodents moving stealthily about.

Here in this untraveled, abandoned and forbidden area of desolate emptiness, Jiao, after having traversed interior terrain clearly hostile to all footing and daring to step deep and continuously along the winding pathway of the convoluted folds of these magnificent caves and daring to thrust himself through a sliver of a "vaginal" opening in the stone discovered that such a separation was situated there to facilitate his "giving birth" to the creation of his "holy room of worship."

He knew that the spirits had directed him to find this room and so he knelt and gave thanks to them by first striking his chest in a most profound manner that caused the very walls surrounding to shudder and threatened to dissemble. Then Jiao began to walk about the room, pounding his seemingly leaden fist into sections of it, crumbling and reassembling parts of it to fashion it into his vision, his "Holy room of prayer."

The cave is fastidiously cloaked in a luminous dimness which appeared to come to life when Jiao roared out thundering commands in a language the walls understood and so they all dissembled and reassembled themselves in the faint but increasing light until each of Jiao's demands were completed and were now the construct, the very shape of his dreams.

Seeing that all had been completed, Jiao knelt again and smiled, opening his arms wide seeing that one large area of wall was now shelving with a prominent, newly carved altar jutting out with deep, long furrows at its base for those who would kneel before it. For those who would sit cross-legged, there were a few wide, and rounded pits, not deep, but comfortably sunken for purposes of worship.

He exited the cave momentarily to retrieve his canvas bag that he dropped outside his cave in order to achieve entrance, once again he squeezed through the opening that was now became noticeably wider when he neared it. When he had passed through and was back inside, he saw that the opening had closed again to less than a sliver, an opening no person would ever fit through.

Jiao smiled, knowing that the opening now "knew" him and understood that only those with true purpose and blessing would ever be able to enter. He knew that the cave was from this point on, was forever closed to all infidels.

Next, Jiao removed objects from his bag that he gently placed on the altar: the first was an exceptionally thick, deeply blue, rectangular candle that he lit with a touch of his finger. A brilliant flash from the candle swallowed all the darkness immediately replacing it with a searing white that was blinding, even to Jiao. But just as quickly it dimmed to a pleasant glow from its wick and this from the white flame that danced over the top of the candle.

Jiao smiled. He knew that from that moment on this candle would be the only source of never ending light in the huge space. Nothing now, no power on earth, other than Jiao's command could ever cause it to be extinguished.

Jiao next placed a large candelabra holding thirteen black candles on the altar, lighting each of the candles: each of them emitting a blue flame. After saying a solemn prayer over them, he then, with a quiet whoosh of air, extinguished each candle.

Then, with extreme reverence and ceremony, Jiao retrieved from his bag, five leather bound volumes, each of them the thickness of a laborer's balled fist. These volumes are the teachings Jiao has been embroiled in for all of his life, these precious secrets of sorcery, each page scribed painstakingly in blood were to be the source of instruction for his son Baofung starting on his eighth birthday as Jiao had been taught by his father starting on his eight birthday. Finally, Jiao placed several bowls of food on the altar as offerings; Into five glasses Jiao poured different whiskies and wines; all of these items were for the pleasure of all visiting spirits.

And so, he was done.

Jiao knew that there was little chance of human trespass since rumors were rife then and even now that the cave houses supernatural entities within them. He dropped to his knees almost without his will to do so an thanked the gods bringing him here to this perfect area.

Then, on Baofung's eighth birthday, his father told him the story of his discovery of the cave and brought him to it; and then began Baofung's instruction in sorcery.

Baofung and his friend, Wo-Ling, both of whom shared the same day and precise hour of birth had long ago declared such a matter as far more than a coincidence; they were sure that their friendship was a sign from higher powers and vowed to protect the welfare of each other for as long as they both lived; and so, upon this sacred vow, they shared everything and were inseparable.

So it was understandable that Baofung wanted to share with his friend Wo-Ling the secrets of sorcery. And one day Baofung managed to gather the courage to ask his father for his permission to allow him to bring his friend Wo-Ling to visit their cave of worship and to introduce him to sorcery.

But he made it clear that it would not be for the purpose of Wo-Ling ever practicing sorcery, or for learning it on any level of expertise, it would be merely for the experience of him being exposed to such overwhelming knowledge and to develop a real appreciation for the terrifying powers sorcery provides to certain practitioners.

After studying his son's face for several minutes, he granted him permission to bring Wo-Ling to the cave, but never on the three days Baofung was receiving instruction. But his father made it very clear that if Baofung's friend Wo-Ling ever committed any offense against the "order" that Baofung would be entirely to blame for it and so would pay the dire price along with Wo-Ling for any such nonobservance; and in the end, his father solemnly advised his son, he and his friend would not be the only ones to pay for any transgression…he, Baofung's father, would also pay the horrible price, a punishment that his father said was too terrible to describe to his son. Readily agreeing, he brought his best friend Wo-Ling Cheung into his father's holy room to show and introduce him to the many methodologies of sorcery. His father told him that he was allowed to explain sorcery to him and to let him read from some of the sacred texts from which he was being taught.

Baofung wondered whether the thin slit in the cave rock was going to widen to accept Wo-Ling as it always did for Baofung and his father. Jiao assured his son that the opening will accept his friend Wo-Ling as long as Baofung was with him, but never if Wo-Ling is alone. And so once again Baofung's father reminded him that it is okay for his friend to learn some of the aspects of sorcery, but he must never practice it. Never attempt any of the spells or wonders he has been shown by Baofung, even the simplest, seemingly most harmless spell. He reminds his son that the punishment would be unimaginable torment heaped upon the two of them, both Wo-Ling and also on Baofung for allowing a traitor's inferior mind to be "bathed" in the "never ending light of all impossible knowledge of sorcery only to be betrayed."

Presently, eight-year-old Baofung gingerly opened he hardcover of the volume in front of them opened the hardcover of the volume in front of them and gently turned to a page filled with drawings of a human eye, with labels in Cantonese characters describing functions and special powers within it when a person has the necessary knowledge to harness them.

Baofung explained to his friend that those drawings illustrated the many weaknesses as well as strengths of each part of the human eye and the myriad powers different parts of the eye has and how those powers can be harnessed by a knowledgeable person, to be used for or against another person—to heal or destroy someone by a simple look.

Then, Baofung turned to his friend and asked him to touch the volume. Wo-Ling, clearly reticent to even consider doing such a thing, and though he trusts his friend Baofung, he still asks, "Is it okay?"

Baofung smiles and nods his head, saying,

"Yes"

"But I don't want to learn sorcery for hurting people. Besides, I'm kind of afraid of magic," Wo-Ling said, nervously.

"I never said it is a complete lesson, only some of the knowledge of the magic that is boundless and goes on forever in all ways; in this way, you will soon learn not to be so afraid of what you think of as magic," Baofung replied.

Wo-Ling Cheung did not understand the purpose of his touching the volume if not to learn sorcery. But, again, trusting his friend, he tremulously took his hand, which hovered over the volume, but before lowering it, he looked at his friend for assurance.

Baofung smiled warmly and nodded,

"Lower your hand."

He lowered his hand to touch the volume. The moment his fingers made contact, there was a blinding white flash of light that illuminated the room and a giant man appeared on the opposite side of the ebony table and candles, causing Wo-Ling to wet his pant. Then, the giant man spoke to him, "And so, little one, the circle of your aura is not yet separated and so shall remain true to the words you have agreed to and that is seen clearly by me here and in this place and at this time. Be as one, my two children."

Then, the giant was gone. Wo-Ling begins trembling so badly that Baofung holds him to calm him. Then, he explains, "That spirit we just saw is the True Master of all sorcery. And when someone who is not properly invited to see and touch this volume, he will appear the moment the volume is touched and decides the intruder's punishment. All the punishment will be terrible and lasting. But you are my friend, my true friend, and he knows that and I knew you are safe within these walls as long as you are properly invited."

Then, Baofung smoothly closed the cover of the volume and placed it back near the others. He sat next to Wo-Ling again and reassured him,

"You and I will visit this place many more times over the years and I will continue showing you some sorcery but not be for you to practice; you must never try to use it. I am your forever friend and if such magic is ever needed by you for justice of your design, you will call upon me to request that it is done. But then I shall be the one who decides if the magic needs to be done. But never can this be done as matters of caprice. And don't worry, my friend; one day, as you progress in your education in this holy place, I think you will be more amazed than afraid."

Wo-Ling, who'd grown much calmer by then, agrees,

"Yes, maybe so."

Many years later, as adults, Baofung is now well-known as one of the few practitioners who're given the title of Supreme Master Sorcerer; at that time, his friend Wo-Ling Cheung, has become Dr. Wo-Ling Cheung, a Harvard educated Research Chemist and like Baofung, and is living in Hong Kong, after having earned and completed his studies on a full scholarship to Harvard University in America. After completing his studies abroad and returning as Dr. Wo-Ling Cheung, he received great praise from the government and was granted an enviable and newly created position as Master Research Chemist. For the next several years, Wo-Ling is treated with great reverence and decorated by the Chinese Government for the several vaccines and medicines he had discovered during the past next twenty years of his independent medical research. He retires to his private practice, but still holds the highest position as Master Research Chemist in Hong Kong and continues to work a few days a week in his labs in two of Hong Kong's largest hospitals where he is allowed to continue his medical research.

Thanks to his uncanny memory, Dr. Cheung as a result of his friendship with Baofung is also the surreptitious holder of an unusually broad and comprehensive knowledge of sorcery for one who does not practice it; but his friendship with Baofung over the past thirty years has never for a moment weakened.

Sorcery and medicine, in many aspects, Dr. Wo-Ling Cheung has discovered, coincided at certain junctures in rather spectacular ways. But never for a moment had he even considered breaking his vow to his friend Baofung to never practice sorcery, in any manner and on any level though he felt capable of doing so.

There was little doubt of that ever happening because although Wo-Ling had gotten over his fear of sorcery and most of the magic he has been shown, but he is still in awe of what seemed an infinite depth of magic within the realm of sorcery; and so, he was approaching this evening with Baofung with an appreciable amount of trepidation.

This session was to be a very special night. Baofung promised to show Wo-Ling some profoundly dark secrets of sorcery and some of its most horrific spells and reality defying incantations. And as he knelt at the altar next to his friend, Wo-Ling felt chills rushing up and down his arms and back and a strange desire to run out of the room into the surrounding caves knowing that he would become instantly lost but free of an all-consuming anxiety.

Baofung opened one of the volumes to a section that had adjoining page illustrations of the human eye in great detail. Baofung explained to Wo-Ling that the drawings illustrated the many weaknesses as well as strengths of each part of the human eye and the myriad powers to be derived from different parts of the eye by "grand focus." It teaches how to disable or destroy a person by simply looking at him; such focus also enables the sorcerer to destroy inanimate objects or any life form. It can also be used to heal a sick person, something it would be chiefly used for. This "grand focus," however, generally takes close to a lifetime to achieve. Baofung explains further that:

"The reason it takes so long to acquire this skill is that it is a desired and often necessary weapon for an aged sorcerer who is otherwise incapable of defending himself or herself from an assailant he is otherwise powerless to defend himself against."

After spending time on the powers within the eye, Baofung became noticeably disquieted as he closed the volume and opened another one. He placed the volume closer to his friend and said to him:

"Read this with me, Wo-Ling…and be afraid, for this is the one instance where those with my title of 'Wielder of The Way' are moving within the most holy of all precincts: the creation of a life. Unless I am mistaken, I believe that only five Supreme Sorcerers have been chosen to deserve the title I have been so honored. We are the only holy ones allowed to pursue that which is written upon these next few pages:" Baofung very gently smoothed the page and then he and Wo-Ling begin reading aloud together:

'CREATING *THE SHADOW DESCHONG*

A shadow deschong is always to be a female and cannot be created, defeated or exterminated except by the direct and ardent engaging and judicial use of those precious and magical abilities vested only in a Supreme Sorcerer or Sorceress who has achieved the rank of "Wielder of The Way." After the completion of the purpose of her "birth," she will be given an honorable death by her creator and although her "human body" will deteriorate, once she has moved beyond the mortal disguise of life and into what results in a semblance of death, she will be given a state of existence albeit in a most unnatural form, in a region beneath hell, where she is available to be summoned by magicians who may use her only as a spirit demoness with no powers other than a remarkable ability to terrify humans by assuming many forms horrific to human eyes.

However, if she has, on any level, committed an act of disobedience to her creator, then it is an affront that will never be excused and by such an offense she will have brought about her own quietus and will be returned to the abyss from whence the life essence placed into her is plucked; and that horrific place is a world of perpetual darkness, a region beneath hell that is too frightening, lewd and fearsome to name here.

As her punishment, the Shadow Deschong will be eliminated by her creator and then she will be consigned to remain in the dankest region of hell forever in some vulgarly fashioned pose of horrid petrification where verbose insults are endlessly heaped upon her by other condemned creatures. She will periodically scream from the pain of teeth, fangs and claws sinking into her flesh by tormenting horrors she cannot see in the total

darkness. And between her screams she will beg for final death but it will
never arrive as entities rip at her flesh tearing it asunder, flesh that only
moments later is replaced for more abuse at the pleasure of any passing
wretch deciding to indulge itself.

And so now, heed ye all these words: that upon this earth or even
within the depths of its bowels only a sorcerer or sorceress has the required
power to deceive, delay, or momentarily turn away a Shadow Deschong
from its duty to her creator by the most skillful use of sorcery or legendary
magic; nothing other while she is upon this earth, can invade and defeat
such a horrific veil of evil.

—Observation attributed to Abe No Semei (c. 921-1005)'

Baofung and Dr. Cheung finished reading the document.

"Yes, my friend, few practitioners of sorcery are known to have achieved the ultimate status of *'Wielder of The Way;'* This is an honor enabling me with the ability to turn a human female into this creature known as a *"Shadow Deschong."* This an entity that, during her existence lives in a two dimensional world of shadows. When not carrying out an assignment, her life is as a simple image, an innocuous black shadow immersed in the reflective silhouette of some object near it. Her creator can allow her to remain in this existence if he has another task for her to fulfill; otherwise, he is not permitted to continue her life here on this earth. And he is only entitled to two tasks for each Shadow Deshong."

Wo-Ling slowly nodded, but was fathoming things out when he asked:

"But what would she be used for?"

"More often than not, she will be instructed to perhaps drive a person to distraction, insanity, or suicide. The *shadow deschong* is also used as an assassin, a brief assignment that's simply a matter of the victim being located and then summarily destroyed. This is one of the few times a *shadow deschong* is allowed to take human shape due to the physicality needed for her assignment to be completed. When her task is finished she will be given to **Woequi,** as the human payment due her for granting the sorcerer, during my trip to hell, permission to create this entity. Woequi is a very powerful sorceress in hell that is sometimes referred to as, *The Divine Mistress of All Hell."*

Then, taking a moment to stand and walk about, Baofung studies his friend's features before kneeling again by his side. Then he whispers to Wo-Ling

"...You see, Wo-Ling, there are means for a human to find ways into hell, but if one wants to leave hell, then that requires the permission of a high-ranking demon or demoness of the region they have entered or Satan himself; of course, Satan will never grant such permission."

Dr. Cheung is transfixed by what Baofung has told and thinking about the many uses he could find for such a creature. Wo-Ling is startled by the suddenness of Baofung's voice:

"The shadow deschong has been known to turn herself human without permission from her creator for her own personal pleasures. This is a betrayal and the same way you must remain true to your word never to use sorcery..." Baofung's fingers traces over that part of what has been written, "it is written that absolutely no betrayal is ever forgiven and so she will be given to Woequi who awaits the disloyal creature; her garrison gathered behind her gnash their teeth and rip and tear off pieces of their own flesh in anticipation of serving out some of this horrible punishment. awaiting the offending deschong who betrays her master."

Dr. Cheung is thinking of what a magnificent enforcer the shadow deschong can be and he wonders:

"What are the limits of her power?"

"Whatever her creator chooses. She is never given any strong or dark powers. Perhaps we can think of her magic skills as beginner's magic. The strongest temporary magic she will have is to return herself to being fully human, but such a transition will be imperfect without her creator's touch, not much more than a crude resemblance in some cases. But without using much magic, a shadow deschong remains human for the most part and has use of her ingenuity to help her in carrying out her task. She is more likely to employ her human skills of trickery and deceit."

Dr. Cheung nods, "I see."

Baofung continued:

"When a deschong comes off the wall which is always the place it is to remain unless otherwise instructed by its creator, birth, so to speak…it is still two-dimensional, and such an appearance is frightening to humans and so she can use it to terrify, encourage heart attacks and so on; a 'reality separation,' a breakdown. As an assassin she can never be apprehended. And once she completes the task her master has given her, she returns to him."

Dr. Cheung was really impressed, and he says,

"This is fascinating."

Baofung nods and agreeing says:

"Indeed. If she serves her master loyally, she is rewarded by being sent to hell to Woequi and is likely rewarded by becoming a member of Woequi's horde of demons." Baofung smoothly closes the volume and bows his head.

Dr. Cheung knows that this has been the best of magic he has learned and remains fascinated. He looks at his friend whose head is now bent in prayer and he knows that Baofung will remain that way for the next hour as he sends out prayers of thanks to spirits.

And so, as always, Cheung remains at his friends side. He takes a deep breath and thinks back to his own personal experience with still another kind of magic the day that changed his life.

The fateful day that he met Welleck Chauncier….

CHAPTER 2

A CONSIGNMENT FOOLISHLY DREAMT OF WILL BE THUSLY DISTORTED

Cheung's breathing slows dramatically as he looks at the ashen face of the thick-bodied man sitting across from him at the library's shiny table. Cheung tries to return the man's smile, but it is far too difficult a thing to do as his mind is racing about for an answer to something it is sure it has just witnessed. Less than a second ago, this man, Cheung is positive, was at least fifty feet from this table at the other end of the library room. And now, in less than a second, it appears to Cheung that the man has moved that distance to sit directly across from Cheung, who is astonished and in awe of what he thinks he has just seen and at such ability.

He glances at the mysterious man in black and flashes another thin smile before delving back into his own book about plants and life forms expected to be found in Jianfengling Tropical Rainforest, a forest not far from Dr. Cheung's rented home in Dongfang City, in the Ledong County; it is purported to be the largest and well-preserved in forest in China.

The private hospital that employed Cheung had finally and, he knew, begrudgingly granted him special leave to attempt to locate certain plants and herbs possibly attributable to unusual and unrecognized early life forms. He was able to convince the hospital's governing board to award him a meager but large enough grant to do a year's research ostensibly to prove a reciprocal pathway between mind and gene action, a way to show that the mind can heal the body; this study always fascinated him as much as the etiology of some peculiar life forms. But even using the money they granted him, he was still living on a shoestring budget…a very thin shoestring at that—one that would wear too thin for use after and likely long before the year is over.

"…Dr. Wo-Ling Cheung, I believe?" It was the man in black speaking to him, but this time, sitting next to him. When Cheung looked up and saw the empty space just across from him where the man had been earlier, he knew that the man should be, by all sane reasoning, still sitting across from him.

"Yes I am, sir. But, I am afraid that you have the advantage of me."

"I am sorry, doctor," he told Cheung.

Cheung marveled at the brilliantly pearl-like gleam of his teeth. He imagined the man likely paid a small fortune to some dentist for such a whitening process. Nodding to him, he took the man's card and looked at it. ***Chauncier Welleck, Mortician***, it read.

Curious, Cheung thought, *there is no phone number or business address or email—no way for a client to contact him for his services.* Then, pointing to the card, Cheung said, "How does a prospective patron reach you?"

"…It's all word of mouth, sir. I do not provide services to anyone outside my…community or those very much like my own. Mine is a very highly selective service," he replied.

Cheung smiled and tried to return the card, but Welleck held up the palm of his hand and refused to take the card back. Cheung slipped the card into his jacket's lapel pocket.

"I don't think I understand, Mr. Welleck. And by the way, how do you know my name? Have we met before?" Cheung asked.

"We have, but it was quite brief and unceremonious, not something you would very likely remember. I am, after all, not the most memorable person. It was at your hospital's fund-raising affair. As a generous donor, I was given the privy of being introduced to you and allotted time to remain in your presence along with a few other gentlemen while you all discussed things far beyond my scope of interests or conversance. That is, until you began to discuss life forms and their generation and regeneration: 'I am especially interested in your views on unusual life forms and on how errant observations that may be the cause of matters thought to be happenstance degeneration of the unrecognized and uncredited life forms thought to be false life due to scarcity and how the absence of numbers may contribute to the demise and possibly or creation of consequences blocking the prevention of unnecessary and unnatural demise and the possible interim states of life only barely recognized pre-primordial lifeforms so severely affected by the contributory factors inherent to the former but at least incidental to the pathology created due to the blatancy of lifeforms too often allowed to die in oceans of disregard.'"

After reciting the reason for his attraction to Cheung's postulates, Welleck withdrew a rectangular envelope from his inner jacket pocket and laid it on the table between them after taking a very deep breath. Cheung was wide eyed that Welleck has recited, his words, word-for-word during a part of the conversation between himself and nine other medical researchers at the earlier affair.

Welleck continued, "Yes, my dear Dr. Cheung, let me tell you that I could not possibly have been more enthralled by your discussion and views on the beginning, interim, and final states of primordial and unrecognized life forms. It was your touching upon that area of discussion, which let me know that you are the one person who hopefully is going to be able to perform a magnificent service for my community." With that being said, Welleck tapped his finger on the envelope, and then continued, "And it is all going to be research within the area of your present work." He then glanced around the library room quickly and held the envelope between two fingers as he leaned closer to Cheung. "The amount of money that is in this envelope is what you will get on the final day of every month while you are working on my community's personal research." Welleck smoothly pushed the puffy envelope to Cheung, who hesitated for a moment before letting his fingers tilt it upwards as another finger fanned the contents—a wide series of one hundred American dollar bills. "I think when I explain it to you you will find it within the boundaries of the research you are preforming at this time." Welleck slid the money filled envelope beneath Cheung's jacket. Cheung finished sliding it into his inside jacket pocket, no longer caring how this man Welleck appeared to move opposite any possible law of gravity.

Welleck leaned closer to Cheug when he said, "I...my community and I need to have you create a drug that can be taken, which mixes well with the blood and one that will allow the body to do certain things: it must remove the need for sleep for much extended periods, for months. This, I imagine, will need to be a serum, but I am not the doctor here. Then, your creation has to dull the need for the person to take certain nourishment for the period I have specified with no degrading of any bodily functioning or appearance. Also, it has to be able to give an abnormal amount of strength to the recipient and, much like steroids, enhance bodily appearance when the subject is awake and this must be nonexistent when he or she is asleep. But, mind you, the subject must be able to awake himself at will. It must give the subject immediate recovery from both body-piercing wounds, whether accidental or inflicted, and the same from ingested substances capable of causing either death or internal permanent injury leading to the degradation of bodily tissues and functions and death. Finally, this product you create must never—mind you, sir—in any fashion, remove or compromise whatever abilities the subject now is capable of accomplishing on his or her power, quite the contrary; I am absolutely hopeful that it may find a means of enhancing such abilities, something perhaps, again, akin to but positively superior to any steroid or super stimulant."

Welleck straightened and leaned back in his chair, all the while keeping his eyes on Cheung who began laughing, but very softly.

"Sir, on one level what you're asking me to create is just not possible. You're talking about a regenerative ability that science has dreamed of forever," Cheung answered.

"Dr. Cheung, I have followed you for years and in my own crude manner, I have researched you and assessed what I know to be your undreamed-of potential. And when you are almost at your end goal with this assignment, you are going to find that you will falter and find a compulsion to move into another direction but one that is eerily similar. And then, at that point I will have the remedy to allow your brilliant mind to make the final choice and advancement. I will then, at that point, have the substance to introduce to your body."

Saying so, Welleck stood. "I will remain in touch with you, sir."

Cheung turned, wanting to object, but Welleck placed his hand on Cheung's jacket, touch the money filled envelope in Cheung's inner pocket. "A scientist with your brilliance requires freedom of thought and expression, the ability to explore and improvise and broaden contemporary thought on traditional science of human existence. Only I am capable of offering you that kind of freedom…financially," he said.

Then, Welleck spun about and walked away, heading for the library exit. Cheung clutched his jacket, gripping the envelope telling himself that he wanted to get up and stop him and give back the money.

But he knew better.

They both knew.

CHAPTER 3

JACOB, PAUL, AND ELIZABETH JENNINGS

Standing on their front porch with her husband Paul Jennings, Elizabeth Bonaveau Jennings had no idea what the two uniformed soldiers climbing from the green sedan and approaching them meant, but she greeted them with a bright and friendly wave and smile.

But her husband, Paul Jennings himself a veteran of the Korean Conflict many years ago, knows exactly what dreaded news the two Army Officers have come to deliver and his expression, like the solemn look of the two uniformed visitors, is grim.

Paul takes a really deep breath and briefly manages to hold back his tears as the Army Captain stops in front of them, stiffens, and salutes, asking, "Mrs. Elizabeth Bonaveau Jennings and Mr. Paul Jennings, parents of Army First Lieutenant Roger Jennings?"

Paul thought he nodded in the affirmative, but he had turned numb and was not quite sure of what his body is doing. He was only able to look helplessly at his wife as his chest began to tremble with horrible remorse that Elizabeth had no means of recognizing. Paul wished he could spare her the devastating words he knew were about to come.

She answered the captain, "Yes, sir, we are."

The captain turned and nodded to the lieutenant at his side. The Lieutenant handed Elizabeth a Bible on top of a folded American flag. The captain looked at Elizabeth when he next spoke, "The secretary of the Army has asked me to express his deep regret that your son, First Lieutenant Roger Jennings…"

Now Paul's tears freed themselves, leaking profusely down his cheeks.

The captain continued, "…Was killed in action in Vietnam today. The secretary extends his deepest condolences to you and your family in your loss." The Captain then took a single step back and saluted again, this time holding his salute for longer.

Elizabeth's mouth is open and her lips moved wordlessly. She gasps when her three-year-old grandson, Jacob, excited at the sight of the two uniformed soldiers, runs over and wraps his arms around her legs. Little Jacob Jennings looked up at the Army Officers, grinning.

"Hello Mr. Policeman," he said.

The stern-faced captain flashed a cold smile down at Jacob before handing Paul a small box.

"These are the medals awarded your son during his tour of duty. His personal effects will be forthcoming to you by a special courier within a week. I am truly sorry to be the bearer of such terrible news." He handed Paul the letter and saluted him once again.

Paul attempted to hold himself together by coughing hard and snapping to something that resembled attention.

Paul briskly returned the captain's salute.

"Thank you, Captain."

Again, the Captain saluted Paul, "Sir."

Then, he took still another step backward, saluted once more, spun about, and he and the lieutenant returned to their waiting vehicle. After the two climbed in the rear, their driver nodded sadly at Paul and his family, and then slowly, quietly pulled away.

Jacob looked up at his sobbing grandfather, asking, "Grandpa, where are the policemen going? And how come you are crying?"

Paul was only able to attempt to smile at his grandson. Then, he picked him up and held him in his arms. Elizabeth hugged them both for a very long time.

The three of them sat on the porch and Paul stared blankly ahead while Elizabeth tended to her fidgety grandson Jacob squirreling around and asking, "Granny, why you an' grandpa not happy no more?"

When Elizabeth managed to stop crying, she and her husband looked at each other for a long, silent moment.

"Grandpa, I wanna make ice cream," Jacob said.

Paul smiled. "Okay," he replied.

Jacob jumped up with a gleeful scream and started running in the back porch.

Giving Elizabeth a kiss Paul very gently wiped away one of his wife's last, errant tears attempting freedom and quietly says, ""…Baby girl, I reckon that you an' me kin sit an' deal with this heah biz'ness tonight when our baby go to sleep, huh?"

Elizabeth smiled and nodded, "I guess so."

"Before it were you and me what was gonna be takin' care o' our grandchild just while his daddy is overseas. Guess it weren't enough that our li'l grandbaby mama up an' died a year after givin' birth to Jacob and what with her comin' outta an orphanage, an' now' his daddy gone an' your daddy done up an'died on us an'—!"

Elizabeth gently pressed her hand against her husband's mouth and softly said, "…Paul, please stop making a death toll and let's just deal with all this later."

"Sure, baby girl; I'm jus' kinda sayin' you an' me is the only kin our grandbaby got now an' we gotta be strong an'…" Paul could feel his own tears pushing against some kind of wall or something in his eyes and he had to stop speaking.

"Yes, we are now, dear," Elizabeth said and bowed her head.

"So, like I say, I'm scared of it, like you know, but you gonna have to teach our baby that stuff you know. He jus' might be needin' a whole lotta that magic stuff that you kin do. You gonna have to teach it to 'im, baby girl." Then shaking his head, he added, "I nevah thought I'd be tellin' you that. Heah me, a Baptist Christian man, tellin' a witchin' woman to teach our baby grandson magic to protect hisself with. Jus' don't do it when I'm around. You know how I feel about witchin' magic. Anyway, knowin' you, I reckon you was gonna teach the boy anyway no mattah what I might'a thought or objected to. Ain't I right?"

Elizabeth did not answer him; she simply brushed some invisible dirt or dust from her husband's short sleeved shirt, kissed him, and then gently pinched the end of his nose and grinned, saying, "Old man, I always told you I wanted to teach Jacob. You know I won't let that boy go out into this sad world with no family and no protection. Now, you take yourself on out of here to the store. I'll have the machine set up for you and Jacob to start your churning by the time you get back."

He turned to go, but she grabbed his arm and looked in his eyes in a way he had not seen before, and that did not help the tears knocking at his eyelids.

He broke free almost running to the car, hollering back, "Yeah, you right, baby girl. I'm gonna drive down to the store an' find us some ice to put in that contraption. I reckon, we kin all use us some ice cream right along up in now."

After getting in the car, he did not look at her before driving off. But, it did not matter to her, because… She knew why.

LEARNING TO TEMPER

It was a bright sunny day, and Elizabeth was on a "sweetness" hunt with her ten-year-old grandson Jacob. Shielding her face from the bright sun, Elizabeth was a bit nervous looking up at ten-year-old Jacob who was high in a tree and precariously positioned only inches from a huge hive swelling with a swarm of honeybees.

From Elizabeth's point of view on the ground at the base of the tree, she could see that the hive above had hundreds aggravated bees, angrily starting to swarm around Jacob. Now and then, she could barely make out that some of the bees were flitting about and bouncing against Jacob's face, investigating but not yet stinging him.

But now, the investigative swarm was growing thicker, swelling to obvious threatening numbers. Jacob smacked his small fist against the palm of his hand and the entire swarm of honeybees spread wide, distancing themselves from him, but they continued to hover there though allowing Jacob to dig a small shovel into their hive and loosen and free three large, dripping honeycombs from their hive lodging, dropping them into his bucket.

Then smiling down at his anxious grandmother below, he says, "Granny Elizabeth, I got 'em." Jacob smiled and held up his bucket for his grandmother below to see.

"Come on down then, Jacob. And be careful climbing down," she replied.

Instead of climbing down, however, Jacob slid half the way down to his grandmother's loud gasp and then eased himself down the remainder of the way, grinning widely at her and his mischief.

"Oh, Jacob, I wish you'd stop doing that. It can be dangerous sliding down such a distance," she said in angst.

"I'm sorry, Granny," he said.

"Oh, no you're not, either," she said laughing and pinched his nose softly.

Jacob handed the honey-filled bucket to his grandmother and they head for an open nearby field to pick blackberries for the cobbler pie Elizabeth has promised to cook for supper.

On the way, she stops to congratulate her grandson, "Jacob, I'm happy to see that you chose the right choice of magic to use on those bees; you didn't choose to kill them, only to move them away." She pinched his nose and added, "And you know that fist smack that I taught you, along with what you're thinking when you smack your palm, can be used at strength to truly harm a person or a thing or something less. And with something as small as bees, you could easily have killed them if your thoughts about the magic you are using are not clear."

"Yes, ma'am, but I didn't need to kill them just for some honey; it wouldn't be right," he said.

Elisabeth pulled her grandson's head against her generous hip and smiled. "You're right, baby boy. Never cause harm to a person or even a thing if you don't have to do it." Then, she suddenly stopped and turned him to face her. "What's our first rule of using magic?" she asked.

Jacob smiled boyishly and folded his arms, saying proudly, "We first affect magic against those who would harm others."

Elizabeth bent down and hugged her grandson enthusiastically. "Oh, yes, Jacob. Yes!" she exclaimed. "Granny's only been teaching you magic for a short while now; only taught you five magic things. But I can see you are suited to it and you are a really good person inside; that is really important for using our magic—the real magic." Saying so, she gave him another squeeze.

Jacob, who seemed enthused at the prospect of learning still more magic, replied, "Granny, I'm gonna learn more magic? Even more 'n what you already taught me?"

Elizabeth nodded and held her grandson close against her thick breasts. She said, "Jacob, I am going to be teaching you magic right up until the day you are ready to leave here and go out on your own. But the magic will get harder and harder and more and more difficult to remember, so you will have to devote your whole self to practicing it with me watching."

Then she kissed him on the cheek.

Jacob blushed, saying, "Yes, ma'am."

"Now, let's go and get us some blackberries and just drop them on top of all this honey you've gathered and we will be able then to make us a beautiful cobbler."

They skipped the rest of the way to a wide field of berries where they drop low and began picking and munching berries.

Cheung's breathing slowed dramatically when he looked at the ashen face of the thick bodied man sitting across from him at the library's shiny table. Cheung tries to return the man's smile but it is far too difficult a thing to do since his mind is racing about for an answer to what it is sure it has just witnessed. Less than a second ago, this man, Cheung is positive, was at least fifty feet from this table at the other end of the library room. And now, in less than a second he has moved that distance to sit directly across from Cheung, who is astonished, in awe of what he thinks he has just seen and at such an ability.

He glanced at the mysterious man in black and flashed another miserly grin before delving back into his own book about plants and life forms expected to be found in Jianfengling Tropical Rain-forest; the forest is not far from Dr. Cheung's rented home in Dongfang City, in the Ledong County; it purported to be the largest and well preserved rain forest in China.

The private hospital that employs Cheung finally and he knew begrudgingly granted him special leave to attempt to locate certain plants and herbs possibly attributable to unusual and unrecognized early life forms. He is able to convince the hospital's governing board to award him a meager but large enough grant to do a year's research ostensibly to prove a reciprocal pathway between mind and gene action; a way to show that the mind can heal the body; this study always fascinated him as much as the etiology of some peculiar life forms. But, even using the money they granted him, he is still living on a shoestring budget…a very thin shoestring at that; one that would wear too thin for use after and likely long before the year is over.

"…Dr. Wo-Ling Cheung, I believe?" It is the man in black speaking to him, but this time he is sitting next to him. When Cheung looked up and saw the empty space just across from him where the man had been earlier, he knew that the man should be, by all sane reasoning, still sitting across from him.

"Yes, I am, sir. But, I am afraid that you have the advantage of me."

"I am sorry, doctor." He presented to Cheung.

Cheung marveled at the brilliantly pearl-like gleam of his teeth. He imaged the man likely paid a small fortune to some dentist for such a whitening process. Nodding to him, he took the man's card and looked at it:

'Chauncier Welleck, Mortician'

Curious, Cheung thought, there is no phone number or business address or email—no way for a client to contact him for his services. Cheung pointed to the card:

"How does a prospective patron reach you?"

"…It's all word of mouth, sir. I do not provide services for anyone outside of my…community or those very much like my own. Mine is a very small service."

Cheung smiled and tries to return the card but Welleck held up the palm of his hand and refused to take the card back. Cheung slipped the card into his jacket lapel pocket.

"I don't think I understand, Mr. Welleck. And by the way, how do you know my name? Have we met before?"

"We have, but it is quite brief and unceremonious not something you would very likely remember. I am, after all, not the most rememberable person. It was at your hospital's fund raising affair. As a generous donor, I was given the privy of being introduced to you and allotted time to remain in your presence along with a few other gentlemen while you all discussed things far beyond my scope of interests or conversance. That is, until you began to discuss life forms and their generation and regeneration. But I am especially interested in your views on unusual life forms and on how errant observations that may be the cause of matters thought to be happenstance degeneration of the unrecognized and uncredited life forms thought to be false life due to scarcity and how the absence of numbers may contribute to the demise and possibly or creation of consequences blocking the prevention of unnecessary and unnatural demise and the possible interim states of life only barely recognized pre-primordial lifeforms so severely affected by the contributory factors inherent to the former but at least incidental to the pathology created due to the blatancy of lifeforms too often allowed to die in oceans of disregard."

Welleck withdrew a rectangular envelope from his inner jacket pocket and laid it on the table between them after taking a very deep breath after reciting the reason for his attraction to Cheung's postulates. Cheung is wide eyed that Welleck has recited, word for word the conversation between himself and nine other medical researchers at the earlier affair.

Welleck continued:

"Oh, but, my dear man, let me tell you that I became especially interested by your discussion and views on the beginning, interim and final states of primordial and unrecognized life forms. It was your touching upon that area of discussion that let me know that you are the one person who hopefully is going to be able to perform a magnificent service for my community." With that having been said, Welleck tapped his finger on the envelope, then continued:

"And it is all going to be research within the area of your present work." He glanced around the library room quickly and held the envelope between two fingers as he leaned closer to Cheung. "The amount of money that is in this envelope is what you will get on the final day of every month while you are working on my community's personal research." Welleck smoothly pushed the puffy envelope to Cheung who hesitated for a moment before letting his fingers tilt it upwards as another finger fanned the contents; a wide series of one hundred American dollar bills. "I think when I explain it to you, you will find it within the boundaries of the research you are preforming at this time." Welleck slid the money filled envelope beneath Cheung's jacket. Cheung finished sliding it into his inside jacket pocket no longer caring how this man Welleck appeared to move opposite any possible law of gravity.

Welleck looked at a young man who sat at their table. He spoke to him:

"And how are you young man?" He smiled at him.

"Eh? Oh, I'm fine, sir, thank you. I—." The young man looked at the book in his hand, "What am I doing with this book? This isn't what I thought I took from the shelf." He stood and walked hurriedly away disappearing behind shelves of books far from their table.

Welleck turned back to Cheung, but now with a very serious look.

"I…my community needs to have you create a drug that can be taken that mixes well with the blood and one that will allow the body to do certain things: it must remove the need for sleep for very extended periods of time, for months. This, I imagine, will need to be a serum, but I am not the doctor here. Then, your creation has to dull the need for the person to take nourishment for the period time I have specified with no degrading of any bodily functioning or appearance. Also, it has to be able to give an abnormal amount of strength to the recipient and, much like steroids, enhance bodily appearance when the subject is awake and this must be nonexistent when he or she is asleep. But, mind you, the subject must be able to awake himself at will. It must give the subject immediate recovery from both body piercing wounds, whether accidental or inflicted, and the same from ingested substances capable of causing either death or internal permanent injury leading to the degradation of bodily tissues and functions, and death. Finally, this product you create must never—mind you, sir, it must never, in any fashion, remove or compromise whatever abilities the subject now is capable of accomplishing on his or her power, quite the contrary, it must find a means of absolutely enhancing such abilities; something perhaps, again, akin to but positively superior to any steroid or super stimulant."

Welleck straightened and leaned back in his chair, all the while keeping his eyes on Cheung who began laughing, but very softly.

"Sir, on one level what you're asking me to create is just not possible. You're talking about a regenerative ability that science has dreamed of forever."

"Dr. Cheung, I have followed you for years and in my own crude manner, I have researched you and assessed what I know to be your undreamed

of potential. And when you are almost at your end goal with this assignment, you are going to find that you will falter and find a compulsion to
move into another direction, but one that is eerily similar. And then, at that
point I will have the remedy to allow your brilliant mind to make the final
choice and advancement. I will then, at that point, have the substance to
introduce to your body." Welleck stood. "I will remain in touch with you,
sir." Cheung turned, wanting to object, but Welleck placed his hand on
Cheung's jacket, touch the money filled envelope in Cheung's inner pocket.
"A scientist with your brilliance, requires freedom of thought. Only I am
going to give you that and I believe you know that."

Welleck spun about and walked away, heading for the library exit.
Cheung clutched his jacket, gripping the envelope telling himself that he
wanted to get up and stop him and give back the money.

But he knew better.

They both knew.

CHAPTER 4

HOME
SCHOOLING

Five years had passed since Elizabeth began home schooling her grandson Jacob and several of her neighbor's children. Jacob was not only an eager student, but also a bright ten-year-old with a seemingly impeccable memory for even the minutest details. The neighbors were also impressed with the way her grandson Jacob spoke, always sounding so intelligent for his age. Jacob's intelligence and fantastic memory got Elizabeth all the more eager to teach him more and more magic at a faster scale. But she realized that she had to be careful not to overload him with his school academics and his lessons in magic.

Elizabeth was very popular with most of her neighbors as she was very adept at curing small medical issues by using special herbs, salves, and lotions. She was even more in demand for clandestine matters by her neighbors for her handling personal matters of the heart. And so, between husband Paul's raising and selling of hogs and goats and the modest fees Elizabeth charged for her holistic and personal relationship services, the Jennings family lived very well.

Every so often, she reminded young Jacob never talk about magic with any of the young boys and girls that I'm teaching here at the house. Their mothers let them come to be homeschooled by me because they know I'm doing that with you and they trust me to teach properly."

"Yes, ma'am, I know."

"You see, Jacob, people are funny about some things. If our neighbors know that I am a witch and not just a witch but what they know of as a 'Death Witch,' then they would all be really afraid of me and even of you." She thought about it for a moment. "Actually, some of them do think I'm either a root worker or just a witch, but they need one of both and so they come to me on Saturdays or Sundays to hopefully solve their problems."

Truly, although some of their neighbors feared what they only suspect Elizabeth's powers to be, they were quick to secretly seek her help in solving their marital and love problems; some neighbors met each other while waiting for Elizabeth's services, but some of them who were married, pretended to be seeing her for a health issue and never for witching—it was generally assumed by most that any treatment of relationship had to involve witchery. Soon, because her clients were so many, Elizabeth had to begin seeing people only by appointment.

One of the few times Paul witnessed his wife's use of playful magic which delighted him no end is one evening when Elizabeth, using her magic gathered thousands of fireflies in a wide swarm over their garden at the rear of their house. Paul is brought to tears as was his grandson Jacob.

The moving swarm of green lights, some of them are yellow and some orange but most of the fireflies are a glowing bright green and lit up the air; Jacob and Paul held each other as they watched in awe, the dancing, bouncing tiny creatures flitting about playfully as though each of them realized they are putting on a display specifically for the family.

Elizabeth has her little ways of bringing her family closer and of making magic a little less frightening and warmer to her husband Paul a devout Christian. He has always been really terrified of the potential he imagines that magic has for doing harm; especially in the wrong hands. And though he trusted his wife with magic, he is daunted by the power of it but since he has never seen his wife use it for anything but good, the few times he is aware of, his brain holds it in a careful but precarious balance.

But Elizabeth has a mischievous side. Once she spied Paul about to take a bite of his wedge of tobacco while in the living room and she turned his tobacco wedge into a wedge of chocolate. But the next time she caught Paul gong against house rules of conduct, she turned his tobacco wedge into a wedge of "ghost pepper," and then pretended she did not hear him scream and beg her to put out the fire in his mouth.

After a couple of minutes, she decided to finally and mercifully put out the fire in her husband's mouth, replacing it with the offering of a huge bowl of large scoops of his favorite flavored ice cream…and a warm kiss… as she stole a huge spoonful of his ice cream, then the entire bowl, giggling loudly as he playfully chased her around the house. He finally caught her… in their bedroom…but neither of them any longer has any interest what-soever in ice cream.

But young Jacob is always fascinated by magic and always paid rapt attention to his grandmother when she is teaching it to him. But now and then he is also curious as to the reasoning of some things that he did not understand:

"But, granny must we always keep our magic a secret? I know that you would never hurt anyone." Then he wondered: "Would you?"

"No, dear, but people still think that all witches are bad and that they are all very dangerous. So if they—."

Jacob thought he knew the rest of her sentence:

"So if they knew you is a witch, they would wanna burn you at the stake like the stories you read to me about the Salem Witches?"

"Jacob…actually, even in Salem, witches are never burned at the stake; traditionally, witches are hanged; but it's like any story that is told and retold and over the years the truth often gets…well, let's say it gets misplaced. For instance, there's is a famous saying about Pandora's box in mythology that she opened and let loose on mankind all the most terrible evils but did not allow one remaining item to go free; and that item is hope. So it is imagined by those who believe that means mankind has no hope ever escape the evils of this world."

"Really granny?"

"Well, it depends on what you are willing to or need to believe. But to begin with , Pandora did not have a box to open, it was a jar, not a box. So, maybe if they have that part wrong, then maybe…well, who knows?"

Jacob's eyes and mouth popped open wide.

"And granny Elizabeth, you say they hung the witches?"

Elizabeth corrected his grammar:

"Well, grammatically the proper word is 'Hanged,' Jacob. You use 'hung' for a thing like a bird feeder; he 'hung' the bird feeder high so no other animal could reach it, only the birds. But for people it's always the word 'hang' or 'hanged;' all the bad men in the west are hanged. Remember your grammar, dear."

"Yes, ma'am. So the truth is that all witches are hung—I mean, hanged. I'll remember that."

"Oh, yes, you will, dear. Your memory is practically flawless."

"Flawless?"

She nodded.

"That means it is without fault; your memory is just about perfect. You don't forget things." She pointed to the backyard. "Now, don't forget that you need to go gather up the eggs from the chicken coop before the hens decide to start 'nesting' on them. We already have more than enough baby chicks."

"Yes, ma'am."

Jacob quickly hustled off to the rear of the house and Elizabeth headed for the kitchen.

At the gate to the henyard Jacob hesitated, knowing that the rooster seemed to hate him and sometimes tries to attack him when he entered the yard and headed for the chicken coop.

Elizabeth usually gathered the eggs and the rooster never gave her a second look, but for some reason the few times Jacob has to go get eggs, the rooster eyed him with great suspicion.

And this time his grandmother is not with him as he stealthily opened the gate to the henyard and after making sure that the rooster is not around, he closed the gate quietly and made for the coop.

One inside he gathered the eggs in one of the baskets there for that purpose and, having filled the basket, he opened the coop's door and looked around again for the rooster. Not seeing him anywhere, he stepped out and tiptoed towards the gate.

A loud, familiar squawk froze Jacob in his tracks and he turned in time to see the rooster scramble from beneath the elevated chicken coop and screaming loudly it angrily rush in his direction.

Eager to get away, Jacob turned and ran for the gate entrance to the yard but tripped but somehow held onto the eggs and faced the vengeful feathered creature. The rooster jumped at his face and Jacob swung wildly and brushed the feathered fury aside.

Looking up, Jacob saw a soaring hawk flying above. Jacob stared at the hawk and it changed direction and swooped down at the rooster, missing on his first lunge. The rooster screamed loudly, glanced at Jacob then ran back beneath the chicken coop, seeking sanctuary, the hawk following close behind.

Suddenly the hawk's wings begin fluttering frantically as something invisible is pulling the bird backwards from beneath the coop. Jacob stood, confused at what is happening with the bird until heard his grandmother's calm voice behind him:

"…Release the bird, Jacob."

Jacob looked back at his grandmother and apologetically and rather weakly smiled at her before he turned back to the hawk whose wings are still fluttering wildly as though it has been caught in some track from which it could not free itself.

He picked up the hawk and is immediately bitten. Uttering a very silent cuss word, tossed the frantic bird high in the air, cupped his hands, whispered the words: "Lamron return." to his mouth and stiffly blew air into his palms and the hawk is instantly transported very high in the air precisely where he has been flying before Jacob summoned him down to the chicken yard. The bird recovered in midair and continued on his way, complaining in a few loud screeches.

Jacob, ashamed at not controlling his temper with the rooster, looked at his grandmother. But Elizabeth is smiling as she entered the yard. She stands near him and takes a cautious look around to assure no one is about, then she folded her arms, chastising him:

"Jacob, I'm just a bit disappointed with you. If I didn't know better, I'd say you are going to treat that hawk to a chicken dinner."

He lowered his head.

"I was, but the rooster was trying to—."

"He is trying to protect his hens, Jacob." She added, softly, "And you know that's his job."

"But, granny, he knows me enough to know that I don't want his stupid chickens. What would I do with 'em, anyway?"

Elizabeth burst out in hearty laughter, grabbed her grandson's hand and led him from the chicken yard, laughing all the way to the kitchen. Once inside they sat at the kitchen table.

"Now, Jacob, you have to remember to be careful using your magic, in fact since you're seven years old now, I believe it's time for you to begin learning more serious magic."

"Yes, ma'am."

"Ordinarily, a child of your years would be far too young to be trusted with real magic. But with your lineage I trusted that you would be capable of taking 'Instruction,' and that you would also not use it foolishly or in some dangerous fashion." She looked at him without saying anything, waiting for her grandson to acknowledge, and he did:

"Yes, ma'am, the way I did tonight outside in the chicken yard."

Elizabeth nodded to him.

"Yes, Jacob. That was not a very responsible way to use magic."

"Well, I fell running from him." Jacob looked suddenly sad. He knew that he could not offer any good excuse for his behavior. He knew he may have been using magic out of anger more than necessity. "I'm sorry, granny. I'll not do that ever again."

Elizabeth tussled Jacob's thick, curly hair then went to the refrigerator and took out a wide pan of peach cobbler and Jacob's eyes lit up. He rubbed his hands together and Elizabeth reminded him:

"We will see, dearest one." She spooned out two heaping spoons of cobbler then she went back to the refrigerator and returned to the table with a large tray of homemade ice cream. Jacob rubbed his hands together even faster. Elizabeth laughed at his eagerness.

"Listen Jacob, before you start a fire rubbing those hands of yours together, get into that bathroom and put some soap and water on them. And while you're at it, slap some on your face, too."

"Yes ma'am." On his rush to the bathroom to wash up, Elizabeth is surprised that at the speed he is running that he has not attained flight

When he returned to the kitchen, Jacob's grandmother kissed him gently on his forehead and finished her caution to him, saying:

"I think it's time for you to start learning more advanced magic and potion making." Elizabeth's expression turned serious when she said, "From now on, the magic I'm going to be teaching you will be more serious and also more dangerous. As I've always told you, use it when you just have no choice but to help another person who is helpless; of course you use it anytime you are in danger and have no choice. And as always you must try and keep it secret.

"Yes ma'am."

"Since it's almost summer and I don't teach the children during the summer, you and I have all summer for you to learn an do so much more magic. Of course there will be the occasional person; coming to me who is in need of healing or some sort of help since all of our neighbors think of me as a Shaman. But I will set up specific hours to see those people and that will leave plenty of time for you to learn more magic and for me to see you perform it."

"Yes ma'am. But what's a Shaman?"

"Well, it's a kind of magic person, I guess."

Elizabeth hugged Jacob but then he saw that special, almost frightening look in her eyes again. She sensed his perception and leaned close to him and whispered:

"…Jacob this is as good a time as any to tell you that you were born with a 'veil' that covered your face. That veil portended that you are destined for magic and that it will always be a large part of your world forever. And it will occasionally give your sights and feelings of things past and things to come; things that can be sometimes pleasant and sometimes dreadful."

"Granny, what does that word 'pretend' mean?

"Portend, dear. And the word portend means something that is very likely to happen. Something important, something that is going to be very big and maybe…maybe even very scary. Jacob when you become an adult using some of the magic you will get to know, you are going to come across demons and some people so evil that they seem to evil to even be demons and sometimes they won't be human; they will actually be demons only pretending to be human, perhaps they may have found a way to invade a human person's body; but such an invasion is almost always temporary. But you know even temporary can be a long time. One such demon is thought to be a creature called Corpo Seco; he is so truly evil that even Satan would not take him."

"Wow! What'll I do, granny? Demons. Evil people."

"Over the coming years, and from this day on, you are going to be learning only the most powerful of magic. That means spells, potions, chants and a way to do magic with using your thoughts. You will be much more powerful than almost any creature or person you have to deal with."

"Wow, granny. But you know, I do magic now with my mind and words. You taught me that. That's how I got the hawk to come down to the chicken yard just using my eyes and thinking what I wanted it to do to that rooster."

"Yes, I know, Jacob. Maybe that wasn't your best moment."

"Huh?"

"It just kind of reminded me of your young age."

"Huh?"

"Anyway, when I have taught you all the magic I know, then that will be the time for you to be instructed by 'The Enchanters.' You will be an adult then, Jacob. An adult and ready to go out into the world on your own."

Jacob stared at his grandmother, suddenly not feeling very happy.

"Granny, why would I ever wanna leave you an' grandpa? I'm gonna be livin' here forever."

Elizabeth pinched Jacob's nose and smiled, then she cut him another large slice of peach cobbler and plopped a scoop of vanilla ice cream on the middle of it.

Jacob hardly gave her time to pull the ice cream scoop away before he speared the pie.

CHAPTER 5

JACOB EVOLVES.
BUT HOW?

Jacob's fifteenth birthday and he and his grandfather Paul are saun-
tering along, heading for a local ice cream parlor. Paul is studying
his grandson. Something about Jacob has changed noticeably since he had
learned the abundant magic grandmother Elizabeth taught him over the
past years.

Paul did not believe it is simply the magic that has created a coldness in Jacob's demeanor, but, he thought, maybe the thought of having the
responsibility of carrying such a huge load. Jacob is, after all, a teenager,
but he never really had the opportunity to be young and silly the way Paul
imagined he should have been for the years past.

No. Jacob has proven to be a very serious and dedicated student of
both magic and of his academics. He showed little interest in playing with
children in his age group; his main and basically only love is for magic; but
his grandfather Jacob is wondering at what cost.

"Grandpa, look!" Jacob said, breaking into Paul's thoughts.

Paul and his grandson have come upon a dog lying in the middle of
the road. Paul knew the animal but Jacob did not and he wanted to make
friends with him but Paul warned him:

"Son be careful of that old dog. He's old and sometimes he kin be kinda cranky. So, I don't know if you really need to mess with 'im right along now 'cause it is right hot out heah today an' even I feel kinda outta temper."

Paul bent down and smiled at the old hound, knowing it likely has been in the woods earlier attempting to chase rabbits or raccoons as it has always been so fond of doing.

But arthritic age has caught up with the now partly feeble animal and its current efforts of the chase have become pure folly. However, it continued to go alone to the forest where Paul has several times witnessed the elderly hound dog enjoy a faux chase, closely simulating the activity it once enjoyed with its owner, a man named Chester whose body old age has also found and inhabited and caused him to become housebound and unable to accompany his faithful animal chasing memories in their declining years.

When Paul Jennings, no youngster himself, went hunting, now and then he would come across the old hound collapsed on the ground, panting, tired, exhausted from its folly chase. Paul always gave it water and waited until the dog regained its composure and then watched it slowly wander from the woods towards its home.

"Jacob, that's ol' man Chester's dog. Be careful now..."

Jacob beckoned to the dog who began wagging its long spindly tail with such gusto that it is difficult to tell whether the dog is wagging the tail or if the tail is wagging the dog.

"He acts friendly, grandpa." Jacob bent low and called out for the dog to come closer to him.

The animal struggled hard to stand; once it accomplished this obeyed as it always did with anyone, but as it neared Jacob, it slowed its approach and the fur on the back of its neck abruptly flared high, a clear sign that the animal is tense. Its legs begin trembling badly and the dog suddenly became unsteady standing.

Jacob reached out to pet the animal. It snarled and bit his fingers; but instead of Jacob yelling, the dog yelped several times as if in great pain, curled its tail between it legs and slinked back several steps with its eyes locked on him.

Paul's eyes widened. He is unable to comprehend what is happening. How can a dog bite a person and the dog react with main? At this moment Paul, experienced some kind of vague, unrecognized fear, not of the dog rather of some present danger that he sensed Jacob posed for the creature.

Paul stepped between his grandson Jacob and the dog and he tries to shoo the animal away for its own good but the old hound is frozen, appearing to be mesmerized by Jacob's piercing glare at it. The dog is only able to stand and tremble badly, unable to look away from Jacob and run to freedom. Occasionally it emits low, intermittent whines, moving its head from side to side, furtively looking about for an avenue of escape that it would likely be unable to take. Paul thought Jacob's predatory stare is the reason the old hound clearly has become terrified of Jacob.

Finally the hound dog began to feebly back away while still urging a low growl from deep inside its throat that it could never get to quite reach a confident pitch.

Jacob shook his balled his fist at the dog and suddenly the sad animal screamed an abrupt loud whine as though it has just remembered the pain it is in and its rear legs gave way beneath him. After several more anguished moments, Jacob turned away and when he did, the old hound turned and feebly regain its footing but could only move its front legs.

As the animal very slowly began to drag itself away by use of its front legs, its rear legs are useless now. Paul is staring at his grandson sure that he sees something similar to a smile on his grandson's face as Jacob watched the old, whimpering hound dog struggle along.

As he watched the dog struggle to get away, to reach home, Paul's emotions struggled with what his grandson may be turning into or may have already become. And knowing that he is the one who asked his wife to teach their grandson magic, caused an old saying he has heard several times to keep running back and forth in his thoughts:

"Be careful what you wish for."

MAGIC NOT WELL DONE

Five months later, Jacob, Elizabeth, Paul his friend Jessup are swinging back and forth in the Jennings' wide backyard swing and singing silly songs with made up silly, spontaneous lyrics and having a delightful time. The incident with Jacob and old man Chester's hound dog has never been mentioned to Elizabeth or to Jessup by Paul or Jacob and is the furthest thing from Jacob and Paul's minds Jessup, between liquor belches, mentioned the dog:

"Well, I reckon y'all done already hear tell 'bout ol' man Chester's hound dog, eh?"

Paul's breathing slowed and he cautiously allowed the conversation to proceed, though he has a dull feeling that he is going to regret doing so.

"Can't say I have, Jessup.' Paul slapped at a stinging mosquito at his neck. I ain't one fer gossip, an' I ain't never knowed you to be neither."

Jessup shook his head emphatically and help up his hand to Paul.

"Oh, now, Paul, I ain't passin' none o' them 'who shot John?' tales. I hear this for myself from church sister Lena an' I'm still shakin' from what she done up an' tol' me."

"What you hear, Jessup?" Paul is a bit impatient, not really happy that his friend is about to revive the gory hound dog memory.

"Well, Lena tells me that old man Chester's hound dog done gone an' got 'bigged' an' done gone an' give birth to eight puppies."

Elizabeth looked at Jessup and sadly shook her head, siting up on the swing as Jessup kept on with his story:

"From what everybody knowed…the dog weren't never showed pregnant in the first place for what nobody knowed, it ain't never showed that it done gone an' got 'bigged' by some ol' dog whilst it were wanderin' around' like it always do."

Jessup pulled out a pack of cigarettes and off one to Elizabeth that she politely declined; then to Paul who also refused and so he lit one for himself and blew the first puff of smoke down between his legs before continuing with his tale

"You know the church sends sister Lena by to Chester's house once a week to clean up for the ol' man what with him not no good for nothin' much wit' his poor health an' all. Anyway, sister Lena tell sister Lizzie that she say she seen it for herself that ol' dog give birth in ol' Chester's kitchen while ol' man Chester's in his bed sleepin'. Jessup looked around the area suspiciously then leaned close and hissed: "... Lizzie tells me say that sister Lena say the dog give birth to the puppies right through its mouth! Through his mouth, I tell y'all. Doggone if she ain't says she stood right there and watched that ol' hound throw up them newborn puppies from the mouth—chokin' near death on each one of 'em! Kin you believe that? Sister Lena say she don't never wanna go back in that house again, no matter what the church say to her to do."

"Well, Jessup, I gotta say that I ain't never hear of no dog havin' puppies that way, but I guess it's what God wanted." Paul took a deep breath and shut his eyes against the memory of Jacob and the hound dog, but he is not successful in trying to blank out the terrible image.

Again Jessup shook his head emphatically.

"Naw, Paul...it ain't what God wanted. An' if ain't God what wanted it then you know who that leave wantin' it."

"Jessup, jus' what the heck're you carryin' on about anyway?"

"Paul, you know better. You know that ol' hound."

"I reckon that I do for the best part of fifteen years now."

"Well, in all the time you ain't knowed that ol' dog, ain't you knowed that ol' man Chester's dog is a boy dog?" Jessup took a long swallow of whisky, frowned, smacked his lips and belched loudly. "Well, anyway, he been a boy dog all these past twenty five years an' you know that, Paul, as many times as you an' me done seen him hoppin' up on some female dogs. You know how you an me used to laugh at him. But now Lizzie say the ol' hound ain't a boy dog no more. She say he ain't got no more pee-pee. He done lost it after pukin' up them puppies. She say she looked down theah where his two little balls is s'posed to be but she say she see something what shouldn't a been there in his backside. Even though he give birth outta his mouth, sister Lena say she seed a woman's thang back theah where it shouldn't've oughta be. She say she see a woman's thang, Paul!"

Paul stared at his friend for a long time

"Jessup, you tryin' to tell us that the dog done grown hisself a pussy?

Jessup shrugged.

"Whatever they calls it." Jessup seemed embarrassed. He glanced at Elizabeth who is smirking and took a quick drink. "But, anyway somebody up an' poisoned that ol' hound and all them puppies too. Killed 'em all dead is what they done. Then somebody who I reckon were that same identical somebody what killed up them puppies an' the hound went ahead an' painted the words: 'Satan lives here,' on old man Chester's front door. They say ol' man Chester died with his ol' hound dog an them puppies."

Elizabeth frowned and turned uneasily on the swing's cushions.

"That was a terrible thing to do." She said.

Jessup nodded in agreement and said:

"Yes, ma'am, it is for a fact. An' lawd knows but I feels sorry fer ol' man Chester but I swear I can't bring myself to go by theah to see if it's true or no. It's all jus' too scary if you was to ask me—even though you ain't—but…"

Jessup's voice seemed to be fading out as an icy waft of very cold air shimmied over

Paul's shoulders and down his back. Paul looked at his friend's mouth moving but he never heard the rest of what Jessup is saying. It has been replaced by his terrible vision of the memory of Jacob and the cringing hound dog who appeared terrified of Jacob even before Jacob brutalized the poor animal.

It has always been clear to Paul that his wife Elizabeth has given Jacob very strong powers but what he has done to the old hound dog did not seem like a power that would have come from any Godly place; and certainly, what Jacob has done with it is far from Godly.

Jessup stood and extended his hand to Elizabeth and then to his friend Paul.

"Paul. I bes' be headin' home. Look to me like it's gittin' ready to rain. I got some stuff hangin' on the line I needs to take in."

Paul stood, smiled and put his arm around his friend.

"Okay, Jessup. But I'm gonna stop by your place three weeks this comin' Saturday it'll be my turn an' I'll have a fresh batch of whisky ready an' done for you to be tastin."

"I'm gonna hold you to them words, Paul." Jessup grinned, then nodded at Elizabeth. He waved to Jacob and unsteadily walked from the backyard to his car. Before getting in, Jessup hollered out at Paul: "Yeah, maybe we kin talk some more then. But right now, I done got tired o' talkin'. Good day to you all." He climbed in his car, started the motor and after a very long pause…his car tires screeched forward a few feet, stopped abruptly then smoothly ambled forward.

CHAPTER 6

STRANGE AND
EVEN STRANGER

Three weeks later on a late grey and brooding Saturday afternoon, Paul arrived at Jessup's home with four plastic water containers and a large mason jar all filled with Paul's homemade white lightning whisky in the rear of his pickup truck. Jessup met him at the truck and helped Paul carry the whisky to the backyard; both men paused for a moment to wipe away the sweat that has saturated their bodies and faces. The men sat the plastic bottles on the porch and the large mason jar on a small wooden table near the rear of the porch.

Paul swiped the sweat from his forehead.

"Lawd have mercy but it's hot as all hell today, ain't it, Jess'?"

"Damn sure is, Paul." Jessup looked up at the sky, frowning. "An' still, it ain't the first sign o' no kinda sun no place up yonder in this sky." He looked at Paul and grinned. "Paul, you reckon that maybe that God got Hisself another private sky up yonder behind the one what we're seein' what he use for hisself only?" He laughed. "An' maybe that' where he's hidin' the sun what's got all this heah heat what you an' me is feelin.'"

Paul unscrewed the top of one of the mason jars and handed the jar to Jessup.

"Well, I bought my new batch o' white lightnin' over for you to taste but it sound like to me like you done already got hold of somethin'

55

stronger'n anythang I kin whip up." Both men laughed and Paul added, "But o' course if he is got somethin' like that what he's hidin' up yondah, I wish he'd hide some o' the heat, too." Paul laughed and wiped away more sweat and pointed to his liquor:

"Now, Jessup, them four jugs yondah is for buyin' but that mason jar I jus' give you is for you and me to be tastin' an' drinkin' wit', my friend." Paul said, patting the top of Jessup's balding head. "An' I think you gonna be right fond o' this heah batch, boy. I done messed aroun' an' made some whisky so good that I'm scared to drink it myself! All I do is sit an' look at it."

Jessup snorted out a hard laugh and grinned widely. Paul could tell that something other than liquor is on his friend's mind. He has never seen him with such a concerned expression on his face. He also noticed a suitcase at the front door that looked full. They sat at a small table in the backyard and Paul filled the mason jar he has given Jessup.

"Jessup, you okay?"

Jessup shrugged, looked around and then began to explain that all the people in the neighborhood felt that due to a few recent scary events, it is no longer safe to walk around at night, and he is starting to think that it is no longer safe to live in his house.

"Somebody told me that Simpson boy up the road come walkin' by Jessup's porch and sure enough somebody snatched open the door and stuck his head between the open door and tries to get young Simpson to come inside, but he run away and told his daddy." He took another swallow. "But guess what? His daddy ain't go to ol' man Chester's house to find out, neither."

Paul waved him away.

"Jessup come on. Is you serious? What in the worl' is you talkin' about?"

"It's 'bout ol' man Chester an' his ol' hound dog again," Jessup replied. "Paul, I thought you tol' you at your house somebody poisoned the dog an' its puppies too. An' do you 'member I said that 'ol' hound dog were all he had?

"Yeah."

"Well, now can't nobody find ol' man Chester."

Paul stopped at mid swallow and looked questioningly at his friend. "What?"

"You heard me right. Now can't nobody seem to find out where ol' man Chester is. He don't come out on his porch for sun like he used to be doin'. But ol' wider Louise say she passed by his house the other night and somebody cracked open the front door long enough to grin at her and slam it back shut. She say his eyes was just a glowin', too!" Jessup took the mason jar from his friend Paul and took a long swallow. "Some peoples done come to start believin' Chester's done died an' gone behind his dog to the grave an' is in his house dead." Jessup took another long, hard swallow of Paul's white lightning, but this time he frowned as though he may have been in excruciating pain. "...Or somethin'. Some peoples is sayin' that ol' Chester jus' might be jus' a li'l bit dead." Then he handed the mason jar back to Jessup who almost dropped it for staring in disbelief at Jessup and his statement and thinking about his friend's packed suitcases.

"Jess', what the hell're you talkin' about?"

"Peoples is scared to go into Chester's house to see if he's okay or not. They all of 'em scared o' what they might find movin' around in theah with 'im."

"Jess', you tellin' me that everybody is scared to go into his house— even if they's all bunched up together?"

Jessup nodded solemnly.

"They ain't goin' in that house. Even if the KKK's chasin' a nigger, he ain't goin' to run in theah! Reverend Moore say he went to the door an' it smell right peculiar. He go onto say that he thought he could hear some-body on the inside o' Chester's house movin' around an' when he knock... they stops movin'. He say it sound to him like somebody is in theah drag-gin' something aroun' an' aroun' an back an' forth like they can't decide where to drop it or put it."

"Well, the preacher's a good Christian, God fearin' man. So I know he did the right thing."

"Oh he did the right thang all right. He got the hell outta theah."

"How come nobody call the sheriff?"

"Oh, they call Putney, awright. That ol' cracker knock on the door an' they say somethin' on the inside knock back. They say that ol white man got so scared he stand theah shittin' in his drawers 'fore he could get his feet to movin' and get outta theah!" Jessup took another long swallow from Paul's mason jar then he continued with his tale, "…Now, mind you, what I'm gittin' ready to tell you, I ain't seed for myself yet, but word is that ol' man Chester's hound is done come outta the grave an' done come by the house an' got ol' man Chester and done took 'im away."

"What? Where'd he take 'im?"

"Lawd only knows, Paul. I hear tell they's both been seen walkin' the streets at night, side by side at night. Hear tell one time somebody come near him an' his dog an' ol' man Chester jus' stan' theah lookin' at the person an' smilin' an' they say his teef's done come to look for the worl' like a dog's side teef's with two long teef's hangin' down on the side near the front of a dog's mouth."

"Yeah, you talkin' about his canines."

"Am I? Well, anyway, they say they both walks real slow like, almost like they feet ain't movin' 'em along, almos' like they are sliding and gliding along the ground or somethin'. Some peoples is callin' that they 'death glide' an' that they lookin' for the one what poisoned the dog an' his puppies."

Paul nodded and accepted the mason jar from his friend for a quick swallow while he continued listening to Jessup's tale:

"But, some peoples think they lookin' for whoever done messed up the hound's legs to start wit'. They somethin' happen where that ol' hound couldn't go chasin' rabbits no more 'cause he were draggin his hind legs for some reason."

Paul stood, a bit arthritically, gently pushed the mason jar and its remaining whisky to his friend and smiled.

"Jessup, I gotta git to gittin'. I'll git the money for them two jugs later. I tol' Lizzie I'd be back in time for supper."

Jessup frowned, "Aw, boy you jus' got heah a good minute ago. Well…" Jessup looked around the area suspiciously. Then he stood and leaned close to Paul, hissing: "… Lissen, Paul, 'fore you go I wanna tell you somethin'." He looked around again. "You might wanna keep your misses kinda close. I hear tell some peoples is kinda wonderin' if maybe she might got some kinda hand in this mess. I mean, what with her knowin' so much 'bout…well, you know…'bout stuff like healin' people an' the like." Jessup lit a cigarette, looked around again then leaned even closer, warning him: "Jus' a friend to a friend. You an' the missus might need to be right careful."

"Thank you, Jessup. We will." They shook hands and Paul started walking to his truck.; when he climbed inside, his truck would not start up. Jessup came over and lifted Paul's hood and examined the motor. He turned to Paul and shook his head.

"Your truck's jus' as dead like somebody don' shot it. You leave it heah an' I'll fix it for you later on. I'll call you tomorrow an' I kin drop it by you an' then maybe you kin drive me to the Greyhound Bus depot. I'm gonna stay with my brother in Wilmington for a bit. But you gonna have to walk home, 'cause my car's worse off than this thang you drivin'. I'm ready to junk it."

"Okay, Jessup and thanks. I kin walk home. It ain't that far." Paul started out and decided that since it is getting dark, he needed to take a shortcut through the nearby woods. Halfway through, an uneasy feeling came to him, a sense that some dreadful thing pending is following him.

He stopped for a moment and looked around. He is sure that he heard a branch snap somewhere in back near hm. Then there came a conglomerate of noise of birds twittering sounded as though the forest has decided to help him or maybe something was moving through the forest disturbing everything but then it became instantly quiet and the daylight seemed to dim more than he thought it should have. He took a deep, tremulous breath and let it out slowly as his eyes searched the darkening woods.

He assured himself that there is absolutely nothing to fear in these woods that he hunted so often and knew every inch of. And so he knew that any animal with it superior knowledge of its forest home is capable of hiding itself from him until it is too late for Paul to defend himself. And if it came to something beyond an animal of the forest, something only bordering on being human, then Paul looked around with as casual a look as he could manage to affect…then he leaned forward, bent low in the direction of home and since he thought simple running was going to be far too slow and after careful and thoughtful contemplation, he decided that he now needed the required speed to…—Disappear.

CHAPTER 7

AND SO,
INTO THE DEPTHS

Jacob's grandmother Elizabeth draped him in a black robe that almost reached the tennis shoes he is wearing. The two are standing at a tall altar in the spare bedroom of the house that Elizabeth used for teaching the neighbor's children in her home schooling program; she uses another room in the house instructing Jacob in magic as on this day and this very special occasion.

She normally keeps that door closed, but once it was left open and a parent, bringing her child for schooling, questioned Elizabeth about the altar. She wondered what kind religion an altar holding fresh fruit, candy and bottles of whisky could possibly represent. Elizabeth explained away everyone's worries by saying that the altar is a curiosity, simply an attractive conversation piece she has picked up during her travels abroad when she was a young woman. Elizabeth's clarification easily satisfied the neighbor and nothing further is ever mentioned about it; and she saw to it that the door was never again open for anyone other than Paul and of course Jacob and she tells them to see that it is always closed.

Observing his grandmother Elizabeth's solemn demeanor on this Sunday, Jacob is just a bit uneasy watching her kneeling at her altar and he wondered why he and his grandmother are dressed in black robes. Never before have either of them ever wore anything but their regular clothing during his instructions in magic.

Elizabeth stands at the altar and turned to face her grandson. Her expression is grim and wearing a tightly wrapped deep burgundy scarf wrapped around her head, that is covering her hair. She is holding a purple book whose volume of pages appear to be at least five inches in height. She holds it for twenty year old Jacob to look at while she tells him that:

"Jacob...this writing is known as *'The book of skins,' and it has been* written by a witch whom other witches call, *'The most unholy of all things human.' These writings contain* some of the most despicably horrible spells and it is a very dangerous book to use. If a person makes a mistake using any of its teachings, it is not somethin that is easily if ever forgiven by the words written herein or by the person who wrote them. These are the strongest spells and incantations ever created. You can only use these contents by touching the book; there will be occasions when, while you are using this book, that it will burst into flames. |When this does happen, then you must put out the flames with your bare hands. If you dare to try to put out the flames with anything other than your hands, if at that time of fire you allow anything other than your hands to touch this book, then you yourself will be the one to burst into flames. And if such a thing does happen, then no one will ever be able to extinguish those flames, my dearest child; not even I am able to perform such a task. Please see that that never happens."

Elizabeth places her hand on Jacob's chest while holding the book against her breasts, she says:

"The pages of this book will always appear to be sealed to outsiders who look at it. There is no penalty for them touching it, but if it is ever opened by you and someone touches it, then the flames will be upon them, Jacob. And that will be that. Forever. Flames that will burn everything other than the person who is engulfed by them.

Jacob Jennings stares at the thick, purple book and he could swear that it is actually moving while in his grandmother's hand. He looked at

Elizabeth and then at the book, positive that intermittently it flashed very subtle squirming motions.

Elizabeth turns back to her altar.

"Kneel with me, Jacob. Kneel quietly and with grace as you believe it to be."

It took him a moment to reconcile his grandmother's phrasing and the he took a breath and knelt beside her as she gently placed the book on the altar.

Elizabeth smoothly, very evenly begins opening the volume as she spoke to her grandson in a very low voice, almost a murmur:

"…Jacob I can only administer the teachings extant within this volume to you in whispers. If I attempt to speak these horrible chants, spells, and curses to you in a normal volume of speaking then you and I will both be damned by those very words and the book will seal itself, never to be opened again."

She turned to her grandson and placed her hand on his forehead.

"…And of equal importance, you must be able to concentrate far and beyond what you may consider yourself capable of doing because I am not allowed to ever repeat an instruction to you. Ever. Once I have told you a thing from this book, you may ask me to repeat it, but I will never be able to; I am not allowed. This book demands that you give it a place in your life while you are learning where no other reality exists. You may ask any question as we go along, but you are not allowed to ever ask me to repeat anything from this book that I have once said to you while teaching. But I will be taking a great amount of time explaining everything that I teach you from this book. We, you and I, will move very slowly with these particular lessons. Do you completely understand me, Jacob?"

He is staring at his grandmother when something came over him and instead of responding, he turned to her altar, took a very deep, tremulous breath, then bowed his head without speaking. He could only think to pray for the ability to be able to negotiate the new avenues his grandmother is availing him of through this book, a thing he sees in his purple book of dreams…that harbors certain nightmares.

But Elizabeth understood and knows that the very fiber of esoteric spirit has searched for and found and entrance to her grandson Jacob's very being; she realizes that he has just been "reached" by *the book of skins*. She smiled and hugged him, then, for the next five hours, began her teachings cautioning her grandson here and there to be careful when using these new and profound abilities he will learn from this book.

She took special care to slowly explain every possible detail to Jacob, pausing when she thought she needed to give him more time to take in what she has imparted to him. Even her cautions to him are gentle and slowly paced and, as she has told him earlier, her words to are always a whisper:

"…Another punishment for the person using these teachings improperly or for their own selfish desires is that, once done, he or she will shed his or her flesh and be made to carry it worn around their shoulders like a terrible cloak until the flesh is renewed over the person's skeleton; then, it will, upon thirteen midnights from that day, shed its entire body of flesh again and have to carry it worn about their shoulders until such time as it is once again renewed; renewal of one's flesh requires a period of a year each time only to be shed thirteen days later. The violator will bear this horrible punishment forever and the blasphemer is sentenced to be forever shunned by all human society and made to live where other humans do not gather or arrive."

Jacob listened to his grandmother making sure that he heard every word she whispered to him. He knew that he dared not miss a single one and at the same time, he knew that he has to grasp the full meaning of the content she is relating to him.

But watching his grandmother, she did not appear to be reading from the voluminous book, rather she only glanced at the words now and then but gently turning pages long before she could have completed reading the entire content of the page; it seemed to him to be obvious she apparently well remembered or had known the words. Then Elizabeth turned to him, her voice continuing in its soft whisper:

"As I have told you earlier, this book is created by the witch *the most unholy of all things human* in a most horrendous manner. She chose two witches from among her most faithful followers, those she knows to be most loyal to her, to do as she commanded and that is to pull the flesh each from the other. She reckoned that such a choosing would cause the flesh to be even more horribly as they are horribly chosen in a way that would never have been expected. Then, she has those followers carry their flesh and follow her back to the coven and so they did, their skeletal bodies drenched in blood and ravaged flesh remains."

Elizabeth looked around the room and then back to the explanation to Jacob:

"The wailing women did as they are bid and once there she commanded the lower witches, none of whom are in favor with her, to scrape the flesh free of all dermis. When the lower ranked witches began this arduous task, the flesh, yet alive, resisted and tormented beneath the blades of the scraping knives of the lower ranked witches and those favored witches from whom the flesh has been removed, toiled about on the ground, writhing and screaming and begging for her to stop the horrible pain. But she would not.

Jacob is making a face, appalled by the cruelty of the process and of the creating witch.

Elizabeth continues:

"Once the lower witches completed the cleaning, she commanded them to bring to her paper upon which to begin creating her horrendous spells, chants, methods of magic and means of committing the most egregious acts any human would be absolutely incapable of even imagining. Once they have done this he began to write on the pages, each of which burst into flames that engulfed her hand but she did not acknowledge any pain, instead seemed to delight in whatever discomfort there may have been. And for the next thirty days and thirty nights, none of the witches bringing her paper are allowed to either eat or drink. When the volume is finished, she commanded that two lower ranked witches volunteer to have the flesh removed from them, each one to remove the flesh from the other. And when this is done, the two high ranked witches are allowed to take the removed flesh and place it upon themselves and with a smoothing of her hand, *the most unholy of all things humans* affixed the flesh upon her most faithful and all is well one again with them.

Jacob feels a very icy wind blow through the room and so does his grandmother Elizabeth. He rubs his shoulders but Elizabeth simply continued with the origin of the volume, *the book of Skins:*

"Then *the most unholy of all things human* slapped her hands together and the two skeletal women burst into flames, screaming as they did so until their voices are silent and only ashes remained of them. And then *the most unholy of all things human*, recited a prayer in a language no one in the coven understood or has ever heard before. As she recited the prayer, she slowly and meticulously sewed the flesh of the two chosen witches to cover and bind the book; but even with each piercing of the needle into the flesh, the two chosen ones, though newly clad in the flesh of others, screamed in pain, as the flesh being adhered to the book, remained originally theirs. And when this is completed, she assured the two highly ranked witches that their flesh shall cover and bind the huge volume she has written and will forever be guardians to it."

Elizabeth held the volume to her and looked around the room, speaking to her grandson:

"All witches are forbidden to use *the book of skins* but high ranking witches have the ability to do so but not the permission. Only she, *the most unholy of all things human*, is allowed to use the book or even so much as to open it. And so even now, Jacob, those two witches whose flesh her binds and covers this work, are seeking me and have been doing so for oh, so many years. But though they may be closing the distance between us, they will not find nor take possession of this horror, because it belongs in the hands of a righteous person who will only use it for good. It will be in the hands of you, my grandson who is, simply by his knowledge of magic and what I know to be his purity of soul, easily superior to both high ranked witches who are the volume's guardians."

Jacob, the witch who, as I have told you, is the unholiest of all things human created the spells in this book hoping that the title *The book of skins* would be enough to stop anyone from attempting to use it if ever it fell into the wrong hands. I want you to know that even I should not be in possession of this work…but I am." Elizabeth looks around the room as though expecting to either see or hear something or someone agree with what she has just said.

Jacob wondered earlier why his grandmother kept glancing around the room as though to make sure that they are alone. Now, he understood.

She squeezed her grandson's hand.

"All the many years gone by, and long before you were born, witches of very high ranking have been in pursuit of me because of my leaving their ranks and for the thievery of this horrendous literature. But I was and am determined that it never reach the hands of some infidel who will misuse it in some terrible manner and for some horrific purpose. I am old now and before you depart this home, I will give you this work but not before I apprise you of many of the spells and works herein. You are going to be taught how to make a drawing of your enemy, but it must be a just enemy, and that drawing alone can be manipulated by you to either guide him to misfortune or death. This book will instruct you on how to develop your mind so that your thoughts become what you desire them to become. You will learn, in a very temporary way, how to control anyone and any living creature; you will be able, briefly, to even control nature."

Elizabeth placed Jacob's hand on the book and he felt heat radiating up, down and around his hand, heat that ran up his arm and circled around his shoulders, up his neck, down his spine and flashed through his upper body only to be abruptly drawn out of him.

"But, there is so much for you to know and learn from this book and it is to be used only when the powers against you cannot be handled by you and your current knowledge of magic. This magic in this book is to be used by you only as a last resort when nothing else works and you need, in some desperate way, the most powerful of all magic. And yet, most of the magic you will never know by memory for the instruction is far too lengthy to commit to memory and there is much in this book that you will be frightened to hear or read; some of it you will feel daunted and perhaps too much to even finish reading. But let me tell you that you will always be protected by me no matter what, as long as you are acting in the proper manner in which you have been taught by me. The largest portion of this writing is for your reference and not for your memory. You must see to it that no one ever touches this book because when and if they do, your skin will burn terribly and you will know that you have failed as keeper of this volume of fear and that you must act quickly and resolutely to discover who the int ruder is and do what is necessary to resolve the matter."

"I'll always do my best, granny."

"Oh, I have no doubts about you, dear." She kissed Jacob on the forehead. "Now, understand that the things I will teach you, the chants, the conjures, methods of creating manifestations... I want you to understand clearly that most of the prayers from '*the book of skins*' are truly evil and great care—Jacob, I mean, truly great care must be used when saying them. I know I have told you this before, but if you make even the smallest mistake, the slightest mispronunciation of a single word when reciting certain prayers from this book...that will be enough to reverse the prayer; to turn it on you instead of the intended person."

"Yes, ma'am." Jacob did not know exactly how to ask his grandmother a question that is bothering him: "Granny...did you ever use a spell or prayer from this book?"

Elizabeth looked at her grandson for a long moment then she sighed and returned to *the book of skins,*" rubbing it gently.

"If this book is ever used, then those witches who are seeking me will know precisely where I am and how to find me. |So, no, I have never used it for anything, Jacob. It is not likely you will ever need to use it, but if you do, then be prepared to do battle with the two highly ranked witches who are forever seeking this book."

"What will happen if they are able to find us, granny?"

Elizabeth smiled at her grandson and pinched his nose playfully.

"You'll be more than prepared, Jacob."

"But, which spell or command will I use against them? We haven't talked about that."

"Jacob, there are any number of things that you and I have not discussed concerning your magic. That is because, when you need to use it, the kind you need will be instinctual."

CHAPTER 8

DEEPER INTO
THE DARKNESS

The years seemed to dissolve before his very eyes, and now at the age of nineteen Jacob is considering what he is going to do with his life and where he needed to be to do it. He felt a sense of importance in the knowledge that he is likely the only person his age who knew the things he knew about magic, the occult and something his grandmother Elizabeth called **the darkness.** Elizabeth has also seen to it that Jacob is well versed in homeopathic treatments for certain illnesses and of course the use of herbs for certain dastardly reasons.

Jacob has always imagined that after learning so much magic that he is going to feel quite superior to other people. Instead of feeling all powerful, he felt strangely humbled, especially when he is reminded by Elizabeth that he needed to keep his magic skills secret unless the circumstances called for him to reveal it; and so she taught him many ways in which to do that in his lessons: *art of the deception.*

Jacob loved both his grandparents, but he simply adores his grandmother. He is an avid student of his homeschooling studies and proved to have an incredible memory for his academics as well as the magic Elizabeth is teaching him. In fact, Jacob eventually proved to possess an even better memory for magic than Elizabeth's.

What gives her cause for concern her is that her grandson exhibits far more interest in the darker sides of magic than she is comfortable with. He is also more adept at using them the and proving so each time Elizabeth tested Jacob his ability to perform the magic she has taught him. His prowess with dark magic always proved superior to his use of lesser magic though abilities with both are superb; yet, he seemed to have a greater interest and intensity in learning and using *dark magic.*

One day, Jacob and Elizabeth are sitting near her altar, but instead of holding the purple volume, *The book of skins,* she is holding a holy Bible, stroking it gently. She kissed the Bible and when she spoke to Jacob, her stare is still locked on the Bible in her hands.

"Jacob…*Darkness* does not exist only in areas of magic and the occult, there are also *Dark* parts in the Bible. It is a holy book, but just like in life, not everyone in it is a good person and not everything contained in it is a good thing. There are some evil things and evil people spoken of and depicted in the Bible."

Elizabeth opened the Bible and moved her fingers along the paragraphs, murmuring words very lowly as her finger moved along. Jacob assumed she is reading Bible passages, but her voice is getting lower and after several minutes, Elizabeth's lips are moving but no words are being issued from her throat.

And then it happened.

Jacob sat up at the table when he saw an exceptionally tall person with sunken cheeks and black eyes and mouth standing at his grandmother's side, staring at him. His sallow complexion is lifeless, more like a grey sheet someone is using to cover parts of his face and his prominent cheeks are so bulbous that they appeared to be ready to burst.

Jacob is trying to remain calm, but it is not an easy task to accomplish.

"Granny, there's somebody right next to you. Can't you see him?"

"No. But you can see him, can't you?" Elizabeth is delighted.

To his surprise, Jacob became calm.

"Yes, granny, I can see him."

"Good." His grandmother touched his arm. "It's okay, Jacob. I'm not able to see him. It's part of your *veil* gift that you can. He is one of the angry angels and he is never to be trusted and yet, he may come to your aid if you need to call him. Our time together is short, Jacob and so instead of continuing instruction from *the book of skins,* because it is limitless, I will also be teaching you to conjure from the *Dark* parts of the Holy Bible."

Jacob is keeping his eye on the figure standing at his grandmother's side who has not allowed his eyes wander from Jacob.

"Jacob, you will see people like the demon presently in this room and at my side, from time to time all of your life. Sometimes they will be present to help you, and other times you must be careful of them because they might have been sent by someone to harm you. Other times they will be moving through and have been stopped by the beauty of your aura; yes, sometimes simple curiosity will draw them to you, but never consider being friendly with them. Demons are never to be trusted. There may come times when you summon one spirit and a second or even a third one just might accompany it. Beware them all and be prepared to destroy them. But when a creature or spirit appears to you that you have not summoned or mistakenly brought forth, it cannot do things to harm you but can still cause you grief. Never use a spirit whose presence you have not commanded, because it can turn on you since it is not there at your command."

"Do all spirits look so...grim?"

"No. In fact, some spirits are very young and joyous. I will teach you the differences between the good and bad ones and also how to send them back to the person who sent them to you or back to the terrible shadows from which they came. I am moving you along now to clear your aura to for whenever '**The Enchanters'** are ready to give you your final teachings. But that may be years from now. Sometimes they will wait until your current magic knowledge ages a bit and you have shown sufficient promise in using magic. Those will be brief, but ever so deadly. When they have completed your instructions, you will then, like me, become an *enchanter.*" a member of When your instruction from this book is over, you will be ready to become, like me, a member of this sublimely *Dark sect: the enchanters.* Your magic abilities and knowledge will then be infinite."

"Who? *the enchanters*? Who are they?"

"They are exceptionally powerful beings who have hidden themselves in the deepest part of the *Dark,* the subterraneous world of *'phantom continuance.'* They appear at will into this world or retreat instantly back into theirs. Their power is awe inspiring."

Elizabeth held her grandson's hand and looked deep into his eyes with an expression he did not quite know how to interpret, only that it seemed kind.

"I desire you to learn the absence of fear, Jacob. Nothing can ever harm you with me present even when you believe I am not near, I promise you that I shall be. You have need to fear nothing, no man or creature human or otherwise."

"Grandma, that spirit next to you is acting nervous, as though he's about to do something."

"That's because I've turned this room into an 'expulsion plane' that can send him either back to where he came from or to limbo—total blackness forever. I did this so he would stop trying to 'eat' your energy."

"He was 'eating' my energy?"

"He's been staring at you, hasn't he?"

"Yes, ma'am, he has been. Was I supposed to do something?"

"Not at this point in your instruction. This creature near us has been hoping for certain of your energies to leave your body, as it slowly does with anyone who is fearful. If enough of your energy left you, then he could sneak into your body fooling it by pretending to be energy being restored, and your body would welcome him, unwittingly allowing a demon to sneak in believing it to be energy." Elizabeth takes a chained pendant of a black man's head from her altar and hands it to Jacob, explaining:

"Jacob, this is a black Moor. All the Moors are black."

"Yes, I remember that from your home schooling classes. The Moors are of the Arab and Berber races and they are of noble blood, breeding and position."

"Yes that is correct and this is a blessed pendant left to my great grandmother many years ago by her great, great grandmother who, it is said, owned many African slaves. One and one of them told her she is a princess in her native country and that she has been kidnapped and sold into slavery by an angry African suitor whom she continually refuse to marry.

One day, in appreciation of my great, great grandmother's mother's kindness, the princess gave this pendant to her for protection, giving it a special blessing that turned it into a formidable weapon of special defense. The slave princess said a very special prayer and pressed the face of the pendant until its tongue sprang forward. Then she pressed the pendant against her breast, letting it pierce her there while continuing to pray for several minutes before returning it to my great, great grandmother, saying: '…Now it has powers from the grave.' The princess died that night."

Elizabeth placed the pendant around Jacob's neck.

"Jacob, never remove this pendant for any reason. It is your protection. My spirit will live forever in this pendant. Simply press its face and allow the tongue to spring forward and pierce your finger and I will come to you from wherever I am. But when I do come you may not recognize me"

Jacob is examining the pendant.

"Thank you, Grandma. It's beautiful."

Jacob held the pendant and there is a tremulous warmth that suddenly washed over him, giving him a sense of comfort, and he knew that, indeed, he is being watched over…

Forever.

CHAPTER 9

THE ASSAULT
REVEAL

The black man's fist slammed into the side of the young woman's face, immediately blushing her bright-beige cheek into a wide circle of angry, dark red flesh. The muffled crunching noise in her mouth is caused by several of her teeth smashing together and then crumbling onto her tongue, where they settled in the blood pooling there until she spat it all out.

Her assailant, a beast of a man well over six feet in height and 280 pounds of rippling muscles glares at Jacob until deciding to change his focus to the slowly growing crowd looking at the woman who is collapsed on the ground, shaking. The small, curious crowd moved cautiously closer to the woman on the ground as she stirred and slowly regaining consciousness and sits up.

The burly man glanced menacingly at the crowd as they whispered encouragement to her, then he knelt to beside the woman and began pummeling with his thick fist. This caused the crowd to immediately withdraw as the woman curled into a fetal curl, then into a state of merciful unconsciousness.

The burly man stood straight and now focused his ire on Jacob, walking slowly in his direction. Jacob has watched the brutality with anger building.

Obviously the man has not missed Jacob's interest:

"What chu you fuckin' lookin' at, pretty boy? You want some o' this ass whippin' too, young blood?"

Jacob is moving slowly in the man's direction but looking down at the unconscious young girl. The giant of a man curled his fists into two swollen knots of flesh as he and Jacob walked towards each other.

"I said what the fuck is you lookin' at, fool? Pretty as you is maybe I'll make you one o' my hoes like this one heah an' put you on a corner to make me some dollars. But don't hold out money on me like this bitch layin' here did." He laughed, and his smile betrayed a missing upper front tooth and one absent canine on the left. The man and Jacob are standing face-to-face now, each staring into the other's eyes and not blinking.

"Matter o' fact, you jus' might be prettier'n my bitch heah, young blood."

Jacob's fists are balled and he is only a second from punching the man in the face, but instead he mumbled something and stepped back several feet. Suddenly the brute's entire body began spinning. As it continued whirling around and around, its speed began increasing, and he screamed for someone to help him. Soon his revolutions are so fast that his body is not more than a blur.

The terrified crowd watching the man spin, murmured a communal groan of surprise and slowly moved further away, some of them stumbling over each other as they fearfully watched Jacob who bent to give the beaten aid girl and while still attending to the beaten girl on the ground, Jacob turned slightly towards the spinning man and whispered several indecipherable words and the unconscious man stopped spinning and collapsed to the ground.

But the young girl heard the words Jacob spoke, a language she did not understand and it frightened her. When Jacob held out his hand to help her to her feet, the young girl drew away from Jacob and managed to get to her feet on her own. Keeping her eyes on Jacob, she walked over to her abuser and helped him to his feet.

Once the man has gathered his senses, he yanked a pistol from his pocket and pointed it at Jacob. But his arm began trembling so badly that he has difficulty aiming his gun.

Jacob beta his fist against his side and called out:

"Sic! Sic! Sic!"

The sound of numerous dogs barking and snarling thundered through the air centering on surrounding the young girl's assailant. The crowd backed away even more, many of them trying to call out but terror has locked words in their throats though their mouths remain open with their lips moving but no sound is uttered by anyone as they watch the man's clothes is being torn from him by some raging, invisible thing snarling; then the man's flesh is pierced and bleeding from deep slashes on his neck, arms and legs.

Then the man is gripped by something that tossed him back and forth and about, tearing away the flesh on his hand that is holding the gun, forcing him to finally drop his weapon. His screams could barely be heard above the din of snarling and barking. Terrified and confused, he looks at Jacob and begs him for help.

"Please, mister! Whatever they is—please call 'em off me!"

The petrified people gasped when the man is suddenly yanked off his feet and into the air by the invisible assassins. He attempted to reach into his pocket for something but a snarling creature snapped its teeth over the man's hand and the terrified man screamed in pain, his eyes pleading again with Jacob to help him while he continued trying to defend himself. The people are all struck dumb at the strange sight of the man being torn apart by invisible, barking animals.

An elderly woman in the crowd pointed to the man under attack but she is looking at Jacob, yelling

"Hellhounds! Them's hellhounds!" And she pointed to Jacob, "Boy, where you from? How you git here? You got Satan's hellhounds! Oh, I know where you from!" The old woman turned to the crowd. "He a conjurer! That yaller nigger boy's a conjurer!" She held up her hand as though shielding herself from a blow. "Turn away from him! Don't let him look at chu! He got the evil eye! He'll hex ya'!" Everyone turned from Jacob, shielding their faces with their arms.

The barking stopped and the man is no longer under attack. The young woman began tending to her abusive pimp, but then he is suddenly being chased by the barking dogs that no one can see. He is chased while the abused woman follows, calling out to him, wanting to help but unable to do so. Soon they are too distant from everyone to see or hear.

The crowd then began to slowly disperse, but they all kept cautious eyes on Jacob. The elderly woman held up a thick Bible and begins approaching Jacob, continuing to fan the Bible's pages at him, but taking care not to look into Jacob's eyes.

"Get thee hence, student of Satan!" She slapped the top of Jacob's head with the Bible. "Do not allow him to make his home here! Move thy form from his door Beelzebub!"

The elderly woman continues to fan the pages in Jacob's face as a series of low growls suddenly surround Jacob and the sound of loud barking, baying and snarling, all of it menacing and surrounding Jacob.

He seemed to not notice the growls, but the old woman gasped and stepped back, taking the crowd, who has ventured near him, with her as she retreats. She clutched the Bible against her huge, deflated breasts, falls to her knees and rolls her eyes skyward while slowly sinking to the cement in a shudder of trembles.

Someone in the crowd hollered:

"Them hounds is back! He done called 'em back! Oh, yes, Lawd Jesus—they's back! An' they protectin' him! Protectin' they master is what they doin'!" Then, with her eyes locked on Jacob's, she began singing, "Yes, Jesus loves you…yes, Jesus loves you. Yes, Jesus loves you, 'cause the Bible tells me so." She held her Bible high. "Oh, yes Satan!—I mean, Jesus! Yes, Jesus is Lawd!"

The jeering voices are making it clear that Jacob is no longer wanted or needed and as always the old woman's voice is the loudest, screaming at him.

Satan's son! Satan's son!" She got to her feet and began strutting about with one hand on her hip, sashaying in a sassy manner. "Satan's son walkin' his dogs what can't nobody see! Yeah, you go on an' walk them dogs, Satan! You jus' keep in walkin' an' git thee hence, boy of Beelzebub! Get thee hence!" She fell to the ground again, her Bible raised high above her head while she screams: " –Oh! Jesus! Lawd of mine!"

Jacob turned and begins walking away and now thinks he might understand what his grandmother meant when she said that often their magic gifts came with great difficulties in life. Also he clearly understands now if not before, just why his grandmother Elizabeth told him to always keep his magic skills secret.

But a part of him is furious with the girl for rebuffing him and though he tries to employ reason concerning the thankless behavior of her and the crowd, he is angry at the behavior of the young girl whose life he was sure he likely saved.

He wanted to do something to get even with them all but is glad that he left before he attempted to do so. And as he walked on and calmed his emotions a bit, he felt ashamed that he had imagined the vengeance he felt against them all could be justified.

After walking a long distance, Jacob is finally calm and seeing things more clearly[and he is understanding how he has expected too much from the crowd and especially from the elderly woman who is obviously a religious fanatic. But he kept walking until he no longer knew why he is trying to sort out things when he knew that when all is said and done, none of the entire incident and the people involved are not going to fit into what could be considered as logical. His grandmother has long ago taught him that humans, especially when acting angrily or violently, rarely would logic or reason fit into their situations.

Later that evening, Jacob has tired of walking and returned home. He is greeted by his grandparents Elizabeth and Paul both of whom are having a snack in the dining room. Jacob plopped in a chair near at the table where his grandparents are eating. `

Paul is just finishing up and he walked over to his grandson and put his arm around his shoulder, inquiring:

"Are you okay, son?"

Jacob nodded and touched Paul's hand.

"Oh, I'm fine, grandpa. Just kinda tired from walking so much. No, I'm fine thanks.

"Well, I'm off to bed then." He kissed Jacob on the forehead.

"Goodnight, son."

"Goodnight, grandpa."

Paul walked to his wife and started to kiss her on the forehead but instead he grabbed her and kissed her on the mouth long and deep, shocking Elizabeth who immediately flushed almost as red as her hair. When he allowed her to sit up free of his embrace, she fanned herself frantically with her hand, grinning unabashedly and happily embarrassed. Elizabeth playfully slapped at her husband while looking at a grinning Jacob who loved seeing them so happy with each other; and they always are.

"Paul, I'm going to slap you, mister." She is still fanning herself and still flushing. "You see our baby sitting here and you carrying on like that."

Paul gently slapped his wife's behind.

"I ain't nevah seen no baby that big an' ugly. Just you don't waste no time gittin' on in the bedroom, 'cause I'm waitin.'"

"Paul!" Elizabeth is grinning and looking at Jacob. "Jacob, I don't know what's gotten into your grandfather." She is really fanning herself now at double speed and glancing at her husband as he sauntered off, glancing back at her now and then. She stood, sighed loudly and walked over to Jacob.

"Jacob, baby, are you really okay? You look kind of bothered."

"To tell you the truth, granny, I'd much rather talk about it tomorrow, if it's okay with you."

"Jacob, are you sure?"

"Yes, ma'am. Fact is, I'm headed for the 'fridge and a ham sandwich." He stood and kissed his grandmother on the cheek. "Now, it looks like you'd better get outta here before our caveman comes looking for you." Both he and Elizabeth laughed at that.

Then Paul's voice sounded out:

"Elizabeeethhhhh."

She shook her head and pulled her robe tightly around her.

"Oh, that man…" She kissed Jacob. "Goodnight, Jacob."

"Goodnight, granny." Jacob headed for the kitchen, grinning and feeling better about the day's earlier incident. His grandfather's voice called out again:

"Elizabeeeethhhh."

"I'm coming you fresh old buzzard." She is giggling almost beyond control as she hurried for their bedroom. When Paul closed the bedroom door the real giggling began. A moment later the room is bereft of giggles but burgeoning with love.

CHAPTER 10

IMMEDIATE
REVEAL

The next day, word of Jacob's incident reached his neighborhood. The exciting retelling of his "underworld powers" he used when levitating the man and spinning him around in midair and the invisible dogs that Jacob made attack the man and tear him to shreds and making the man tremble so badly that he couldn't shoot his pistol at Jacob and him telling the dogs to chase the man away while still in midair, and Jacob calling the dogs back to protect him from the old woman and her Bible and his evilness succeeding in dropping the old woman to the ground a few times and the terrible warnings from Jacob's invisible dogs blocking him from the old woman and her Bible or maybe just the old woman or yes, maybe from both of them—are verbally reenacted, embroidered and spun in practically one breath in lavish, fictive style for to those who are not there and would never dare be there by others who dare and who will, one day, lie and pretend they at least attempted to intercede.

Of course the retelling of the tale completely overshadowed and negligently disregarded the fact that Jacob saved a young woman from a more advanced vicious beating, maybe even death at the hands of her pimp, a giant of a thug with hands like a bear's paws

It took less than a week after the incident for Jacob and his family to become feared pariahs whose reputation for causing manifestations of unnatural phenomena is known to be true and their ire to be avoided. Visits to Elizabeth by their neighbors for personal problems of love or some kind of sickness slowed to a trickle. This is fine with her since it meant she is able to spend much more time with her husband Paul and her grandson Jacob.

One Sunday, fall afternoon after Paul and Jacob returned from hunting, while helping her husband and Jacob "dress" the deer the men have taken, Elizabeth wanted to have an important conversation with her grandson:

"Jacob, I'm going to ask you something that may strike you as incongruous with my years of teaching you magic, but I need to ask you this and I hope that you will decide in my favor."

"Sure, Grandma. What is it?"

She stopped cutting the deer and looks at him, searching his face for something she needed to see there. She smiled and touched the side of his cheek.

"Jacob when there comes a time you have to use your magic skills, please try and use only the lesser ones; use the least harsh and less dangerous magic if you can. If you don't have to harm people, then don't."

"Yes, ma'am. I believe I think that way anyway. I don't really want to hurt anyone."

She looked at him for a long moment without saying anything. Jacob wondered what his grandmother is thinking:

"Granny, what're you thinking."

Elizabeth started slicing into the deer again and then stopped abruptly and looks at Jacob.

"That man who was beating up the woman you helped. You angry at him and you wanted to hurt and humiliate him. You could easily have chosen a binding spell to lock his feet to the ground or just locked up all his muscles so that he would have been unable to move."

Jacob looked away from his grandmother, knowing that she is telling the truth about him. He is feeling greatly ashamed.

"…Yes, ma'am. You're right."

"I want you to try and remain objective when helping people, Jacob. If you make it personal, you are going to make mistakes the way you did with the pimp."

He did not understand why she is calling what he did a mistake. It is not an appropriate choice of magic, but why a mistake?

"Granny, why do you call that a mistake?"

"Jacob, the mistake you made is letting people witness you doing magic. And look what it's led to here. Now, as I warned you years ago, now people are afraid of us, of you of even your grandfather."

He hung his head down.

"I see what you mean, granny, and I'm really sorry."

She wiped a smudge of deer's blood on the tip of his nose, smiling at him.

"Jacob, every mistake needs to be a learning lesson for you. Just look at it that way. I am not chastising you, just making you aware of something that you may be hiding from yourself. Your magic is oh so powerful and can be oh, so dangerous and yet an absolutely wonder. But, as I have always tried to instill in you…please, please, Jacob…use it wisely and only when there is no other choice for your purpose which I am sure will always be a selfless one." The two hug and after a long hug they returned to cleaning the deer. Elizabeth points to her husband. Paul has fallen asleep with his deer skinning knife in his hand. She took the knife and smiled at her husband, taking a long, loving look at him. Then Elizabeth covered his legs with a small blanket and pinched his nose. He snorted, began snoring and brushed away her fingers. She laughed softly and this time she lovingly plinked the end of Paul's nose with her finger, smiling.

"…Old buzzard."

…giggle.

IT'S TIME

Jacob wiped away tears from his grandmother's eyes and is fighting really hard to keep his own tears from making a like appearance. He looked at his grandfather Paul who is standing next to Elizabeth. Jacob abruptly locks his grandfather in a loving embrace and at that moment both their tears broke free. Jacob and Paul held onto each other tightly in order to subdue their chest heaving silent sobs. Everyone knows...

Even the thick faced black bus operator's eyes almost appeared crestfallen as flashed a brief grin at Jacob, Elizabeth and Paul while he tosses Jacob's two suitcases into the lower baggage compartment of the bus...so, well, of course he knows...

But it is for certain that Elizabeth and Paul Jennings know that their grandson Jacob Jennings has passed the test for New York City Police Officer and is due to start in the Police Academy in lower Manhattan in two weeks. Thanks to an amendment, prospective police candidates living out of state are allowed to take the exam as long as they are living in the state of New York at the time of their appointment

Months ago Paul and Jacob scoured Harlem for an apartment for his grandson and are fortunate enough to get Jacob into a new apartment complex on riverside drive in west Harlem. He moved his grandson into the apartment over three months earlier and thus the onset of the "empty nest" syndrome that visited Elizabeth and Paul, even though Jacob remained living in their home, commuting back and forth from the farm in Louisiana to his apartment in west Harlem in New York.

But now it is time, time for Jacob to say his goodbyes to his family, repeating his promise to spend as much time visiting them as he could manage to do once he is situated in his new job and abode. He promised Elizabeth that he would practice his magic techniques often and keep his skills absolutely secret from others. His grandmother, handing him a small leather backpack, wondering:

"Jacob, I don't know why you like taking the bus for such a distance as from here to New York."

"Granny, I love just seeing the sights in other little towns along the way. I like using that time for reflecting, too. I think a lot, you know."

Paul swiped away a few tears and hugged his grandson:

"Now, son, when you git up there in New York, you kinda keep it under cover 'bout them strange creatures you always talkin' 'bout and especially don't let nobody know how much food you kin put away at one sittin.'"

Elizabeth pinched her husband playfully and gigged:

"Hush your fresh mouth, Paul." She turned to Jacob.

"This is a going-away present for you, dear."

"Aw, Grandma, what a really beautiful leather satchel."

"I think it's called a briefcase, up north, dear. That's from your grandpa Paul. What's inside it is from me." She smiled at her husband.

Jacob hugged his grandfather for a long time, both of them fighting back tears.

Finally, his voice cracking from emotion, Paul broke the moment.

"Well, your grandma done put somethin' in that bag, boy."

But Jacob took another long moment to look at his grandfather, thinking of the emotional moments they experienced together when Jacob was growing up. He is thankful for the strength in Paul and for all he has taught him about being a man. He opened the leather briefcase and took out three thick books. Paul is smiling but it is such a sad smile with the corners of his mouth twitching as it fought to continue to imprison the forced grin, the failure of which meant letting loose a flooding of tears.

One of the books is labeled, "Cryptozoology."

Paul is curious.

"Lizzie, what is that you said that book is about?"

"It's about creatures thought to exist, but there is no real living proof of it, like the Loch Ness Monster or the Abominable Snowman. Things that may or may not be real." Then she grinned mischievously at her husband. "Like that six-foot Muskie fish you keep talking about."

"But I'm tellin' you, Liz, Jacob was in the boat, but it started putting up such a fuss, it almost turned the boat over. Jacob was there but the boy had done ate up his lunch an' mine and then fell asleep. I were hollerin' for is him go! I mean, it weren't no room in that boat for the three of us no way." He looked at Jacob and tussled Jacob's thick, curly hair. "I gotta admit I did turn it over in my mind a few times 'bout keepin' that fish and tossin' this heah food vacuum cleaner overboard in place of it. But I throwed that seven-foot monster on back in the water."

Elizabeth and Jacob looked at each other and then burst out in raucous laughter. She patted her husband's behind. "Yes, sweetie, we know. You do realize that fish just grew a foot longer, don't you?" She hugged her husband and kissed him.

One of the books in his bag, Jacob did not recognize and he looked, questioningly, at his grandmother. She touched the book.

"That's called, 'The Cabala,' Jacob, an old Jewish tradition of the mystical interpretation of the bible. You'll understand once you begin studying its content."

The third book caused Jacob to catch his breath. He looked at Elizabeth and she nodded her head.

"Yes, Jacob. 'The book of skins.' I told you it is going to be yours and this is the day, the day you're leaving, for me to pass it on to you. "When you get settled in your new place in New York, you put this books in a special area of a room and be sure to keep that space clear and don't let anything clutter it. It's space should always remain open and kept absolutely clean. Above all, *The book of skins* needs to breathe so never place anything on top of it."

"Yes, ma'am."

"And always remember that magic—our magic comes at a price, sometimes small and sometimes it is a great price. But always a price…an eventual cost to us." She hugged him again and so did Paul.

"Thank you, Grandma." Jacob headed for the bus. He started to climb aboard, not daring to look back but then deciding to do so anyway.

His eyes met Paul's eyes that are dripping with tears.

Jacob smiled at his grandfather. In addition to becoming Jacob's parents after his father has been killed in combat in Vietnam, Elizabeth and Paul gave him unrelenting love. He loved both of his grandparents, but his love for Elizabeth is so strong that he found it to be almost impossible to leave her. But he knew he needed to, and his grandmother, in her own, very subtle manner, encouraged him to do so. Jacob waved an abrupt goodbye to them and climbed on board the waiting bus.

Through the window, Jacob watched his grandparents continue standing for the longest time, until he is barely to see them and he knew that they only saw a blur of the bus from their distance.

Still standing and staring at the far away moving dot that was at one time a bus, Elizabeth and Paul slowly turn away and head for Paul's truck to return home.

She manages to keep her brave face in light of the fact that she knew Jacob's kiss on her mouth and the deep look of acceptance that she saw in her grandson's eyes told her, not surprisingly, that he is able to see what her eyes betrayed to him and that is that she knew what is coming; that when he returned home again, this time she might be…somewhere else.

…She thought he may know where.

CHAPTER 11

NEW YORK CITY

Jacob liked living in New York, especially in West Harlem on Riverside Drive where, from his apartment he watched the boats moor and run up and down the Hudson River during the summer.

He spent a lot of his free time on his terrace where he often ate his breakfast on it watching the cars zip back and forth on the highway near the river. There are also lots of people coming and going in the parks with their pets and their families cavorting

After Jacob graduated from the police academy with top honors as number one Police Candidate almost two years earlier he is given duty as a Special Assistant to the Manhattan District Attorney's Office; a position that allowed him little time for himself.

But at the end of his two year assignment he is promoted to the rank of Detective First Class with NYPD. Still, with crime being at an all-time high in New York, Jacob is unable to get back to his grandparents' farm to visit and has been so involved in his work that he has neglected to remember to keep in touch either by phone or writing.

But a phone call from his grandfather Paul quickly brought to his mind how delinquent his love has been. He called his grandparents here and there, but not nearly as often as he wishes.

Now, sitting in his precinct's locker room, he is ruminating both about his life with his grandparents and his recent promotion to detective first class and what his future offered him as a police officer.

Jacob looked at his gold detective's badge and grinned weakly. He is dubious about his feelings concerning the end of his assignment with the District Attorney's office; with crime occurring at a high rate, it is hard work that seemed never to end but he definitely found investigatory work to be his calling.

He is packing a uniform to wear home as his grandfather, who has requested: "…You make sure you got your police uniform on 'cause I know you lookin' more'n handsome in it. An' you ain't nevah got the chance to send us down no picture o' you wearin' it, so…"

Jacob finished in the locker room and headed downstairs not knowing there is a small crowd of well-wishers awaiting him as he is about to leave the precinct. He stopped and acknowledged the congratulations coming from some of the other police officers with whom he worked. Jacob, from his first day on the job has proven to be a very popular young man.

The loudest congratulations came from his friend Ivan, a white officer with a tall Mohawk-styled haircut colored green. Jacob and he were street patrol buddies until Ivan is assigned to work "clothes" undercover for the Youth Gang Division in their precinct.

The heavily muscled man grabbed Jacob's hand and pumped his arm as though it is a leveraging bar on a water pump. Then he yanked Jacob to his chest and wrapped his arms around him.

"Yo, Jacob, my man! Congratulations! I hear you got your gold 'tin.' You deserve it if anybody does! I'm happy for you, my man!"

"Thanks, Ivan."

"An' I see you got the old patrol uniform ready outta mothballs, huh?"

"Yeah, until there's an opening in our Division, I guess for a 'DT First class."

"How come you still so serious, man? What does it take to make you happy? Man, I think you need to get laid. Let's hang out tonight. I'm off in two hours." He slapped Jacob on the shoulder.

Jacob held up his hand and shook his head.

"No thanks. I've got things to do."

"What things man? I hope you ain't missin' the D.A.'s office like that!"

Jacob shook his head.

"Naw, Ivan, it's not that."

"Then what 'chu gotta do? Do some more readin' from that weird book you used to always have under your arm? What is the name o' that book? Zipology?"

Jacob corrected him with a thin grin.

"It's Cryptozoology, Ivan. Cryptozoology."

"Yeah, that's the one about weird creatures, am I right? How come you're into that kinda stuff, anyway?" He leaned close to Jacob and whispered, "...Jacob, pal, that's why you ain't got no steady woman, man. A handsome dude like you? You gotta ease up an' have some fun." Ivan banged his thick fist against his puffy, muscular chest. "An' ain't nobody no closer to you than me an' so you know I ain't gonna lie to ya'!" He hugged Jacob again. "I love you, my brother! But I can see somethin's on your head so I'm gonna step off for a minute. But chu know I'm here for you!"

Jacob smiled and patted his friend on the shoulder.

"Thanks, Ivan. You know that I already know that and I'll see you later." He waved to everyone and walked out to the police parking lot area.

Inside his car, Jacob eased the windows down, leaned his head out from the window and took in a deep breath of the night air. He laughed thinking about what his friend had said. But he also knew his friend is right. It is exactly what his grandfather Paul is always telling him with one difference; Paul advised Jacob that he needed to be with a special kind of female, maybe someone who is a professional—but not a police officer, but who knew what kind of female? All he knows is that he has not come across any girl during his dating in New York who held his interest for very long and no one, really, with whom he cared to maintain any kind of meaningful relationship.

He sighed and started his car then sat thinking that maybe his grandmother knew best after all. He needed to stop actively seeking love. When it is time, Elizabeth always advised him, love will find its way to his heart.

He glanced briefly at his plane ticket and thought about his grandparent's house and how the neighbors have pretty much shunned his family since those years ago after rumors spread about his incident with the pimp beating up the young girl. Of course there are still those neighbors who shunned Elizabeth until the times they needed his grandmother to solve their personal problems. He felt his temper stirring and, shutting out those negative thoughts he snatched his car out into the heavy evening traffic.

ARRIVAL

Jacob, wearing his police uniform, woke to the sound of the plane's pilot dryly announcing that seatbelts needed to be fastened for the landing. He glanced around the plane and wiped the sleep from his eyes. He called his grandparents' home earlier from the plane. His granddad answered and reminded him to be wearing his police uniform.

Paul mentioned seeing Jacob on television for singlehandedly stopping a bank robbery just before his recent promotion to Detective First Class. Paul said that his promotion and the big bank robbery he heroically stopped has been shown on television and has taken up practically all the news, and that everyone in the neighborhood considered him to be, "Some kinda Eliot Ness or somethin."

The plane landed smoothly except for a noticeable bump that happened in tandem with a bright lightning flash followed by a long roll of thunder that reverberated around the small airport as Paul arrived in his truck to pick up Jacob.

Seeing Jacob in his police uniform, Paul jumped from his truck as though he has been ejected from his seat. He ran over to Jacob and hugged then stepped back several steps and looked at Jacob in his uniform. Paul turned to some of the exiting passengers and pointed to his grandson, Jacob.

"Hey, this heah's my grandson, Jacob! He's a New York City Detective what stopped a bank robbery all by hisself! He's a hero!" Paul turned back to Jacob with a grin that appeared ready to split his mouth open.

Jacob and Paul climbed into his truck and rumbled out of the airport parking area and out onto a narrow dirt road leading to a highway. On the way to the house, Paul's demeanor of happiness is replaced by a somber tone. He glanced over at Jacob.

"I reckon the neighbors will be kinda surprised to see you wearin' your policeman's uniform. But you kin go in the house an' change real quick if you wanna, Jacob."

Jacob knew that there is no doubt that his old, superstitious neighbors are going to be much relieved to discover that he has become a policeman and not as they expected a Warlock.

When Jacob and his grandfather neared their home, many of their neighbors are on the road and waving to them as they approached. At one point, a neighbor put up his hand to stop Paul's truck. He smiled broadly at Paul and walked up to the truck window to take a look at Jacob. He likes what he is looking at and signals to the others nearby to come over to the truck.

"Y'all git over heah an' take a look at young Jacob in this heah pretty police officer 's uniform! Git over heah!"

They all gathered around the truck and a grinning and proud Paul Jennings. As they sat there in the truck, the crowd of neighbors grew and several young girls are very obviously quite taken by the handsome Jacob. Thankfully an increasing rain thinned out the crowd and Paul and Jacob are allowed to move through the few people remaining and continue on their way. When they reached the house, Paul suggested that they remain in the truck for a while to wait out the pouring rain. Jacob agreed and spent the next hour bringing Paul up to date with how his life has been going in

New York. Jacob also asked Paul endless questions about his father, Roger Jennings, who was killed in combat in Vietnam.

Paul and his grandson sat in the truck for almost two hours talking before deciding to stop waiting for the heavy rain to slow and they both made a dash for the front door. Inside the house looked exactly as Jacob remembered. Paul made sandwiches for them and they sat at the dining room table munching and recalling the days.

After finishing off the sandwiches, Paul have been sitting in the dining room for over an hour, both of them, their expressions grim, have run out of words and are listening to the rain beat against the dining room windows. Paul has also suggested perhaps they both needed to remain quiet because of the raging electrical storm outside. As has always been the practice in the home, during an electrical storm, no electrical appliances are to be used or even turned on. Earlier, Paul reminded Jacob that:

"With that 'noise' the sky is makin' out yondah," Paul warned, "we don' wanna call no lightnin' strike in here. Any kinda noise'll in heah kin make God's 'lectricity come inside lookin' for ya'. An' it kin find ya' too. An' God knows you don't want that.

But as Jacob peruses the family photo album, he chuckles at the photos of himself as a child on the farm, helping Paul feed the hogs. He is especially fond of the picture of him with his arm around a very large animal that later became his pet hog.

Paul saw him looking at the picture and shook his head:

"You an' that blame hog. Lawd knows that more'n a minute ago, weren't it, son?"

Jacob nodded.

"More than a minute, grandpa. More than a minute."

"Boy you sure look right handsome in that police uniform if I do say so. You could'a knocked me down with a feather when I first seen you in it. Yeah, you growed up to be a right handsome man like your daddy an' your grandpa."

"Thank you, grandpa."

Paul reached for his small mason jar of his homemade whisky, "O' course you ain't quite as good lookin' as me, but you damn sure tryin'."

Paul went back to staring in the direction of the living room but Jacob is still ensconced in the photos in the family album.

Paul, still staring at the living room, said:

"Yes, sir, you a right good lookin' policeman theah, son. You look for the world like your daddy."

"Thanks, grandpa." Jacob touched Paul's hand.

"Grandpa, how're you doing?"

Paul did not look at him.

"Aw, I dunno, son. I just feel like I should be goin' huntin' or somethin'. Like I should be jus' about leavin' the woods now, an comin' home with a bagful o' squirrels on my belt or draggin' a deer behind me. So you done made detective up north now, have you?"

His grandfather's voice is always strong unless he is speaking to Elizabeth; now it just sounded tired.

"Yes, Grandpa."

Jacob came across a photo that captured his really special Christmas. It is a photo of him kneeling at the base of a very tall Christmas tree, holding his gift of a pellet rifle, something that he has dreamed of but never thought he would get due to his grandmother's aversion to weapons in the hands of children.

"Yeah, I done read 'bout chu up theah, boy." Paul is smiling. "Did I ever tell you we even seen you on the television. You turned out to be a right brave young man. I reckon as how you done took a lotta chances up north theah by bein' a policeman, so I reckon it ain't no wonder they made you a detective. But when you gonna find somebody an' git married, son?"

"I dunno, Grandpa. I just can't seem to meet the right girl."

"Well, you know, you do need a wife. A man ain't much good at livin' alone, even though he thinks he is."

Paul took a deep breath but it turned into a gasp. It sounded weak, desperate, as though about to collapse into something horrible. He took out a square of chewing tobacco, put it to his lips, and called out:

"I'm gittin' ready to chew this here tobacco at 'chur table, girl. You'd better come an' stop me." Tears dribbled down his cheeks and then refused to leave them.

Jacob felt his heart crack open. He and his grandfather are staring at the place in the living room where the Christmas tree ordinarily would have been, where the wonderfully green and aromatic tree has always stood every Christmas for so many years, towering over the gifts; but now it stands almost hidden in a far corner of the living room and now in the space where the Christmas tree ordinarily stood is…

…Elizabeth's body lying in her flower covered coffin.

WAKE OF WITCHES

The wake for Elizabeth Jennings has a surprisingly large number of neighbors arriving at her home for the ceremony. Jacob is very surprised but Paul, morose and depressed took little if any notice of those in attendance, all of whom came bearing pots of food, pies and cakes for the family and for those sitting at the wake. Although it is understandable that neither Jacob nor Paul has even the slightest appetite, it is custom that families of the deceased should never cook during the week of mourning and certainly never at a wake so there is an abundance of cooked foods, enough to last Paul for at least a month.

There are also huge tin pans of baked macaroni, baked hams, pots of pinto beans, black eyed peas and okra, rice, apple pies, potato pies, large tins of cornbread, pots of fried chicken and mashed potatoes, collard greens and string beans.

All of the food is taken to the kitchen to be later parceled out to mourners who would eat in the dining room. Some of this food is to be consumed by the mourners, but that would still leave a huge amount for the family.

Jacob wondered just how many of the visitors have come by to assure themselves that his grandmother Elizabeth is truly dead; to see proof of her demise. After all, superstition teaches that demons, death-witches, creatures of the supernatural night never die.

Jacob looked at a few mourners looking at Elizabeth's coffin with dread and he is sure that some of them are there to make sure that his grandmother did not rise up from her coffin. But he and his grandfather welcomed them all even the people seated some of which are stealing furtive looks at the coffin with some dread.

Someone is knocking on the front door and before Jacob could get up from the dining room a guest let the minister in. Paul has arranged for a Baptist minister to say final prayers over Elizabeth though the minister, knowing some of Elizabeth's background, wondered if that would have been her wish.

The preacher wasted no time getting down to business and he immediately began the Services at Elizabeth's coffin. The minister placed a Bible in Elizabeth's open coffin and said a last prayer over her.

After the ceremony the mourners hummed and half sang a vague gospel song that not everybody seemed top know the words to but are feebly and errantly filling in with their own versions of it. The moment they finished there is another knocking at the door, but it is sharper, far more decisive.

An elderly church sister wearing a wide pink carnation in the center of her black straw hat headed for the door to answer it until a sudden strange and rather loud noise caused everyone to stop and look around the house, wondering where the vibrating droning is coming from.

Some of the guests eating in the dining room, put down their food and gravitated toward the living room, looking around for the source of a sudden droning sound. In just a few moments the living room is crammed with mourners who have narrowed down the sound to be coming from the front door where someone is knocking, the sound of a person striking a cane against the wooden door. Now everyone is looking at each other and moving in closer together in building fear .whoever is at the door now began pounding their firsts against it and this soon replaced by the horrible sound of someone clawing at the wooden door from outside.

The sound turned to a low rumble that danced across the living room ceiling and then began shaking the house. Mourners, some of them now terrified, are beginning to guess that witchcraft is definitely afoot in the house. Then, from outside, at the front door, there came the shrill, shrieking screams, and squealing voices of women who begin pounding their fists against the front door caused the women in the living room to grab hold of each other for fear of collapsing from terror. Then the sound of many nails clawing at the door and it began to tremble at its hinges and the women in the living room are petrified and unable to move, they are not even run out of the living room while those in the dining room with Jacob, the minster and Paul remained in place, but all have move to within inches of Jacob, hoping he was going to take over. But they too clutch their Bibles against their breasts.

Jacob calmly stood and started for the living room the source of the strange droning when suddenly the house is plunged into total darkness. Every one of the mourners including the minister fell to their knees screaming and pleading to God for mercy.

The front door suddenly began to rattle badly and shake. Some mourners clasped Bibles to their breasts and began weeping, while others snatched their Bibles open, frantically searching the pages for some Psalm or prayer to protect them, to save them from the evilness at the door that now is a flashing bright light about to allow the creatures entrance as the mahogany structure began to slowly split in half.

Elizabeth's coffin burst into flames and every mourner, gasping in horror of the sight, immediately prostrated themselves on the floor, some of them speaking in "tongues."

Jacob and Paul rushed to Elizabeth's burning casket and tries beating out the flames but it seemed useless with the flames seeming to intensify though none of the fire is touching her body or burning the casket.

Jacob knew exactly what is transpiring but he is hesitant to use his powers although his grandfather is looking at him with a silent plea for him to do so. He realized that it is the high ranking witches that have come for *The book of skins* and are likely being led by the ranking witch seeking the book for *the most unholy of all things human, and* that she is on her way through the front door at this very moment.

Then, from just outside the front door, a woman's piercing scream that sounds capable of splitting metal causes the doorknob on the front door to tremble. Then the scream from outside the front door turned into a prolonged horrific howl and what little is left of the front door from the entities attempt at entry, abruptly explodes with a deafening crack, sending splintered shards of wood into the assembled mourners in the living room.

The front door space then became a wide sheet of black and purple flames and a woman appeared, slowly walking and covered in a roaring fire, her body covered with an ape's fur and her eyes are bright green and the smell from her is so putrid that everyone, even Jacob, gagged at the stench of rotten eggs, dead rats and decaying meat combined.

When she entered the living room the flames from the door's opening ignited her fur and her entire body erupted in black and purple flames that slowly burned away her fur down to her starkly white flesh that turned red and raw. Then her flesh began melting under the heat of the fire that is covering her as she writhed and moaned in obvious torment from the flames that started to extinguish themselves only to reignite seconds later as they continued to liquefy her skin which as quickly regenerates itself. But apparently nothing is going to stop this creature from her goal of reaching the coffin searching it for *the book of skins.*

The horrible reek of this offending specter is causing everyone but Jacob to vomit violently as she slowly, painstakingly struggled towards Elizabeth's casket. Jacob realized that there is no doubt that this woman is no simple specter, instead she has to be the person his grandmother described as *the most unholy of all things human.*

The flames are no longer engulfing the casket and have done no harm to either it or Elizabeth and Jacob moved quickly to stand in front of the casket, blocking the witch from getting any closer. Then he looked down and saw two young, hunched-over children, scrambling along on all fours like horrible, fleshy crabs, while being dragged along behind the witch who held them captive by metal leashes at the end of each is a thick and large metal hook that pieced the children's spines.

The witch stopped and took great pains to smell the area of the casket and then she turned back to look at the cowering mourners who are all too petrified to flee. She screamed hysterical laughter and shifted her glare to Jacob who stood defiantly facing her.

"Where is the book, boy? I smell it on you! Where's the book!" She turned to point to the cowering minister who is hiding behind several of the mourners. "You there! Either you tell me where this book is or I'll paint the ceiling with those whoring Jesus groupies as easily as their legs part for you!"

"What kind of book are you talkin' about? You don't mean this…" he held up his Bible, "…the Bible, do you?"

The witch screamed out a horribly loud, maniacal laughter:

"No, boy! What would I do with a damned comic book?"

The witch started to reach for Elizabeth's body. "Then we'll take this whore for now!"

Jacob whispered a prayer then wrapped his hand around two of his fingers and twisted. A deep, roaring tornadic wind filled the living room and quickly sucked out each of the resisting specters who managed to grab a couple of the mourners as the witches are swept away.

Jacob gently repositioned his grandmother in her coffin. One of the mourners lying on the floor held her hands up to the ceiling.

"Lord Jesus!" She turned to Jacob and interlocked her fingers, pleading with him.

"Jacob please! Please free us of this place! Please let us outta this hell house! We promise never to return or to cause your grandfather any discomfort! But for God's sake, let us go!"

Jacob glared at each of the mourners one by one with clear hatred. He began focusing hard on them.

But Paul, remembered what Jacob did to the old hound dog and feared that he is about to do the identical thing the living room assemblage of mourners. Paul touched his grandson's arm and whispered:

"…Jacob don't do it son. Think of your grandma! Think of Lizzie, boy! You know she wouldn' want chu to do nothin' to 'em. Jus' let 'em go son."

Jacob immediately relaxed his glare, took a deep, tremulous breath then he pointed to the door and the flames died out immediately.

"Get out! All of you!"

His words immediately galvanized what is left of the frightened group into a single blur of bodies rushing out the door pushing and shoving each other aside in an effort to be the first through.

The minister threw the fee Paul gave him onto the dining room table and joined the others in the melee to flee.

In moments all the remaining mourners are gone and it is once again quiet. Paul watches Jacob tidying his grandmother's hair and her dress.

"Son, you know them creatures that was jus' in heah is gonna be comin' back for that book an' for you, too. They gonna follow you. I know Elizabeth done already warned you about 'em, didn' she?"

"Yes, sir. And that's why I'm not leaving you here alone, grandpa. You're going to have to move back to New York with me."

Paul smiled. He walked over to Jacob and put his hand on his shoulder and looked down at Elizabeth who looked as though she may have been simply sleeping.

"I know your grandma is right proud o' the way you handled things heah this heah night. But don't chu worry about me. When they come back heah an see that that book ain't heah, they gonna go to lookin' for you. They ain't gonna waste their time wit' no ol' buzzard like me. Besides, if you ain' heah then they ain't gonna be able to smell the book. That smell's on you what they was smellin' and if you ain't heah then they gonna go lookin.'"

Jacob nodded.

"Yes, maybe you're right grandpa."

"Besides, Lizzie ain't gonna let nothin' bad happen to me no matter where she is." He bent over and kissed his wife in the coffin. "Naw, Lizzie is gonna be heah with me. I done already prepared her a 'bed' deep in our back yard, right near her chicken coop an' them chickens what she loved so much. That way I kin always sit out theah an' talk with 'er whenever I pleases to do so"

Paul prepared to close the coffin, but he just leaned it for a long moment, mouthing the words to some prayer. Then he turned to Jacob:

"Now, let's you an' me git our gal in the ground for her to finally have some peace." Paul bent over and kissed his wife again then closed the coffin lid.

"Grandpa, I'm going next door to get those three Jefferson boys to help us carry grandma to the back." Jacob headed for the door. His grand-father's words stopped him there.

"Jacob I can't help but think of how many times them same ol' fool neighbors used to come slinkin' through that door an' some of 'em not wantin' to be seen comin' heah, an' my Lizzie helped them ol' fools outta their miseries."

"Granny would probably say that they are just frightened."

Paul shrugged.

"I reckon as she jus' might say that. She would sometimes worry and dote on them peoples like they was her own." He sighed and looked down at his wife's coffin.

Jacob thought about what his grandfather has just said and a faint smile moved across his mouth as he thought about the mourners and smiled, muttering to himself:

"...Yeah, I think maybe in her own way grandma's thinking is right. These poor old souls really are her children."

CHAPTER 12

THE ARMY
WAY

It has been six months since Elizabeth died and Jacob Jennings, though he knew her death is approaching when he left their farm years ago, is finding it more difficult than he imagined it would be to get over his grandmother's death.

He found it curious that he never felt this way about his father's dying in combat in Vietnam, but then he was just a child when he understood what has actually happened to him; only as an adult did his father's death hold any true significance.

Jacob wiped his sweating forehead as he approached the mid-Manhattan recruiting. A Marine recruiter is standing outside the street recruiting post. He waved to Jacob, beckoning to him to come closer.

"Come on, young man. The Marines could use another good man."

The Army recruiter inside the station heard what the Marine recruiter said and he rushed out and grabbed Jacob's hand.

"You must be Jacob Jennings. We spoke on the phone yesterday. Sergeant Louis Wilkins here. Come on inside outta this heat." The sergeant grinned at the other recruiter, "Good try Jimmy." They both laughed good heartedly.

The temperature inside the recruiting station is not much lower than the mid-June numbers outside. Jacob is headed for the fan until the recruiter gestured for him to be seated in the chair at his desk.

"Have a seat here, Mr. Jennings and let's see what the army can do for you."

"Yes, sir." Jacob sat.

"Boy, it is really a hot one out there, isn't it? I hear the temperature's has already reached the mid-nineties."

Jacob looked at the street filled with people moving lazily along.

"Yeah, it sure feels like it. Man, I mean it's hot out there."

The recruiter did not answer. He is thumbing through a small file that has Jacob's name on the tab. He closed the file folder and folded his hands, giving Jacob a very serious look.

"Mr. Jennings...just what is it you're looking for from the army? Are we talking career here or what?"

"I already have a career."

Sergeant Wilkins opened the small folder again, nodding.

"...Yes so I see. You're a cop—a detective." He closed the folder again. "And first class too. Then why in the world do you want to join the active army?"

Jacob stared him for a long moment before saying:

"My father was killed during combat in Vietnam, sergeant and I actually want to go there and, I don't know, maybe get some sense of the futility of it all, maybe. Something." Jacob fanned himself with his hand. He is thankful that he is wearing a low, wide cut white cotton shirt.

"I'm sorry about your father, young man. Really sorry. Where in Vietnam?"

"Bong Song."

That really got the recruiter's attention and he looked at Jacob with a certain appreciation.

"Oh, wow! Your dad is Special Forces."

"Yeah."

"Wow."

"Yes, sir. A first lieutenant. Career soldier with a combat promotion to Captain and he had just completed his overseas tour and he and his men are on their way to the army airport to head back to the States when they get ambushed."

Jacob is obviously on the verge of having to choke back tears. He turned away from the sergeant.

"An honorable man your father." Well, let's see what I can do for you. I might be able to find a spot for you in Military Intelligence and that might get you near there or maybe get you stationed there, if you have any college."

"I have an undergrad degree from Columbia University and I'm fluent in Mandarin."

The sergeant's eyes lit up and he flashed a wide smile.

"Mandarin?" The sergeant extended his hand. "Welcome to the US Army, son. I'm going to put you in for OCS, Officers Candidate School after your basic, and from there you won't have any problem getting assigned to wherever you want after that. Your dad was an officer and I'm sure you're going to want to be one. An officer can move around more freely in our army than an enlisted man. As an officer in Military Intelligence, you ought to be able to reach Vietnam sooner or later. Give me the spelling of your name again. I can have you out of here in a matter of two months." The recruiter and Jacob shook hands firmly.

ARMY LIFE

After his first year in the army, Jacob has completed Officers Candidate School with the rank of 2nd Lieutenant. His flight is just landing at Tokyo Airport the city of his first assignment to work with a semi-intelligence Police unit in Tokyo, Japan as Military Assistance Advisory; His civilian occupation as a Police Officer with NYCPD, with the rank of Detective First Class affords him this rather coveted first assignment.

Jacob followed the line to the plane's open rear exit. As he disembarked, a tall stocky black man several yards from the plane is standing next to a large, black Chevrolet van with darkened windows.

The man motioned to Jacob to join him. When he reached him, he man extended his hand:

"Lieutenant Jennings?"

"Yes, sir?"

He grabbed Jacob's hand and shook it vigorously.

"I'm Colonel Lionel Burney, U.S.Air Force. Like you, I'm military and you will call me Lionel or Burney in public. I'll call you Jennings or Jacob." They shook hands. "As you probably already know, one of the first things we do is in our line of work is to drop all military and police authority title references. Calling a person by his or her police title can be deadly for that individual. Do we understand each other?"

"Yes, sir."

"And let's drop the 'sirs,' too. Okay. I'm your liaison person for the Japanese Community Police Affairs Bureau headed by Usata Onanoka."

Burney gave Jacob a brief once over as though not quite convinced that he is fit for this mission.

"I've worked with him for all of the fifteen years I've been assigned duty here in Japan." He pointed to Jacob's luggage. "Toss your bags in the rear and let's go. I'm taking you to your hotel, and we'll go over a few things there before I pick you up in the morning and take you to meet Chief Investigator Onanoka."

The Colonel's Chevy rushes the van forward into the thick traffic near the airport, moving along rapidly until they are free of all congestion. Then it seemed to melt into the bright lights of the city and the tall, glass structures that has people busily coming and going from its interior. It is almost, he thought, as though the buildings are regurgitating human beings as quickly as they are busily being swallowed at the different glass and steel entrances

Once at his hotel, Jacob registered and he and Burney stepped inside the waiting elevator where a pretty young hotel uniformed Asian girl stood smiling. When they enter she slams the door closed the car abruptly jerks upward, stopping at the fifth floor The young operator pointed the colonel and Jacob in the direction of Jacob's room, saying:

"Your room is at the end of the hall, gentlemen. Thank you for choosing our hotel and please enjoy yourselves."

Jacob did not care for what he thought is the insinuation of her statement and he glanced over at her quickly, but then he and Burney stepped out onto the thinly carpeted floor and the elevator door closed quietly. But Jacob is sure that he heard the young elevator operator giggling as the elevator descended.

Inside the room Colonel Burney sank deep into the softness of a wide, cushiony chair that faced the bed. Jacob took a quick moment to check out his accommodations. His room is a reasonable space with a queen-sized bed facing a large console television.

There is a small sink inside a closet-like room, and several towels, four washcloths, a tube of toothpaste, and a pair of shower slippers. A green and white curtain covered the shower that is adjacent to a toilet, an oblong mirror, a medicine cabinet, and a scale.

On a small table in a corner of the room near another door is a large pitcher of water inside a small porcelain basin. There is also a small working fireplace at a far wall. Several thick logs lay next to it, and though it is early fall and chilly in his room, he appreciated that it would take very little to make his room toasty if need be.

Jacob is happy for the fireplace with extra commercial fire logs at its side that he could light if he so desired, but the comforter covering the generous sized bed is more than enough, he thinks. Even with the very cool Japan evenings.

Adjacent to the bed is a huge picture window with sheer white-lace curtains and a long wooden table with two Ming Trees on either end straddling the base of the large window looking out onto a forest several hundred yards from the hotel that is almost hiding a large lake behind it.

Jacob placed his small suitcase near the bed and took out his constant companions, his copy of the kabbalah and *the book of skins and* a book on cryptozoology. He did not see a clear area suitable for his books, so he sat on the bed facing Colonel Burney who is seated on an oblong green leather couch almost appearing to be ready to fall asleep. But then Burney caught sight of the books:

70

"Uh…stupid question here. Maybe." Burney pointed to Jacob's books. "Are you of the Jewish religion?"

"No sir."

"Okay. Funny book for you to be reading, isn't it? I mean, the kabbalah."

"It is a gift."

"A gift." Burney did not know if he really believed that. "And that one on cryptozoology? Another gift?"

"Yes. Both of them are gifts from my grandmother."

"Are you familiar with the Almasty legend?"

"Somewhat. It's much like the Yeti, Bigfoot—all the ape man sightings except the Almasty is supposedly living in Khazakhstan in Asia."

Burney's expression revealed that he is surprised at Jacob's immediate, and educated response. He looked at *The book of skins* but since there is no label on it, he didn't mention it.

"Yes. You're well into it, I see. Well, okay, Jacob, here's the skinny: I'll meet you in the lobby in the morning at nine and then we go to Tokyo's Police Headquarters to meet with Usata Onanoka. He's Chief Investigator of the Tokyo Police Special Affairs Department here in Japan. He believes that your being black just might be an advantage for the investigation. Certainly no one is going to suspect that you are in any way affiliated with the Tokyo Police Department."

"No, sir, they surely won't."

"Well, if this assignment goes well, you'll get your 'railroad tracks' promotion to captain. And since you're a Detective in New York, I've got a friend who is in charge of a new covert unit there in the NYPD. I think I can get you get you preferential consideration for admission. You book on Cryptozoology tells me his unit will be right up your alley. That is if you decide to leave the service."

"Thank you, sir—I mean, Lionel."

"Yes, that's much better Jennings."

Burney is staring at Jacob's Cabala again.

"His name is Jaegar, Inspector Adelfried Jaegar. And judging by those two books you have there, his new department is going to be of great interest to you and you to them." Burney stood and walked to the door.

Jacob opened it for him.

"I'll give it my best, sir."

Burney shook hands then down the hall to the elevator. He pressed the button and stood staring at it for a while as though lost in thought. When the elevator arrived, he glanced back at Jacob who is still standing in his doorway. He grinned at him and stepped onto the elevator.

Jacob watched the elevator descend through the iron grating surrounding it then he closed the door and headed for his bed, yawning. He sat on the bed and picked up *The book of skins* and began reading.

He thought about the view of the forest from his window across from his hotel. Now, again he marvels at the scene of pristine snow surrounding an explosion of black trees and bushes.

The trees' snow-covered limbs looked like dark, slender arms of ghosts, throng together, stretching, reaching their phantom white atrophied slender limbs out for something not quite within reach. In the farther distance he could see rows of single story homes, all of them lit by lanterns, glowing yellow and orange and other colored similar shapes blurred by distance are no less appealing to him. Jacob took a deep breath and exhaled slowly. He could hardly wait until the morning arrived.

He could feel that he is going to love this assignment and Japan. He stretches out on his bed, but just for a moment to get the kinks of flight out of his bones, he believes. He has no idea that the moment was going to last until..

The next morning when Colonel Burney knocks on his hotel room door and gives him ten minutes to the three army "S's" and no more than that, chiding him that:

"It's not my fault that you love to sleep. This is not a unit for sleeping, I can tell you that much. But Director Onanoka is high on you after having read your resume. Must be one helluva piece of paper. Okay, let's roll!"

After miraculously negotiating the rapid Asian traffic in Tokyo, Burney's black Chevy van glided to a stop in front of one of the buildings of Tokyo's Police Headquarters. Jacob is sitting next to him, his heart is racing with excitement of what felt almost like a police chase. The main Police Department building is walled in with uniformed officers stationed in front at intermediate places within the entire block.

Stepping out from the van, Jacob looked around the area. Directly across the street is a small park with long, rectangular patches of grass and a large sprouting water fountain near the front of it. He thought of the difference in scenes between the police headquarters and his hotel which is closer to the forest.

Burney led Jacob to a guarded side door entrance where he slid a card into a slot in the wall next to the door and in a moment a tall, very thin Japanese woman is walking down the hall towards them. She stopped at the thick glass door and disturbed her austere countenance by smiling at Burney and opens the door for him using an electronic card signaling device.

"Good morning, gentlemen." She bows to them.

"Good morning, Isha." Colonel Burney returned her bow and then he leads Jacob to an elevator far in the rear of the floor. On the way, they walk past two large open office pools of male and female uniformed police officers.

In the elevator, Jacob is surprised that there are no numbers on the elevator's button board. nor any other kinds of designations; the buttons are all blank and far too many buttons for the height of the building.

Burney presses one of the buttons and smiled at Jacob's confused expression. The door opened to a blank wall with coded lock on it. Burney slid a card along a slot in the coded lock and the "wall" slid aside, revealing a long corridor of offices with their doors closed.

"Don't worry, this isn't an entrance you or anyone else will be using. It's really an emergency entrance and exit."

Exiting the elevator Burney and Jacob walked through another corridor with doors where along the way several armed uniformed police officers are rigidly standing at the "ready" with their M16-A2 rifles held against their chests.

Finally, they entered a wide area with several desks that are "manned" by females, all of them uniformed policewomen but for one female sitting behind a desk in civilian clothing. Burney stopped at a mahogany door with no name on it and knocked. The door opened and a smiling Usata Onanoka bows to them.

Colonel Burney spoke first:

Director Usata, this is Lieutenant Jacob Jennings."

"Lieutenant Jennings! It is so great to meet you!" Onanoka gripped Jacob's hand and began shaking it with great enthusiasm while doing a really quick assessment of Jacob's muscular physique. "Looks to me like you're in great shape, too!" Onanoka gestured to his office, "Gentlemen, please have a seat." He stepped aside and pointed to the refreshments on the table. "And please help yourselves; maybe you haven't had a chance to grab a bite." Onanoka sat at the round table and clasped his hands together.

Onanoka tells Jacob:

My name is Usata Onanoka and I have been recently appointed to the position of Chief Investigator of Japan's Special Affairs Department, a division of the Tokyo Police Department. But we're like the Intelligence part of our Police Department. I don't know if he's told you or not, but Colonel

Burney here and I have worked together for about fifteen years but in different departments. But all of them dealing with the Tokyo community."

"Yes sir, he mentioned that."

"I personally have been with the Tokyo Police Department for over twenty-five years and think I still look okay for an old forty-six-year-old ex-prizefighter. Even though I can see that I'm nowhere near your top condition, Jennings but let's get down to business. I'm sure, Lieutenant Jennings, that your department has brought you pretty much up to date on our concerns here about some of our local gangs."

"Yes, sir, I think they have but I'm anxious to hear your take on things, too."

"Good. I'm glad to hear that. We are just a bit concerned about the many different gangs migrating to Tokyo recently and we have no idea why. Now, they are not breaking any laws here yet, it's just that this congregation of so many different gangs in our city. It's really unheard of. There is even a local subculture but I don't really think we need to consider them a gang as such, but they are a kind of reckless motorcycle group of young Asians and we keep an eye out. We call them 'Bazooka,' literally meaning, I believe, that they are out of control. But they have not presented a problem, but now who knows? I mean, we've got gangs here from

Vietnam...Hong Kong—Mongolia, even; and these are all Asian gangs!"

Colonel Burney concurred:

"And just where did these gangs get the financing for traveling and living here? And they're living somewhere—but where? We can't find them anywhere. It's almost as though once they get here they disappear."

Onanoka looked at Jacob.

"Jennings, we're hoping that you can find out something about these gangs. As I have mentioned to Burney your being a black man, no one is going to suspect that you're working with local police authorities. And I am more than familiar with your vitae. You have graduated number one from the military academy, are said to be the most outstanding student that the

Military Intelligence has come across in many years. I am thrilled that your unit has agreed to assign you on loan to work within my department for this assignment. And I'm anxious to hear if you have any idea on how we might give this a new approach."

"Thank you, sir. I was thinking that I could assume the role of an American college student researching a psychology thesis paper on ancient Asian gang behavior. In that way he could ask questions of local people without drawing suspicion."

"That sounds great to me." Onanoka said. "When do you want to start?"

"Tomorrow sounds fine to me." Jacob said, with a shrug.

"Burney, you are right; you said this young man is on the ball."

Burney smiled.

"Yeah, he's hitting the ground running, Usata."

CHAPTER 13

THE
DREAM

Late night. Raining heavily. Wide sheets of gray water undulating through the air in floating waves of visually impenetrable rain struggling but defiantly holding its own against a hostile, blustering wind. Even the velvety night bristled against such harshness but it has nowhere to retreat until morning.

Nikki Ozaki, a tall slim Asian woman is also having to brave the relentless torrents and the abusive cruelty of the angry night monster ravaging the city of Tokyo. Nikki braced herself against the stiff winds and stinging rain while she cautiously follows Jacob and a young Japanese woman through the back streets and alleys of Tokyo.

Although the pouring rain made it much easier to follow them unnoticed, the noisy wind continued to press the rain against Nikki's face with such force that the tiny pellets has begun to feel like so many small pieces of metal about to pierce her skin.

Finally, Jacob and the woman reach their destination: a solitary, orange house standing alone on a wide street bereft of any other structure or persons but blessed by many trees just across the street from the lonely single story building.

Nikki has only the shelter beneath a thick tree next to which she has crouched with such fidelity that she could have been mistaken for being part of the tree. She wonders just how it can be possible that the day's pre-winter weather began as medium snow but the moment evening arrived, suddenly it has turned to splattering, stinging rain.

Nikki pulls her light coat tightly around her and tucks her legs in closer to her body. She finds it remarkable that Jacob managed to find such a valuable gang contact on the first day of his fieldwork pretending to be an American college student doing research on gangs for a paper he is working on for his thesis paper; and he has come into contact with the one person he really needs to find; she is certainly one person who could elucidate this curious gang activity. The problem, however, is that she is the one gang member who has been declared the most dangerous female in Tokyo: Yatsuko Desirlee Sakura, War Contessa for The Last Order gang.

Meanwhile, outside the gale winds are whistling tunes not meant for listening pleasure. Nikki is still bedeviled by the indifference of the elements producing intermittent wide areas of a cascading deluge that it seems to delight in spreading over her face. Again, she pulls her coat collar higher around her neck, then after a shudder quickly rushed up and over her arms, she pulled her coat tight and tries to lean even closer to the tree.

Nikki could only watch the front room of Desirlee's house from where she is crouched.

But from her position she can see anyone approach the house outside and any activity taking place in the living room.

Nikki gasped aloud and sat up at the tree when Desirlee came back outside and stared directly across at her. Then she looks around her own house as if she expected someone to be there.

Nikki's heart tripled its rate when Desirlee turned her back to her and began waving her arms about, screaming a chant for several minutes. Then she turned back to stare at Nikki. After a long moment of staring, Desirlee covered her face with her hands and lowered it. When she removed her hands from her face and looked up, Nikki's breath freezes in her throat at what she sees:

Desirlee has turned into and old hag with a protruding chin and she is now slightly bent over. She smiled at Nikki with a sadistic grin, displaying no teeth in the front of her mouth. She wipes her face and is transformed back into the beautiful young woman that Desirlee is. Again, a wind, a more violent one, slams Desirlee against her front door, momentarily forcing the wind from her, but she recovers quickly and goes back inside her house, but not without a scowling glance at Nikki across the street.

Nikki drew back against the tree when Desirlee slammed her front door.

"Oh!" Nikki's hand is trembling. "She has been given the power of shape shifting! She is the way a Soucouyant might appear. I believe the old woman in Desirlee's body is not so much a transformation as it is simply the source of Desirlee's power. The old woman is the source of her power. If that is true, then it means Desirlee has reached the level in sorcery that gives her The old woman is her power. If that isn't true, then it means that Desirlee been reached the level in sorcery that gives the power of shape shifting. My God I hope not!"

Across the street, once more Desirlee's door is snatched open and the old crone in Desirlee's body stepped out pointing an accusing, arthritic finger at Nikki, screaming above howling winds:

"You can die with him in here, bitch! You interrupter! Come inside and die with him! With us!" She turned around and walked back to the door which this time opens by itself as she neared it and slams behind her after she enters.

Nikki is suddenly exceptionally cold and it has nothing to do with the relentless torrents tormenting her. What she has just seen, no—what she has just witnessed is terrifying and certainly contradicts any sense of reality she always held dear. But what is of the utmost concern at this moment for her is that she knows that Jacob may think he is visiting Desirlee, but he is not a visitor. He does not realize it yet , but he is no visitor—he is a captive; Desirlee's prisoner.

Her instincts are telling her that she needs to find some means of backup before she attempts to protect Jacob inside Desirlee's house. But what backup is there against this kind of strong magic—magic that is far deeper and more insidious than ordinary black magic; this is what she knows to be *Dark* magic.

But she has to try and do something to get him out of there. There is no way she is going to allow him to be at the mercy of such a powerful sorceress one that she, too, is powerless against. But she has to at least try to come to his aid and she is positive that he is going to need someone to do precisely that very soon.

Determined to do what she knows has to be done, Nikki stood and, in a battle against a suddenly wildly gusting wind, she presses herself into the gale and makes her way across to Desirlee's house after being knocked off her feet a few times. Once there, she leans against the side of her front window and looks in to see if Jacob and Desirlee are in the living room.

Jacob is sitting in the living room alone, waiting for Desirlee. The room is filled with rather unusual objects: there are mural murals of Asian Peasantry working farms, strapped to their oxen with their feet deep in the muddy soil; on a few tables there are Ming Trees, some of them are bearing tiny drupaceous offerings on their branches of plums, cherries and olives.

There are pastoral paintings on a wall of families boating in row boats, children fishing in ponds and other little ones picking flowers and holding ice cream cones poised for imminent ingestion. A ceiling that held a barely fan is whose white blades are lethargically, perhaps, she imagined, even agonizingly barely managing to complete revolutions, is oddly painted black and orange.

But there is another curiosity in the room that she has read bout; a thing that is reeking of evil magic and is incongruous with the other items: it is the infamous exceptionally large bird bath fountain that she has often heard about; it occasionally belches up spurts of multicolored streams of water "painted" by lights flashing sporadically from somewhere at its base. But Nikki is unable to locate the precise source of the lighting and she knows the purpose of the terrible fountain, swimming in the *Darkest* of magic.

Jacob is sitting on the edge of a purple crescent-shaped couch with large yellow pillows spread across it that partially encircles a round smoked-glass coffee table.

Nikki draws back from the window when she sees Desirlee, who his once again her original, youthful self, entered the living room, smiling at Jacob who stands.

"You have a beautiful home, Desirlee and I am absolutely fascinated by the paintings of the farm workers on your walls." Jacob feels his Moor's head continuing to vibrate, it's very slight movement is enough to draw a subtle glance from Desirlee who is careful not to let Jacob notice.

"Thank you, Jacob. But, please have a seat." Desirlee handed him a long narrow glass filled with the orange liquid that Jacob could have sworn was white at first when she poured it. "Please drink and be comfortable and let's have our discussion on gangs." She leaned close and kissed him then coyly sipped at her wine. Her breath is ice cold and he involuntarily pulled away the second time she kissed him, but she kissed him even harder, as the wine in her mouth slide into his, sweet and strong.

Jacob easily senses the house has magic moving through it, but it is a different kind of magic, not one that he is familiar with from his lessons. His Moor's head warned him earlier of danger in the house when he entered with Desirlee.

He pressed a thumb hard into the palm of his hand and twisted it once to summon his "witching nose," a great heightening of his senses. Immediately an odor from Desirlee rose and repulsed him. He recognized the smell as one his grandmother Elizabeth taught him marked the person as a witch or sorcerer, in this case the strength of the odor told him she is a sorceress and someone with malefic abilities; she is able to resort to supernatural means for her personal purposes.

Desirlee, though frowning in an attempt to keep the old hag from reappearing at this moment, begins rubbing her fingers against Jacob's crotch.

"You will if you give me two hundred dollar for sex, yes? Here, I will dry your raincoat in my kitchen sink.

When Desirlee leans across Jacob, he notices that her complexion is pasty, sallow, maybe, he is thinking, a bit wrinkled. When her cheek brushes against his, her flesh and breath are frigid.

Desirlee grabs his poncho and rushes from the room. He sees that Desirlee is moving almost arthritically now, not like a young woman; and when she left the room, she looked stooped.

He knew these things may well mean that her magic is not fully under her control and that she rushed from the room maybe feeling that her "mother," the woman from whom Desirlee gets her power, is about to force herself to be visible, to take over Desirlee's body even if only for a moment. His grandmother has taught him that demons want much to be human and to have as much time in the real world as they can manage so much so that, at times, they do not mind ruining the agenda their conjurer has for them.

Watching it all outside the window, Nikki knows from her research into sorcery and gangs exactly what is happening now with Desirlee. As a sorceress using a level of magic above her station, she has insufficient means to maintain control the level of magic she is using, perhaps it's simply too unfamiliar for her to use competently and thus the presence of the old hag who is supplying Desirlee's with her present power.

So the old hag that appears in Desirlee's body is in control of Desirlee's power and is making her appearance to show that she, not Desirlee, is in power; and that Desirlee rushed from the room to keep Jacob from seeing her old hag facilitator whom she probably feels is taking over her body again.

Nikki is wondering how Jacob ended up going with Desirlee to her home. She has no idea that Desirlee has agreed to give him a lot of information on gangs since, as a coincidence, she, too, is writing a paper on local gangs and gambling. But Desirlee suggested to Jacob that since people might be listening to them talking about gangs, it would be safer for them to further discuss things at her home.

Even though Jacob remembered Onanoka's warning not to interact on any personal level with the locals while pursuing information, he decided to go with Desirlee to her home. He is especially intrigued by her mentioning that she even knew where some of the recently arriving gangs are living. He does not suspect that a woman as strikingly beautiful and young as Desirlee could ever be a gang member, much less into magic.

Jacob flinches as the bird bath water fountain suddenly erupts in a geyser a few feet high. When it subsides, he walks closer to examine it. The fountain's gold stand was surrounded by flowers around the surface rim, though not rooted in dirt of any kind— an immediate sign, he knew, of witchcraft, of something unnatural. And some kind of sound is coming from within the fountain and he feels compelled to lean closer, listening:

He is able to distinguish what he is positive sounds like a congregation voices growing louder and clearer:

"Stupid goddamned lieutenant."

"Is he a soldier?"

"Too late to leave now, lieutenant."

"There's a demon in the kitchen smelling your poncho."

"Come. Come here. Hurry. Come in here and join us. Be safe."

"But, no. She thinks to help you find us.| "Many numbers here, lieutenant. Your father is here, but he is always running. "There is no running from death."

The loud voice of a woman from the fountain warned:

"… Jacob, get out."

Jacob finds he has to struggle to back away from the fountain, but he succeeds. His thoughts are fogging and he headed for the door but realized that it no longer exists where it did before. He wanders the hall looking for it. There is only a strange and vague kind of dimness at both ends of the hall, not really dark rather a terribly incompleteness; and though he knew he should logically be within several feet from the entrance, still he is not able to see the front door.

He returns to the living room and sits on the couch—immediately feeling the soft cushion next to him depress at the same time as though someone with a great weight is sitting next to him. He recites a short prayer and spat a spray of his saliva at the space above the depressed cushion.

He waved his hand up and down rapidly over the depressed cushion and the image of a person sitting there appears; a fatAsian woman is staring angrily at him, but her staccato image staggers in and out very much like the drunken flickering an old fragmented film negative struggling through the gate of a period movie projector.

Then a strong woman's voice behind him screams:

"Why do you spit on my couch? You are a crazy man."

He spun around. The old hag has taken over Desirlee's body again and holding a red snake that she throws at Jacob who deftly brushes it aside.

Facing the old hag, he tries thinking of what magic would repel her. He brushed his hands together and a wind shoved the old woman all the way out of the room. Nikki rapped at the window and pointed towards the door:

"Front door! Go to the door!"

He ran to the place where the front door should be but again, there is only darkness there and no door.

While he frantically feels the darkness for the front door, the old woman is slowly, her feet dragging, coming towards Jacob. Visit my fountain young man. And now she is really bent over with a heavily curved hunched back and crystal white maggots crawling over her lower eyelids, each of them, slithering and fighting to be free but unable to struggle loose.

Nikki is screaming behind him from outside:

"Jacob! Are you in there? Are you still inside? Stay away from the old woman. She has taken Desirlee's body! Open the door!"

He hollers back:

"There is no door!"

"Is Desirlee or the old woman with you?"

"Yes!"

"Move away from her! It's '*the dream*'! She is pulling you into '*the dream*'! Wake up! Wake up, man! Wake up before it turns into a *travel dream* and traps you there! She wants to place you in her fountain in the living room! You have to really focus and force yourself to wake before '*the dream*' turns to a 'travel dream' and traps you inside it! Wake up! She wants to place you in the bird bath! It is her *fountain of souls!* Wake up and go to the door!"

Nikki is banging on the door that is visible outside, but still invisible to Jacob inside.

Jacob trembling finger presses his Moor's head face and its tongue slid forward and pierced Jacob's finger. The old woman raised her hand but, not waiting for the Moor's head to help him, Jacob spoke words from *The book of skins* that caused the old woman's legs to shrivel and she collapses to the floor and the front door reappears behind him.

The old woman pointed to Jacob from her position on the floor:

"Ah! So. As I thought! I smelled you even at the library! Foul pretender! So something is there after all. But it is not strong enough for us, you silly American."

The old hag makes a weeping gesture that turned Jacob upside down and slammed him against the front door. She ripped off a part of her dress and threw it at Jacob and it flew into his mouth in a great ball that began swelling, gagging him. After a long struggle, he is able to yank the dress from his mouth.

He locked his fingers together and the front door flew open. Nikki held out her hand to him:

"Please hurry! Even there from the floor, she is trying to ensnare you again. But she is having difficulty. Let me interrupt her concentration!"

She pulled out a small automatic pistol and fired a shot near the old woman, not trying to actually hit her. Desirlee's recognition of the mortal danger from a bullet returned Desirlee to her young self.

Nikki grabs Jacob's hand and they run from the house and out into the driving rain. After several minutes they see a huge field in the distance and they run towards it. Only then did Nikki slow down, but not by much.

"There is a huge barn over there and it looks empty."

Jacob looked at all the tents spread around the open field.

"What about those tents? Is the property theirs?|"

Nikki shook her head.

"No, I don't think so. If it belonged to them, they'd likely be living in the barn." As they enter the barn, she looks at him with wonder, slowly shaking her head. "But, she poisoned you. Otherwise you would have been able to see the front door. How are you still living? It's a real miracle that you have survived 'The Dream' she placed you in! But there was no exit ceremony performed by anyone, so how is it you are not dead? No one is supposed to able to survive outside 'The Dream' once they are ensnared. To leave without a ceremony means death.|"

Jacob is out of breath and they are both drenched.

"What's this 'the dream' stuff?"

Not knowing anything about Jacob's background in magic, Nikki looks at him with a condescending smile.

"Oh, you are not going to understand or believe what I am going to tell you. But, that fountain in her living room holds souls she has imprisoned through *the dream,* using sorcery. "Don't worry, I'm not nuts. If I didn't really believe it myself before, but now, well, after tonight I have seen proof of it. But, she will not forget this and will try and get you again at some point. This is sure to be an embarrassment for her; losing you, I mean. That's why she is trying again to place you back in 'The Dream' before you left her house."

"Oh." He nodded.

"I told you it would be impossible to believe. But you're alive and that is all that matters." She breathes a sigh of relief.

He catches a glimpse of a handgun on Nikki's side beneath her blouse when the wind flipped her jacket open for a second. How many women, he wondered, are walking around Tokyo with Glocks on their sides?

"Miss, I don't know who you are, but I thank you. Now, I don't want to look a gift horse in the mouth, but just how did you just manage to be here to save me? Also, you seem to know Desirlee. How is that? Are you following me or something, or is it all just a coincidence or what? And who in the world is this Desirlee?"

"Desirlee is a member of The Last Order gang and an even more powerful sorceress."

"Wow. The people you meet in a library."

Nikki smirked and said:

"Are you sure you don't mean, the beautiful women you meet?"

Jacob sees that Nikki understands the real reason he followed Desirlee which is because of her being so beautiful and he felt a bit embarrassed at being so easily deceived by Desirlee because of her beauty and as easily detected by Nikki. But then he realizes that since he has no idea who Nikki is, it does not really matter what she thinks.

"By the way," he took a deep breath, "I'm Jacob. Who are you?"

Nikki is looking through the barn window at a small group of young men and women coming their way in the heavy rain.

"Is something wrong?"

"We need to move quickly! Please follow me!"

With Jacob behind her, Nikki looks around and decides to climb up a retractable ladder that she and Jacob pulled up behind them once they are on the platform above. She gestured to him to crouch in the dark amidst old furniture and large empty wooden cartons.

A moment later the young men and women pursuing them ran inside. Immediately each of the young men and women begin searching the ground floor, looking behind old animal stalls, empty crates and refuse that has been left there over the years by others.

They ae all breathing heavily and satisfied that no one is hiding on the lower level, they look up at the platform where Jacob and Nikki are hiding. But it is really high and several of the men look around for something to stack high to enable them to climb up to the next level and begin their search. Meanwhile the others are standing in front of the exits and entrance of the barn, blocking any possible escape.

Jacob whispers to Nikki:

"…Who are these people?"

"… They might be intoxicated street punks looking for trouble but I am not sure. They have come along way for a simple fight. When I saw them earlier I was hoping that they are not following us. But I think they trying to get closer to us without being noticed. They are probably gang members that Desirlee has sent after us."

Jacob counted them.

"There are eight of them. Three of them are girls."

"Yes."

Nikki took out her weapon and held it ready to use it if necessary. "I just hope they don't find a way up here."

Jacob saw a huge rat and thought of a possible way out of the situation without having to really harm anyone. But, he has to distance himself from Nikki, not wanting her to hear him murmur a spell.

"I'm going over there to see if there's another way out." He quickly moves away from her and into deeper shadows He crouched behind a large crate and looked down on the gang and began whispering words of a conjure:

"…explitus nimrev idelaxtius wide."

He finished the spell but in the dark he accidentally knocks over a board that fell to the floor below. One of the gang members pointed up.

"They're up there!"

But the entire lower floor is suddenly besieged by really huge, squealing rats jumping at the young men and women. It took only a few minutes before the rats cleared the bottom floor and Jacob and Nikki quickly lowered the ladder and climbed down to ground level.

Nikki rushed over to the door through which the gang members exited. She peeked out and then broke out in hearty laughter, beckoning for Jacob to come over and see why she is laughing. He looks through the barn window and he begins laughing too. The rats he conjured are still in pursuit of the gang members and they are screaming and splitting up and yet unable to avoid the raging rodents.

But then Nikki looked down at something that is shining on the ground. She reached down and picked up a silver and gold dagger embroidered with golden snakes wrapped around the hilt and handle. She is handling the dagger with care and examining it with some awe.

Jacob is curious:

"What's that?"

"Something one of them dropped. It's a ceremonial dagger. Meant for you.":

"For me?"

"This is a very special instrument, a sacrificial one, I believe. So these are not ordinary street thugs after all. Certainly they are gang members sent by Desirlee to get you." Nikki wedged the knife into her small gun holster.

"This stiletto is a ceremonial dagger evilly blessed for *Dark* purposes. It would have been stabbed into you and that would have placed you in a kind of coma but it would have been very much like the Haitian death "coma" that is used on a victim to simulate death so that later the victim can be removed from the grave and made into a kind of zombie slave."

He stared at Nikki.

"Oh? Desirlee was going to make me a zombie?"

"Actually, I am not sure that she has the power to make zombies. No, her purpose to have you in the 'coma' would be to incapacitate you so the gang members could bring you to her without bother. Then she would have returned you to *the dream'* and... well, I have already explained how that would or might end for you."

The rain slowed to a drizzle and Nikki is able to hail one of the few empty cabs not off duty and they climbed in.

"I'll drop you off first, Jacob."

He hesitated to give his address, but he has gone through thick and thin with her, and he is sure she could be trusted. He gave the driver the address to his hotel, and moments later the cab stopped at its entrance.

He extends several dollars to Nikki:

"I hope you don't mind if I ask you again. Who are you?"

"I thought I had already told you." She refuses his money. "I'm Akinisha Ozaki. Nikki for short. Actually, Nikki's my nickname."

"I'm glad you were around, Nikki." He shook her hand .

"Yeah, me too."

He gave the driver his address and Jacob settled back for a ride in silence. When the cab arrived at his hotel, Jacob asked her:

"Nikki, would you care to stop in for a coffee or something? We also have a pretty nice bar inside the hotel. I at least owe you that."

"Thank you, but no. Another time, perhaps." Jacob stepped out and closed the door. As the cab pulls away, Nikki sticks her head out and says: "And please, no more student studies trips with strangers." She laughed , rolling up her window.

Jacob laughed and stood in the rain watching the cab disappear with the mysterious young woman. As though reminding him that he is standing in the rain, a huge wind rocked him to one side and slams a wide curtain of rain against his face. He ran to his hotel front entrance.

Inside the hotel as the elevator lifted Jacob up and delivered him to h is floor, he walked down the hall wondering just who in the world Nikki might be. A real mystery woman, he is thinking.

CHAPTER 14

TIME TO LEAVE

The next morning at Onanoka's office, Jacob is reluctant to mention last night's adventures to Onanoka and Burney. He knows he has no reasonable way of explaining why he took the word of Desirlee that she is a student and followed her home where he became her victim. It is the kind of mistake a person with his experience both civilian and army should not have made. He is very disappointed with himself knowing that he has allowed Desirlee's beauty to turn him into a victim; and in his private thoughts, he has been an absolute fool. Well, he thought, this is going to be one faux pas that he is definitely going to keep in silence.

The men have settled and about to begin the business of the day when someone knocked on Onanoka's office door. Onanoka interrupted his sip of morning tea to say:

"Yes, come in please."

The hinges on Jacob's jaw disintegrated and his mouth simply fell open when he saw who enters the office and is smiling at him. He hardly realized that he called out her name:

"Nikki?"

"Good morning, Jacob." Nikki said. She looked at Onanoka and Burney, "…Director Onanoka…Colonel Burney." Everyone except Jacob is wearing a knowing grin.

Onanoka turned to Jacob.

"Jacob, I believe you have already met Detective Akinisha Ozaki. We call her Nikki."

Jacob is astonished.

"De—Detective Ozaki?"

"Yes. She is my best officer. Detective Ozaki tells us that you are quite a brave man. But we are not surprised to learn that. I assigned her to surveil you last evening. After all, it was your first assignment and since you are not really familiar with our culture and our people, it seemed to me an appropriate thing to do at the time. And it appears fortunate for you that I did.

"Yes, sir." He is still staring at Nikki, and she continued smiling at him.

"It seems you had a very...peculiar evening. You managed to run into some gang members."

"Well," Jacob explained, "it is more like they ran into us."

"You took a dangerous chance by going home with a female you didn't know."

"It is my first time doing that, sir. I really thought that Desirlee is on the up and up, though I should have known better than to take such a chance." Jacob tries to grin but it is not working.

Everyone at the table except Nikki, sat up, surprised at hearing the name, "Desirlee."

Onanoka is very bothered:

"Jacob, you said her name is Desirlee?"

"Yes, sir." He looked at Nikki and then at Burney and Onanoka. "You said that you knew about last night's incident."

Onanoka looked disapprovingly at Nikki for not having given him the information that the person Jacob met is Desirlee; Nikki quickly offers a defense.

"Sir, I thought I'd let Lieutenant Jennings give you his version first."

Onanoka took a deep breath, leaned back in his seat, and gestures to Burney who lit a cigarette and reached for a cup of coffee, saying to Jacob:

"Jacob, her name is Yatsuko Desirlee Sakura. Her street name is Desirlee and she is a most important member of *The Last Order* gang. She is also a beautiful young woman as you obviously have already noticed. She is the 'War Contessa' for the gang; this means she is advisor to the gang leader, Yuuta, who their enemies are and when, if and how to eliminate them. She is heavily involved in sorcery and holds a high office therein, and so her opinion carries a great deal of weight in the gang's major decisions and actions. It's rumored that during one of her black magic rituals, she contacted an entity called, **'*She Who Is Most Evil*'** and it gave her special powers in exchange for her surrendering her soul to her. This entity is rumored to be as diabolical as America's **Satan**."

Onanoka patted Jacob on the shoulder.

"But Jacob, you have made a most important contact even though the odds of you coming into contact with her is one in maybe a hundred thousand. Nevertheless, Desirlee is the one person we most need to contact but there was no way. Well, until now, that is. We believe that even Yuuta, who is the founder and leader of the gang is somewhat afraid of her powers. I would think that is why he has never made her second in charge, for fear of an insurrection led by her. But having her as War Counselor, he is able to keep a closer eye on her activities." Onanoka looked at Nikki. "By the way, Detective Nikki is our gangland expert. Ever since her first year of hire, she has been doing research on gangs especially the new advent of those working with sorcery and Dark Magic." He picked up his tea and leaned back in his chair.

Jacob turned to listen to Nikki. She smiles pleasantly at him and began with an apology:

"Jacob, I'm sorry I neglected to identify myself to you last evening.

He returned her smile with:

"It's okay, Nikki, it's just that it is such a surprise."

"Anyway…I have spent most of my career here at police headquarters researching gangs and tracing their activities. But not just local gangs in Japan, but all Asian gangs and American gangs in social and psychological comparison. And yes, the most recent development in gang activity is the interest in the practice of sorcery and magic. Dark magic. Something I found to be rather extraordinary considering that sorcery is foreign to the formulaic thinking of most gangs which is usually militaristic and not using magic. However, I found that their magic is not the prestidigitation that we are familiar with. No, I am talking about magic derived from some ingredients in sorcery, somehow." Nikki looks at Onanoka, "Magic that appears to actually be real. Magic that, at last on the visual level—is real and really does work."

Jacob looks at Burney and Onanoka both of whom shrug in tandem, but Onanoka offers:

"We try to keep open minds here Jennings, after all even your Shakespeare wrote: 'There are more things in heaven and earth, Horatio, than are dreamt of in your philosophy.' Didn't he?"

Jacob agrees:

"Oh, yes. Yes, he did. He did write that."

Onanoka stood and begins pacing his office floor. He is holding a paper and reading it as he moves about. He stops and walks over to where Jacob is seated and holds out the sheet of paper for him to take. Then he says:

"Lieutenant Jennings, this is really a very great disappointment for me and this office, but you are the military property of the United States Army Office of Military Intelligence. And you are here on loan to my office and I greatly regret that I must allow you to be relieved of your present duty here in order that you be reassigned to work with Hong Kong police authorities. Now that you have made unreal inroads into a matter that is presenting itself as possibly an impending disaster for Tokyo, you are no sooner being taken away."

Jacob has read his orders from his military unit in Taiwan.

Onanoka shrugs:

"Well, it seems there is a very pressing and urgent matter taking place in Hong Kong that is threatening to possibly become a pandemic. Your unit wants you there to assist in an active investigation that is perplexing everyone."

Onanoka sat down hard in his chair at the head of the round table and bangs his fist.

Jacob finds difficult to believe, but being in Military Intelligence, he knows that being relieved of duty and reassigned without prior notice is not uncommon.

Colonel Burney has taken Jacob's orders and is reading them. He laughs aloud and shows Jacob's reassignment orders the orders to Onanoka and points to a name on the sheet:

"I think you overlooked something. Look who Jennings is going to be assisting."

Onanoka takes the paper and his eyes light up. Both he and Burney begin laughing. Onanoka hands the paper back to Jacob:

"Jennings, the man you're being assigned to assist is Chief inspector of Police, Owen Chang! One helluva man."

Onanoka is joined at his side by a laughing Burney, who agrees. Onanoka points out:

"Oh, brother! You have no idea! Burney here, me and this Inspector Chang go way the devil back in time. Chang was the class instructor for me and Burney way back in—."

Burney stopped him:

"Never mind the year! But, we go back to the days when it was like the old wild west here in Tokyo. Man, those were the days. But now old man Chang's a big shot over there in China. And you're gonna love it in Hong Kong. But be ready for a real 'soldier' of a cop!"

Burney started laughing and he and Onanoka slapped hands together. Burney dreamily said:

"Beautiful women, buildings, the most modern of everything, the best foods, the most elegant restaurants and places to visit and all of them…"

Colonel Burney and Onanoka held each other and in tandem hollered:

"Will never be seen by you!" Onanoka and Burney burst out in loud, raucous laughter. "Not with old man Chang at the helm! It's gonna be all work!"

Onanoka hollered:

"Your work starts immediately after you're introduced to him! He is a workaholic. If he ain't doing it physically, then he's doing it mentally!"

Calming down a bit, Burney added:

"But, if you want to learn how to get a job done—not always by the books, mind you, but you're in law enforcement in your civilian job, so hooking up with old Charlie Chan is the best thing that could happen to you.

Jacob is confused.

"Charlie Chan?"

Onanoka explained:

"That was a name we all had for him, and that includes all his students. He had mad respect from everyone he taught in his 'Special methods of Law Enforcement and Encoding Criminal Behaviors.' Chief Inspector Owen Chang is one fantastic cop. So get ready to start really learning about law enforcement from a real law bulldog! But I've put in for you to be reassigned to my office the moment you're free from Chang in Hong Kong."

Jacob felt grateful:

"I thank you, sir." He shook hands with Onanoka, then with Burney and lastly with Nikki who held his hands with both of hers, saying to him:

"I wish it could have been longer, Jacob. But I feel that we shall meet again. I am sure of it." "So, until then…" She kissed him lightly on the mouth and they hugged.

Jacob then glanced at his reassignment papers and felt so much better now about leaving Tokyo and going to Hong Kong.

And he surely is looking forward to meeting this legend: Owen "Charlie Chan" Chang.

CHAPTER 15

HONG
KONG

Heat. Even as he walks through the jet plane's boarding tunnel connecting the plane with the Hong Kong International Airport terminal, Jacob Jennings felt the searing Hong Kong heat attempting to eat its way through the seams of the exit bridge's protective gray tubing. He blots the perspiration on his forehead and cheeks then places the dampened cloth into his jacket's lapel pocket for easier retrieval. He adjusts the leather straps on his briefcase and repositions them on his shoulder. It is just too hot. Even inside the tube's cooling system, the thick, merciless heat commanded an omnipresence, demanding that the air cooling mechanism be reduced to the basic operation level or to full capacity Ineffectual.

Jacob enters the freezing airport terminal that is flush with hordes of people rushing to greet each other, some of them sidestepping to avoid collisions, while some stop here and there to observe rights of way. There are some people standing or milling around or wandering aimlessly, appearing to be lost or having only a vague idea of where they are or need to go.

Jacob is somewhat fond of airport scenes although this one did seem just a bit unusual that many of the travelers are black. He marveled at the numbers of young people arriving and either waiting in the ticket line or listening for their departure announcements or looking for someone to meet them; some have signs on their short sleeve shirts with names that he assumed are either the wearer's or the one the wearer is looking for.

He marvels at the architecture of the palm trees along the moving sidewalk and the white columns stretching up and reaching through the glass ceilings. The terminal's rotunda seemed boundlessly futuristic. His Army M. I. Unit has instructed him to report to Hong Kong's police headquarters. He casually looked around the area hoping the person sent to take him where, is holding a sign with his name on it.

Chief Investigator Onanoka and Colonel Burney have received orders from Jacob's M.I. unit in Hong Kong and he is to report directly to Police Inspector Owen Chang; Jacob smiles recalling the joyous reaction the name "Chang" got from Colonel Burney and Onanoka in Tokyo when they saw his name.

A grinning Chinese child wearing a Mickey Mouse hat that has the words Disneyland, Singapore printed on it is smiling up at him. His mother is thumbing through a small booklet. Jacob crouched and spoke to the boy, pointing to the child's hat.

"Hi there young man. I like your hat."

The child gave Jacob a long, curious stare and his smile turned into a frown. He begins crying, yanks on his mother's skirt and steps behind her for protection. The child's mother closed her booklet and looked at the eta boards, paying her child no attention.

"Mommy!" The child peeked out from behind his mother at Jacob, scowling up at him. He smiled at the child and made a silly face. And now the infant is furious and begins screaming in anger. Finally, his mother notices and she yanks him behind her and frowns at Jacob. He tries an apologetic smile that is refusing to form. She thrust a sudden finger in Jacob's face, scolding him:

"You a crazy man!" she chided Jacob, shaking her finger at him. "What's a mattah with you?"

Jacob straightened. smiled at the woman and apologetically pointed to the child's cap.

"I was just thinking that Mickey Mouse really is international, isn't he?"

He hoped to see a smile from the woman, but instead she mumbled something that has an unpleasant sound and walked away, pulling her son behind her. After reaching a short distance from him, she crouched and pressed her face close to her son's and began shaking her finger and scolding him for something, every so often glancing back at Jacob with a disapproving frown.

A moment later the boy is smiling at Jacob again, but a firm yank from his mother ended that. She walked away again, this time dragging him behind her as the terminal's bustling swarm of bodies eventually swallowed them up.

"Excuse me sir," a gentle voice purred behind him, "are you Jacob Jennings?"

He turned to see a beautiful young Chinese woman with light-green eyes smiling at him. Her tight silk blouse accentuated her perky breasts, almost commanding him to stare at them; and while he is doing his best to refuse, he did allow himself a prolonged look before moving his eyes back to her face. He bowed to her.

"Yes."

"Lieutenant Jacob Jennings?"

He bowed again.

"Yes."

The aroma of her perfume made him feel closer to her almost intimate than he assumed he would ever be. Its hypnotic fragrance slapped him into a monosyllabic state of verbal brevity and he bowed again:

"Yes."

He managed to muscle his smile into continuing to flower though it is more of a vacuous device grin. Still it kept his eyes aloft, well above the horizon of her mammary attraction.

The woman laughed softly.

"I am Detective Liao Maotze." She briefly displayed a badge and bowed slightly. "We are here to escort you to Chief Inspector Owen Chang's office."

That caused Jacob to look around.

"I'm sorry. Did you say, 'us?'"

A voice, older, more authoritative and behind him, responded:

"Well, actually I said 'we,' but who's counting?" She laughed.

Then there was a more authoritative voice behind him and Jacob turned around to a Japanese woman who looked to be in her early forties. He bowed even deeper to her when she says:

"I am Agent Margaret Che sir." She discreetly held her badge and photo ID low, cupped between her hands, and bowed slightly to him.

"May we please see your identification?"

Her stern expression indicated that she might have been becoming impatient or annoyed.

"Yes, of course." He jams his hand into his pants pocket and yanks out his army M.I. badge and picture identification.

Che looked at it and handed it to Agent Che who read it and gave it to Detective Liao. While reading his I.D. she informs him that:

Mrs. Che is an Assistant Commissioner with Japan's Interpol Office. She, like you, has been assigned to us on a temporary loan agreement."

Jacob bows again.

"I am pleased to meet you, Mrs. Che."

Mrs. Che's rich brown eyes did not have the warmth of Liao's green ones, and though she is much older than Liao, her attractive and rather curvy shape is not so dissimilar.

"It is my pleasure, Lieutenant Jennings."

Margaret Che, for an older woman, has an exceptional figure, Jacob thought. Che's much thicker breasts are conservatively subdued beneath the thick lapels of her light-colored and light weight summer skirt suit. Her waist is thick but well-defined.

"If you are ready, sir, we have a car outside. Inspector Owen Chang is awaiting your arrival."

Before Jacob could answer her, Liao and Mrs. Che began walking away. Detective Liao smiled back at him.

"Please follow us."

Jacob's eyes are appreciating both bouncing behinds. He thought surely that his escorts would have been men but, under the circumstances, he is glad that they are not.

Mrs. Che whispered to Detective Liao:

"…Our American seems quite fond of bowing."

Detective Liao nodded in agreement, quickly glancing back at Jacob, then whispering to Mrs. Che:

"… And that isn't all he's fond of." Both women giggled softly and then Detective Liao spoke in an exaggerated Chinese accent: "… he believes it is old 'Chi-a-nese' custom." Mrs. Che pressed her fingers hard against her mouth to stop an unexpected laugh from escaping as they approached the counter of a security check.

A Chinese officer behind the counter snaps to attention upon seeing the credentials Liao and Mrs. Che presented. After she spoke with them for a few minutes, the officer waved them through and motioned for Jacob to follow them. They passed through a low, metal gate in front of a door marked "No Admittance."

Once past the gate, they entered a long hall leading to a rear exit where two armed Chinese policemen are holding American M-16A2's. They instantly shifted their weapons to the "ready" position but allowed them to walk by and through the exit door.

Outside, the midday furnace-like heat cloaked Jacob's face and twisted it into an immediate frown. Liao led the way to a rear lot where their car, a recent model of a Mercedes Benz is parked. Jacob is accustomed to seeing the car being used for police work in some countries overseas, but he has always found it curious since it is a luxury vehicle in the States and would never be used for police work.

Liao climbed into the driver's seat while Agent Che held the car's rear door open for Jacob. He bowed a thank you and leaned forward to climb in but a sudden wall of heat met him and caused him to quickly abandon that idea for the moment. Mrs. Che noticed his discomfort.

"I'm sorry, sir, that the car is uncomfortable, but today is an exceptionally warm day." Mrs. Che apologized. "The air conditioner will cool the interior in a moment, and then you will be able to enter."

Agent Che left the door open for him and walked around to the front passenger seat and climbed inside, joining Liao. But, giving it a second's thought, she climbed back out and gestured for Jacob to come to the front of the vehicle to climb inside:

"Perhaps you will be more comfortable if you sit in front where the air conditioner is stronger. Please allow me to sit in the rear." She held the passenger door open for him.

He bowed to her and climbed in, at once grateful for the freezing air breeze of the roaring air conditioner. He turns around to Agent Che:

"Thank you, Agent Che." He bowed his head to her. This time he is positive that they both giggled.

Detective Liao. slowly pulled out of the lot and into city traffic but after several blocks, she snatched the steering wheel to the right as though she has just averted hitting someone or something in the road and accelerated.

Liao pressed her slender foot hard against the accelerator and the car sprang forward up a hill rushing past food vendors and other street peddlers on either side of the narrow street; some of the people cast annoyed eyes at the police sedan while other pedestrians assumed protective crouches and other kinds of evasive maneuvers, none of which are actually necessary.

After glancing in her rearview mirror, Liao turned sharply once again, but to the left and onto a narrow side street that snaked its way down and up a very steep hill. Once again pedestrians, women and men pushing hugely high carts that are stacked seemingly skywards moved aside as best they could manage.

A woman tending a small herd of chickens, moves them quickly out of the way while another woman shouts words in Cantonese at Liao as the car almost runs over one of her frantically fleeing ducks who are complaining loudly.

Jacob is fascinated and caught between watching Liao's manhandling the steering wheel while he gasps as quietly as he could at her near misses of the pedestrian and avian traffic.

He clutches his seat and watches through the front windshield as the sedan charges on at high speed, bumping and leaning right and then left as Liao continually adjusted her steering to adhere to the irregularities in the road. He looked at Agent Che whose expression is stoic and then at Detective Liao, but she has put on a pair of dark shades and it is impossible to read her expression; only that she appeared to be fully alert.

Then there is another abrupt left turn, this time their car plummets down a steep incline that causes the vehicle to become momentarily suspended in the air where it floated for a long moment before dropping abruptly to the ground bouncing several times, then nosily it settles in with an audible crunch in the dirt road; the car's motor screamed and the vehicle appears to crouch and then roar forward in a bravado mode. Although on tenterhooks Jacob marvels at Liao's auto gymnastics and driving skills; and it seemed that she has some idea of what he is thinking;

"Our training as police officers included automobile tactical maneuvers, Lieutenant Jennings. I hope you don't mind, but with a guest as special as you, these maneuvers are certainly called for to assure that no one with some interest in you is following us."

"Oh, no, not at all, Detective. Everything is fine."

But Jacob breathes easier seeing that the path ahead of them is barren of civilians and livestock and his thoughts will no longer be troubled by the possibility of people, vending carts, and animals flying through the air after being tossed there by the hastily driving Liao.

Then Liao spins around another corner and leaned the vehicle forward in a rapid ascent up a hill with such a daunting incline as to cause its zenith to appear to lead straight into the bright sky and oblivion.

Jacob shut his eyes as their car reached and bounded over the top of the steep hill landing and after what seemed to him an indeterminate amount of time, lands smoothly on the opposite side. Detective Liao turns another corner hard then slows the sedan to a pleasant cruising speed. She glances at Jacob and smiles.

"I am sorry for the speed I employed, Lieutenant, but I have been instructed to take very careful measures to assure that we are not being followed. You are a very valuable asset to our investigation and if you are seen with us, then it might be dangerous for you, and it would most certainly end the effectiveness of the worthiness of you to our department."

Agent Che agreed.

"That is the reason that we are using the circuitous route to police headquarters."

Jacob took a low but deep breath and let it out smoothly.

"I see. Well, that was surely some ride." He is smiling. "Kind of cool, really."

Detective Liao reaches for a magazine.

"Lieutenant, are you interested in history?"

"Yes, I am."

"We have a while before we reach headquarters, so perhaps you might enjoy some reading material on the way. There is an article on some of the history and etiology of our Police Headquarters Building in this magazine. I think it will be of interest to you. One of our local magazines printed a series of articles on several landmark edifices in Hong Kong and they did a magnificent job researching the origin of Police Headquarters." Liao hands the magazine to Agent Che and she offers it to Jacob.

He accepted the magazine and leaned back in his seat.

"Thank you, detective Liao." He opens the magazine.

Detective Liao suggested:

"This article I am referring to is on page thirteen.

"Okay." He turned the pages until he reached the article. "I have it."

He settled in and began reading the long article:

The History of Du Lam
Police Headquarters—A Devil of a Place
Article by Chunhua Jing-sheng

Citizens understandably think of police precincts generally as a place for some type of punitive action, and our own Police Headquarters at 399 Hinshung Square in Chou Lien in Shengdou Province, has, in its five-hundred-year history, served in that capacity, but there is much more to its history. Even to this day, the twenty buildings are as erect as when first built, thanks to their creator, Du Lam. Much the way the Romans built their aqueducts, baths, and the Pantheon, Du Lam constructed the buildings of a kind of hydraulic cement mixture formalized by the French and British engineers in the eighteenth century. According to historical records, the police headquarters buildings are believed to have been constructed circa fifteen hundred, a complex of twenty connected, two-story buildings, perhaps loosely modeled after the Forbidden City. It is said the elderly Du Lam, who is just a passing stranger, designed the buildings. Clearly he has some formal training as an architect. The locals, in appreciation of his creation, named the complex after him. During that period, some five hundred years ago, the mazes of two-storied buildings described by superstitious locals who chose not to live within its walls as, "Chengshi Buneng," which loosely translated means "the dwelling that cannot be." But faced with the choice of living in straw huts or other inferior housing, eventually most locals moved into the complex with their families. Du Lam is considered the organizer of what eventually became an infrastructural community of farmers, fishermen, politicians, and artists, all living together in complete harmony.

Within ten years, Du Lam became a small but prosperous community. Its occupants of diverse Chinese ethnicities /3a2 a rapidly evolving society whose doors /3a2 open to all sorts of foreign trade and communication. The tenants of Du Lam were living much in the manner of those in the Holy City, with the exception of Du Lam's free enterprise, which is not only welcomed but also encouraged. Du Lam was a self-sustaining community, even choosing to bury their dead on the rear section of the property's acreage. For many years, Du Lam enjoyed great prosperity, trading with itinerants who exchanged merchandise and fashion along with news of the outside communities with those living in Du Lam. According to designs and certificates found by anthropologists, plans were being made to expand Du Lam. Daring to dream of becoming a city within a city may have been construed as a vague threat by certain powers within the Holy City itself.

However, before such an elaborate construction could commence, the creator of the complex, Du Lam himself, disappeared. It was rumored that he simply went fishing in the nearby Duang Sin Forest and is never seen again. It is believed that he has been caught by the Special Imperial Guard of the Forbidden City and executed for daring to copy its design. Such closeness in design to the Holy City may have been considered blasphemous, and if so, such construction would never have been tolerated. It is believed that the powers within the Forbidden City may have taken steps to bring such a matter to a halt.

A year following the disappearance of the creator of Du Lam, the entire community also disappeared. And so it followed as a logical conclusion by the locals that every member of the Du Lam community has been spirited away during the night and executed for their pretensions.

"This is really a fascinating piece of writing." Jacob said, enrapt as he was in the article.

"I thought you'd find it of interest." Liao smiling.

Jacob mutters something but quickly returns to the magazine article:

Another theory about the disappearance of the people of Du Lam is that a powerful sorcerer, wanting the buildings for his own esoteric black-magic practices, scattered them from their home by using certain dark spells. It is whispered that he has been hired by certain powers within the Holy City to use his fearsome magic to evacuate Du Lam, and in return he would be allowed the use of a single building for his own purposes. It is thought that he conjured up frightening images for every member of the Du Lam community, specters that demanded they leave and never return.

It is said that this sorcerer later betrayed the persons who hired him and occupied all the buildings with his followers. It is written that the companions of the sorcerer and his followers are creating phantasmagoric images and screaming voices that rushed through the entire complex day and night. In addition to the voices that sorcerer raised from Du Lam's own graveyard in the rear of its largest building, he also resurrected fearful, terrifying images of spirits of the dead and dying wandering about the complex, terrorizing all outsiders who ventured near any of the buildings.

At that time Emperor Guangxu lived in Beijing 's Forbidden City. Records indicate that Guangxu may have been a highly skilled sorcerer who murdered the betraying sorcerer and his followers then took control of Du Lam for the purposes of clandestine ceremonies with his own secret society of followers of his cult called "Children of the Most Ancient."

He selected the main building, the largest of the twenty, to use for himself and his secret society to live in and hold their rituals, all of which today remain secret. Only a single person, a beggar, Din Xseung, thinking it to be deserted, sought shelter in Du Lam from a storm. He is said to have accidentally seen or heard Guangxu's dark rituals.

The next day a local fisherman found the beggar Din Xseung floating in midair high among the trees in Duang Sin Forest near Du Lam. He is weeping loudly, begging for someone to release him from the horrible curse. According to records, the curse could not be undone, not even by Emperor Guangxu who it is believed placed the curse. So to cover up the horror, that evening the entire forest was burned, reportedly by Guangxu, in order to remove all evidence of the bedeviling. The emperor returned to the Forbidden City and is never seen by outsiders again.

Later historical records of the period state that the Emperor Guangxu is murdered during his reign, and today's modern science proved that he is poisoned by the use of arsenic. There is no shortage of suspects including his adoptive mother Empress Dowager Cixi, but no charges are ever brought against anyone. The heaviest suspicion rested on a eunuch who, at the emperor's request, served him a dish of yogurt moments before his demise. It is certain, however, that the eunuch has nothing to gain by such a murder. Many believed that the emperor's murder is a way to close off all loose ends to the Du Lam mysteries.

Near the end of the Qing dynasty, Pu Yi, China's last emperor, gave the abandoned building to the locals, but it is later requisitioned by a bandit leader, Ju-Guang Lee, who is thought to have been the ghostly reincarnation of a conscripted Chinese warlord from the feudal period in China's Zhou dynasty. His soldiers are also cursed to follow Ju-Guang Lee and serve him for eternity, sentenced by a revengeful king or his demons to serve their sentences of penance for sins committed when they are alive.

It is believed that he defected from the lord he protected, and for that he is assassinated by ninjas hired by the lord he betrayed. As further punishment he is thereafter doomed to roam the earth forever as a ghost bandit plagued by misfortune for betraying his master.

Ju-Guang Lee housed his men, horses, and weapons in Du Lam and used it as his sanctuary between battles and raids. He is said to have committed all manner of atrocities against his prisoners, both men and women, including the practice of cannibalism done in the pursuit of ultimate power over his enemies. Some locals believed that Ju-Guang Lee could only maintain his human shape and form by the consumption of human blood and flesh something he has to do every three days.

During that time, villagers who lived nearby claimed to constantly see the ghosts of dead men and women facing the building and praying for prisoners being held inside. But if Ju-Guang Lee happened by, the specters would cringe and hide from him. It is said that these same ghosts often visited the homes of the locals, begging for food that, once given, they are unable to eat. They appeared unaware of their death, and they would stare at the food, perplexed, while weeping and continuing to lament that no one would feed them.

In the end, the locals are unable to rid themselves of Ju-Guang Lee and the victims of the warlord and his soldiers. Eventually, more from sadness for the spirits they saw and those that visited them, the villagers moved farther and farther away, deeper into the mountains and hills, to distance themselves from the place they came to call "the buildings that weep."

After that, due to fear and superstition, the buildings stood abandoned for many years until later considered a landmark. The Chinese Conservation Board appropriated the land and buildings and set about preserving Du Lam as an historical site. After restoring all the buildings, the board charged a conservative fee to visitors. When interest in the buildings declined years later, the buildings are abandoned once again but left as a historical site reflecting an era of early Chinese culture.

Later the Chinese film industry began renting the buildings for the purpose of filming adventure movies loosely tied into the history of Du Lam. A few documentarians filmed some of the history of Du Lam before it once again fell into a lull from lack of interest.

Fifty years ago, Hong Kong's board of zoning decided it is an ideal location for a newly proposed correctional facility. And so after extensive refurbishing and reconstruction, the buildings are donated to the city to be used as the location for the construction of a new Police Headquarters.

Jacob stopped reading and looks up as their sedan left the rural back roads and pulls back into city traffic. After driving for another half hour they merged into an area that has very few buildings and almost no traffic other than a few police patrol cars. In the near distance is a very high cement wall with encircled "concertina" wire spread along the top of the thick walls. A very large metal sign emblazoned on the fertile grass lawn in front of the walls announced that these are the grounds of Police Headquarters, No. 1.

A narrow wire fence reveals that there are several other buildings behind the walls.

Liao stopped at the narrow entrance to the police compound, where two uniformed officers stand behind the gate holding M-16 rifles. Two more officers are outside the gate.

"We're here, Lieutenant." Liao looked at Jacob, who is obviously impressed by the headquarters grounds, and smiled. "Do you like our new 'home,' Lieutenant Jennings?"

"Very much."

He watches a young Chinese police officer approaching. As he came closer, it is clear that Liao and the uniformed officer recognize one another, but she held out her badge and identification for him. He scarcely glanced at her ID but he studies Jacob for a moment, bowing slightly to him. The officer took a single step back and saluted Liao then quickly spins around and signaled for the gate to be opened.

Jacob appreciated the "ceremony." It exhibited a certain pride in the officer's position, even his khaki uniform seemed permanently starched with collar and neck cuff edges that appeared capable of slicing bread or inflicting cuts to anyone carelessly touching them. And though Jacob knows the temperature outside the car has to be mid-nineties, the man's uniform showed not the slightest wrinkle and there is no visible sign of perspiration or of any discoloration. Jacob smiled, wondering if somehow the officer has trained his flesh to not dare not allow even a single drop of sweat to appear anywhere on his person while he is on duty.

How, Jacob is wondering, is such a perfect specimen as these officers possibly created, amazed that this perfection does truly exist.

Their sedan drove past the slowly opening gate and enters the compound. Liao continues driving to the rear of the buildings, pausing behind one of them. Jacob could hardly believe the enormity of the compound.

Police Headquarters is a complex of interconnected pagoda-roofed concrete buildings that, thanks to the article he read, he now knew are originally part of a village named Du Lam. The article has given him a true appreciation of the history of these reddish-brown single and double storied edifices that are spread out over a huge area.

Jacob wonders which of the building houses the much-revered Chief Inspector of Police Owen Chang who, according to Onanoka and Burney's description of him is rumored to be a fearsome individual, and that even many of the Hong Kong underworld are daunted by him.

Liao drives to another gate. The guards standing in front immediately wave her on to a modest sized brick building and another security stop. Jacob is aware that a big difference at this checkpoint is that this gate has an electrically charged fence that he recognizes from some of his city police training. He knew the fence could issue a medium to deadly voltage charge of electricity; easily enough to easily render a violator unconscious.

A number of uniformed policemen and policewomen are outside the buildings conversing with one another. While most of them are Chinese, there are also several Americans among them in civilian clothing. A black man in a white pin striped suit is lecturing a large group of seated Chinese men and women all of whom are wearing civilian clothing. Jacob assumed the Americans to be mostly administrative personnel, part of a Military Assistance Advisory Group.

Nearby, several men and women in shorts are running around an oblong track, which has an area next to it where judo and karate training are being held. He is very surprised to see what appeared to be a Kensyobudo sword class being taught. He knows that Kensyobudo is a thoroughly rigorous and exceptionally realistic Japanese sword-fighting martial art, and he is impressed that it is included in the training of the Hong Kong police officers.

The last area there are four men in wrestling gear sparring for position while a group of eager-faced young uniformed officers sat in a large circle watching them. Other officers are in jogging outfits sitting on benches adjacent to them listening to a tall female uniformed Asian police officer lecture them on some subject. But a sudden sprinkling of rain is causing all outdoor activities not enclosed to be slowly, one by one, curtailed.

A few of the civilian men casually glance at Liao's sedan as she slowly cruises by them. One of the officers smiles at Liao and she nods o him then slows down for another checkpoint gate.

After being cleared for entrance, Liao drives to a ruddy colored building with terra cotta shingles over its façade and sides, the largest of the buildings. The sun casually slides behind a cluster of dark clouds as though sneaking up to frighten them.

Agent Che and Jacob emerge from the car to a thick fragrance in the air to greet them that let Jacob know from experience that an "important" storm is possibly imminent. He looks up at the clouds and watches the sky become darker, emitting sporadic wide flashes of yellowish light that blankets the area. He is slightly jostled by a chilling wind that rose and moved across the compound. Everyone but Jacob hastened their walk towards the building's rear door where the guard who is stationed there abruptly snapped to attention. But Jacob for just a second, caught sight of a graveyard at the rear of the building. He stopped walking and turned back to take another look to make sure that what he has just seen is a graveyard.

Detective Liao walked back and looked at it with him.

"Lieutenant Jennings, you read the article I gave you. Do you recall what this area is?"

"That's the Du Lam graveyard, isn't it?" The moment he spoke those words a bright flash of lightning flooded the area immediately followed by a crack of deep, reverberating thunder that rolled hoarsely over the dark sky, preceding a sudden rush of wind. Both he and Liao glanced up at the sky, chuckling. It is just too perfectly timed not to resemble some old horror movie where lightning is used to let the audience know, in case they did not recognize it, that this is the part where they ought to be frightened.

"Yes, it is the Du Lam graveyard. And those are the graves of some of the people from early Du Lam before all of its occupants just simply disappeared. Police Headquarters considers it a sacred burial site now and once every six months we allow the public to enter and pay their respects if they desire to do so. There are many who claim to have ancestors buried in there."

"It isn't under guard?"

Detective Liao shook her head.

"No. There is no reason to do that these days. During the time of Du Lam, warning signs are posted throughout many graveyards warning in Cantonese: **'no witchcraft'** and subscripted in English. Such signs are thought to be blessed and carried a very strong curse on those who disobeyed by stealing bodies or disturbing the graves in some other manner. There is such a warning remaining displayed on this sign but it is in the form of a single, tiny eye; the only way to see it is to be at the grave itself. It's on each and every grave in here but nobody has any idea who painted them on the graves. Some say a wizard simply floated over the graveyard one night and waved his hand and the next morning each grave has an eye on it."

Agent Che has joined them and she added:

"Yes, as you may remember from reading the article, hundreds of years ago, graveyards—including this one—are routinely robbed for the benefit of certain magic ceremonies. But now, there are only gifts of food, drink, toys, and personal items on the graves, left there by the loved ones of the deceased.

"I see." Jacob nodded.

The gravesite is of great interest to him. He vividly recalled what he has read in the article on Du Lam about these buildings. Sudden gunfire startled him. Detective Liao pointed to the firing range several hundred yards from where they are standing where police officers, men and women, are firing at targets on the range. Jacob watched the officers firing at their targets for a while.

More targets abruptly slid out of hiding from behind rocks or out of the ground and either presented a threat or persons being held prisoner by an armed gunman. Jacob remembered seeing a similar obstacle course when, as part of his rookie training with the nypd, he visited an fbi training facility.

Liao and Che are already walking towards the entrance to headquarters. They waited at the entrance for Jacob, inquiring

"Lieutenant Jennings, are you coming?" Mrs. Che is holding the door open.

"Yes, yes I am. I'm coming." He joins Liao and Che at the door and just as he is about to take a step inside the building, a large drop of rain splatters against his nose. Inside, he takes a final look back at the guard standing at the entrance, knowing that his mission is to stand there in the rain or snow or whatever until he is relieved. The British Queen's guard has nothing on these officers. Discipline.

CHAPTER 16

OWEN
CHANG

Once inside the building, Jacob continued following Agent Che and Detective Liao into a wide room of glass partitions with names and titles printed on metal panels on the glass. Overhead, several ceiling fans turned lazily. Most of the large cubicles are occupied by uniformed as well as plainclothes police officers, men and women, all of them wearing side arms with their police badges pinned on their belts or underarm holster straps.

There is so no buzz, Jacob thought. Very much like the inside of a library. There are many conversations, people talking to each other or on the phones, but little sound, as though everyone felt speaking softly is called for almost as though observing some grim occasion. Asian, he imagined, this adherence to decorum.

Only a few of the people in the offices took any special notice of him as he follows Liao and Che through a hallway of long and twisting corridors with swinging doors. In the halls he is surprised to see that some of the historical remnants from the time period when the buildings are a community named Du Lam are still in place. Rusted relics of metal benches are still positioned against the cement walls and metal wrist restraints attached by thick chains to walls appeared to be still functional; all of these items are grim reminders of how truly pagan the warlord Ju-Guang Lee must have been in his method of dealing with prisoners.

Jacob is sure that, under the circumstances of being Ju-Guang Lee's captive, it would not take very long before anyone would confess to anything and that it is likely many prisoners died before and after confessing. His imagination drudged up a sign that should have been posted in huge letters above the entrance to Du Lam housing Ju-Guang Lee and his soldiers:

"Even those who are innocent need take heed. Beware, shun and hope never to enter this wretched place for it is bereft of all mercies."

Liao walked to a bare office door at the end of the corridor. Jacob thought how eerily innocuous Chang's office compared to rest of the office doors and office they have just passed. It appears almost as though his office is little more than an afterthought. Liao knocked on the door.

When the door opened, a wide-jawed, thick-bodied man whose neck and broad shoulders appeared borrowed from some much-larger person stepped out. Chief Inspector Chang looked like a power weightlifter.

He walked by Liao and Che and stood silently facing Jacob who, at six feet four inches is looking down at Chang who is easily four or five inches shorter. Chang's emotionless eyes locked on Jacob's. Then he abruptly smiled and grabbed Jaco in a fiercely tight hug, sucking the air temporarily from Jacob's chest. Then, releasing him, he stepped back and grabs Jacob's hand in a vise-like grip, shaking it with great enthusiasm; so much so that Jacob is hoping that his teeth did not begin to rattle.

"Welcome, First Lieutenant Jacob Jennings. Come inside, please." Inspector Chang led them into his modest office but not before smiling briefly at Liao and Mrs. Che. "As always, a wonderful job ladies."

Inside the office, he gestured for Jacob to be seated at a large table that has a very large pot of tea, several cups and saucers, a quart bottle of scotch whisky, a large pitcher of water, several sweet rolls, a large bowl of butter, a cinnamon cake ring, hard rolls, a small platter of cookies sitting in a wide pot surrounded by ice cubes, and silverware almost centered.

"Please help yourself to whatever your pleasure happens to be Jennings. We are far from formal here and make no judgements. That is the reason I chose this obscure little office that isn't much more than a supply closet but it makes me happy. I'm here for work not luxury. So feel at home and dive in."

Jacob poured himself some tea. Chang lit a cigar and leaned back in as leather swivel chair behind his small desk that has a small metal name plate with the name: "CHANG".

"Jennings, I've heard quite a lot about you and if what I heard isn't true then you'll probably be a dead man a few days into your assignment here."

Liao and Mrs. Che glance at each other then they looked at Chang.

"Lieutenant Jennings, Mrs. Che cooked these cookies expressly to welcome you to the department. I'm sure that after the airline food, you might welcome these sweets."

Jacob smiled at Agent Che and bowed.

"Thank you, Agent Che." Jacob bowed to her.

Inspector Chang came over and grabbed a cookie himself and sat at the table.

"Now, I realize that you have just arrived, and you might be tired from your flight, but please allow us some of your time before we get you to your hotel."

"Yes, of course, Inspector and I'm not really tired."

"Good. And please call me either Owen or Chang. I'd like us to get used to not using titles. You know how that can become not only awkward, but even dangerous. So kindly call Detective Liao either Maotze or Liao. As for Agent Margaret Che, well, I prefer that we call her Mrs. Che." Chang smiled at her and then at Jacob. "I hope you've no objection to being called either Jacob or Jennings."

"Not at all sir."

"Good. Which do you prefer? Jacob or Jennings?

"It doesn't matter, sir. Either of the two is fine with me."

"Good. I like the name Jennings. Of course, as we get to know each other better I am very likely to call you by another name." Chang glanced at the two women and chuckled.

He lit a cigar then adjusted his chair at the table. Chang poured himself a cup of tea. "Mrs. Che's specialty is the tribal behavior of gangs, both underworld organized gangs and local thug groups. She focuses on the psychological rationale involved in their herd mentality. She is a graduate of Harvard. She has given us a great deal of insight into some of the thinking of the largest gang here in Hong Kong, *The Chinese Blood* and the civilians who might be connected or attracted to them."

"I see."

"And Liao is my personal administrative assistant and computer person. She is an expert at hacking computers, a skill she may use sometimes when doing her research for the department. She gathers all the information that is available on the cases that come to my desk. You will usually find Liao in her office down the hall; Mrs. Che is more my field person. Now and then detective Liao hits the streets with her." Chang draws in a long puff on his cigar and lets the smoke slowly curl out from his pursed lips, all the while keeping his eyes on Jacob. "Now, Chief Investigator Onanoka and Colonel Burney have described some of your background to me, both army and civilian, and I consider all of that priceless. But perhaps you can describe to me just how you are going to be of use to us in this investigation?"

"Well, sir—"

"Onanoka tells me you always come up with a workable plan. What do you know about *cherry berry*?"

"Only what Director Onanoka and Colonel Burney have told me and that's that it's a new drug that you have not been able to find or figure out yet."

Chang bristles slightly at that remark but quickly let it go.

"Yes. It's a new drug that my street sources tell me is created by Dr. Wo-ling Cheung and his friend Yongli Baofung who is a sorcerer. Dr.

Cheung is a well-known and respected research scientist here in Hong Kong. He has also been associated with several hospitals here over the years and has come up with some wondrous drugs beneficial to us all. Thus over time he has become well respected, almost revered."

"Yes, I can imagine."

"But he has recently become wealthy very quickly, and that is suspicious. I'm sure that, like us all, the good doctor has a dark side, a greedy side, and if this *cherry berry* drug is all it's said to be, its continued distribution will make him scandalously wealthy. But at the same time it could become a pandemic addiction. According to our street informants, this drug is many times more addictive than crack cocaine. But no one has ever seen it. Naturally we're assuming the users have seen it but even *The Chinese blood* gang members have no idea what the drug actually is or looks like, and we're told that they're the ones who package it. How that's possible, I don't know."

"Yeah. That is pretty strange." Jacob is intrigued by that.

"And the really weird thing is that this drug is only available to a single clientele and they're in the U.S., located in New York."

"Sir, with all due respect, are you sure this drug even exists, that it's not just some rumor?"

"My most reliable informant tells me this drug is real and that it's being exported in copious amounts for the past almost two years; but only to a single country; and to only one locale in that country. That's why you're here Jennings because that one country is the United States."

Jacob is shocked:

"What?"

"And the locale is New York."

"New York?" Jacob repeated, still unsure he was hearing it right.

"Yes. Dr. Cheung works in research for different hospitals here in Hong Kong but he has a private research practice here and a modest facility in New York and has a facility at his estate here in Hong Kong. My informants tell me that Cheung has a client that, for years, has been paying him extremely well to perform some kind of medical research in search of the creation of some exotic drug. Cheung is kind of untouchable here in Hong Kong because of his status as a top research scientist both here and abroad and his very heavy political connections. So that makes it difficult to get search warrants with the fluidity I require to pull surprise raids at his facilities or places of employment. And it is absolutely impossible to get a search warrant for his estate. Of course, I don't let that stop me. I've intercepted several of his shipments…kind of illegally and searched for the drug but can never find it. But recently, his political allies here in Hong Kong have really been bringing down the heat on me. I've had to drastically cut back my activities against him."

Jacob is thinking how involved Dr. Cheung's operation seems to be..

"Yes, I can understand why."

"I am positive though that Cheung has come up with the drug he's been paid to create and is getting it out of the country hidden in some of his medical shipments from the hospital to his New York facility."

Jacob shrugs:

"But the paradox here is that we don't know what the devil the drug looks like. Are the authorities in New York aware of your suspicions sir?"

"Yes, but since I have nothing to back it up, they're pretty much powerless to do anything and they are not about to go after China's leading research chemist alleging he's invented some kind of dangerous super drug worse than crack cocaine and meth combined."

"No, they're not going to do that. Even with proof they're going to be reticent to proceed without the most extreme caution."

"But the fact that you have been so quickly reassigned to me shows your government has some concerns that it might be true. And everyone fears the word, pandemic."

"But if this drug is that addictive, wouldn't American authorities in New York see it on their radar?"

"They should, you would think, but its rumored this new drug is being used by a highly select and affluent clientele in America. And the drug is always delivered personally by some stateside member; maybe one of *The Chinese Blood* gang positioned there for that purpose. So since only gang members are the ones. And you and I both know that American Police Officers do not really sweat Asian gangs; that's always an Asian community matter and handled there by them."

Jacob is wondering:

"Maybe there's a large population of them and not just the one sect in New York. Maybe there are others of them in other cities, even in other countries and maybe New York's the kind of epicenter; the distribution point, maybe, for others to either come and get it or have it delivered to them. This is a new idea in drug dealing and one that is going to pay off better than selling it on the street."

Chief Inspector of Police, Owen Chang, is mulling over what Jacob has just said. He has not thought along those lines. And it all made sense. Now, he is really happy to have Jacob on board with him.

Jacob continued with his thoughts on the operation:

"Yeah, it sounds like they might be running a drug delivery service." Jacob gulped his coffee. "So the gang members are the drug's messengers. And in America gangs are not at the zenith of police concerns since they tend to be, at times, nomadic and other than sporadic shootings and small time drug dealing, they go pretty much unnoticed. But our problem is how in the world can we ever find a drug that we have no idea what it looks, never mind where to find it?"

"That's the conundrum, Jennings." Chang said, reaching for his stubbed out cigar.

Jacob shrugged.

"Undercover. It's the only way."

For a long while no one in the room said anything. The idea seemed preposterous to everyone. Then Chang noticed Jacob's briefcase on his lap. He is curious;

"By the way, Jennings, what's in the briefcase?

Jacob gave it a moment's thought then he took out two of his three books.

"This book is the Cabala and this one is on cryptozoology. They're presents from my grandmother. I usually carry them around with me in case I have time to sit and read them."

Chang is studying his face. He glanced at one of the books Jacob is holding and then back to Jacob.

"The Cabala, isn't that a book on Jewish religion or mysticism?"

"Well, yes. It deals more with the esoteric or mystical understanding of the Bible."

"So then you're of the Jewish faith?"

"No, sir, but I have a great interest in this book and abstruse things."

"I see. Onanoka tells me that you're not easily rattled."

Jacob shrugged with a smile.

"I rattle, sir, but I don't usually break."

Everyone in the room found Jacob's remark amusing.

"I don't see how you will. Getting back to my question, how do you suggest we approach this, Jennings?"

"Well, it's my thought to make some kind of business contact with them as opposed to some kind of surreptitious joining of the gang. I could pose as a drug and arms dealer—small scale, of course but flashy; not too flashy though. Just enough to seem a braggart who is something else undercover. A garish appearance is good, but a kind of cheap one; almost laughable. You know, a stereotypical hustler type. Nice car, gold everywhere, Carrera shades, the works."

"Okay, I think I'm following you." Chang chuckled.

"That's really flashy."

Even Jacob laughed.

"Yeah, we'll cut back on the gold and even then the gold will be fake gold. The glasses a knock off. But the car has to be real and registered to me. I'll drive my car around town and walk around with great panache sooner or later I'm bound to come into contact with the wrong people, and hopefully one or more of the gang members will be among them."

Detective Liao nodded, reflecting on the image.

"I think that just might work, Inspector."

"I'll let it be known I'm in the business of making 'paper', you know, money. I'll tell them I can get them shipments of drugs and weapons or I can buy drugs and weapons from them for resale."

Chang liked the idea, but Mrs. Che inserted a very important point:

"Yes, it is a good idea. But that means we must upgrade the present hotel we have for him."

Chang is giving it serious thought and warned Jacob:

"Move carefully, Jennings. *The Chinese Blood* gang are very dangerous people And I mean very dangerous; nothing we've ever been able to prove because they totally intimidate citizens, even more so than the underworld gangsters."

Chang goes to his desk and takes out a small cell phone.

"Now, this cell phone leaves no trace of calls made or received; that way if a gang member gets hold of it, they can't tell who you called or who called you."

"Sounds good, sir."

"I am going to assign one of my veteran undercover officers to secure work as a maid at your hotel. She'll make herself known to you at her first opportunity. Her name is Mrs. Susan Wong. Hold on a moment. Why should we wait for this?" He smiles at Liao, "Detective Liao, will you please go get Mrs. Wong?"

"Of course, sir." She leaves the office.

Chang, Jacob and Mrs. Che continued in discussion, examining the good, bad and the dangerous parts of Jacob's plan.

Moments later, Detective Liao returned to the office with an older Asian woman. Owen stood and hugged her then held his hand out to Jacob.

"Jennings, this is Mrs. Susan Wong, my most experienced undercover policewoman. Mrs. Wong, this is Jacob Jennings, an First Lieutenant Jacob

Jennings from the American U.S. Army Military Intelligence Unit stationed in Formosa. He is on loan to us to assist in the *cherry berry* investigation.

Jacob extended his hand to her.

"How do you do, Mrs. Wong?" He bowed.

She returned his bow, saying softly:

"Oh, how wonderful. It is my pleasure meeting you, sir."

She will secure a position at your hotel. This particular hotel is very large and they have an enormous cleaning staff. They constantly seek fresh staff for cleaning.

"Yes, they are very fussy about staff making mistakes, even the cleaning staff. They have quite a large turnover in workers.." Mrs. Che added.

Chang continued:

"So Jacob, if you ever have a message of importance for me, rather than risk calling me, you will leave a note in your bottom dresser drawer. When that happens, leave a sign on your room door asking for your room to be cleaned. Mrs. Wong here will check your room for the notes whenever you leave. In fact, when she sees you're gone, she'll check anyway.

"Sir, I'm just curious … if the phone you're giving me makes untraceable calls, why can't I call you?"

"Because walls often grow ears. Once you meet the gang, they might bug your room that Mrs. Wong may have missed. They will be able to hear our conversation. Not good. But keep this phone on vibrate. You don't want it to ring at the wrong time. When you answer, always say 'Jake'. If you don't I'm hanging up. If it is a mistake you call back, otherwise I'm on the alert and looking for a way to get you help—fast!" Chang turned to Mrs. Wong.

"Okay, thank you, Mrs. Wong. Detective Liao will get you a letter of reference and fill you in later."

"Okay, sir." Mrs. Wong smiled at Jacob and bowed, slightly. "I look forward to working with you, Lieutenant Jennings."

"It's going to be my pleasure, Mrs. Wong."

Chang thanked Mrs. Wong and she left the room. He returned to Liao and her photographs of the gang and its members.

"Now, in the meantime Jennings I want you to become visually acquainted with some of the gang members."

Mrs. Che pulls out a very thick folder from a large filing cabinet and brought it over to the table and lays +it in front of Jacob.

Chang opened it and pointed to the photo on top.

"This is the one you must be careful of and I mean careful. He is called 'Chop-Chop Chewy. He has orange, spiked hair. We are sure he's knifed and killed at least five men and one woman. And a stiletto is his weapon of choice; and from what I hear, he is equally adept using it by either throwing or sticking. And his best friend and 'enforcer' is another thug named 'Jub-Jub Tai.'" Chang looked at Jacob with a serious expression. "I'm going to say it again, Jennings, this man and this entire gang are the most dangerous people you will likely meet in Hong Kong. But Chop-Chop and Jub-Jub Tai are the most lethal members. Remember orange spiked hair with Chop-Chop and Jub-Jub Tai wears his hair slicked down with pomade parted in the middle. It kind of gives him the unusual appearance of some Chinese person from the nineteen twenties." Chang stood and relit his cigar. "Now Mrs. Che will fill you in on the remaining photos of the gang members while Detective Liao will go to her office and make the hotel reservations for you and find you a suitable for lease."

Liao headed for the door, Chang points to the book of photos of gang members:

"You make sure you learn as many of those faces as you can but see to it that you burn Chop-Chop Chewy's face into your brain."

"Yes sir."

Then it struck Chang that he has overlooked something and he thumbed through the photo book again, stopping and stabbing his finger against a photograph. Mrs. Che became uneasy looking at the image and even more so when Chang said:

This man is Yongli Baofung. He is a Supreme Sorcerer. Both his parents are very accomplished in the practice of sorcerer. He has been raised in the *Dark Arts*. Many who know of him say that Baofung is easily in his late nineties but he looks no more than fifty—really even younger. I am are positive that he helped Cheung create this new drug, *cherry berry*. The two men are lifelong friends."

Chang put out his cigar again and sat next to Jacob.

"Jennings, I'm sure you think of black magic and sorcery as nonsense. Old wives tales. Superstition brought to life, and so on. I only ask you to not be too quick to judge; and don't come to conclusions about the occult based on what you may have heard or even believe about it all being superstitious foolishness."

"I won't, sir."

"Baofung is a practitioner of, among other Black Arts disciplines, a sorcery practice known as, "Tao of the Left." And though we hope not, he may have become either a member or a consultant to *The Chinese Blood*, and he may be willing to use Tao of the Left for the gang's purposes. And whether a person believes in it or not, trust me, you don't want to come up against that level of sorcery."

"What is Tao of the Left?" Jacob inquired.

Chang shrugged.

"I am no expert in magic, but some say it is a very fierce form of sorcery, much like the *Guman Thong* but not nearly as vicious or as strong.""

Mrs. Che added:

"All the members of *The Last Order* gang are involved in some form of occult practice. In fact, these days many gangs are involved in one form of the occult or the other."

She cleared her throat and took a very long sip of tea, then she continued:

"We are aware of gang and underworld gangster activities and mindful of being always alert to the possibility of any merging. The last thing we want is gangs joining in with organized crime; and if this drug is what it is rumored to be, then it will only be a matter of time before organized crime will be sniffing around. And so, concerning that, for the past two years we have requested some form of assistance from the OCTB but the request remains at first level.

Jacob does not understand.

"What is the OCB?"

"The OCTB," Chang corrected him. "It is a division I was in charge of before attaining my current position. The letters stand for Organized Crime and Triad Bureau. The purpose of the Bureau, as you might imagine, is to monitor triad leaders and their activities."

Mrs. Che poured herself more tea and pointed out to Chang:

"But sir, there is an upside of sorts. If the triads allow *The Chinese Blood* and other gangs to become affiliates, it will be for the sole purpose of taking over the distribution of this drug. And if they learn how to make it, they will surely eradicate the gang. So there's a good side and a bad one, well…kind of, anyway."

Chang frowned.

"Yes, I imagine." He walked to his desk and reared back in his chair, looking at Mrs. Che.

Jacob has another thought:

"There is one other possible reason that you have not been able to find the drug during your searches, sir."

Chang is very interested in this.

"And what would that reason be?"

"Well, maybe Cheung and his people are being warned in advance about each of your impending raids by someone here in your headquarters. So the doctor would know not to ship the drug on those days, or to hide it better."

Chang straightened himself in his chair behind his desk and stared at Jacob for a very long time. Then he bit his cigar in half.

CHAPTER 17

THE
HIGH LIFE

Eight days have passed since Jacob's arrival in Hong Kong. Detective Liao, following Chief Inspector Owen Chang's instructions, before booking Jacob in a fashionable hotel, leased him a luxurious current model Jaguar convertible, a faux Rolex diamond watch glittering on his wrist highlighting his two gold-filled diamond rings. A thick, ten carat solid gold chain around his neck is dazzling in the sunlight against his bronze flesh.

Jacob is quite handsome in his Armani summer suit, one of the seven bought for him and one that allows his muscular body to be tastefully displayed. He is wearing deep blue shoes, his favorite of the department's purchase of ten pair of designer shoes. Jacob, while leaning against his jaguar convertible and looking over the people in the large public park, he comments on his own appearance:

"…I imagine that I must appear either quite the 'rake'…" he chuckled lowly, "or quite the fool."

Jacob is hoping that his attire is taken for the rather gauche taste some associate with the hustling trade. A few passing pedestrians grinning at him but most people pay scant attention to him as he strolls about, flirting with some of the passing young females.

Some of the young Chinese girls near him appear to be attracted to him, but when he tries to speak with them, they giggle and quickly turn and run away.

Jacob has spent the past few days majority hanging around the city's pool halls thinking them to be ideal places for gang members to spend time. Detective Liao told him that they are often in Larry Song's nightclub but she warned Jacob against considering the club as a good place for a first meeting Jacob has all the trappings of either a small-time hustler or one of the nouveau riche who has absolutely no idea how to dress themselves properly without advertising their wealth in the most extravagant fashion.

Either way, he has not managed to find anyone who is a gang member except a few young men and girls. After brief conversations, with them, he found they members of a gang, but not *The Chinese Blood* gang.

Today he is parked near the Pang Tung River, a wide body of water part of which is adjacent to a huge public park. Jacob is pleased that the river is crowded at this time of evening and at this area with Chinese Junks and smaller sailing vessels docked near each other. He finds it fascinating attending the water scenery from the shore where he is parked.

On a few of the Chinese "Junks" women are bathing their children, stoking fires, frying foods for dinner while others pour cups of tea or hot water into large circular receptacles, some of which are being used for washing clothes, and others for cleaning fish or feeding their geese or ducks on board their vessel. Young girls are washing rice, preparing potatoes and green vegetables, a few of them are scrubbing the decks of their boats.

The men are either bathing or repairing their fishing nets, or eating, smoking pipes; some are playing with their younger children and watching a few of the older ones help their mothers clean fish the men have caught for the day. Other youngsters help strip feathers from ducks and chickens and scale fish; the very young children are cavorting about the decks of the boats.

Jacob has stopped near the docks and is parked near a female vendor who is selling octopus, squid, and fish with vegetables and rice. He spoke briefly with her in Mandarin then purchased fried fish and vegetables. She smiled, remarked that his Chinese is very good and handed him his change and they exchanged brief bows.

At sat on the fender of his car eating his meal and watching the young women passing by his car, some of whom are impressed with the vehicle; others with him. Finished eating, Jacob bought a Coke from a nearby vending machine and took a long grateful swallow and tossed the remainder of his meal in a nearby trash can. He climbed in his car and turned on the air conditioning. Leaning back in his seat, he relaxed until he began snoring.

But giggling woke him. Two young girls are standing at his car, smiling and pursing their lips at him. One leaned close and pressed her lips on the window, leaving a round, dark-red perfect lip print.

"Whassuh mattah, big boy? Too much party time? Eh?"

Jacob sat up and grinned at the young girls. One of them began wiggling her tongue at him. He stepped from the car.

"Hey, girls, whassup?"

"Whassup, baby?" She stopped wiggling her tongue and rubbed her hands under her large breasts, giggling. Her girlfriend laughed and pulled her away, but she pulled free and walked back to him, sticking out her breasts. "Hey, sailor, baby, can we ride, baby?" Both girls giggled even louder.

Jacob laughed and playfully reaching for one of the young girl but she backed away and wagged her fingers at him, still grinning.

"Come on, girls. Let's go riding. You can show me around."

"Sorry, sailor. No can do." They walked away, giggling and glancing back at him a few times, blowing him kisses. Then they ran away.

Jacob shrugged and sighed loudly and leaned against the Jaguar's, checking his Rolex watch. It is growing dark and Jacob believes that it is going to be another dry run in the search for the gang.

He is about to call it a day when he sees two young white American men walking with two young Asian women approaching. The men stopped to look at the car. One of them gently runs his fingers over the body.

"Hey, yo, bro. You score this over here? It's a fuckin' monster, man. A fuckin' monster. What's under the hood, son?"

Jacob shrugged, "A motor, I think."

The guys laughed at that.

"Yeah, this machine is big bucks and one of the faster models."

Jacob shrugged and got into his act.

"It ain't no thing, really. Just some paper, my man. I just drive 'em. I don't analyze 'em.

The two young Asian girls are becoming interested in Jacob and his Jaguar. The youngest one walked to the car and stroked the side.

Jacob is closely watching the exceptionally pretty girl who appears to be the youngest, though they are both pretty young.

She is wearing a very short miniskirt and her medium large breasts are fussing about a bit beneath her loose silk blouse. The older girl, almost equally pretty, is wearing tight short, shorts. But Jacob is appreciating the long, slender, well-shaped olive legs of the younger girl.

"So, what's up with the girls?"

The older Chinese girl quickly answered, stepping up to Jacob.

"We're just showing them some of the city. They tourists." She turned to the two American men. "Well, we showed you some of it, now we see you later. Now we with Jaguar man." She leaned close to Jacob. "I know you already see some of the city, now maybe you wanna see some of me an' my sister."

The two Americans gloomily sulked away, glancing back angrily at Jacob as they left. The younger girl spread out a paper on the fender of Jacob's car and sat, letting her miniskirt ride all the way up to reveal her orange panties. She yanked her skirt down but only by a bit while she watched Jacob stare between her legs. She parted them just a bit wider while she lit a cigarette.

"So, what's up, big boy?" The younger girl asked, then she, obviously not a smoker, hacks out several coughs from her cigarette smoke.

Jacob manages to tear his eyes away from between the girl's legs.

"Hmm? Oh nothing really. Just out for some fun in the sun. Ready to blaze paper trails, if you know what I mean,"

She leaned back on the fender and blew the smoke out slowly.

"Maybe we do and maybe we don't." She looked up at the cloudy sky. "But it's kinda hard to have fun in the sun when there ain't no sun." She slid down from the car fender and let the paper fall to the ground as she slinked over to Jacob. "How you make your paper, big boy? You make big paper in Hong Kong to buy car maybe? Huh, big boy?" The young girl slid her hand between Jacob's legs. "You plenty big boy down there too I betcha."

Jacob knew a street hustler doesn't blush, and so he attempted a nonchalant shrug, but before he could complete it, while the younger girl is rubbing between his legs, the older girl kissed him, a long wet kiss that took him by complete surprise.

"My name's Delilah," the older girl said as the other rubbed him even harder between his legs. "What's your name, big boy?"

"Ja—" Almost a mistake. "Jake." He found it hard to make up his mind whether to stare at the older girl's beautiful, bulging cream colored breasts or to just keep enjoying the younger one's rubbing him. "My name's Jake. What's yours?"

She playfully shoved him. "Hey, whassa mattah wit' you, silly boy? I already told you my name. I'm Delilah, and she's my little sister, Ginger."

Ginger moved away from him, grabbed the newspaper from the ground and, leveling it on the car again, she hopped up on the car's fender. This time she crossed her shapely legs. Jacob is more transfixed on her legs and thighs.

Delilah slapped him on the behind.

"You like real young pussy, huh?" She gripped him hard between his legs, and he grimaced. "Yeah, I see you want my li'l sister. How bad you want her, Jake?" Delilah, still gripping him between the legs, looked at her sister. "Ginger, this boy got a donkey dick." Both women laughed. "So you wanna sex up my little sister? You give me two hundred dollars and maybe can do."

He turned to look questioningly at Delilah.

"Did you say two hundred dollars?"

She shrugged.

"Did I stutter? It's only paper, Jake. Remember?" Delilah patted the Jaguar. "It's only paper, Jake With Jaguar." Then she held his wrist, pointing to his Rolex. "And you must got plenty paper, baby."

"Nah, I don't want her." Both women knew he is lying.

"Jake With Jaguar is lying to Delilah. You know you want my baby sister." She kissed him again. Her full lips are soft, moist, large and perfectly round. "You like the real young stuff, huh?" She held the gold chain around his neck. "One hundred and gold chain can do. You gimme gold chain and the gold rings on your fingers and we can do two for one, me and my sister together. We fuck you crazy." She grabbed his hand and shoved it beneath her dress, rubbing it against her panties. "This good stuff, Jake. Pure gold pussy."

His decorum deserted him, and he grabbed Delilah between her legs. She gasped then giggled. It is warm and moist there and her gentle, female fragrance is rising. He inhaled it deeply and appreciatively, and when her mouth softly presses against his again, her almost liquid tongue darted inside his mouth. His self-control is making a run for it, but he manages to stop, gather himself and release her.

"Nah, I'm working, baby." He is doing his level best to be cool and collected. "Pussy's good, but since you can't print it on a check, so it won't pay my rent."

Delilah laughed softly and turned from him to light a cigarette. She glanced at Ginger, who slid down off the car's fender and came over to him.

"What chu do for paper, Jake?"

Ginger slips her arm around her sister and looked at Jacob.

"Yeah, me and my sister Ginger got friends who got friends. They make paper, too. Maybe you give us money to meet them, huh?"

"I already know people. I wanna meet some paper, not people."

"You meet our friends, you make paper. Plenty money, Jake, but you pay us first. Two hundred dollars, Jake With Jaguar."

He shook his head.

"Naw, I ain't stuck on stupid. First you bring your friends to me, and if it works out, I'll give you one hundred."

"You wait here. We'll come back. You got money with you?" Delilah squeezed his pockets.

"You'll get paid. Don't worry."

Delilah and Ginger started walking away. Delilah turned back to Jacob.

"You wait one hour. One hour, we'll come back with our friends."

"I'll be here."

Jacob watches them start to walk away. Even from this brief meeting, he is able to discern that the girls probably spoke the language as well as he but are toying with him by occasionally speaking broken English. He thought it might be the way some local Asian hustlers are used to speaking to some of the Americans on the lookout for sex or some other illicit activity. But he suspected that they are simply playing a game with him, pretending to be street hustlers when they are much farther up on the cloak- and-dagger scale than that. Ginger stopped and walked back closer to Jacob. She squatted and began tying her tennis shoe.

"You want I stay with you?" She is making sure that her legs are open enough for Jacob to see her soft orange colored panties and her womanly fur sprouting out from the edges again. Her eyes are on Jacob and his are lost between her legs.

Delilah is also watching him and she calls out:

"Well, what chu say, Jake With Jaguar?"

He didn't answer. He couldn't answer. He didn't have to. His eyes revealed what both women already knew. Ginger walked to the car and climbed in the rear, beckoning with her finger for Jacob to join her.

"Put the top up, Jake With Jaguar, and come on back here with me." She is holding up a small bottle of whisky.

Delilah is laughing softly to herself as she watched Jacob close the roof of the convertible and then climb in the back with Ginger.

Delilah turned away and muttered:

"…Now soon you gonna get pussy whipped. Soon you gonna give up your gold and your cash, maybe your head too slick baby." Delilah smiled and walked faster. She giggled, thinking about Jacob. "I didn't know that they still made this kinda Americans who's wearin' so much phony gold that it looks like he's caught fire." She laughed harder and louder. "Jake is young man but old school and so lit up with gold he looks like a walking sunrise."

She hums a tune as she walks on, knowing that her friends *The Chinese Blood* are going to be very happy to meet this "bright" American.

CHAPTER 18

MEET
THE MAN

A not very gentle tapping on the fogged window of Jacob's car and the terrible heat inside it interrupted Jacob's dream. He sits up and looks out at several young Chinese men watching him through the car's window. Slipping his pant on, and glancing around, Jacob saw that the young girl Ginger has absconded with his Rolex, his two rings, gold chain and cash. He wipes his eyes and rolls down the car's window and sees Ginger's sister Delilah and two young Asian men approaching.

When they came closer, one of the young men stops and waits, apparently in some sort of deference to either Delilah or the young man with spiked, bright orange hair, whom Jacob knew immediately is Chop-Chop Chewy. And he assumed that the heavily muscular man at Chop-Chop Chewy's side is the person Mrs. Che told him is Chewy's enforcer and sidekick Jub-Jub Tai; his black hair is pomaded flat against his scalp and parted in the center. The three of them stand at the window, smiling at Jacob.

One of the young man with Delilah has orange spiked hair laughed as Jacob tentatively opens the car door and steps out. A large group of several young Asians are surrounding Jacob's car and are watching him. Delilah leans close to the orange hair man and whispered something to him that he found amusing. Jacob is looking around the crowd wondering where Ginger might be.

"Yo, my man, my woman here says you wanna make some paper. What kinda product you talkin' about? What chu got for us?" The man with orange hair asked.

Delilah laughed.

"An' zip up your pants, lover boy."

Embarrassed, Jacob zipped up his pant as Delilah bent over and peeked in the rear of the car. She turned back to Jacob.

"Hey! Jake With Jaguar! Where's my sister? What chu do with my sister?" Delilah is grinning.

Jacob knew this is the time to be really careful because there appears little doubt that he has found *The Chinese Blood* gang—some of them, anyway. There is certainly is little doubt that the young man with the spiked, orange hair has to be Chop-Chop Chewy and the man with pomaded hair is Jub-Jub Tai Chop-Chop's partner.

Jacob shrugged.

"I dunno where Ginger went. I guess she went where my Rolex, two rings, gold chain, and cash went."

Delilah stopped grinning and frowned. She walked close to Jacob and shoved her finger in his face.

"You tryin' to say my sister stole from you, clown?"

One of the young men moves close to them and assumed a threatening posture near Jacob. But Chewy holds up his hand to stop the man and then turned to Jacob with a very concerned expression on his face.

"Yo, my man, that's some serious shit you poppin'. How you gonna come outta your face with some seriouslip like that? How you know her sister stole from you when all the time you sleepin'? You don't rightly know who took your stuff, so step off, yo." Chop-Chop Chewy moves closer to Jacob and pokes him hard in the chest with his finger. He grins and leans his face close to Jacob's. "Now, it looks to me like you owe my woman an apology for putting' her sister down like that."

"Yeah, well, I'm sorry. It's just that when I woke up and saw all my gold is gone I didn't realize that the gold fairy made collections in the park."

Chewy is incensed. He walks closer but Jacob steps back and points his finger at Chewy, warning him:

"If you try to shove me in the chest again, then you and me's gonna be two chest shoving motherfuckers in this park."

He and Chewy stood glaring at each other for a long moment before Chewy begins laughing.

"An' what are my boys here supposed to be doin' while all this shovin' shit is goin' on?"

"They gonna be watchin' one of us get a beat down."

Chewy laughed even louder and harder but then he stopped abruptly. "Really?"

He slowly advanced again on Jacob who balls his fists but quickly undoes them, knowing that this is not the way. He needed Chewy more than Chewy needed him and an all-out fight is going to defeat his purpose. He knew that he is going to have to really control his temper this time and maybe many times after this. He walks up to Chewy and when their faces are a most meeting, Jacob says:

"Look, I ain't got time for this. My missin' stuff ain't really no thing. It's just some jewelry. You feel me? It ain't the first time it happened, and it might not be the last. This time somebody gets me, but maybe next time I don't get got. Besides I got three more Rollies at my hotel, and I shit gold chains."

Chewy burst out in raucous laughter at Jacob's last remark. The others joined in as Chewy lifted his sleeve and revealed a gold and diamond Rolex watch that Jacob knew is the one Inspector Chang has gotten him. Chewy held out his fingers which has two gold rings and a thick gold chain is hanging around his neck. Now, at least, Jacob knew what Ginger has done with his gold. She has turned it over to Chewy who he imagines as head of the gang, takes what he wants from whomever in the gang. Chewy is laughing really hard now.

"Yeah, ain't that the truth? We all got Rollies an' gold an' shit up in here." Chewy walked to the Jaguar and leaned in the open driver's window and inspected the dashboard.

"Yeah, this car is sweet. What year is it?"

Chewy pressed the horn, but it remained silent. Jacob is glad he did not wait for an answer, because he has no idea of the year of his car even though Inspector Chang told him the year earlier when he turned it over to him. Chewy pressed the horn again.

"Yo, how come this thing ain't blowin', my man?"

One of the young men informed Chewy, "The car's gotta be turned on, Chop-Chop. The horn don't work without the car being turned on."

Chewy, furious by both the intrusive, informative response and the fact that the man knew more about the car than he did, turned and grabbed him by the shirt collar. He yanked the man's face to within an inch of his own.

"Well, ain't we just the chatty little motherfucker today? You wanna give him my address too while you supplyin' so much info?"

The young man, apparently too frightened of Chewy to speak, shook his head and swallowed hard. He never saw Chewy pull out his knife that is suddenly pressed into the flesh just beneath the terrified man's eye.

"Say goodbye to this eye, dumb ass."

Finally, the trembling man is able to speak, though it is a subdued plea.

"... Please Chop-Chop,, I'm sorry. Please." He began crying.

Chewy pressed the blade against the man's cheek and drags it down the side of the man's nose all the way to the top of his mustache, drawing a thin line of blood. When Chewy stopped, the man's trembling fingers quickly traced the wound on his face. He backed and hid behind the other men who are standing around hoping not to next. Chewy wipes the point of his blade against his dark slacks, spun around and smiled at Jacob.

"Well, you already heard my name, so let's talk, my man. You got some kinda product for me to check out or what?"

Darkness has begun shrouding the park and Jacob did not want to be in it too late at night with the gang. He needed to get this first meeting over with as quickly as he could. He shrugged.

"I'm Jake.

"What kinda product? You tell me what you need, and maybe next time I might have some news for you, depending on how much and what it is. What're you looking for?"

Delilah walked over to Chewy.

"Jake With Jaguar says he wanna make big paper. Maybe he got bang bangs."

Chewy thought about it for a moment.

"You got guns, Jake With Jaguar?" Chewy asked. "You got nine millimeters? Rifles? Army shit, like grenades?"

"I can get it."

"But I'm talkin' big bunches o' army sniper rifles, grenades—all kinds an' army gear, even flak jackets." Chewy leaned his face close to Jacob's: "We wanna be the best we can be."

"How many you need?"

"How many can you get?"

Jacob sensed this might be the time to make a daring move.

"Look, my man, I ain't got the time to be out here all night lip flapping with you. You give me a number and I'll get back to you tomorrow. We can meet here."

Chewy's body stiffens and the features on his face drain to a blank. He obviously does not care for Jacob's brusque attitude and he pushes Delilah aside and took a few steps closer to Jacob, still holding the knife in his hand.

Jacob stepped back and slips his hand into his empty jacket pocket as though he may have been holding a weapon of some sort there; but he is not. Chewy stops and looks at Jacob's pocketed hand and laughs.

"So, what chu think this is, Jake With Jaguar? The OK Corral? You got enough rounds in that piece to shoot us all?"

"No. But I sure got enough to shoot some of you. And guess who's gonna be first." He is looking at Chewy.

Again Chewy stares at him for a long moment before he bursts out in maniacal sounding, humorless laughing. But this time no one around him joined in. They are all watching Jacob and edging closer until Chewy waved them back and said:

"We might be needin' several hundred pieces. That bother you?"

Jacob shook his head and smiled.

"Come on, man. I'm almost carrying that many in my pockets. Say a number that won't make me go to sleep. Gimme a number that makes sense."

Chewy laughed hard, and this time the others joined in.

"You okay, Jake With Jaguar. I'll let chu know." They shook hands. "We gonna be wantin' some other stuff to go along with the guns. We thinkin' like M-16S, Glocks, you know an' ammo an' stuff. Don't worry, we'll give you a list."

Jacob shrugged. "Like I said, no problem. I'll check with my people, and we'll see if we can come up with some ballpark figures. Might not be a big enough order for them, but we'll see. Now when and where do I see you again? We gonna keep using the park?"

"Why not? What time you gonna be here tomorrow, Jake With Jaguar?"

"Maybe about three if I don't oversleep. Orders this small bore me into snoring."

Chewy snorted out a short laugh.

"Maybe I can give you something to help you wake up, my man."

He took out a cell phone and, turning his back to Jacob, he spoke in very low Cantonese. A few minutes later Jacob sees an aloof Ginger walking towards them. She stopped next to Chewy, but he motioned with his head for her to join Jacob.

"You ain't gotta worry now, Jake With Jaguar. She gonna look out for you this time an' see that nobody takes nothin' from you again like that fei who got 'chu before. You know what fei means in Chinese?"

"No." Of course Jacob knows it means "bandit," even before Detective Liao used the word at the meeting in Chang's office he knew; but at this point he does not need Chewy to know or suspect that he knows or understood any of the Chinese language.

"Well, 'fei' means bandit. You got guts, Jake With Jaguar, an' I like that." Chewy giggled and draped his arm around Delilah. Leaving Ginger with Jacob, everyone began walking away, blending into the smoothly arriving dark.

Ginger smiled up at Jacob.

"This time, Jake With Jaguar, no making love in car. I'm more wonderful in a soft bed." She grabbed his hand and led him to the car. He wanted to resist, but his will power is no longer present, he relinquished it to her earlier in the backseat of the Jaguar, along with Chang's gold chain, Rolex, rings and cash.

As they drove to his hotel it bothered him that Chewy never asked how much the guns are going to cost. But then the answer is abundantly clear. Chewy has no reason to need to know their cost, because…

…he has absolutely no intention of paying for them.

After he and Ginger arrived at his hotel, the first thing she did was to slip out of her outer wear down to her blue panties. Then she rushed over to turn on the radio and tuning it to a station that is playing music. She turns to him and says:

"Will Jake with Jaguar please teach me how to dance?" Then she began doing her own version of a dance that is almost keeping time with the music playing.

It is a silly made up dance and Jacob finds her step, sexy but also amusing and he laughs at her. She is not insulted, instead she joins him and they laugh together until she slips her arm around his neck and slowly grinds her hips against and into his groin. She kisses him warmly and pulls him toward the bathroom, saying: "You're gonna have to teach me dancing later. Now, I want you to be dancing inside me, but we gotta shower first."

The next morning when Jacob woke in his hotel room again Ginger is gone, but this time nothing is missing. He glanced at the clock on the night table. It is near the time for him to meet with Chewy in the park. He showered and left a note in the bottom bureau drawer briefing Chang about his meeting *The Chinese Blood* gang and they expected him to be able to deliver weapons in high numbers. He wrote that he will keep him informed and that they are meeting again today in Pan Tung Park.

He slipped the note into the lower dresser drawer for Mrs. Wong to retrieve and on the way out, he slipped in a *CLEAN THIS ROOM* card in his door's slot for Mrs. Wong whom Chang has assigned to work as a maid undercover in his hotel.

As he is about to close the door, he sees that Ginger has dropped her silk handkerchief on the floor. He picks it up and presses it to his nose, inhaling deeply with a pleasant smile as she recalls last night with her. Once again, her image alive in his thoughts and he laughs at how she danced to the music from the hotel room's radio. How she cavorted and jumped up and down and twisted and turned with not even a hint of how to dance or keep time to the music or apparently even what dancing looks like; but she was having fun.

As he stood in his room he thought of last night and how she has proved to be such a different and pleasant person when away from the gang. He remembered after they showered together, she left the bathroom before him and waited for him to come out and letting out a very loud hiss like a cat, she pounced on the unsuspecting Jacob who was startled and they both fell to the floor, laughing loudly. Then she made loud cat howls as she playfully clawed and bit him and pretended to be eating him. Then, dropping to all fours she hopped onto the bed and curled up, meowing softly, waiting for him to come and pet her.

A gentle knock at his partially open door broke Jacob's reverie and he turns to see a smiling Susan Wong. She bows to him, furtively looking about the hall and then quickly entered and closed the door behind her.

"Good morning, sir. What a coincidence that I was cleaning a room down the hall when I saw you preparing to leave." She looked around the hall again. "We are alone on the floor at this time."

"Good morning, Mrs. Wong."

She is wearing a maid's black-and-white uniform that she seemed perfectly suited for. He figured that, as part of her role as maid in the hotel she has been working pretty hard and judging by the number of soiled bedding on her cart, she certainly appeared to have been doing so. Her hair is a bit disheveled and she looked just a bit tired.

"Mrs. Wong I left the note for the inspector in the dresser drawer for you. I'll go get it."

She stopped him:

"Oh, no, sir. You go ahead and I will go retrieve the note as though you are not here."

"Oh. Fine, then.

"I will wait for a safe time and location to call the inspector and relate the message of the note to him."

Mrs. Wong read Jacob's note which stated that Jacob:

I made contact with the gang, and that they wanted guns. Big order. I told them it was a small order. I think I will need to know is there is a limit to amount or caliber and they will be needing army rifles and Glocks. I will need pricing by the next day on all army weaponry, including grenades. Any other weaponry he could stall them for a moment on prices and availability. Since this is their first order, we have time to play around with them without looking like we're stalling.'

"I will call this in soon, sir." She bowed to Jacob and he left the room. "Fine." He said.

Jacob opened the door, but before stepping out into the hall, he cautiously looked up and down the hall before stepping out, closing the door and briskly walking to the elevator.

Ringing for the elevator he noticed that he is still holding Ginger's silk handkerchief. He smiled and once again pressed it against his nose. He could almost hear the tunes from the radio but he has absolutely no problem seeing and feeling Ginger.

CHAPTER 19

MISSING
SOMEONE

It has been five days since Jacob met Ginger and Delilah and Chop-Chop Chewy, all members of *The Chinese Blood* gang at the Pang Tung River Park area. Other members of the gang are also present but Jacob's main interaction is with Chewy and the two sisters Delilah and Ginger all of whom are members of *The Chinese Blood*.

Most of those five days since meeting her, Jacob has spent with Ginger who has been staying with him in his room or the two of them going to movies. Having developed seemingly genuine feelings for one another, Ginger and Jacob spend almost every hour of each day either going for walks in a nearby park where they have ices and foods on chopsticks from sidewalk vendors.

When he inquired about the next meeting with Chewy, Ginger told him that he is doing business for the gang and that he has not forgotten him. She explained that she is not privy to all gang business but that maybe he is determining how many army weapons the gang needed and what kind of weaponry they wanted to purchase through him.

But he wondered if Chewy has been simply testing him to see if he has any real connections, or if he is just having some fun with him by saying he wanted guns. Ginger told him several times that they would contact him at his hotel especially since they know she is with him. She told him that he has to be patient, that the gang is involved in many things.

The day after first meeting the gang, Jacob a phone conference with Chief Inspector Chang who assured him that he could get the weapons but felt this may have been some kind of setup and he cautioned Jacob to be careful with Chewy. He suggested that at his next meeting with the gang that he tell them he needed to be shown they are capable of getting the cash for the weapons before he came up with them. Chang also warned Jacob that he needed to be careful with his affair with Ginger. On the one hand, it is good but at the same time he suggested that perhaps she is a plant; that she is with him at the orders of Chewy to find out all she can about him. Inspector Chang also cautioned him to remember that according to the department's research, Chop-Chop Chewy is a psychotic who possesses a brutal and vicious temperament and is predisposed to acts of violence even when not aroused.

Ginger has gone shopping with her sister Delilah and Jacob is alone in his hotel room. But the real absence that bothers him is that of the Chop-Chop Chewy. He realizes that he is being impatient and he constantly has to remind himself that it has not really been that long since his first meeting them. He is also reminded that whenever Ginger is with him, he does not often think of the gang; and he believes that she feels the same way then

But, he has not seen her since last night when she left to spend the night with her sister Delilah so they could get an early start in the morning to get their clothes shopping done worried him, not to mention Ginger's absence.

Jacob told himself that he is bothered by her absence because he is concerned that it might be part of some scheme Chop Chewy is concocting but he is having difficulty convincing himself of that. He knew that he is growing far more than fond of Ginger. Far more. And his real concern at this juncture is the hope that she is feeling the same way.

And no matter how many times he chastised himself for being so unprofessional, he could not help his feelings for this young woman so vibrantly exudes life with each and every breath and step she takes.

He found he has grown quite fond of her. She is great fun to be with, more than with any other female he has known.

Just then the phone rand and he started at the sound of its ringing. He grabbed the phone and heard Ginger's purring voice:.

"Hello, Jake With Jaguar." Ginger's cheery voice rang sweetly in his ears.

"Ginger! Hey, I was wondering what happened to you."

"You miss me, baby?"

"Oh yeah."

"You miss your Ginger doll?"

"I miss you a lot." His room felt empty without her clowning, dancing and acting silly. "Yeah, I do miss you." He wished he was lying but he knew he is not.

"Does Jake With Jaguar know where Chowdien Square Park is?"

"Uh…" He has no idea. "No, but I can find it, I guess."

"You got the stuff for Chewy?"

"No, not yet, but my people say they can do it. But they want a big order and a show of some cash."

"Good boy. I come to your hotel tonight, then tomorrow night you and me go back to the park." She hung up.

He stretched out on his bed overjoyed at the thought of seeing Ginger again, holding her, kissing her and of course making love to her. He thought he is wide awake until Ginger knocked on his door and woke him. It is two o'clock in the afternoon. Jacob sleepily opens the door thinking it could be Mrs. Wong, but seeing it is Ginger, he is really happy.

"Hey, Jake With Jaguar."

Ginger playfully punched him on the chest. Then she pressed her full, soft lips against his, letting her silken tongue slip through his slightly parted lips; it played inside there as she melted into him at the door. He loved kissing her. Ginger's mouth is warm and aromatic, smelling of some kind of mint but more flowery he thought, and when she leaned her slender body against his, he felt their bodies have melted one into the other.

Theirs has become an instant relationship and now when they are together, especially sexually, she made him feel as though she is relinquishing every part of herself to him, maybe even her soul, he thought; Jacob knew that she wanted him to do the same and he knew that once he allowed that to happen, he would be free to do with her as he wished.

But it has all happened between them with such rapidity that it actually frightened him. Jacob has never known such feelings as he has for Ginger but then he has never known anyone like her. He is sure that he sensed something different about her but he has no idea what that could be and when she comes to his room later that evening, he felt like a school kid about to receive his first kiss. He is just delighted to see her and though he has tries to fight the feeling, he realized that he has long ago lost the battle to keep their relationship a clinical one.

He could scarcely recall the moment when he crossed over that ambiguous border into the first ethereal stages of love. As they stood in the doorway, Jacob is kissing Ginger as though he fears he is never going to see her again, never this close and maybe never again feel the heat from her mouth enter his.

The kiss surprised Ginger and took her breath away for an instant; but then she gladly joined in her body essentially dissolving into his and no matter how insane, how improbable how absolutely ridiculous a matter such as this could prove to be, there is no doubt, albeit his first time, Jacob is well done the road of a centuries old well-traveled route long ago carved the most esoteric emotion embraced humans: love. And now, seeing the way she is returning his kisses and the way they are holding onto one another with such fidelity, clearly his concern is without a whisper of merit; it did not require a visionary to see that he... is not traveling this path alone.

The next afternoon, Jacob and Ginger are driving to nearby Chowdien Square Park. On the way there, Ginger pressed her generous breasts against his arm, and locked her arms around his neck. Jacob's hand gripped Ginger's slender thigh firmly and they held this position until reaching the park.

The air in the park is profuse with the aroma of freshly blooming morning glories and newly mown grass; these delicious fragrances have been stirred up, created by the several elderly park workers cutting grass and trimming hedges.

Jacob buried his face against Ginger's neck inhaling the wonderful sweet smells it offers him. He marveled at how she never wore perfume and yet there is somehow always an intoxicating and splendorous scent wafting over her flesh.

Climbing out of the car, he smiled at her knowing that things have gone too far for him to be clinical in his investigation in regard to Ginger. He wondered if Inspect or Chang really believed him when he said that he is just using their romance as a means of gaining more acceptance in the gang. But when he and Ginger walk through the park holding hands as they are doing now, he finds himself not caring or thinking about anything but her. And cherishing the time they spend together.

Ginger is laughing and he knows that she is not laughing at anything or anyone in particular but simply finding humor in any and everything she sees. She has not lost that wonderful innocence that allows her to fully engage the random silliness of youth though every so often he thought he detected something in her eyes, and sometimes there is a vague trace of it in her laughter, a pronounced sadness that lurks somewhere beneath the heavily blanketed covers of her mirth. And yet she has the power to cause a special energy to surge within him as no one has ever been able to do; at times he felt his chest swelling to the point of nearly shattering into a thousand shards of uncontrolled giddiness.

Ginger's cellphone begins ringing. She blew out an exasperated puff of air and grabbed it from her pocket.

"Hello." She began smoothing out Jacob's yellow cotton shirt while she spoke. "Yeah? We're in the park. Yeah. What?" Ginger's face lit up. "What? When? Really? Yeah, okay. Yeah, he's here with me. Chewy who else would I be in the park with?" She slipped her arm around Jacob's waist and pulled him against her. "Okay. Sure. Okay. Right now? Okay, we're coming." She eased the phone back into her pocket and kissed Jacob. "Okay, let's go."

"Go? Go where?"

"To Larry Song's night club. Chewy's there and he's got some people he wants you to meet. Come on." She pulled him in the direction of the Jaguar. Then she put her arms around Jacob. "No more waiting, baby. Let's go an' meet the big shots."

CHAPTER 20

LET'S MEET
THE BOYS

It has taken them no more than half an hour to reach their destination. Ginger pointed for him to pull over to a dark building that has a huge pair of brightly lighted, glowing red lips sign above its front door entrance. Just below the lips is a neon sign blinking, "BABY BABY." And above the lips are two large slanted eyes with black mascara and green pupils surrounded by glitter and beneath all this is the black door entrance.

Jacob drove into the nightclub's front parking area. Ginger exited the car first and skipped around to meet Jacob as he got out. She kissed him, and they walked hand in hand to the front door where they are met by Ginger's sister Delilah who slipped her arm around Jacob's waist, and the three of them walked through the seven-foot-high, five-foot-wide door above which are the flaming-red lips.

Inside the dimly lighted club, an all-girls band composed of eight young Japanese girls are performing on a stage in the center of a wide, oblong all-glass bar glittering orange and lavender. Strobe lights blinked rapidly appearing to accelerating the movements of the dancers on the floor, throngs of young men and women, some of them drunkenly crashing into one another in attempts to dance.

Some of the other young women dancing with women are barely moving, they seemed to be marking time and waiting for something to happen to liven them up. A heavily muscled guard stood in front of a gold-colored chain and a sign that read "VIPS ONLY." Seeing Delilah, the guard quickly stepped aside and allowed them entrance. An older Chinese man and a middle-aged woman are sitting at a large table speaking with Chop-Chop Chewy and Job Jub Tai. The woman is holding a thick, dark-brown snake. Seeing Jacob approach, Chewy rose to greet them. The man and woman remained seated and simply smiled their greeting at Jacob. But, Chewy seems enthusiastic:

"Well, it if ain't Jake With Jaguar." Chewy gestured to a chair. "Have a seat, my man. I was just talkin' about you. Jake With Jaguar, it is my pleasure to introduce you to"—Chewy turned to the man and woman. "This is Mr. Nianzu Zhihuan, but to simplify things we call him Mr. Larry Song. Mr. Song owns this club and this is Misao Diayu. We know her as Geraldine Taipan because of her fondness for Taipan snakes. I have told them about you and the wonderful resources you have."

Song smiled and nodded to Jacob.

"Oh, indeed he has been telling us of you, sir, and we are very impressed." Song snapped his fingers and two scantily clad young women rushed from behind velvet curtains over to their table, bowing deeply.

Jacob glanced at Larry Song. He recognizes him from the photographs in Chang's office.

Song smiled again at Jacob.

"And what will Jake With Jaguar have?"

"Just a rum and Coke is fine." Jacob is watching the snake move lethargically over the woman's wrist and hand as she very smoothly manipulated it from one arm to the other, all the while keeping her eyes on Jacob.

"Does Jake With Jaguar like snakes?" She held her snake out to him.

"What kind of snake is that?" He hesitated then backed away a bit, trying to remember what Liao told him about the snake.

"It is a Taipan. Are you familiar with snakes?"

"Not very." For the life of him, Jacob could not recall what Liao mentioned about this particular snake.

Chewy laughed.

"How come Jake With Jaguar don't pet'im?"

Geraldine is gently rubbing the belly of her snake.

Jub-Jub Tai tries to provoke him to touch the deadly snake.

"You scared o' snakes, Jake With Jaguar?"

"I don't have any fear of snakes."

Jacob did not like the feeling of being challenged, it is something he likened to being bullied and so he started to reach for it, but in the back of his mind he recalled Detective Liao having said something negative about Geraldine Taipan and her snake and he wanted to pull his hand back but seeing Geraldine smiling at him, almost as a dare, he continued to reach for the snake.

Ginger grabbed his hand and jerked it back. She frowned angrily at Geraldine.

"What're you doing?" Ginger's voice is demanding and she is looking at Geraldine who is smiling at Ginger.

She has no intention of allowing Jacob to touch the deadly serpent; perhaps she is more interested in seeing Ginger's reaction:

"I am sorry Ah Cy Mingzhu; or, as you prefer: Ginger. But I have no intention of we allowing your American touch my snake or anyone else." Geraldine's face turned blank but her eyes are leveled at Ginger in a vague, disapproving way. How wonderful to see how protective you are of your acquiesces."

Ginger chastises Jacob:

"You ought to know that it is not considered wise to interact with creatures you are not familiar with." She held Jacob's hand.

All the while, Chewy has not taken his eyes off what is going on at the table:

"Aww, ain't love grand." But not to worry, Jacob with Jaguar. Chewy waved the creature away. "It just looks like an oversized worm to me."

Jacob shot a very brief, disapproving glance at Chewy.

"Well," then lemme see you pet 'im."

Chewy's features hardened.

"I don't pet nothin." He is looking at Jacob.

A long, awkward thick silence.

A sudden burst of loud music interrupted the uneasiness at the table as three nude female dancers appear on a slowly rising small stage just behind and slightly above the bar, but Chewy is still glaring at Jacob.

And not for one moment did Jacob forget where he is and with whom he is dealing. He acted casually interested in the voluptuous naked young women on stage. Ginger is watching him all the while with furtive side glanced.

Jacob sees that that Chewy's constant grin is gone and that he and Larry Song are glancing at each other, possibly ethereally passing back and forth some ideas about him.

Larry Song, is dressed a dark suit with grey stripes, black and white shoes and orange open neck shirt.

"Does Jake With Jaguar like my nightclub?"

Still watching the dancers, Jacob nodded.

"This is a very nice place you have here."

Jacob is still trying to think of some way to approach discussing the guns Chewy said they might want. "Real nice."

The topless girls arrive with the drinks, holding the tray out to Jacob first. He is appreciating the glitter around the topless waitresses' areolas. The girls appeared to be very young, maybe some of them early teens and exceptionally pretty with no need of the heavy makeup they are wearing. Jacob is rather appreciative of the young girls.

Chewy, watching Jacob appraise the young girls, snickered and he looked at Ginger, who is not too happy with the Jacob s conduct in general.

"Does Jake With Jaguar likes the girls?" Chewy fondled the breasts of the two young women, surprising Jacob. "Go ahead, Jake With Jaguar, these titties are real soft, an' the girls really don't mind." Chewy glanced at Ginger again. She is watching Jacob. He is watching the girls. Chewy slapped one of the young girls on the behind and then guided her to Jacob.

She smiled at Jacob, pushed her breast near Jacob's face, rubbed her erect nipple across his lips, and then leaned her face close to his.

Chewy guffawed:

"What's a-mattah, Jake with Jaguar? If you don't like girls then I can get you some young boys1"

One of the pretty waitresses kissed Jacob lightly on the mouth. Chewy guided Jacob's hand to the girl's breasts, all the while he kept looking at Ginger who is watching it all. Jacob, in spite of himself, began to rub the waitresses breast and then he squeezed them once and held them.

Chewy leaned over and whispered in Jacob's ear.

"Ginger's not happy with you, my man. Look at 'er."

Jacob, as though snapping out of a trance, quickly dropped the young girl's breast and turned to Ginger, who is staring blankly at him. He smiled at her, but she did not in any way acknowledge it. Instead she took a sip of his drink and set it down hard on the table.

Ginger's sister, Delilah, laughed and slipped her hand between Jacob's legs then leaned her face close to her sister's.

"Your boyfriend's a 'butterfly' boy, Ginger. You need to cure 'im of that. Maybe you need to show him some more of your panties."

Delilah leaned back and laughed in a loud voice and is immediately joined by Chewy and Jub Jub Tai.

Larry Song tapped on the table for attention or perhaps decorum. Frowning and seeming a bit impatient, he motioned for the waitress to leave when he said:

"Plenty time for play later. Chewy tells me that you have access to certain items that we may be in need of in the future. We will discuss that matter after you have a look at my place. Perhaps one day some of your friends may want to come and enjoy some of our atmosphere." Larry Song rose. "Ginger, do you care to show your friend around the club?"

Ginger is pouting.

"No."

"Well. Delilah, kindly give our guest a tour of the premises. He may even have ideas on bringing it up to date with some American clubs."

"It already looks pretty much up-to-date to me now." Jacob takes a big swallow of his drink and follows Delilah up the stairway to a long hall with a single door. Walking through the door she showed him glass-partitioned gaming rooms and what appeared to be an Olympic-sized swimming pool.

On another floor are the executive suites for special guests with large bankrolls, Delilah told him these special high rolling guests are called, "Whales." She whirled around with her arms wide and explained:

"Mr. Song calls these rooms the 'whaling suites,' and they are meant strictly for the really high rollers, usually politicians and dignitaries. Any and all forms of entertainment are supplied for these prized guests and no request, short of murder, is too bizarre to be accommodated.

On another floor they come across a series of doors. She opened one and they step inside the huge room with a dining table, an immense wall television, a picture window reaching the dimensions of the room, telephones and two more doors. Delilah opens one of the doors and inside thee is a really large round bed with a gold canopy overhead with gold colored drapes festooning the windows behind it. She closes the drapes behind the bed, telling him:

"All the suites on this floor have a huge round bed with a silk canopy above it, three complete baths, a panoramic window, crystal chandeliers, a very large cabinet with the best bourbons and whiskeys, and Waterford crystal glasses and as you can see you sink almost up to the top of your ankles in the rugs."

Delilah pours them a drink and they sit on the edge of the bed. Delilah places her drink on a nearby end table causing her skirt to rise to mid-thigh. Jacob glances appreciatively at her rounded, cream-colored thighs, perfectly shaped knees, and thin ankles.

Delilah is a beautiful woman whose body is close to the shape of her sister's, only a bit heavier but Jacob knows that Ginger is prettier and he is starting to feel guilty about his conduct so far at the club.

She is wearing a tight fitting T-shirt, and her large breasts bounced crazily up and down and side to side as she rearranged herself on the bed, half-heartedly trying to pull her skirt down.

Jacob tries to look somewhere in the huge room other than Delilah's very large, bouncing breasts and her full, shiny, beige thighs.

"This is a really beautiful suite, Delilah." I can see that you need plenty of money to occupy these suites.

Delilah leans back and stretches out on the bed and purrs:

"… Jake With Jaguar. Maybe you wanna stay here tonight? Only five thousand a night."

"I don't think I could sleep well spending that much for a room—no matter how beautiful and well stocked the whiskey cabinet is."

She drains his glass and drops it on the rug then curls her legs up on the bed looking seductively at him. He did not know what to do at this point. If he made a move on her, she might tell Ginger. Besides that, he is not sure that he even wanted to do such a thing to begin with. Also, something like that might discredit him with the gang and he surely did not want to hurt Ginger. He is already angry with himself about the way he allowed Chewy to get him to touch the waitress; even that could possibly have discredited him with the gang. More importantly is how Ginger is feeling about his behavior.

And he realizes that this all might just be a test to see if he is a trustworthy person as far as loyalty went. But then it could be possible, he is thinking, that maybe the gang does not want to deal with someone who is trustworthy. Also Ginger's professed affections for him just might be something that Chewy set up. Maybe Ginger is acting under orders from Chewy. His head feels as though it is ready to explode. Anything, he reasons, can be everything and everything is quite possibly nothing.

Delilah leaned back and stretched out on the bed and coos:

"…Just lay back and relax Jake With Jaguar and let's just talk for a minute."

She patted the space next to her and gently pulls him down to lay next to and against her and she drapes one leg over his legs. Again Jacob immediately is engulfed in an intoxicating mixture of expensive perfume and Delilah's body fragrance filling his senses.

She turns to him, and he sees her lips are wet—not moist but actually wet and open, and now at this one moment in time, he did not care about right and wrong.

Delilah's breasts are only slightly flattened by her lying on her back and they are heaving and he leans over and presses his mouth against hers, and she quickly pushes her tongue into his open and all-too-willing mouth.

When they parted, he is out of breath, and so is she but his breathing difficulty is caused by constrictions of guilt.

"Jake With Jaguar…my knees are itching me. Scratch them for me."

Immediately he raises up a bit as she lets her legs part slightly. He began gently scratching them, and she began to writhe and moan.

"How's that?"

"Now my thighs are itching." Jacob began scratching her thighs but she grabs his hand. "No, that hurts me. Use something softer than your manly fingers."

He kissed both thighs and then let his tongue begin "scratching" them, going from thigh to thigh. It took only a few moments for his tongue to convince her legs to smoothly, widely part, pushing her short dress all the way up to the top of her stomach revealing her bright pink panties from out of which spring sprouts of silken, thick strands of vaginal hair, including a thin stream of the smooth fur leading upward from the top of her panty's elastic hem.

Delilah moans and slowly pulls his face even more against her panties as he pulls his face away to grab a breath. Then he slides his tongue up and down her heated cream colored thighs until she grabs his head and presses his mouth against her warm cushion of fleshy wetness.

Jacob's fingers gently pulls aside the edge of her panties as he presses his mouth there in her bushy forest of delight and only seconds later he sends it into a thick creamy voyage in exploration of Delilah's fleshy inner caverns.

Delilah holds his mouth firmly there and starts to slowly gyrate her hips against his mouth, urging her purse of sexual wonders forward, if there is a hilt—then find it. But, no matter what—demand what you need.

Delilah's body quivers, then begins suddenly convulsing spasmodically and each spasm is timed with to the slow and gradual movements of Jacob's tongue. In a moment she is making noises that sounded to Jacob as though Delilah has begun to gasp out deep sobbing preluded by thick groans crying, concluding with loud uninhibited gasps.

Her slender fingers are pulling his face harder against her, scarcely allowing Jacob the space for his tongue to continue licking and slapping against her cushiony vaginal flesh and suddenly the predictable trembling arrives and is so profuse as to seemingly have turned violent. And then, no longer indecisive, Delilah can stand it no longer and caring not that he is now bereft of breath, she greedily locks her thighs against Jacob's temples, vaulting him into a world of painful, throbbing silence, Delilah's body shudders mightily and all that is left is the finality of it all. And gratefully after moments when the shuddering, the terribly delicious trembling subsides to a simple shivering, there is only a single destiny left her and so Delilah collapses into a light fainting.

Jacob lowers his pant and underwear and moves to between her legs, entering her in a single smooth gliding motion. Delilah moans lowly and her nails press deep into Jacob's sides. She begins slowly gliding her hips side to side in a smooth and then undulating manner that caught Jacob unaware and though he tries to right his ship, to alter, undo and readjusts his rising ecstasy—it is too late and Delilah gripped his mouth with hers to muffle his growing scream.

And then it is over. They both lay there for several minutes with Jacob breathing heavily on top of Delilah but she kissed him and then eases herself from beneath him, stands and rearranges her clothing. She slips out of her panties and walks briskly to the bathroom. He joins her.

She drops her panties in the sink and washes them with one of the several bars of soap on a wire shelving at the side of an oblong medicine cabinet. She pulls down Jacob's pant and his underwear, letting them drop to his ankles, commenting lowly:

"…No wonder my sister is falling in love. Hurry. We have no time for showering but we can take what the American's call … is it a 'pink bath' that they say?"

He chuckled and shook his head.

"It's called a 'pimp bath.'"

She laughed and shrugged.

"Okay." She took a bath towel, soaped it and began washing him between his legs. "I do not want my sister to smell me on you. She is already furious with you. You must stop looking at other girls when she is with you. You know she is beginning to fall in love with you and Chop Chop does not like that. He thinks Ginger is losing her focus with you. And so do I but I will never say it. She is my sister. I love no one other than her and our parents. He thinks if Ginger loves you then she is young and that you will be able to control her. He does not want that." She looks at him with a very serious expression. "Be very careful of Chop Chop."

He nods. He knows that even if he tells Delilah how he really does love her sister, she will not believe him. After all, he can hardly believe it himself. But he knows he loves Ginger even though he certainly has not demonstrated it at this club today.

Jacob really feels badly now and overwhelmingly guilty.

"Yeah."

Delilah finished washing him then she did the same to herself and placed her panties between a dry towel and wrung it dry as she could manage, then she slipped her underwear back on.

"Ohhh—that feels nice and cool. Come on, we have to get back downstairs to Larry Song.

"Now, look, Jake with Jaguar. Nothing happened between you and me up here in this room. She kissed him deeply before they rushed out the room for downstairs.

When they returned to the table, Jacob is surprised to find that only Geraldine Taipan is there. She glanced at them and when they sat she asked Jacob.

"Is there something else we can give you, sir?"

Busted, Jacob thought.

He looks at Delilah and shakes his head:

"No, I think I've had enough for today."

"Well, look who's returned to the land of the living." Chewy is coming to the table, laughing.

Jacob is surprised to see Chewy returning with Larry Song, Jub Jub Tai, and Ginger. He assumes they must have had a meeting about him and he does not think it could have been a very positive one. When they sit at the table, Larry Song has a smirk on his face but Chewy's facial expression is serious, even grim.

Larry Song takes a swallow from his drink and looks at Jacob.

"My people need large numbers. Army rifle, Sniper, McMillan TAC-50. 50 heavy caliber sniper rifles for the start. One hundred." Song produced a large wad of hundred dollar bills.

"Tell your people to please be assured of the money is here."

Jacob held up his hand

"It's not just the money, sir. My clients want the order to be large enough to warrant the risk. My people have gotten to the point where they expect big things from me and huge returns on their investments."

Chewy laughed.

"Jake with Jaguar sound like he got hisself some stockholders."

"You can say that, in a way."

"Well, then, I agree," Song said, putting away his roll of bills, "nothing trivial. And if your price becomes uncomfortable, then perhaps we can find something with which to barter away some of the costs. But we will see once we get an estimate on this order from your people."

"Sounds good. If the price is too high for cash then maybe something else. I'm thinking diamonds, gold bars—platinum is even better or—."

Chewy interrupted him.

"Or cocaine?"

"Naw, too common and way too much heat. Too easy for the feds to find If it ain't gonna be diamonds and gold or platinum, it would have to be something better, and I don't know what could be better payment than that. I mean something more costly than diamonds or gold or platinum that can go right by you; right past the authorities with them looking at it and now knowing."

Jacob's last remark caused Chewy, Song and Delilah to look at each other. Jacob saw it and realized he has said the wrong thing and needed to clean it up quickly and so he jokingly added:

"I got it! –Invisible cocaine!" He snorted out a very brief laugh that even he did not find to be amusing. "Aw, I dunno. Besides, who knows if we're even gonna be able to do anything. But, we'll see. And if it's gonna be diamonds, we have to check that there's no serial number inside the stones. I know you guys know that's one of the latest things some diamond dealers are doing to protect against theft; they laser serial numbers in the stones."

Everyone is looking at him with solemn expressions, and for a long moment, it appears that either they are surprised that Jacob is aware of the tattooing of diamonds or they are totally unaware of the practice.

Jacob leans back in his chair and again finds himself hoping he has not said the wrong thing or advanced too much of what should be exceptionally privileged information. But he knows that one way or another he will find out.

CHAPTER 21

GINGER
IS ANGRY

Something is wrong. Jacob just has that feeling although it has only been two days since the meeting at Song's club he has not heard from Chewy or any other members of *The Chinese Blood* gang, including Ginger.

Jacob is more concerned about not having heard from Ginger and he hopes she is not still angry about his fondling the waitress' breasts. He is sure that the waitress he fondled at Larry Song's club was paid extra money to allow his hands to roam over her body.

But he really misses Ginger and feels guilty about his sexual encounter with her sister Delilah at the club and hopes that she has not mentioned it to Ginger whom he is sure is fuming over his touching the waitress' breast. He vowed to himself never to be with another woman sexually as long as he and Ginger are together, no matter how tempting.

Jacob wants to contact Chewy but the gang leader has made it clear that they will do the contacting. And Jacob knows that he has to be careful with Chewy who often exhibits the characteristics of a typical sociopath; even his laughed evidenced no sign or sound of real pleasure in it neither did his facial expression when he laughed; always stoic, almost blank.

His hotel phone rang. He is excited but has no idea if it's Ginger or Chewy. He is thrilled to hear that it is Ginger who sounds dulled out, almost tired. She tells Jacob:

"Chewy wants to see you. He is going to be at Suzy Q's Bar and Grill on Hyuzi street. He wants us to meet him there in an hour."

Jacob is really glad to hear Ginger's voice:

"Ginger, you okay?"

"Come downstairs. I'll be in your parking lot."

"Ginger why don't you come upstairs for a minute? Let's have a drink. It's been a while since we've been together."

"We can drink at Suzy Q's. Please come down. I'm waiting." She hung up.

He does not like this at all, especially the monotonous tone of her voice. Obviously she is still out of sorts with him over the waitress incident at Larry Song's nightclub. But this is not the time to dally and he slipped on a light jacket and rushed down to the hotel's parking lot where Ginger greeted him with a vague grin.

The ride to the bar did not lighten matters between them since Ginger has very little to say to Jacob during the twenty minute ride; and he senses that it is better to keep the conversation to a minimum until he can figure out a way to diffuse her anger. And so he settled in and followed her instructions, all the while wishing that he could touch her; finally, he could take it no longer and he placed his hand on her thigh. Ginger simply looks a Jacob then turns her back to him. He feels really badly and he murmurs:

"…I'm sorry, Ginger. Please forgive me. If you do, I promise you that nothing like what happened at Larry Songs will ever happen again. Please. I promise you that I will be completely faithful to you from now on; and I mean completely."

After a long moment, Ginger turns and looks at Jacob. He hated himself for causing the tears on her face.

Ginger's voice is calm almost to the point of being lamenting when she said to him:

"If Jacob with Jaguar ever disrespects me again, he will pay dearly. Never must you do this to me again."

Jacob's eyes are filled with tears flowing down his cheeks when he vowed:

"Ginger, I will never—ever do anything like that again. I swear this to you!"

They kissed and embraced there for a very long and loving time and after quite a while they managed to pull themselves apart and head for Suzy Q's Bar and Grill which proved to be a short distance Jacob's hotel.

Inside **Suzy Q's** Bar and Grill, Jacob and Ginger are seated in a booth with their drinks. As usual they are so caught up with each other that they are taking little if any notice of any of the customers. But Ginger is being annoyed by two customers and is keeping a wary, furtive eye on them.

These few Asian male patrons are opposed to Ginger being with Jacob and whenever Ginger kisses Jacob, one or two of these patrons tosses peanuts into their booth. Every so often one of them makes a lewd remark in Mandarin directed more at Jacob than Ginger, thinking he did not speak the language.

Ginger, though watching them from the corner of her eye, tries to ignore the occasional rudeness and the lewd gestures that sometimes accompanies the peanut tossing. But then, Jacob, aware of the insulting behavior of the men, has become furious and over Ginger's objections he gets up to face the men, ready to deal with their boorish behavior. Then the men, are joined by two more men and they all slowly approach Jacob in threatening postures.

Ginger cusses the men in Mandarin and angrily jumps up from the booth and stands next to Jacob and is ready to fight the men. Jacob moves her in back of him and hopefully out of danger but Ginger refuses to stay out of the impending brawl and she shoves his hand away and steps back slightly in front of Jacob. He tries again to get her to sit back in the booth but she refuses.

The men are laughing at what they believe will be a very easy fight and they move in closer. Ginger side-kicks one of the men just beneath his chin and he falls unconscious on the barroom floor, much to the amazement of the other men confronting them.

Their laughter is suddenly replaced by looks of abject fear registered on all their faces, fear of something behind Ginger and Jacob; this sudden change causes Jacob and Ginger to turn around In back of them are Chop-Chop Chewy and Jub Jub Tai both watching the men whose brave posture has now wilted, degenerated into weak smiles and a halfhearted wave to Chewy and Jub Jub.

Breaking into wide smiles, Chewy and Jub Jub slowly saunter past Jacob and Ginger without speaking and over to the four men, laughing and joking and ordering them all a free round of drinks for everyone.

The man has been the most demonstrative of grins and then speaks to Chewy:

"Hey, Chop-Chop. What's happenin'?"

Chewy looks back at Ginger and Jacob:

"Oh, I dunno, Danzi. Suppose you tell me what's happening here with my two friends. Looks to me like you got them in some kinda circus center ring; you know, like maybe you think like they supposed to be your clowns or somethin'." Chewy walks back a few steps to stand in front of Jacob and Ginger to face the four men. "Why are you guys clownin' my friends here?"

The thick bodied man that Chewy called 'Danzi' is into an immediate, seemingly urgent apologetic explanation:

"Aw, naw, Chop-Chop. Nothin' like that. Naw, me an' the guys here…" Danzi turned to gesture to his three friends who are complicit in the crude behavior but one of them who has already sensed the imminent arrival of pain has disappeared, "we was jus' having some fun with your friends here who we figured are acting like newlyweds. Just some fun stuff, you know."

"Oh. Sure." Chewy smiles.

Chewy introduces the men to Ginger and Jacob and explains that they are special friends of his and that Ginger is a member of *The Chinese Blood*.

When the men hear that Ginger is in *The Chinese Blood* gang, the men bow deeply and apologize to her profusely for their behavior. One of them is still on the floor unconscious from Ginger's kick.

Then Chewy reminds them that they owe Ginger's boyfriend Jacob an equal apology and they quickly bow and apologize.

Now, the men having finish their free drinks, are saying goodbye to everyone and Chewy bows to them then immediately he spins around with a kick to the head of one of the men, rendering him into a unconscious, bleeding heap on the floor. The two remaining men turn to run but Jub-Jut Tai is blocking their way and his fist crunches into the face of one of the men causing the man's mouth to explode in a spray of blood and teeth.

Now there is only one man left and with his back against the wall, he decides that he has no choice but to fight back. He swings at who intercepts his fist with one hand using his other hand to bang his elbow into the man's ribs. There comes a muffled crack announcing the breaking of ribs and the man goes limp at Chewy's feet. He begins begging Chewy not to kill him, to let him go. But Chewy yanks the man to his feet to face him. Now, Chewy's knife is pressed against the man's face just beneath one eye.

Chewy looks at the crowd of people who have now crowded around. He points to Jacob and Ginger as he addresses those assembled:

"I don't like people screwin' around with my friends. And most of you know me and you know when it comes to abuse, I ain't the one you lookin' for. The same goes for my two friends here." He presses his knife against the man's flesh until it bleeds and then he drags it on down his cheek, at the cent er of his eye. "I know you're sorry an' you're gonna prove it by this here eye that's gonna be always cryin' for the rest o' your life, fool. Be glad I ain't the time to leave my initials on you like I usually do."

When Chew finishes, the man's left eye looks as though it is crying a wide stream of blood all the way down to the corner of his mouth. Then Chewy turns him around and kicks him into the gathered bar customers.

"Nobody clowns my friends."

Chewy hugs Jacob and Ginger tightly. He kissed Ginger on the cheek and looked at Jacob with fondness. At this point, Jacob felt in his grip that Chewy, if nothing else, is certainly exceptionally strong. But what makes him uncomfortable as he looks at Chewy is his stare; it is cold, maybe even calculating, and at that moment as he and Chew stare at each other, he is sure Chewy's mind is off somewhere in the distance, concocting something that is going to be very unpleasant for someone. But then he realized that his own mind is also off somewhere, analyzing Chewy's and also concocting something; a means of being prepared for unexpected actions from Chewy; this one, however, is appreciated and certainly well-timed which creates an enigma of an already existing enigmatic, fathomless person.

Chewy ushers Jacob and Ginger from the bar and grill whispering to them:

"…Looks like meeting here wasn't the best idea. I'll contact you guys later and we'll get together then." Then, speaking at a normal level: "Now you two crazy kids get the heck outta here! Move! Go on! Get outta here you guys! And keep away from this dumpy bar from now on."

Chewy and Jub-Jub Tai wait at the bar entrance until Ginger and Jacob climb in his Jaguar and drove off. Standing in the doorway of the club, only when Chewy sees Jacob's car turn the corner does he turn to Jub-Jub Tai asking him:

"What chu think, Jub-Jub?"

Jub-Jub Tai shrugged.

"You know what I think. I don't trust 'im an' I don't like 'im, neither, 'specially with Ginger. You can't see they done got kinda on the real cozy side?"

"Yeah, like you wish you was, huh?"

Jub Jub, shrugs.

"Not really.

Chewy looks at him and smirks.

"…Yeah." He and Jub-Jub walked to their car.

Meanwhile, reflecting on the night's events while driving his jaguar, Jacob before is totally confused. Jacob blinked as the flashing red and blue police car lights zipped past him, heading, he imagined, for the Suzy Q's Bar and Grill. He listened to the distant, faint fussing of whooping police car sirens announcing the coming of law and possible order to the bar they just left.

Just moments after that, Chewy's car zipped past them with a fathomless look at Jacob from Chewy. Though he came to their rescue in the bar, Jacob sensed that he should never relax himself around him. Jacob thought that there is part of Chewy that appears to like him, but another part, perhaps the larger part perhaps suggests that Jacob needs to always be on his guard whenever he is around Chewy.

It is clear to him that Chewy is a person on constant verge of unpredictable and likely violence behavior; savoring almost any opportunity to show how adept he is at revealing his savage side.

Ginger's pressed her hand against Jacob's knee, reassuringly. She likely has a very good idea about his concerns, he thought. He feels that she is good at picking up his concerns or worries. He likes that. She presses her head against his shoulder.

"Jacob with Jaguar should stop worrying so much. Things will be okay. Relax." And he did precisely that as he smoothly turned another corner and headed for his hotel room.

SOMEONE IS IN LOVE

Jacob turns on the hotel radio. Three weeks have passed since the Suzy Q's Bar and Grill incident. Jacob still has a problem figuring out why Chewy has them meet there and then why did he intercede when the men are about to attack him. Was it all just a set up? Chewy could have let the five men jump him and if he did not like the idea of Jacob being serious with Ginger, it would have been over, but Chewy did not let that happen. Why? Is this just more of Chewy's unpredictable behavior?

Jacob stretched out across the bed, listening to Ginger in the shower. She loves showers and takes maybe three or four every day if possible. His hotel room has more than adequate central air conditioning so it is not the heat that she is escaping. No, she simply liked taking showers.

Jacob closes his eyes and takes a deep breath, trying to fathom out what his position of trust is with Chewy since he is the one who seems to represent the gang. If the amount of weaponry they want is high volume then he will be able to charge them a large enough amount of money to force them to have to barter to make payment. This way they might have to consider trading the *cherry berry* to resolve their arms debt.

He smiled, thinking of Mrs. Wong, the undercover policewoman. She and Ginger are always totally at odds. He never realized until the two women met just how truly jealous Ginger is. He hopes that Mrs. Wong is not reporting to Inspector Chang that Ginger is more or less living with Jacob. But he knew that she probably is.

On a few instances when Jacob did not leave the room and no one has heard from him Chang instructed Mrs. Wong to check his room, concerned that he is alright. She does so on the guise of needing to clean the room. Unfortunately, each of those times although Jacob is there and he is okay, Ginger comes to the door.

And there the problem began. When Ginger sees Mrs. Wong at the door, though she is old enough to be her mother, Ginger only sees a quite shapely and attractive woman. And she suspects that Mrs. Wong has an interest in Jacob that has nothing to do with cleaning his room.

Of course she is right but not for the reason her jealousy suspects. And after the second or third time, Ginger is so furious with her that on her last visit, Ginger's temper and jealousy exploded:

"Now, what the fuck you want this time, ol' woman?" Ginger's angry eyes are flashing like neon signs.

Mrs. Wong kept her composure.

"I am Mrs. Wong. Maid service, Miss." Detective Wong bowed to Ginger. "Room service, please to clean room."

"Why the hell are you always knockin' on my man's door anyway? Is this the only damn room you get to clean?"

"I'm sorry Miss. Cleaning service, Miss." Mrs. Wong stood with her head bowed in humility.

"And just how the hell are you gonna clean the room with us in it granny? We don't want none today, ol' lady. Go wave that pussy at some other damn door!" Ginger slams the door in Mrs. Wong's face, but not before hollering something apparently even more unpleasant in Mandarin, some of which he picked up. Ginger turns to an embarrassed Jacob and asked:

"Ain't the maids supposed to just clean rooms that got a sign on the door askin' to clean the room? An' ain't they supposed to clean a room when you ain't in it?"

Jacob knows she is right but he also knows to say nothing rather than to risk being the second victim of her violent temper so he makes her a cup of tea in an attempt to calm her. He relishes Ginger's gentler side, the part of her she showed him when she told him of the poem she wrote for him.

That particular evening they are sitting on a park bench and watching children play, she told him she has something for him to read and she unfolded a small sheet of paper and gave it to him. He read it:

Jake With Jaguar I think of you sometime,
So I write you this poem I hope I can rhyme,
I see you run and want to be free,
Maybe you can stop and take time to see me.
I hope you do not see me because it will mean
That I am not there before you. It will mean that
I am hiding from you and perhaps you can find me.
But you must take care when you seek me out,
You will never fine me, because you see,
I am inside your heart.

Jacob has absolutely no idea what to say, so he kisses her, and they sat on the bench holding each other until the sun came up.

Later that morning, after showering, Jacob just finished shaving. Walking from the bathroom he yawned and almost choked on his yawn when behind him:

"Boo!" Ginger sneaks up behind him wearing a towel.

He is startled and turned around to kiss her. As soon as they embraced, the hotel phone rang. Jacob's heart thumped once before he hesitated, took a deep breath, and picked it up.

"Hello?"

"Whassup, Jake With Jaguar?" As always, Chewy's voice is loud.

"Chewy?" Jacob is greatly relieved to hear his voice.

"Yeah. What you been doing these past few weeks, my man?"

"I just been lying dead."

"Oh yeah?"

"Yeah."

"Lying dead, huh?"

"Yeah."

"How about that."

"Yeah."

"Meet me. We gotta talk."

"At the club?"

Slight pause.

"Naw. Write down this address."

Jacob grabbed a pen and notepad.

"I'm ready."

Chewy spoke slowly.

"Twenty-three Shang Rung Road. It's an apartment house near Shung Rei, east of the club. One hour from now. We'll be in apartment number—!" The line went dead.

"What apartment number?" Jacob clicked the phone several times. "What apartment number, Chewy? Hello? Chewy?" Jacob hung up. He grabbed a sheet of paper and wrote:

3 Shang Rung Road,
No apt. number.
Be careful in approach.
They could be anywhere.

He hid the sheet of paper to be left in the drawer and meant for Chang, but Ginger heard him repeat the address.

"I know where that place is. Lonely place. Not much there."

"Chewy said one hour from now so how much time does that leave us?"

"It's about half an hour from here. Later let's go to the park on our way back Okay?"

"Okay. You'd better get dressed."

After getting dressed and while Ginger is still putting on her clothes, Jacob slips the hotel card: "PLEASE CLEAN ROOM" into the slot on his door. Then as he is about to put it in the dresser drawer:

"Boo!" Ginger is right behind him. "Okay, your little Ginger is ready! Let's go!"

Jacob balls the paper in his hand and turns around and smiles. Now it is going to be impossible for him to get the note in the drawer without her seeing him do it. Ginger is becoming anxious:

"What's wrong? How come we're still standing here?"

Jacob started feeling for his car keys, pretending he did not have them. Ginger locked her hands on her hips:

"Now what?"

"The car keys! Where'd I leave them?" He begins pretending to search the room. Then someone knocked at the door.

Ginger and Jacob are staring at each other wondering who could possibly be knocking. Ginger went to the door, looked back at Jacob, shrugged and opened the door.

"Maid service, Miss."

Jacob's heartbeat hastened. This confrontation between Mrs. Wong and Ginger was going to be entirely his fault. He forgot he had placed the "Clean This Room Please" in the door's slot.

Ginger glanced back at Jacob who is staring at Mrs. Wong. He momentarily forgot he placed the clean room placard in the door's slot.

Ginger stepped closer to her and jabbed her finger hard against Mrs. Wong's forehead

"Oh hell no! Uh-uh. Not this time you horny old cow! What the fuck you want this time, old woman?" Ginger is absolutely beyond furious. "An' while we're at it, lemme ask you again how come you always at my man's door? You got a cleanin' lease on this room maybe? What is up with this visitin' shit? You lonely or somethin'?"

"I am sorry, Miss. Please. I am sorry. But there is a request in the door."

Ginger looks at the cleaning card Jacob put in the slot in his room door for the maid to clean his room.

"I will come back later. I am new and cannot seem to remember my place. I am new and I try to remain busy so I do not lose my position here,"

Mrs. Wong tries to bow again, but Ginger snatches her by her hair, her grip is tight and unrelenting, and she moves her face very close to Wong's. Ginger lifts her chin higher and takes a long, careful look at Wong's face, pacing her words:

"Wait…a… minute. I know you from some place. I know you, Grandma. What's your name?"

Mrs. Wong forced some tears to appear.

"I am no one. I am Susan. Susan Wong. I clean rooms. You have spoken to me other times of my stupidity. I am sorry, but I am new here and I sometimes become confused. I sometimes make mistakes. I am an old woman."

Ginger emphatically shakes her head.

"No. No. You ain't that old! An' I know I've seen you somewhere outside! Where do I know you from? Tell me before I kill you, dog-faced woman!" When Mrs. Wong lowered her head again, Ginger grabbed Mrs.Wong's hair and yanked her head up so they are face-to-face. Mrs. Wong pleaded:

"I am a maid, Miss. A maid." She avoided Ginger's eyes.

Jacob, caught up in what he thought is imminent violence, still has not taken the opportunity to place the note in the drawer for Mrs. Wong but knows he has to step in.

"Ginger, stop. Please. She's crying. She is right, you know. I did put the card for cleaning in the slot on my door. I forgot I put it there but you can see it's there. Let her go ahead and clean the room. We're leaving anyway, that's why I put up the sign. I was leaving when you came in. And look I found the keys! They were in my pocket all the time! Come on, let's get outta here. Come on."

Ginger, not at all satisfied, allowed herself to be pulled down the hall towards the elevator by Jacob, but her eyes lingered on Mrs. Wong while she mutterers:

"I dunno…maybe she's the only bitch in here that can read English 'cause it looks like none of the other maids know what that 'clean my room' card means. But that one there's like a fucking Chinese bloodhound with a damned boomerang up her ass; the boomerang brings her back and her godamn bloodhound nose always finds your room."

Catching Mrs. Wong's eye, Jacob dropped his note to Chang on the carpeted floor as the elevator arrived. But Ginger saw what he did and placed her foot in the elevator doorway to keep it from closing.

"What's that paper you just dropped on the floor?"

Jacob grabbed Ginger and is trying to pull her into the elevator, insisting:

"It's just some notes I was doodling. Let the maid get it. That's what she gets paid for."

"Liar. What is Jake With Jaguar hiding? So now you Jake With Secrets, huh?" Ginger's voice is cold.

"You writin' love letters to ol' grandma maid lady maybe or maybe you write love letter to some other China ho?"

"Ginger, don't be ridiculous."

He tries to hold her arm, but she pulled away and stepped into the elevator, glaring at him.

"So now you're Jake With Secrets, huh?"

"Ginger, it was nothing, really."

"Then why didn't you let me go pick it up if it's nothin'?" Ginger's eyes seemed to narrow and she pointed her long, thin finger at Jacob's eye.

"You got love letter to some China girl who ain't me? If it's nothin', then lemme go get it and read it, butterfly boy. I know it's a letter to your Chinese ho?" She slapped him hard. Tears are in her eyes and she jabs a finger against Jacob's chest.

"I forgave you for Larry Song's little nasty young girls, but now I see you jus' a big ho monger!" She stepped into the elevator, folded her arms and pouted mouth looked like a large, perfectly ripe cherry.

The elevator door closed but not before Ginger issues a screaming, liberal amount of profanity in mandarin to Mrs. Wong just before the elevator begins its descent.

Outside, once they reached his car, Ginger took out her cell phone and dialed a number all the while keeping her eye on Jacob. She speaks softly into the phone, now and then nodding and glancing back at the hotel. When she finished, she climbed into the rear seat of the Jaguar and locked the door, then coldly watched Jacob climb into the driver's seat.

He sat there for a moment, knowing it would do no good pleading with her to get in the front with him, and so he started the car.

Ginger leaned forward and hissed:

"Come on an' drive, Jake With Secrets."

She is so livid her lips are trembling. She closed her eyes and calmed her breathing.

"Ginger come on, don't be like that. Sit up front with me."

Though it is obvious she is determined not to ride in the front with him, he still pleaded with her:

"You're gonna have to help me find Shang Rung Road, Ginger, and it's easier from up here."

She sucked her teeth and leaned back in her rear seat, looking out the window.

"Drive to the club, a maid? She looks old enough to be your mama. She's a hotel maid. Everybody probably fucking her!"

"Ginger, you know that I don't 'float' that way."

She sucked her teeth loudly and spun to face him:.

"Oh, you think you just so cool, don't chu baby? You don't 'float' that way." She is fit to be tied. She made a wry face, sucked her teeth loudly again, crossed her legs, and leaned even further back in the seat.

Later, as they drove along, she leaned over the front seat and kissed him lightly on his cheek. He is delighted, but only for an instant. She reached down and grabbed him hard and painfully between the legs.

"So you don't 'float,' huh? Yeah, all you butterflies like to float. But you floatin' with the wrong girl. I'm gonna clip this wing here that you floatin' with!"

She squeezed his crotch even harder and he hollered so loud that it even startled her and she let go of him and slapped him on the back of his head and leaned back.

"No more of this young Chinese pussy for you, Jake With Secrets, unless you already fucking Larry Song's babies at his club. Your secrets done nail my pussy shut." She is weeping.

"Ginger, I—"

"Shut up an' leave me alone!"

The tears flooded down her cheeks. She dug a small hankie from her cleavage and held it to her face. He is feeling really bad that she is crying. He wishes he could explain to her what the note is about, but that cannot happen.

221

He hates seeing her hurt this way and wants deeply to do something to alleviate her pain. Every so often as they rode along, he reached back and touched her leg, but she shoved his hand away each time.

"Ginger, if I pull over for a minute, can we kiss and make up or at least talk about this?"

"No! My mouth is nailed shut too. Keep driving!"

For the rest of the ride, a silent Ginger stared through a flood of tears at blurred, passing images.

CHAPTER 22

A 23 SHANG RUNG ROAD CHANGE OF PLANS

Jacob imagines that maybe the sun, like Ginger, is angry with him too because as they drive along, even with a breeze splashing into his face from the car's top being down, the blistering midday heat is relentlessly felt purgatorial.

They drove past Larry Song's club over half an hour earlier and have been going nonstop since. Then, from the backseat, Ginger points to a narrow street to their left and then up to the end of the block where a four-story building stood in the center of a large square, bare area baking in the sun. Judging from its dilapidated appearance, it has long since been the victim of many thousands of such malicious suns.

Jacob eased to a stop and he and Ginger got out. He shaded his eyes and read the address on the sad edifice: 23 Shang Rung Road. He looked at Ginger, who is still glaring at him. He turned back to the building, not at all eager to enter the shabby brick thing that is listing to one side as though on the verge, through simple sweltering exhaustion, of thankful collapse and respite in death.

The building seemed so pitiful to Jacob, its posture so precarious, he thought it has decided to condemn itself rather than wait for some itinerate, disdainful inspector of buildings to press his disapproving stamp on its aged self.

Why did Chewy choose to meet in such a building? And just what is he supposed to do without knowing what apartment to seek? He looks at Ginger who is leaning against his car and looking away. He thought it strange that she did not make any attempt to enter the building; as strange as Chewy choosing an apparently abandoned building to have a meeting in.

"Ginger, what apartment would we be looking for in there?"

No response.

"Well I'm not going in that building. I think it's abandoned and it looks like it's about to fall down or something. I mean, look at it."

He waited for a response from her, but she still refused to speak or look at him. Instead she continued to hone her glare at him She folded her arms and briskly walked over to a black sedan parked not far from them with its rear facing the building. She opened the car's rear door, climbed in and slammed the door behind her.

What is going on here, Jacob, thoroughly confused, is wondering. From where he is standing he cannot see through the car's darkened windows. He cautiously approached the Bentley but as he neared the car but he still could not see through its dark windows; and he instinctively reaches for his sidearm, something he has done several times as a policeman under similar circumstances.

But then realizing he is being watched—he quickly pretended that his hip is itching him badly that he has to stop scratch. When he reaches the parked car, the darkened driver's window rolls down and a smiling Larry Song reached through the window from behind the wheel to shake hands with him.

"Mr. Jake with Jaguar, it's good seeing you again, sir." Song's handshake is as thin as his smile as he watched Jacob examine his car.

Jacob returned his smile and tries to glance at Ginger in the rear seat.

"This is a nice car you have here, sir. I didn't know you drove a Bentley." Jacob immediately regretted saying that, knowing it is possibly going to be construed as condescending.

Song stopped smiling and turned away as he rolled up the window, he says:

"Please get in."

Jacob grabbed the rear door handle where Ginger is sitting, but she has locked the door.

"Your girlfriend seems to be displeased with you. Perhaps you should sit in front with me." Song features remained expressionless.

Jacob tries once more to open the rear door, but Ginger hisses through the partly open window:

"Jake With Secrets can ride in front with his secrets." She rolled the window all the way up.

Jacob sighed and walked around the car and climbed in front, sitting next to Larry Song.

"What's going on, Mr. Song? Where's Chewy? "I thought we were going to meet him at building 23 back there."

'I have no idea, sir, since I did not make the arrangements."

Jacob glances back at Ginger. Glancing back at Ginger.

"I am afraid that Ginger won't speak to me."

"Oh? I wonder why." Larry Song replied sardonically. He put the car in gear and started driving.

No response from Jacob who is wondering about his car.

"Uh, excuse me, Mr. Song. But my car is still back there. Is it going to be safe there?"

Song turns his car around and drives back where he was parked originally with only one exception: now his car is across the street from 23 Shang Rung Road facing its entrance. He rolls down the windows and switches the motor off.

Jacob's eyes scan the streets examining the faces of the rare few pedestrians in the area. The streets had the appearance of a ghost town. He begins to imagine the worst, knowing that an abandoned building in a business district on a Sunday when the entire area is almost completely deserted is be the perfect place to commit a murder; and absolutely the most perfect location to leave the body.

Now he really wondered what is going to happen when Chewy arrives. He senses the sinister purpose for this business at 23 Shang Rung Road is not likely to harm him, because it is far too elaborate. No, there is something else planned. But what could it be?

Four black vans with black windows slowed to a stop on the opposite side of the street about a hundred yards from where Larry Song's car sits. Several young men and women climbed out of the vans. Jacob recognizes some of them as members of *The Chinese Blood*. Several young women also climbed from the vans, carrying large bags that he is sure holds guns. The men milled about, talking, laughing, and joking among themselves, but the five young girls are serious and quiet and standing with their backs against the building.

All of them, however, appear to be taking special notice of the building 23 Shang Rung Road. Jacob cannot figure out what is happening. And where is Chewy?

Larry Song turns to him.

"Is Jake With Jaguar bothered by something?"

"Hmm? Oh. No. Just a little bored sitting here with my lady not speaking to me."

Jacob glances back at the brooding Ginger. It kind of pleases him that Ginger is clearly and genuinely jealous of Mrs. Wong whom he hopes has picked up his crumpled note for Inspector Chang that he dropped in the hall for her. If she did, then she called Chang, and that means Liao and Mrs. Che should be nosing around somewhere at some time soon, he thinks.

Jacob catches his breath. Could that be what this gathering is for? Is this all a trap? Of course it is. What else could it be? Nothing else adds up. It makes sense that before they seal the gun deal, they have to check to see that he is not in some way involved with some local of international police authority. Especially if they plan on doing more business with him.

So, now they are all waiting to see if some kind of backup followed him to this place. They have to know he'd be worried about going to some remote location to an apartment with no number and would request backup under these suspicious circumstances.

So, if Detective Liao and/or Mrs. Che show up, they are sure to go into the abandoned building, the address that he will have given them. Once they do that, the gang will surely follow them in. He did not want to think of what they will do to Liao and Mrs. Che. There is no doubt they will torture them and they will name Jacob as working with the Hong Kong police in the investigation of their new drug.

If they come, then he is going to have to resort to using his magic to save their lives and that would create incredible complications. He must do it before they are captured and he cannot let it be known that he is doing he magic.

All Jacob can do is pray that no one shows up from Chang's office.

They waited for two hours. Jacob thanks God no one has come However, he knows that Mrs. Che or Liao might still be somewhere in the vicinity watching and waiting for the proper time to approach the building, after all, they are well experienced in police matters.

Finally Chewy arrives but he remains in his own car with Jub Jub Tai. Chewy's car is also facing the entrance to 23 Shang Rung Road clearly waiting to see if some kind of police backup arrives. Jacob knows now that he needs to be especially careful of what he says and does, perhaps even with Ginger. He pretended to need stretch his legs and he starts to open the car door to step outside, but Larry Song touches his arm.

"Do not leave the car…please."

Jacob knew the word "please" is clearly an afterthought. The statement sounded more like a warning than a request. After an hour, Chewy and Jub Jub Tai walked over to Song's car, and Jacob almost jumped out to greet them. Chewy laughs.

"What's up, Jake With Jaguar? How come you sweatin' so much?" Chewy bends down and asks Larry long, "Mr. Song, did forget to turn on your air conditioner again?"

Ginger is laughing, and said:

"That's strange. The one back here with me is freezing. And his name is now Jake With Secrets."

Chewy has a surprised look.

"What? You mean Jake got secrets? I thought he only got a Jaguar." He stopped smiling and looked seriously at Ginger. "What kinda secrets?"

"He's screwin' his maid, and he writes letters to her and won't let me read them. He likes to spread the legs of old women." She waved Jacob away with a sweep of her hand.

Ginger's remark causes Chewy to exchange a glance with Jub Jub Tai. Then he smiles at Jacob, saying:

"Aw, is the honeymoon over already, Jake With Secrets?" Chewy is still watching Jub Jub Tai, thinking about Ginger's statement. " So Jake with Secrets is writin' secret letters, huh?"

Ginger is absolutely furious all over again.

"He's a nasty boy. And he all the time saying how much he loves me." She jabbed her finger at Jacob. "You a liar. No more young pussy for you, butterfly boy."

Jub Jub Tai laughed really loud, but Ginger gives him a 'what the hell are you laughing so hard about, you idiot?" frown.

Jub Jub is deflated and turns on Jacob, but is a bit defused;

"Wow, Jake, you a playa. Yeah, me an' Chop Chop always say you was a butterfly."

But Ginger's statement about dropping the note on the floor causes Chewy's smile to crumble into a rigid look of concern.

"So you droppin' notes to your maid, huh?"

Now, Jub Jub and Chewy were looking at Jacob with bemused expressions. Jacob see something in Jub Jub Tai's eyes that causes him to suspect that, much like Chewy, not only is he capable of cold-blooded violence, even murder, but he suspects that Jub Jub Tai, like Chewy, may be in constant search for such an opportunity to do one or the other—or both, for that matter.

But a glimpse of the way Jub Jub Tai looked at Ginger causes Jacob to have the sneaking suspicion that he is a secret admirer of Ginger. Sometime ago Jacob ago imagined that Chewy might have romantic feelings for Ginger but when he got to know more about him, he determined that was not true.

Jub Jub Tai continued to rub it in:

"So, Jake, you screwing the hotel maid, too? Man, you got plenty long dick, huh? You long dickin' all the females, you bad boy?" Jub Jub only quickly glanced at Ginger not wanting her verbal ire.

"The maid cleans my room, and that's all."

Chewy put his hand on Jacob's shoulder:

"I thought you was a businessman, Jake With Secrets, but you a playa and so maybe you not a businessman after all, huh? You don't wanna make no paper, you jus' wanna make some babies with your maid."

Jub Jub Tai burst out in raucous laughter at Chewy's remark but when he saw Ginger's eyes narrow in his direction, he immediately quiets himself.

Ginger turns to Chewy:

"His maid all the time just comes to his room –nobody else's room. That's a big hotel, an' they got plenty maids, but he got his special maid. That old bitch always at his door." She climbed out of Larry Song's car, fuming.

Jacob saw Chewy, Jub Jub Tai and Song all exchange looks. Song nods and starts his car. Larry Song watches Chewy for a long moment.

Then Larry Song says:

"Maybe he's a big tipper."

Ginger shakes her head.

"That hotel don't let nobody give maids money. They know some maids if they see money, they turn ho on the quick-quick; some of them will 'trick out' for people with the right cash."

Chewy manufactured a cruel smile for Jacob:

"Hey, Jake With Secrets,". "I need a drink. How about you?"

Jacob shrugged.

"It wouldn't hurt, I guess."

"Good. Come on. Let's hit the club. Besides, I got somebody for you to meet. An' he got big business, but he ain't got no big paper. He wants plenty o' guns, but he ain't got the cash for the size order he wants. He's thinkin' to make some kinda deal like you said before. I think maybe he got somethin' you can cash in on real big-time back in your country."

Jacob hopes this is the break he has been looking for, but he knew he has to be reserved, not overly excited.

"Well, maybe, but I don't usually deal personally in my country. Too dangerous. And crack is number-one drug back home, but it's too crowded a market. Some junkies are hittin' up heroin again; it's on a kind of a come-back. This is a perfect time for something new on the market."

Chewy is grinning widely.

"Maybe we can make some Asian crack?" He looked at Ginger. "Ginger, you wanna make some Asian crack?"

She shrugged.

"Don't know what that is."

Chewy smiled at Jacob.

"Maybe you think about dealing opium?"

"It can't compete with crack."

Chewy looked at Jub Jub Tai and began laughing.

"Hey Jub, maybe you and me can mix up some crack cocaine an' opium an' corner the market with our new drug. We'll call it, 'very cherry.'"

Jub Jub snorted a brief, very hollow laugh and said:

"Why not?"

Larry Song turns around and nods to Ginger. She climbs out and he drives away. Chewy, Ginger and Jub Jub walk over to Jacob's car. Jub Jub Tai climbed behind the wheel and held his hands out to Jacob for the keys.

"Gimme the keys, playa."

Jacob drops the car keys onto Jub Jub's palm with a clear dislike and starts to climb in front next to him but Chewy stops him and gestures for Jacob and Ginger to climb in the rear.

"I like sitting in front. You two don't mind, right? Besides, you gonna have your girl next to you and you two lovers need to be alone and talk over your problems." This time Chewy's crazy laugh is really loud.

Jacob smiled and looks at Ginger, gesturing for her to get in first. She mumbled something unpleasant and climbed in the rear of the Jaguar, sucking her teeth loudly and moving all the way over to sit against the opposite rear door.

Jacob climbs in behind her and Jub Jub floors the pedal catapulting the Jaguar forward with a violent jerk.

As they race along, Jacob takes a deep breath and wonders if any of the drivers in Hong Kong has ever even so much as glanced at the speed limit.

CHAPTER 23

A BUMPY
RIDE

Jacob is glad to see they are nearing Larry Song's nightclub since it means the car will have to stop traveling at the excessive speed of over ninety miles per hour. Also it means he will be in a familiar area not too great a distance from his hotel.

But as Jub Jub Tai slowed the car, Chewy leans over and whispers something in his ear and once again Jub Jub Tai jams his foot against the accelerator; but this time before regaining the previous high speed, he made an abrupt turn away from the club.

Jacob leans forward:

"Hey, Chewy, where are we heading this time?"

No answer. Jacob leans back in his seat and looks over at Ginger, who is unperturbed by the change in direction. He is glad that at least for now her stare has turned to simple ice, before it seemed liquid nitrogen. He has never seen her so angry.

But he smiles because even her frosty glare does not in the least diminish her beauty or the olive-colored blush of her satiny complexion. Her beauty almost forbade frowning, it simply refused to allow anything negative to interrupt the flow of her prettiness.

He frowns remembering how she once confided in him that her father has promised her in marriage to an elderly farmer which meant she very likely would have become a baby making machine for the much older man who is a vendor of pearls.

But, at the age of five, Ginger was chosen by their village Shaman to be one of his students of sorcery, saying that Ginger, "…Possesses the 'sign' of a child who will become one with magic. She will travel my road." And, she said, with those words spoken to her mother and father, she is given to the Shaman to become her teacher.

This new life vetoed the marriage her parents have prearranged for her. But she is expected to continue her lessons until she became a sorceress or a position even higher if determined by the shaman. Her family became highly regarded in their village and the surrounding areas and they are exempt from any laborious tasks or taxes; everything is done or paid for them. Small sums of money are given to her parents for their support. The parents of Ginger and Delilah lived as royalty.

Three years later Delilah, at twenty, left home and to seek life in the city where she later met Chewy and *The Chinese Blood* gang. Four years after that Delilah returned to the mountains to ask the Shaman for custody of her sister, Ginger, then twelve years old, Delilah twenty four.

Her apprenticeship not fully satisfied, custody is granted by the Shaman with the proviso that Ginger is to return to the mountains each year to spend time with him in order "…To be provided the *Deepest Magic*." And with those words Shaman whispered in Ginger's ear, kissed her on the forehead, bowed to her and turned away from her and Delilah to "pray them away."

She also told Jacob that when her sister first brought her to Larry Song's club, Ginger was fifteen and some of the older Chinese women playfully called her a "glamour chick-ee," because the opal-eyed Ginger, thanks to her sister, dressed in designer clothes even in her teens thanks to her sister Delilah with whom she lives. Even if Delilah sometimes did not wear designer clothing, she saw to that her sister Ginger did.

Jacob never quite distinguished Ginger's age from the stories she related to him, but he knew she is very young and he has managed, perhaps due to his feelings for her, to obscure that part.

Jub Jub Tai suddenly swerved the car off the dirt road and onto another one. Jacob wonders if he did that because he thought they are being followed and if they are being followed. He is immediately reminded of his ride with Detective Liao and Mrs. Che.

The car suddenly bounces over a high mound in the new road and launches itself into a heavily wooded area, swaying, bumping, shuddering its way through a narrow path that, though it allowed passage, is hardly a road; it appeared to Jacob to be no more than a continuous swath of sparse grass mixed with flattened, dry earth created, it seems, by occasional traffic.

He is startled by Ginger's voice when she contemptuously remarks:

"Jake With Secrets not only one who got secrets." She crossed her legs, took out a pack of cigarettes from a small compartment on back of the passenger seat and lit a cigarette. She purposely blew a wide puff of smoke into 'Jacob's face. "You know?" Again she blew more smoke in his face. "We can hide our secrets like American butterflies do." She tries to blow more smoke at him, instead, not a smoker, she choked on the next mouthful.

She only did it occasionally at the club, in order to appear sophisticated and even then she only knew how to puff the cigarette and blow out the smoke.

Through her anger Ginger is smiling at Jacob, but it is not the kind of smile he likes. This one is vacuous and insincere, the kind of smile that hides a terrible sadness or pending retaliation. It is not at all like her, and he wondered if he has done something with that note at his hotel room that is irreparable.

He looked out the window, trying to get a sense of direction, but they are driving through thick woods, and there is no way of even guessing at the direction they are moving. It would not have mattered, though, since he has little knowledge of the different areas of Hong Kong, and certainly none concerning its forests.

Still, he squinted, trying to make out some landmark, but the woods are an infinite blur of trees and thick, leafy bushes, all of which looked dense enough to qualify as a jungle, and one tree looked very much like the others. He reasoned that Chewy has given Jub Jub Tai instructions to make sure they are not being followed by anyone, though this is an extreme means of doing that. No, there has to be some other reason for this abrupt change of destination.

Wherever they are heading, it would be just about impossible for anyone to follow them on this route since there are several possible lanes to choose from and they all looked alike.

He is sure there must have been another means of getting to wherever they are heading, some road that is going in at least the same general direction, a far more linear and certainly more comfortable path; but he knows that this is the way Chewy is sure he's not going to remember.

When he gave it more thought, Jacob realized that this route is also good in case of police observations by air. He figured that wherever they are heading obviously requires the gang to employ extra high security. Not only did they need to know they could not be followed, but also using this kind of route would make it impossible for Jacob to remember anything but woods and there are plenty of places that are wooded in Hong Kong. But he wonders just where could they possibly be going that is so important?

The Jaguar suddenly burst free of the forest and bounces onto a wide dirt road curving left then right. Jacob let his body swerve and lean as the car directed while he quickly tries to find some landmark and at the same time try to lean against Ginger who quickly pushed him off her.

"Ginger—."

"Move off'a me an' shut up!"

He sighed and went back to trying to locate something familiar in the streets they are now on. There are many one-level huts on stilts that elevated the shacks above a vast area of rice paddies and the sour odor that accompanied them.

It is a smell at once familiar to him. On the left of the road is a very wide and long lake with several houseboats drifting lethargically along, most of them are moored and languidly listing from side to side in slow motion. But he knew this could have been duplicated in so many places in Hong Kong and its outskirts.

A darkening sky portends an imminent summer storm. Its bulbous shadows are threatening to cause the early afternoon to become a premature evening with more heat and darkness as thick as syrup.

As they drove on, occasional vendors tending their roadside stand or pushing their carts take notice of the car. Chewy is screaming rude words and insults at the laboring peasants, words that Jacob understands and that show his utter contempt for poor people

"Chewy, how far are we going? And why the big secret?"

"Not to worry, Jake With Secrets. Talk to your girlfriend." Chewy leaned back out the window to holler more profanities at more pedestrians on the roadway.

Jacob turned to Ginger and touches her knee. She moved it away, but he persisted, and finally she gave in with a deep, disgusted sigh and stopped moving it.

"Ginger, I'm not doing anything with the maid. You've gotta believe me."

"Yeah, like all the times you tell me you love me, huh? Do I gotta believe that nonsense, too?"

He took a moment before answering her this time. Then he spoke to her in hushed tones.

"Ginger, I love you."

"Yeah, sure you do."

"I love you, Ginger. I really do."

"Why should I believe you, Jake With Secrets?"

Jub Jub is twisting the Jaguar all over the roads, skidding and sliding, full throttle and then almost stopping and turning to take another path

And speeding along as though hell bent on destroying at least the car if not everyone inside it.

Jacob leaned back in his chair, closed his eyes and let his mind drift back to a recent evening at his hotel with Ginger:

He easily recalled the feeling of her young, lithe body in the sheer nightgown he purchased for her always jolted his thoughts into plain lust. Jacob is watching her spinning around his room, posing for him in very sexy ways, ways that completely deleted his entire commonsense functioning.

"Does my Jacob with Jaguar mean it when he says I will return to the America as his wife?"

"Of course I do, Ginger. I love you."

"As your wife?"

"Yes."

Even though they are in his hotel room, she warned him in hushed tones:

"…Do not let Chewy know that—not even my sister. Well, maybe I'll I tell her. But Chewy is married to *The Chinese Blood*. My sister is loyal to them but not before she is to me, I don't think." She playfully locked his lips between her two fingers. "You keep this secret between us." She kissed him then began dancing all around the room. "When we go to your country, you will teach me the dances everyone does, and we will go dancing every night. I love to dance, but I do not know how."

"You dance fine."

"No, I dance clumsy."

"No, you don't."

"Yes, I do, but I don't care. If I knew how to dance and still danced clumsy, then I would care. Come on. Now I want to see you dance for me."

"I'm not a much better dancer than—" Before he could finish the sentence, Ginger jumps on him and begins tickling him mercilessly.

"You were going to say that you dance almost as badly as me, weren't you? You rat! You make fun of your girlfriend's dancing, huh?"

Eventually, as with most things with her, he gave in. Yes, indeed, he did love her. He has tried so often to tell himself that it is all in the line of duty but he found that to be a really impossible sell. He has never been able to convince himself that their relationship is just part of his undercover assignment. And he wants so much to tell her what is going on but that would be disastrous, possibly for both of them.

He remembers them watching an old movie "On The Waterfront" on the hotel's television. After the movie finished Ginger abruptly cut off the television and turned to Jacob.

"Jake With Jaguar, do you love me, because I have forgotten everything and fallen in love with you. So, tell me, what are your feelings?"

He has no idea what he should say to her, but something moved his hand to the side of her face, caressing it gently, and from some near distance he heard himself speak the words that caused her to begin crying.

"Ginger, I truly love you. You're the only woman I have ever had real feelings for. I don't know what it is and I sure don't understand it, but I love you more than I can describe. I think I've loved you from the first time I kissed you." And he is being truthful.

For a very long while they did not kiss, rather they simply sat holding each other and looking into one another's eyes, where they both know only truth resides. She touches his arm and then the side of his face and gently presses the side of her cheek against his, whispering something in Mandarin that he did not completely understand but he certainly feels her sentiment and he understood enough of her Mandarin to know the words are so very gentle

Jub Jub and Chewy holler happily when their vehicle suddenly dips deeply in the dirt path and abruptly rises up, causing Jacob's head to bump against the roof of the car; Ginger giggles loudly at him then but quickly returned to her sour demeanor.

Jacob does not know if he should try again to ease Ginger's anger and convince her that he is not having an affair with the hotel maid Mrs. Wong or should if he should just wait until she cools down and let things lie for the moment.

The Jaguar swerves hard, breaking Jacob from his reverie. Chewy turns around and grins at Jacob and Ginger as the car continues to bump and lean from side to side roaring along the dirt road. Jacob is on guard knowing or at least believing that Chewy is always watching him, looking for some sign of weakness, or for … something.

Chewy smiled and brings the palms of his hands together.

"Why don't you two kids just kiss and make up back there?"

He laughed and turned back around whispering something to Jub Jub Tai, who laughs and continues speeding along the dirt road; but suddenly their car emerges from the forest of trees and vague dirt roads onto a smooth street that the jaguar now seems to be gliding over and Jub Jub slows the car; it seems to Jacob that the Jaguar actually takes a breath of relief and lowers itself into a comfortable position of smoothness on the asphalt.

In the rear of the car, Ginger sighed and laid her head against Jacob's shoulder. Jacob's heart screamed out a thousand thanks, and he let his body relax against the seat's cushions. He lifted her hand to his mouth and kissed it then turned to Ginger and kissed her. She did not resist. He has no way of knowing, but like Jacob's heart…

Ginger's lips have also begun silently screaming:

'Thank you.'

CHAPTER 24

THE CHEMISTRY OF DOCTOR WO-LING CHEUNG

Jub Jub Tai has been driving for over an hour now and he turned onto a rather desolate road and began to slow down. Jacob sees what appears to be a huge estate of several black two-story homes several hundred yards in the distance.

After a few minutes the car slows to a stop in front of an exceptionally high gate that appeared to surround the entire property. Chewy speaks through an intercom at the gate entrance and a moment later the wrought-iron gate slides open slowly and their car passes through. Jacob is reminded of police headquarters.

Jub Jub Tai drives to a slow stop in a lot adjacent to the closest building. As they get out of the car Jacob wonders what is on the other side of the wooded area at the rear of the other houses and who owns such an estate and why has Chewy brought him here.

He marvels at the immaculate, well-manicured grounds. The house appears to be living quarters but then so do the other two behind the front house The house in front is a black brick structure with two small golden lions on either side of its front door. Tall trees lined both sides of the path leading to the house, and several wide trees stand at attention along the walk and on either side of the bottom of the front steps. At both ends of the wide porch are wide, two or three person large swings suspended by thick gold-colored chains. Red bannisters adorned the perimeter of the porch and the steps leading up to it.

The fading sun casts its golden iridescence over the surface of a wide, orange cement pond to the left of the front of the home's walkway. Jacob, slowly walking behind Chewy, Jub Jub Tai and Ginger, is amazed by white carp with orange patches flashing their colors as they lethargically glide through the sparsely weeded water.

Jacob is reminded of the fascinating pastoral scenes of a Chinese or Japanese oil paintings, Renoir or Monet-like in the simplicity of pastel colors that depict a kind of virginal innocence.

Chewy knocks at the front door and waits. Under the circumstances of the amazingly exotic atmosphere, Jacob almost expects next to see a golden dragon emerge from the door puking flames; not the East Asian symbol of fertility but one from the depths of some horrible place where monsters are trained to smell out traitors and deceivers such as he is proving to be, creatures that will shred his flesh, and feed on his bones.

As they all stood waiting for someone to answer the door, he and Ginger look at each other. She still appears to be miffed with him, but her vague smile told him that perhaps she realizes that certain dishonesties between the two of them are not unexpected; they have both made the mistake of falling in love.

Chewy knocks on the door again and smiles at Jub Jub Tai who glances at Jacob who hoped he is not being ushered in to face some type of primitive trial and condemnation. He felt the air of some judgment indicting him on charges of being less than truthful, if not outright deceitful, with Ginger and *The Chinese Blood.*

Ginger's lips reveal a thin smile. Jacob believes that she is either thinking fondly of him or feeling sad for what is about to happen.

The front door opens and Delilah standing in the doorway is resplendent in a black silk dress with a large golden dragon's head embroidered perfectly centered beneath her large, very gently sloping breasts.

Delilah bows to them all:

"Good evening. Welcome to the humble home of Dr. Wo-Ling Cheung."

Delilah's perfectly white teeth are accented by the deep red lipstick smoothed over her thick mouth. Jacob has never seen her looking so absolutely beautiful as at this very moment. He stares at her, dumbfounded by her glowing presence. None of his staring went unnoticed by Ginger, who uses her slim hips to bump him aside.

Delilah laughed and moved close to Jacob and plays with his ear.

"Jake With Jaguar, how come my sister mad at you? Hmm? You been a bad boy again?"

A newly fuming Ginger walked stiffly to her sister's side, hissing.

"Some ol' antique bad-tasting hotel pussy has made me put his tongue on lockdown. Now his name is Jake With Secrets." Ginger walked inside the estate.

Jub Jub Tai and Chewy are laughing as they follow Delilah and Ginger inside and down a long narrow hallway that has ornately decorated porcelain walls that empty into a spacious foyer where other members of the gang are gathered seated on black leather cushioned benches.

Jacob is sure something is wrong. He is probably in trouble, and this is going to be the place for his trial. He looked at Ginger for some kind of sign, but it appears that she is not surprised by their presence and she walks over to the seated gang members. After a brief verbal exchange, she turned and glanced at her sister Delilah, then quickly at Jacob.

Delilah leads everyone down the hall to two massive doors at the end. The moment she touched the two half-moon handles on the doors, a single gong echoed throughout the foyer and the two doors slid apart and Jacob is awestruck by the immensity of a beautifully appointed dining room and its marvelous décor.

There are Western and European oil paintings on the walls, objets d'art placed tastefully about the room on glass pedestals. Chandeliers of gleaming crystal hung above several rather long rectangular ebony tables.

Jacob recognizes some of the assembled gang members, a throng of them seated at most of the tables. Gold dinnerware with centers of a single black-stemmed, crimson rose and gold flatware are set in perfect alignment on every tables.

Gold-and-black napkins encircled by gold bands with centers of white pearls are curled inside pale purple glassware. On the tables are large blood red crystal water goblets with shards of gold set into the stems and globes. Huge bowls overflowing with mixed fresh fruit are at the center of each table.

The faces of the gang members give no indication of what they might be thinking. Each member is young, the oldest being perhaps thirty. There is no particular uniform or color worn to identify them. It is clear to Jacob that *The Chinese Blood* are not interested in fighting other gangs, or jostling for position in the streets of Hong Kong, or claiming territories that belonged only to them. Their interests are political and financial gains. They are the largest gang in Hong Kong and as such they are the most powerful without having to prove it. Their ability to easily commit violent acts has instilled fear in most civilians who know of them.

Chewy and Jub Jub Tai see to it that Jacob is seated near Ginger, who sat in a chair at Delilah's table but not before giving Jacob a rather unpleasant look. Delilah walks to the head of the table and gestures for everyone in the room to be quiet before she spoke to them. It is as though a switch clicked off and each and every gang member froze in place with all their eyes locked on Delilah. Her voice was calm and pleasant, yet its tone commanded attention:

"I greet you my warriors."

They all responded with a vibrant but very respectful:

"And our love beholds your presence."

She bowed acknowledgement of their response and then:

"We members of *The Chinese Blood* humbly welcome for the first time at our shared tables, a new friend that we know as Jake With Secrets. It is on this occasion that he is so honored as to be seated within the humblest home of our host the honorable Dr. Wo-Ling Cheung." She held her hand out in Jacob's direction. "Please stand, Jake With Secrets."

Jacob slowly rises from his chair and bows to the polite applause, but he has a feeling the air in the room has suddenly changed; there is a kind of electricity moving about, an energetic rush, almost a static causing his hair to bristle.

Delilah says:

"Members of *The Chinese Blood* and our honored guest whom you have already met, allow me to present your host for this evening. Doctor Wo-Ling Cheung."

A tremendous roar of approval resounded through the large room as the dining room doors smoothly slide apart and a very tall, and wiry man with a short, gray beard enters the dining area through the sliding doors.

Delilah bows and bows to him and every gang member in the room bolts to their feet and stand at rigid attention. Delilah has assumed a very deep and extended bow to him.

The doctor has a slight smile and walks over to stand next to Delilah at the head the table where Jacob is seated. No one changes their posture until the doctor claps his hands smartly; only then do the gang members including Delilah, relax their posture, but all remain standing, their attention completely locked on Cheung.

He smiles and speaks:

"Wayyyy, nee how mah?"

Everyone, except Jacob, responds:

"Woe uhn how. Nee mah?"

His monosyllabic response is:

"Howww."

Dr. Cheung raises his hands and only then does everyone straighten their bodies and once again sit. Cheung bows to Delilah, she returns his bow and sits at the table near her sister Ginger and just across from Jacob. Cheung bows once again to those present and then centers his focus on Jacob, who is wondering if he is an honored guest or the evening's entertainment.

"Mr. Jake With Secrets, I welcome you to my humble home and look forward to speaking with you privately after the evening's meal." He went on to speak about innocuous matters that pertained to the gang's activities, and things that he expected the members to accomplish. It has the content and tone of the speech of a boy scouts leader addressing his Boy Scout Troop.

Completing his oratory Cheung sat again near Delilah, Jacob and Ginger. Delilah stood and spoke loudly in rapid Cantonese. Jacob recognized the dialect as the one Chewy, Ginger, and Delilah occasionally spoke to one another. Jacob has heard Chewy and Jub Jub, who are seated farther down the table, sometimes speak Cantonese. Jacob is conversant with the Cantonese dialect, but very fluent in Mandarin the official language of China.

Delilah claps her hands together smartly and the room is suddenly alive with waitresses dressed in all white entering the room pushing rolling tables filled with huge trays of exotically prepared food sand doing so with such rapidity and precision as to appear well choreographed ballet.

Watching the influx of so many delicacies fascinated Jacob, and though he has certainly not abandoned his concerns for his safety, he enjoys the sights of what he is sure are part of a masterfully prepared menu. All the dishes are taken from the rolling carts and place on the rolling servers on the tables allowing each guest to spin to choose their desired foods.

Jacob easily recognized some of the dishes: dessert dumplings, sweet-and-sour-fish, candied meatballs, steamed and small but live octopuses, tiny fishes, enormous, perfectly rounded mounds of white rice, individual white silk napkins fashioned in the shape of praying mantis and different animals or insects, mixed vegetables, and noodles, roasted chicken, and chunks of fried pork belly. There are several other items alive and moving about in their respective deep bowls that proved to be enigmas to Jacob and not on his taste list.

The servants place small bowls of water in front of each guest, and gold flatware chopsticks and wide serving spoons next to only the gold dinner plates and ivory chopsticks next to the china dinner plates. Jacob has not eaten and is eager to begin the meal. He noticed everyone sat obediently staring at Cheung whose eyes are fixed on Jacob who noticed that his chopsticks are gold, real gold; as are Delilah's, Ginger's and Cheung's. all the other chopsticks at his table are ivory.

Once the food has been placed on each table, Cheung raises his arms wide, and immediately everyone began the feast. However, at the doctor's table where Jacob Delilah and Ginger are seated no one moved until Cheung picked up his golden chopsticks. Delilah then gestured for them to begin eating, and they did with gusto. Ginger, sitting across from Jacob pointed to his flatware.

Ginger dully said:

"You can use a fork if you want,"

"Thanks, but I think I can manage."

But Jacob picked up his chopsticks being quite adept at their use and felt the weight of their gold. Jacob commented to Ginger in a murmur:

"...These feel like real gold."

Ginger snorted:

"Of course they're real gold. Sometimes you are so silly."

Jacob gently placed the chopsticks back on the table and picked up his gold serving spoon to choose his choices of food from the round rotating board in front of him.

But he is still expecting something to happen, maybe for the entire hall of gang members to suddenly converge on him. He has an array of his skills prepared in his thoughts to use against anyone who attempted to assault him.

He did not care that using magic would reveal his secret powers at this point though the first wave of magic he planned to use—if he has to—was going be very subtle. It is possible that they would not connect it with magic at all, the way he imagined that Nikki may have connected the surge of rats on the gang about to attack them in the warehouse as magic.

He began taking food from the round wheel. He looked around at the gang members and the atmosphere has the air of a formal dinner. He found the food delicious, though not always identifiable.

Collectively it is the most delightful assortment of Seafood fishes, clams, oysters, squid, octopuses, swordfish steaks, Dungeness Crabs, pork, veggies, and rice he has ever enjoyed, including three worm-like unidentifiable squishy things he tries and has to force himself to swallow but all other foods that moved he passed on

When the dining is over, Cheung rose, and immediately every guest stood. A gesture from Ginger let Jacob know that he should be standing, and he quickly stood. Cheung bowed to everyone, glanced at Jacob and smiled then exited the room through the huge doors, the reverberating gong announcing his departure as well as another round of deafening applause from gang members.

After Cheung's exit, Delilah clapped her hands, and every member abruptly began leaving by another set of doors including Ginger. Delilah held her hand out to Jacob.

"Come, Jake With Secrets. Dr. Cheung will be waiting to have a conference with you in his library."

She led him from the room and down the long hall and then through another series of long halls. She stopped at a door and knocked. After waiting a moment, she opened it, and she and Jacob stepped inside the room.

Cheung is seated behind a thick, knotted, deep-red mahogany desk and when Jacob and Delilah entered, the doctor rose from behind the desk and walked to meet them.

"Jake With Secrets, I am most pleased to have this opportunity to meet you. I have heard so many wonderful things about you." Cheung extends his hand.

Jacob takes his hand and bows.

"It's my pleasure, Dr. Cheung."

Cheung gestures toward two thick-pillowed chairs at a small table.

"Please be seated. And if Delilah will be kind enough to pour us a glass of port before she leaves, then you and I can enjoy having our gentlemen's talk."

Delilah smiled and pours wine into two large crystal goblets. She served the wine to them then places the decanter of wine on a small tray between them. She bows once more and exits the room. Cheung raises his glass in a salute.

"To wonderful liaisons."

He and Jacob touch goblets, but Jacob is still on edge about whether or not this dinner is a prelude to his announcing that everyone knows he is an agent for the Hong Kong police. Earlier at dinner, he was momentarily convinced Dr. Cheung's speech to be a preamble to announcing his punishment.

Jacob nodded his head.

"Yes, to wonderful liaisons." Jacob took a sip of the wine, found the taste to his liking and took another one. "Tell me, Dr. Cheung, what is your specialty in medical research?"

"Well, that is a difficult thing to answer. My specialty is in attempting in my poor way to make life better for humanity and I am involved in that twenty-four hours a day physically and mentally. At the moment I am doing private research for a client who himself is seeking to improve the lives of others of his kind. Of course I do not impose my private work upon the public facilities that I am affiliated with, indeed, I have my own laboratory on my premises here and abroad."

"Can you extrapolate more definitively on your work, sir? I mean, exactly what kind of research does that involve?"

Cheung seemed surprised by Jacob's phrasing of his question and he replied:

"Please don't think that I'm taking offense, but you're rather eloquent for a...well, may I say for someone in your area of pursuit? In fact, you almost sound like a reporter."

"I'm sorry about that, sir."

"But it is of little concern. Let me further say that you do not have the speech I associate with your kind of entrepreneurship. Allow me to say that you sound rather educated for a person in your occupation."

"Thank you, sir. I have been home schooled by my parents."

Cheung chuckled.

"Oh? Home schooled? Is that correct? How wonderful for you. But to respond to your inquiry, my research is very private. I'm afraid that I cannot really go into it on any specific basis."

"You are also affiliated with hospitals abroad."

"Yes, and one of them is in your country; a modest research facility in New York where I am able to do work on my private research. But let us get down to our business. I am sure you are wondering why the subterfuges, the detours, dodges, deviations, and the out of the way travel to arrive here."

"As a matter of fact, yes, I was, sir."

"Well, it was all done to assure that no one is following you. I am constantly being harassed and persecuted by Owen Chang our Chief Inspector of Police for this province. But then I don't imagine you would have any occasion to know him."

"So that's why such a circuitous route. I was wondering." Jacob is trying to skillfully avoid responding to an inquiry to which it sounded as though Cheung already knew the answer; and now he is really concerned about the reason for his presence in Cheung's estate.

Cheung took a sip of wine then gracefully set the crystal glass on the table between them. But then, thankfully, the subject changed when Cheung said:

"Now, I wish to make matters clear about the purchase we wish to make. *The Chinese Blood* desire to acquire extensive military merchandise. It might even be considered enough to possibly supply a very small army."

"I've heard talk about the possibility of a large order, but I have not been given any real numbers yet. But large is what I need. I don't have any interest in being a common run-of-the-mill gangster, and this order from you, if large enough, is just what the doctor ordered. No pun intended."

Cheung smiled and nodded.

"Indeed." The doctor pours them another glass of wine. "I do find your phrasing to be most interesting: 'a run-of-the-mill gangster,' you say. I have studied communism, and in fact I cherish a book titled 'The Hopelessness of the Proletariat,' a book that led me to consider the subject of crime and why it occurs, whether we are its victims or its creators."

Jacob appreciated how the doctor always takes time to carefully consider his words, letting them flow from his mouth almost subtly. There is no doubt that he is well educated and it is a pleasure listening to him speak. Jacob also enjoyed engaging in sociological discourse and he paid rapt attention as the doctor continued speaking:

"I have come to philosophically classify crime's participants as the common and the uncommon brigand. In the days of our ancient ones, it was necessary for a gang to rule by demonstrated force, not just the threat of it. The presence of these violent power wielders served to let local land barons employ a proven reliable means of maintaining their status quo with no fear of local insurrection. After all, many local police authorities of the period are temporary, and often just roving gangs hired by local landlords for their own purposes. Those thusly employed are what I think of as the common brigand. The uncommon brigand is steadfast and moral and remains loyal to the one baron who wanted justice for the majority but under his rules and conditions."

"Dr. Cheung, I don't know if I understand you. Are you espousing classism?"

The doctor stared at Jacob for a long moment, studying his features, searching for something there.

"Just the opposite. Perhaps I am simply intellectualizing things, but I think the question is, does crime need to be justified?' After all, every man, I think you will agree, has a weakness that will forgo his moral commitment at some point in his life; at the very least it will certainly greatly threaten to do so."

"Yes, doctor, but if he gives in to his weakness then that person is as guilty as any other criminal."

Cheung found that statement curious.

"So you are saying that you find deceit to be preferable; living the lie, so to speak?"

"Well, under certain circumstances. If a person has positioned himself as being the pinnacle of society while covertly, in the dark so to speak, carrying out criminal activities then yes, that deceit is sinful and to be shunned."

Cheung stared at him for a long moment.

"Sinful? One might imagine that you words cause you to sound like a defender of the system rather than one who goes against its grain. If I didn't know better, I might suspect you to be in law enforcement by your responses to my postulates." He smiled at Jacob. "By the way...how is that hip of yours?"

Jacob could swear that he'd just heard the deafening sound of a trap snapping shut somewhere in the room.

"I'm sorry, sir, what did you say?"

Doctor Cheung never for a second let his eyes stray from Jacob's when he took another sip of his wine. Jacob's blood chilled as Cheung continued:

"But let us continue our discussion, Jake With Secrets. In a rather convoluted way, you and I are discussing right and wrong of crime."

Jacob nodded.

"Well, yes, sir, it seems we have different opinions on this subject, perhaps."

Cheung shrugged and leaned his elbows forward on the table as he spoke to Jacob:

"I see crime as existing on three levels that serve as the fulcrum of our societies: the third level, which is the lowest, is for the proletariat to be appointed as a constant working vessel for those on levels above them.

The second level is comprised of the educated ones who protect themselves with laws and education to assure that they do not fall to that third level. Then there is the first level occupied by those with finances strong enough to dictate to those on level two, the meritocracy. Thus, level one suggest and create laws that ensure that those at level two will have safeguards for their continued assurance that they will not likely ever find themselves at level three. To assure the continuance of the level two society, identical laws are continually, and selectively restructured and redesigned. Deceit, might you say?

Jacob looked at him.

"Doctor, you make crime sound almost like a class project on sociological distress, when in reality I'd say that it's—!"

Someone has adjusted the position of the room. It is tilting. Jacob sat more erect attempting to readjust the adjustment. His shaking hand tries to place his goblet of wine on the table between himself and Doctor Cheung and now the table has been moved and Jacob watched his crystal goblet fall and gently bounce on the carpet.

After that, his face is bouncing there.

WHERE AND WHO AM I?

"Mr. Jennings. Please wake up, sir."

Jacob woke to Mrs. Wong's insistent nudging. He sat up on his bed and looks around the room. His mouth is caked, dry, furry tasting, and thick. His throat is raspy, and some kind of dullness is swishing back and forth amidst the throbbing pain singing in arias in his head.

"What time is it, Mrs. Wong?"

"It is two o'clock, afternoon. Tuesday."

He bolted upright on the bed.

"Tuesday?"

"You have been sleeping for almost an entire day." She looks around at the door, and then she lowered her voice.

"Inspector Chang said to keep an eye on you as often as I could until you awaken. I have been coming and going to check on you while being careful not to be detected by staff or anyone else. I'm thankful that you are at last awake."

He grimaced and bent over, gripping the sides of his temples. There is a terrible pain in his head, the worse he has ever experienced. It has begun pulsing through his entire body, even causing his feet to begin throbbing. It even pained him to speak:

"... Mrs. Wong, did you pick up the note I dropped on the floor near the elevator when Ginger and I were arguing?"

"No. I had no idea you dropped it. After the problem with the young lady, Ginger, I thought you forgot the note."

"I dropped it out just as the elevator door is closing. I was hoping you'd see it."

"I think my back was turned to you by then."

Jacob looked at her for a moment before saying:

"I have to call Chang and let him know I need to see him. For now, Mrs. Wong, I think you should leave before Ginger shows up. You know how that usually goes."

"You are correct, sir. By the way, she is the one who brought you home. Alone. I saw her come in with you. Once she saw to it that you were in your room, she left the hotel."

Now he really is worried. If Ginger brought him home, that meant she could have seen the note at the elevator if no one noticed it and picked it up before then. He glanced at Mrs. Wong again, wondering how she could not notice a crumpled up piece of white paper on dark carpeting. And she has to clean rooms on his floor which meant she should have walked by it.

"Thank you for that, Mrs. Wong." He is really happy to know that Ginger brought him to the hotel. That meant she still cared about him though obviously she is still angry with him. When Mrs. Wong leaves he closes the door behind her and, cushioning his badly throbbing head.

He could only vaguely remember passing out on the floor of Cheung's home library.

He sluggishly made his way to the bathroom and leaned close to the medicine cabinet mirror, not at all liking what he is seeing: his lips are swollen, his eyes puffy almost to the point of closing. Even he has to laugh at his appearance. It brought to mind a song his grandfather found pleasure in singing to him about a wayward wife or girlfriend who is a partygoer:

> *"Your eyes look like a roadmap, an' I'm scared to smell your breath,*
> *You'd better shut them peepers before you bleed to death.*
> *When I saw you last night, your eyes was turnin' black,*
> *Go find the guy who beat chu up, an' ask him to take you back.*
> *Don't roll them bloodshot eyes at me, I can tell*
> *you been out on a spree.*
> *It's plain that chu lyin' when you say that you been cryin'.*
> *Don't roll them bloodshot eyes at me."*

The sudden shrill of the phone ringing seemed to electrify the air and it startled him and is threatening to cause his head to explode. He walked to it as easily and quickly as he could manage, not wanting his aching head to move any more than is necessary. He gently picked up the receiver. It is Chewy on the other end:

"Yo, Jake With Secrets. We need to talk. This is the big one. See you in a minute." Chewy hung up.

Jacob is staring incredulously at the phone in his hand as though he has absolutely no idea of what he is holding. He numbly placed the receiver on the cradle. He walked over to the large window, leaned against the side of the wall and looked own onto the streets.

With his head feeling as though it is having small, dull explosions over and over while his brain sluggishly sloshed and throbbed as it excruciatingly slides from side to side Jacob has to fight really hard against an almost overwhelming desire to…

… Just dive!

MYSTERY AND MISERY

Jacob hung up the hotel phone. He has no idea where Chewy has just called from, but wherever it is, he is sure that he is on his way to his hotel. The sudden knocking on his door is threatening to cause his throbbing head to explode. He is able to painstakingly reach it and open the door gently, nursing the pain in his head.

It is Mrs. Wong looking around nervously. She speaks quickly:

"Inspector Chang called me and said that you are to come in immediately if you are able."

"Thanks, Mrs. Wong, but you need to get out of here right now. Chewy may be on his way here and Ginger could be with him! And don't wait for the elevator in case they're on it. Just take the stairway. I don't even want Ginger to see you on this floor."

"Yes, of course." He watches her walk briskly to a nearby stairwell. He closed his door and began pacing the room, but slowly, and wonders what Chewy has in mind this time. Jacob wondered if this has anything to do with the fact that Ginger may have picked up the note he dropped for Mrs. Wong. His greatest concern is that someone from the gang might have paid him a visit and picked up his note. He is sure that probably Chewy and Jub Jub Tai, came by his room to do who knows what and saw the note on the floor at the elevator.

But he wondered had Ginger seen the note. Who knows? Maybe that is why she left the hotel after dropping him off, to give the note to Chewy. After all, the note indicates he is doing something suspicious with someone. He hopes that it has been swept up as garbage.

The hotel phone rang again.

"Hello?"

Chewy's voice is frantic:

"Come downstairs right now, Jake With Secrets."

"Okay, just gimme a minute to wash my face, Chewy."

Chewy's tone changed.

"Wash your face? You ain't gonna get no prettier—now stop playin' wit' me, man, an' get downstairs—right now." He hung up the phone before Jacob could answer him.

Jacob rushed about the room aimlessly. His hangover or whatever it is that he has is causing him not to be able to really focus the way he needed to do. He wanted to leave a note in his drawer for the inspector but again he has no idea if he and Chewy are going anywhere, or if so, where are they going this time. He scribbled a quick note and drops it in the drawer just as someone is banging on his door. He opens and it's Jub Jub Tai is standing in the doorway grinning at him.

"Let's go, big shot. We got somebody waitin' on you. You gonna finally get that big order you been poppin' off about."

Jacob grabs a fresh shirt from the closet, and he and Jub Jub Tai head for the elevator.

"Who're we goin' to see this time?

"Your future, my man." Jub Jub Tai looked at him with a hard stare. "You're gonna be lookin' your whole future right in the face."

Once in the elevator Jacob is still groggy from Cheung's wine and he is looking ahead unblinkingly with the vacant stare of a man who is being escorted to some dreaded, final location; the *dead man walking* feeling.

Outside they approach Chewy who is sitting in the front seat of his Mercedes. Chewy lit a cigarette and casually looked at Jacob then gestures for him to climb in the rear seat. Jub Jub Tai slid behind the wheel, and in a moment they are immersed in almost bumper-to-bumper traffic. Jacob is thankful, for once, that he did not have to drive.

He is watching Chewy in the front seat and he appears to be a bi lethargic. With Chewy it is difficult if not impossible to figure out what his mood is at the moment. He seemed to be kind of distant, pensive. Jacob leaned forward and tapped him on the shoulder.

"How's it going, Chewy?"

Chewy turned around and gave him a short grin before he spun back around and stubbed out his cigarette in the ashtray. Then he took a deep breath and the air out slowly as he shrugged and leaned back on the headrest.

"… It's goin', Jake With Secrets. It's goin.'"

CHAPTER 25

JUST WHO THE DEVIL IS
IN CHARGE, ANYWAY?

The mystery ride this time did not involve traveling through a lengthy, almost impenetrable wooded areas, though the city traffic they have to negotiate is just as congested. Jacob's muddled mind could only make out the traffic as a moving swarm of noisy, mindless metal things all thrown together in a mad rush to be ahead of one another.

Fortunately, the drive is not long, but when they exit Chewy's Mercedes, it looked to be a really dangerous neighborhood with young toughs milling about on the street.

Chewy sighed:

"Okay, let's get rolling. We got a long way to walk and the way we've gotta go we can only go on foot." Chewy turns to Jacob and frowns. "We're doing you a big favor, son, 'cause we hate comin' here."

Chewy nodded hello to a young man with a machete practicing perhaps martial arts moves with it. As they walk on, it appears that many of the people know Chewy and Jub Jub Tai but it seems as though every person is giving Jacob a scowling glance. Even street vendors frown and stare at him.

Jacob cannot understand why he is being given such an angry reception from complete strangers and if he is attacked, is Chewy ready or willing to defend him against so many of these really tough seeming street people as he did in the bar? Is this to be some sort of rescue set up event?

Jacob also notices that Chewy is not screaming profanities at these vendors and street people the way he did when they were driving to Cheung's estate. Jacob imagines the reason Chewy's usual hubris is not present is because he knows he is on the street andnot speeding by in a car. He is easily reachable and easily outnumbered by the hordes of young men wandering about

These people, after all, are not poor and laboring farmers or other workers pulling quite huge loads of goods along the street. Also, these are mostly young men hanging around the neighborhood with little if anything to do.

Still the very sight of the poor seems to stir something inside Chewy that is quite ugly and perhaps defensive; he always seems ready to commit violence against common laborers and poor folk almost as though the violence might erase the poverty or certainly erase the sight of it.

But not here and maybe not against these numbers or perhaps not against these types of people who seemed to have reached the point of desperation. But there is one very important factor in this equation; they are not in a moving car and any insult Chewy hurls will be dealt with on the immediate.

Jacob thought he may know the reason for the looks of anger the people gave him, after all he, Chewy and Jub Jub are dressed in pretty expensive clothes with gold hanging around their necks. The people they are passing appear to be poor, and they might look upon him, a foreigner, as he is wearing such flashy jewelry to perhaps flaunt his financial fortune in their faces.

A second thought comes to Jacob and that is that in some cities with neighborhood such as this a person displaying so much gold on his neck and wrist is an invitation to being mugged. But no one seems interested in doing that or even willing to smile and welcome him the way many others have done in Hong Kong.

These thoughts do not comfort him as they head for a back alleyway. For once Jacob is glad to sidetrack through alleys and connected shacks that seemed to be a maze of mostly empty condemned structures but no people, instead of flying through the streets at drastic speeds.

The air in the alleys and deserted shacks is thick with the smell of urine and, rotted foods and unless Jacob is missing his guess, dead rats and, well…he hopes just dead rats. One alleyway leads into more alleys and stench while and as they are sidestepping horrible smelling things that almost resembled vegetables that have been discarded, rats scramble over their feet; one of them attempts to climb up Jacob's pantleg.

Ahead of him he heard Chewy and Jub Jub Tai speaking Mandarin and cursing the terrible stench of the neighborhood and wondering how people could continue to live among such filth. Jacob and Chewy begin cussing.

But Jub Jub Tai reminds Chewy that the two of them grew up among such garbage and that the reeking smells of alleyways is the way the two of them lived being raised by their poverty stricken parents.

Chewy stops and looks at him and knows that his friend is right. The very alleys they are now traveling through are the same kinds of alleys that they grew up searching for edible foods when not stealing food from local merchants as children.

Finally, after having negotiated their way through terribly suspect and visually threatening "street tribes" of young toughs, the long, seemingly endless alleyway they entered some time ago, at last opened onto a wide street with a single house on it some hundred yards ahead of them, a two-storied structure that looked just a bit like a pagoda surrounded by what appeared to be the near-ruins of tenement buildings.

Jacob is getting a warning from his Moor's head much the same as the warning it gave him at Desirlee's home in Japan but strangely not at Cheung's estate. He held his vibrating Moor's head as they walked on to the building.

They have walked quite a way, and he could see that the walk has exacerbated Chewy's mood. He is not one for anything other than comfort, and he once told Jacob that if he has to walk for more than a few blocks, he preferred driving.

This walk, Jacob estimates has lasted at least twenty minutes but obviously it would have been impossible to arrive by driving; there are far too many adjoining alleyways and private houses to broach. And although Jub Jub Tai reminded Chewy about their background as children, Chewy still did not enjoy being among poor people and he said to Jub Jub Tai that he could hardly wait to get back to "civilization."

At last they reached the wooden structure that stood alone between other congested tenement apartments and rooming complexes. Chewy knocked. A very young Chinese girl answered the door and immediately recognized both Chewy and Jub Jub Tai. She bows and steps back allowing them all entrance, only glancing at Jacob, to whom she also bows, holding her position until he passed her.

The huge foyer is bare but for two long black benches with red velvet seat cushions on them. Along the walls are poster photos of elderly Chinese in ethnic clothing. At the right side of the room is a winding stairway of wrought iron. Clearly the area they are standing in is considered a waiting foyer for guests.

Chewy and Jub Jub Tai, both have both become really uncomfortable men are agitated and restless. This is the first time Jacob has seen either of them evidence any uneasiness, and it surprised him, since he imagined that they are both pretty fearless. He wondered just what in the world is this place that has the power to cause these two real thugs to become so uncomfortable.

Jub Jub Tai is not afraid to whisper his concern:

"Damn, Chewy. I really don't like this place, man—especially after what we saw him do that last time we was here. How come this dude couldn't make this trip alone?"

"Jub-Jub, how the hell would he find this damn crypt when you an' me took forever findin' it our first time? You forgot about that? Beside he wouldn't be able to make it through the streets without bein' jumped with all that gold he's wearin.'"

Jub Jub is looking around the foyer.

"…This place is just creepy. It's scary in here, man."

"Chill. Here she comes."

Geraldine Taipan, her snake coiled around her arm is descending the stairs, wearing a long flowing green-silk dress that shifted and gently flowed lovingly over her curvaceous form. Behind her, a young girl with platinum closely cut hair followed. As they neared the bottom step, Geraldine smiled at Jacob then bows to him.

She spoke to Chewy and Jub Jub Tai in Cantonese, in a low, disdainful yet serene tone and they sat. She next spoke to the girl who answered the door for them and they young girl seemed to almost jump to Geraldine's side, bowing and holding her position of bow.

Geraldine Taipan pulled the young girl's head up to her level and then strokes the side of the girl's face gently; it is as though she is appreciating her beauty for the first time and she leans close to the girl, her lips very near the girl's mouth; Geraldine gently blows her breath against the young girl's lips before speaking to her but this time in English:

"… Please make our guests comfortable. If they desire anything, kindly accommodate them."

"Yes, madam."

The girl bowed briefly to Jub Jub and Chewy, but did not look at them, instead she is looking at Jacob and smiling when she says:

"Please follow me…Jacob with secrets."

She leads Jacob up the winding stair to the next floor and then down a narrow hallway to a closed black door at the end. She knocks softly, and a voice from inside murmured a response.

She turns to Jacob and smiles:

"You will wait here, please, and I shall inquire as to your visit." She steps inside the room and closes the door.

Jacob waits, looking around the bare hallway. His Moor's head has been vibrating from the moment he entered the building and has not stopped. It is sensing something out of the ordinary. The hall reminds him of Du Lam Police Headquarters in its desolation and the unmistakable sadness in the atmosphere. After a quite long moment, the door slowly opens, and Geraldine Taipan steps out. She bows to Jacob again and holds the door open for him to enter.

"You can be seen now."

Jacob enters the room. Lighted candles are everywhere in the room. He stops at the sight of a crookedly shaped person standing, slightly bent over to suit his structure. Jacob's skin ripples a shudder as a wave of ice air washes over his flesh and his Moor's head trembles almost violently. Then he realizes is a life-sized statue of what Jacob sees is a peculiar looking man-creature crouched in position to pounce.

Jacob sees that his host who is seated behind a beautifully carved desk is waiting to see his reaction to the statue and he hopes he showed none, instead he bows briefly to it in some insane gesture or reference of courtesy that he knows his host will understand. But, what an odd thing to have and what, he wonders, does such a grotesque statue represent?

Geraldine introduces him:

"Master Baofung, this is Jacob with secrets."

Baofung is wearing a long, flowing purple robe and is smoothly maneuvering through the many lighted candles to reach Jacob and extend his hand to him. When he gets closer, Jacob sees that the candles cause Baofung's black pupils to turn very tiny, much tinier than should be humanly possible.

Behind him is a massive desk, festooned with carvings of black with red human figures in relief. Each of the figures on the desk's façade is posed in what seems to be moments of agony or of supreme ecstasy festooning it in its entirety. Jacob finds the carvings to be hauntingly fascinating.

At the center of the room is a dark mahogany desk that is barren but for a porcelain wine decanter and two small goblets; there are chairs on either side of this round, wooden table. The very sight of the wine causes Jacob's stomach to feel uneasy and it turned a queasy revolution.

Baofung bows to him:

"I … am Yongli Baofung." He bows to Jacob and grabs his hand the way a serpent would catch its prey seconds prior to injection of venom.

Jacob can see that Baofung has a curvature in his back, almost a hunched back, noticeable more when he bowed but it seems to almost disappear when he straightens his body.

Baofung has terribly deep pockmarks over his entire face which are even more pronounced, Jacob imagined, in this candle lighted room, as are his small, serpent-like black eyes with only a hint of white sclera available to see.

The dim lighting also serves to accentuate Baofung's thin, cruel-looking mouth, a dark, angry, almost serpentine twisted thing, which becomes even more sinister when he twists it into a smile for Jacob. His hands are heavily wrinkled with bulging veins that look as if thick worms are jousting, sporadically squirming, moving in tremulous spasms beneath his flesh, constantly adjusting themselves for better position. Jacob belatedly thinks to return Baofung's bow. As he moves towards Jacob, Baofung's movements appear calculated, precise. He stopped a few inches before reaching him and bows again as Jacob spoke:

"How do you do, sir?"

"It is my pleasure to meet you, Jake With Secrets." Baofung gestured for Jacob to be seated at a small table near a wall, where he joined him. They sit facing each other, not speaking for a long moment.

Jacob is thankful to sit since his head is still swimming and each time he moves it seems to be considering whether to explode or implode. After a few moments of staring at each other, with neither man appearing to be willing to give in, Baofung finally holds up the black porcelain decanter to Jacob.

"I am told you are rather fond of wine. Please have a glass with me. I have made this nectar myself and it is not nearly so harsh as that I believe you may have found Dr. Cheung's selection to be."

Jacob does not care for the reference to his previous wine consumption with Dr. Cheung that Baofung made, thinking he is making fun of him; but with his head throbbing once again, he thought of the old saying about, "… Hair of the dog that bit you." Still, he held his hand up. Declining Baofung's offer.

Baofung smiles with a polite bow and asks:

"By the way, I am curious…just what is the object you are wearing around your neck that is so heavily blessed?"

Remembering that Mrs. Che told him that Baofung is a sorcerer, Jacob is not surprised to find that he knows that he is wearing a blessed object.

Baofung quickly holds his hand up before Jacob could respond to his question.

"I am sorry. I think that I am being…what is the word…intrusive? But the power of your neck piece is very strong, and it has constructed a circle of energy around you that is so easy to feel."

"You can feel that?

"My dear man…I can also see it."

"Oh."

"And my statement was rhetorical. I do not expect you to answer. Forgive me if I have offended you by the impertinence of my foolish words."

"Not at all, sir."

Baofung holds up the porcelain decanter again.

"As I have said, this is a wine that I have made myself. It does not carry nearly the strength as what you have tasted at Dr. Chung's home. Please. I insist."

He poured two small glasses of the brownish liquid and offered a glass to him, doing his very best to produce at least the resemblance of a smile.

"This is more of a plum dinner wine. Here, I must insist. Just taste it, and if you find it not to your liking, then so be it. But it is purely a fruit wine made with plums, hardly deserving of the title of wine."

He hands Jacob a glass and then fills his own and holds it high.

"Let us drink to…honesty in friendship."

Jacob touched the brim of his glass gently against Baofung's, all the while wondering what the toast he just proposed really means. He sips the wine and fins it sweet and fruity with no discernable alcoholic taste. He smiles and tips his goblet to Baofung.

"Your wine is excellent, sir. And you say you made this yourself?"

Baofung shrugged.

"A humble attempt, but yes, and it is a wine that my friends seem to enjoy. But I am sure that you are anxious to get to the business of why you are here."

"Well, yes, I am."

Baofung takes out a sheet of paper from inside the draping sleeve of his silk jacket. Examining it, he traced his finger slowly across the page from side to side, nodding his head as his finger stopped here and there. He looks at Jacob.

"Our order will be for two thousand M-16A2 rifles and ammunition. We will also be needing three thousand armed grenades."

Jacob's mouth dropped open, but he quickly closed it.

"That's a lot of weapons."

"Oh? Have I been misinformed? I am of the impression that you and your people are interested only in large orders."

"Yes, they are—we are. Of course I'll have to speak with my contacts first and get you a price. If the deal is okayed, where do I have this merchandise delivered and when?"

Baofung holds up his hand.

"Please."

"Sorry?"

"Perhaps you are a bit tense. Have more wine. I have not completed our request. I would like to continue with our order." He pours more wine in Jacob's nearly empty glass. Then he presses his finger on the paper, tracing line by line as he reads.

"Now, then, we are also considering certain protective equipment. We are desirous of 500 Sniper, McMillan TAC-50. 50 heavy caliber sniper rifle obtaining two thousand flak jackets and fifteen hundred nine millimeter pistols—with ammunition, of course."

"And helmets?"

Baofung looks at him for a moment then back to the sheet of paper he is reading from.

"Did you say helmets?"

"Yes, sir."

"No. No helmets, Jake With Secrets."

Jacob knew that they did not want helmets meant whoever is going to use this weaponry already have helmets, or they are going to be using guerrilla tactics, hitting "soft targets" and expecting either little or no response from them. Maybe even unsuspecting local police authority. Maybe *The Chinese Blood* is considering some kind of insurrection, or they are purchasing the weapons for some group planning one.

"Oh, but I have been such a wretched host. Can you ever forgive me? I have a wonderful meal prepared."

Baofung claps his hands and in a moment the same young girl who answered the door downstairs enters the room and bows to Baofung. He speaks to her in what sounds to Jacob with the tone of person who may have purchased her services for the day only. She bows and then pulls a second small table over to them and quickly exits the room.

Quickly returning and pushing a cart, upon which are trays of soups and food, she placed an empty plate, a large spoon, and a pair of wood chopsticks from the trays on the table before Baofung and Jacob. She next places bowls of food items and open dishes of food on the table. She dishes food from the covered bowls and the open plates and bowls and then gently places them before Baofung and Jacob.

Baofung smiles and gestures to the food.

"This offering is truly most humble, but please…you must eat. I think you have been without food for some time, and so your body is not in proper alignment. These foods will help heal you. Please try the soup first."

Again, Jacob knows that if the gang wants him dead they already had many opportunities to kill him, so it is obvious they are not going to bring him here to poison him. Besides, he has long ago reached the conclusion that his life is in no danger until and perhaps only when the guns are delivered. And so he tries the heavily spiced soup, and its warmth made him feel much better after the first several swallows. It tasted hot and a bit sour with just a hint of buttery spiced flour on the end; and it super primed his appetite.

After finishing his soup, he ate the boiled fish with vegetables with thick dumplings. Most of the other dishes are chunks and mounds of barbecued and stewed meats that he adorned a bowl of white rice but could not bring himself to follow Baofung by eating from a soupy bowl of live baby eels.

"Is the meal to your liking, sir?"

Jacob feels a bit embarrassed at having eaten so quickly but the food, as he has earlier experienced at Cheung's estate, is absolutely delicious and he has been starving. Also he could feel his head clearing slowly and the throbbing is completely gone.

"The meal was very good, and I thank you for it."

"Please do not. It was such an uninspired attempt as a foolishness that one prays will go unnoticed."

Baofung picked up the sheet of paper from his desk, returned to the table, and carefully placed it before Jacob.

"Of course, an order the size of this just might require more cash than we are currently prepared to pay. But I am not concerned about that, since I think that we have established an element of trust between *The Chinese*

Blood and you. I am sure that we will be able to work out something that is agreeable to us all." Baofung clapped his hands before Jacob could answer.

Jacob knows things are finally coming to fruition and he has to take care not to pounce on it too eagerly. He sips at his drink as the young girl cleared away the dishes. Baofung spoke to her in rapid Cantonese then waves her out of the room with a flip of his hand before turning his attention back to Jacob.

"Yes, we have at least some trust, but even my people have people to answer to. Even though I've done plenty of business with them, it's always been on a cash-on-the-line basis. They are going to want at least half payment and then some kind of foolproof barter for the remainder of the money. As I suggested before to Chewy, it can be gold or some precious metal, diamonds—but no drugs."

Baofung's body straightens at the table, almost as though he is struggling for military form. His body is rigid when he bows from his seated position to Jacob.

"The majority of the fees will be taken care of upon your delivery of the merchandise, and the remainder we may propose to barter before delivery. We have a new product that perhaps you have not heard of. It is called, *cherry berry*."

Jacob steels himself to act as though the name means nothing to him.

"I've never heard of it, and I don't know how much of a payment it's going to be this—what did you call it? *cherry berry*? They might accept it as part payment barter but I imagine that would really depend on how much of the payment you want to cover with this product of yours. Exactly what is this *cherry berry*? My people are going to want definite proof that it is something that will move on the market and move quickly. You know, in other words they're going to want proof that it really sells and can create a big demand for it. I mean, you know, you say it's a new product, so that means there's no track record. How am I going to convince my people that it's going to sell?"

"First, be assured that no one else has *cherry berry* and never will have it and there is no way it can be duplicated except by us. I can further assure you that it will outsell your infamous crack by fifty to one—if not more."

Jacob shrugs.

"That's quite a statement, sir, but it's only words to my people. They are going to want proof."

"Absolute proof will be provided, sir. Of course, you must first prove ability to deliver the weaponry by, perhaps some samples of the order; in that way we will be able to ascertain the quality of these military items. At that point, if the quality is acceptable, we will have not only the amount of cash for you that we can afford to pay. Whatever amount of payment in cash that is lacking on our part, we propose to make up in barter, so do not concern yourself about payment. Once you see a demonstration of our product I would not be surprised but that your clients might, upon hearing your report about it, they might want to do the entire business in our new product, sans cash."

"Sounds good to me, sir."

"The *cherry berry* will be made available to you. In fact, Dr. Cheung is quite eager to demonstrate the efficacy of our product for you. You see, as you can imagine, we have discussed this matter."

Baofung walked to his desk and reached into a lower drawer and took out a small dark bottle. He rings a small bell and again the young woman enters. This time he spoke to her in English:

"Please bring us fresh glasses."

The girl immediately rushed from the room, and Baofung brought the bottle over to Jacob and sat. He gingerly placed it on the small table.

"Now to celebrate our striking an agreement, this vessel contains a very special brandy that predates Napoleon. It is thought to be exceptionally rare. Other than myself and the person who presented it to me, you are the only one to my knowledge who will have tasted this."

The young girl returns with four glasses. She offered Jacob his choice first and after he chose a glass, she holds out the tray of glasses for Baofung to choose one. Once he does, she hastily leaves the room with the remaining glasses.

Baofung opened the bottle and poured a small drink for them.

"This is also my humble way of apologizing to you for my rude question earlier regarding your necklace." Baofung poured them both drinks from the porcelain bottle. "I will see to it that you are given audience to view our new product, *cherry berry* at the time we have reached an agreement as to the delivery of the sample of weapons. Then the *cherry berry* will be made immediately available to you for a demonstration as to its effectiveness. I am sure that you will find it is quite a reasonable trade and a more than profitable investment for you and your clients." Baofung offered a toast. "To he who sees beyond the *veil* of deceit."

Jacob clicks his glass against Baofung's and takes a small swallow; the drink is really powerful, but it is also exceptionally smooth and very rich with a marvelous headiness that floated pleasantly through his olfactory system.

But now Jacob wonders just who is in charge of this gang. Who has the last say in whether or not the deal will be consummated? Jacob knew that now he is going to have to physically produce quality weapons. The real problem may be the increased amount of weapons they want as demonstrations of faith and reliability from him. How many rifles is Chang going to be able to get hold of? And just what did Baofung mean by "*veil* of deceit?

"This brandy is delicious. I've never tasted anything like it."

"Yes, it is quite unique."

Jacob placed his glass on the table.

"Now, sir, is this order definite? I mean, to determine the costs, I need to know how soon the order is needed, and the numbers have to be definite."

"The numbers are definite. As you see, I have listed not only the amount of weaponry we will need to see as a sign of faith between us, but also our projected numbers for our initial purchase...with possibly of more orders of purchase in the very near future, depending, of course, on our mutual satisfaction."

"So the order is a go?"

"Yes, for the initial show of faith from you for the first presentation. You see, if you can produce this large amount of weapons simply to show your ability to acquire them, then we have no reason to doubt your ability to produce the total amount on our actual purchase; the number of which I have placed on the paper you have just read that is in your possession. Seeing the amount we will be buying, and what we need immediately as proof of your ability to acquire, if your people have no problem with this, then we are more than assured of your reliability."

"Are you the final authority, Mr. Baofung?"

"The *Chinese Blood* is the final authority."

"I see."

"Will this be okay with your people?" Baofung asked.

"I am sure that it will be done, but it is always a matter of what terms we can come to agree on. I will need to find out just how much cash they will find acceptable, and from that point we will be able to negotiate a barter."

Baofung finishes his drink as does Jacob who assures him that:

"I'll have a price for you as soon as I can but my people will want me to be fully informed about your product. After I deliver to you the initial shipment of weapons as proof of our ability to procure, then at that time, I will need to see your *cherry berry* and for you to demonstrate to me how it is such a phenomenal seller. Then I will impart that information to my people, and if your product is all you say, then I am sure they will agree to go along with it as a part payment for your merchandise."

"Then it is agreed. When you arrive with the order, we will have the amount of cash we can pay and if that is not acceptable and a barter cannot be made, then nothing is lost. You can simply return your weaponry to your people. To be frank, sir, we believe that once you see the efficacy of our product, you will recommend to your clients that they forego any cash and take payment in full in product. Our will product guarantees immediate return customers that you can charge whatever price you deem appropriate and it will be absolutely impossible for them to resist because our product is more addictive than crack cocaine. And you will be the only supplier—the only possible supplier."

The wonderful thing is that if the authorities seize it, there is no way for their scientist to determine what it is other than what it obviously appears to be. And the cost of manufacture is almost nonexistent compared to the production and preparation of cocaine for general use meaning its export, import distribution.

"Yes, sir. That sounds good."

Baofung finishes his drink then places his empty glass on the table and stands. He bows to Jacob and leaves the room.

Geraldine Taipan enters the room and smiles at Jacob.

"Your interview is concluded, sir. Your host thanks you profusely for the honor of this wonderful visit and greatly anticipates being worthy of such an honor again."

Geraldine Taipan escorts him downstairs to the large foyer, where Chewy and Jub Jub Tai are waiting for him. Geraldine bows to them all then turned and ascended the stairs, never giving them another look.

Chewy and Jub Jub Tai quickly lead the way to the front door where the young girl stood waiting with it open. When they neared her, she smiles and bows to them, but again says nothing though her smile to Jacob lingers.

Once outside, Chewy glanced back at the house and takes a deep breath. He looks at Jacob as though appraising him for damage, then says:

"Let's get to the car, Jake With Secrets."

In the relentlessly increasing heat, although no one looked forward to the long walk back to Chewy's car, but not a single one of them took even a second to or even wished to look back.

And Jacob realizes that if what Baofung is describing about the *cherry berry* is true, then a person would be insane not to grab such a deal. A guaranteed clientele. Detection impossible and implied addiction, according to Dr. Cheung.

But Jacob also knows that once they have demonstrated the product to him…

…that he is never going to leave that room alive.

CHAPTER 26

ANOTHER MEETING, BUT THIS ONE WITH...

Inspector Chang, Liao, and Mrs. Che sit facing Jacob in Inspector Chang's office. Jacob has just reporting his latest two meetings with two apparently senior members of *The Chinese Blood*, Dr. Cheung, and Yongli Baofung over the past few days; it is Inspector Chang's belief that they are also the creators of a growingly infamous street drug, *cherry berry*.

Chang does not seem very happy with what he has been told by Jacob; but he lets it all sink in for a few minutes while standing and pacing about.

Mrs. Che ruminates in a less demonstrative fashion by slowly nodding her head and turning it all over in her mind while sipping her cup of tea.

Detective Liao simply stares at Jacob as though she expects there will be more to his tale of intrigue, but there really is not and so she leans back in her chair and exhales.

Chang stubs out his cigar and immediately grabbed a fresh one that he lights while pointing to Jacob.

"I have to give it to you, Jennings. You moved really fast. But how much of this is on the up-and-up? *The Chinese Blood* is a very dangerous gang, as we have told you over and over. They're not stupid. They surround themselves with people of intellect and other strong influences."

Liao agreed.

"Yes and while you have certainly made fantastic headway within the gang, we have to remind you that this is not a group to be taken lightly, and I think they may be giving you false hope. Why would they reveal themselves to an American and introduce you to their top members if it is not going to benefit them in some immense way? That is, considering that Cheung and Baofung are actually members of *The Chinese Blood.*"

"Actually," Jacob carefully corrected her, "neither man has actually admitted being a member of *The Chinese Blood,* only that this order of guns is for the gang. But my mission is to get them to commit to such a purchase and I've done that. I have to admit that I am a bit surprised and very disappointed that instead of around the room congratulations, instead I'm getting series of question marks."

Inspector Chang is thinking things over and studying Jacob. Things sounds perfect but just a little too perfect. However, if it is all true, then this is the time he has been waiting for. He can get the drugs where he knows they are probably being made and stored: Dr. Cheung's estate.

"Sorry about that, Jennings. and you surely are right. We ought to be congratulating you instead of questioning your great results; you've certainly made fantastic inroads into the gang and I have to be the first to admit, you have achieved far more than I ever thought possible. A helluva lot more than all us in this office now could have accomplished. I apologize but it's just that we've never been able to get anywhere and when we see accomplishments such as yours, well, I guess we're awed and more than amazed but it all."

Chang grabbed Jacob's hand and shook it vigorously. Then he returned to his desk and leaned back in his swivel chair. He said, lowly:

"...And just between us and the walls...I have already broken into Cheung's office and there is nothing there. Of course, I never said that because that would be wholly illegal. But, man, that's an awful lot of weaponry for just a show and tell. But we never put a limit on it so we surely can't change the amount now."

Oh, no sir. And I would never want to go through what I've gone through again, not for the purpose of renegotiating amounts."

Chang leaned forward on his desk:

"I think we've got him just where we need to have him. When he accepts the weapons, I have no doubt that he will want to take them some place that is safe to sort it all out. That will have to be on one of his properties."

Detective Liao agrees:

"Yes, sir. But which property will it be? He has a few of them."

"Well, it doesn't matter since the trucks that my friend General Syongrui will have each of the trucks monitored by hidden devices that will give a constant signal as to the whereabouts of each truck; we will simply follow the signals. As long as they don't get more than 25 miles from us. And that's not very likely to happen."

Jacob shakes his head:

"No sir. Not likely.

"Also the general will have armed uniformed soldiers on each truck. And several of my men in army uniforms will be interspersed between his men."

Chang banged his fist on the table.

"This is the perfect time for us to strike and Jennings we have you to thank for this. Dr. Cheung and the gang will be unprepared for such a raid and doubtless the *cherry berry* will be somewhere on the premises not far from the weapons. You mentioned that they said they are going to give you a demonstration of it. Am I correct, Jennings?"

"That's what they told me, sir."

Chang continues:

"Of course this will be a renegade raid because we'll never be able to get a search warrant for the doctor's estate, not for drugs and military weapons or anything else for that matter."

Detective Liao cautioned:

"This will be a great undertaking, sir. Perhaps one that requires more planning and consideration." She is hoping Chang picks up on her hint to not rush ahead without careful thought on the possible consequences.

Chang could not disagree.

"Yes, I know what you're saying, Detective Liao and you are right. But we don't have the time to be careful. The longer we wait the more we are all in danger of this drug becoming a pandemic. It is clear that it is meant to be available and used in other countries, possibly beginning with the U.S. Now as I have said before, I have spoken with my close friend General Witcho Zhong Syongrui who has not only agreed to loan us the necessary weaponry, but, as I have mentioned, to also be part of the raid. General Syongrui is the commander of a Naval division doing an exercise with the American Seventh Fleet in Yokosuka, Japan and so the weaponry is readily available to us through him; with the proviso that his men be in attendance in the immediate vicinity of all the weapons."

Detective Liao suggests:

"It is a sizeable amount of weaponry, sir. But as we know this looks like the chance we've been hoping for."

Chang is wondering again:

"Yes, this is really a huge order for any one gang."

Liao turns to Jacob:

"Lieutenant Jennings, just what is your take on this size of order?"

"Well, either the gang is planning an insurgency, or they're ordering these arms at the behest of some other group, and they plan to sell them at a substantial markup."

Mrs. Che wondered.

"Lieutenant Jennings, just to cover all of our bases, can we discuss your relationship with the young woman Ginger? Have you been keeping it on a professional level, sir?"

Jacob swallowed quickly.

"Yes."

"Truly?"

"Yes, on a professional level."

"You and she are not involved in any personal way?"

"Only as part of my role."

Chang came right to the point.

"Jacob, we do believe that you may have developed a romantic interest in this girl. Not that it matters at this point. You have achieved what we needed you to. But just what is your situation there with her?"

"The gang believes Ginger and I have a relationship and now they trust me. I have to keep that belief going, sir.

"Yes, but, do they trust her? In fact, do they trust you?" Liao wonders.

Someone knocked on the inspector's door.

"Come in."

An expressionless middle-aged female entered holding a small slip of paper that she gives to Chang, exiting immediately. Chang reads the note and drops his head. After a moment he read the paper again and crunched it into a small ball and looked up, slamming both his fist on his desk. He looked at Mrs. Che, then at Detective Liao and finally his tearing eyes rested on Jacob when he muttered:

"...Everyone...Mrs. Wong is dead."

Jacob got to his feet and heard himself repeating Chang's words without having the will to form such dreaded words: "Mrs. Wong is dead? Officer Wong?" Jacob is in an utter state of disbelief: "But what happened to her? What happened?"

Angrily swiping away the tears in his eyes, Chang stared at Jacob:

"I sent Mrs. Che to your hotel this last time during your incommunicado period you know—when you were somewhere being interviewed by Baofung. Not knowing at the time where you were and there was no note in the drawer, and after your last disappearance with the gang when they took you to Dr. Cheung's estate, I was worried and I asked Mrs. Che to go to your hotel to check your room. But, Mrs. Che says that she was okay then, isn't that right, Mrs. Che?"

"Yes, sir. She said that nothing unusual has happened except that she has not seen Lt. Jennings that day. And there was no note. I checked it myself."

Jacob is confused.

"Wait a minute! I did leave a note for you in the drawer. I said Chewy—unexpected trip again to nowhere.' And I dropped it in the drawer! Of course, in the shape I was in, maybe I missed the drawer but…I don't know. I was sure I put it in the drawer."

A furious Chang waves him away and shoves a finger at a befuddled Jacob:

"The hotel is saying that she committed suicide by jumping from your window, Jennings."

"From my window?"

"Yes! Your window!"

Detective Liao found it inconceivable:

"This really doesn't make any sense. The gang has no reason to harm her. It could only complicate matters for them. But who else would do it?"

Mrs. Che tapped her pencil against the table and looked at Jacob.

"This is a grievous matter and may be most important concerning your safety, Lieutenant Jennings."

Chang agreed.

"Yes, it could be that someone in the gang found some kind of link, and they're sending a message. Did the gang ever mention her to you, Jennings?"

Immediately Jacob thinks of the note he dropped on the floor and that Ginger may have found it when taking him to his room after being drugged by Cheung. Did she find it on the floor? Then he thinks of the constant battle Ginger waged against policewoman Wong, and he knew if her name entered into Chang's investigation of Mrs. Wong's death, that he would have to "bend" some of the truth to protect Ginger, otherwise the contentious rapport would doubtless point to her as an excellent suspect.

"No, sir, the gang never mentioned her to me."

Chang very slowly walked over to where Jacob is seated and stood over him for what seemed an interminable amount of time to Jacob. Jacob is thinking that Chang wants to bang his fist into his face as payment for losing one of his officers. Instead, Chang crouched to face him.

"Jennings, we all know that Officer Wong, if anything, was thrown from your window by person or persons unknown. She did not commit suicide. But the fact that it took place in your room makes me think that the gang has their suspicions about her being connected to you in some way. You have to be especially careful now. This isn't some random act. Now I wonder if you should even go back to that hotel again. Maybe this entire business with you undercover should be a wrap." He stood, exasperated. "In fact, maybe this entire *cherry berry* business should be dropped."

From the corner of his eye, Jacob thought he saw something flash past. He rearranged himself in his chair at the table while taking a furtive glance around Chang's office and he saw it again. It is a person's shadow darting back and forth against the walls, stopping here and there ostensibly to, Jacob assumed, stare at him but it has no eyes or mouth or any facial features; but it has a head and body shape of a female.

Chang noticed Jacob's preoccupation, and he turned around to look at the walls.

"Jennings, is there something wrong?"

"No, sir," he lied.

"Well, okay. Let's get back to this business of Mrs. Wong's death. Jennings, you may be in danger here."

"I think I'm safe, sir. Ginger would probably know if something is wrong with the gang and me, and she'd surely tell me."

Jacob is watching the shadow, which is now on the wall behind Chang's swivel chair.

Chang lit a cigar.

"Jennings, I can't help but feel you're leaving something out about the girl. It's vitally important to let us know if you've been compromised."

Mrs. Liao agreed.

283

"Yes, and we certainly do not blame you. After all, she is really quite an attractive young woman. But before you say anything more, let me tell you I recently reported to Inspector Chang that I observed you and the young woman Ginger in coital behavior one evening in the rear of your car while you were parked at the NinShung River Park. The two of you are often in that park shall I say posing as lovers?"

That took Jacob by complete surprise. His face registers shock and embarrassment simultaneously. But he recovers quickly and answers:

"That's all part of the game. There is no way to convince her that we are a couple without intimacy at some time."

Chang put his hand on Jacob's shoulder.

"Yes, Jennings, and at certain places. And let me tell you, Jennings, when Liao gave me that report, it is dispiriting. But you'd better get back to your hotel in case the gang is trying to reach you. They don't seem to have any regular schedule for getting in touch, so let's try and always have you available for them."

"Yes, sir."

Jacob leaves the office feeling uneasy with Chang's abrupt dismissal of him and he hesitates outside the office door. It's clear that no one is happy with his relationship with Ginger and he hoped inspector Chang is not going to do something to compromise Ginger for the good of his investigation.

He put his ear to the door and listens. He heard Inspector Chang's chair squeak the way it always did when he is agitated and twisting about in it:

"Well, ladies, do we go on the assumption that Jacob can still be trusted and that he hasn't been totally compromised?"

Liao answered first.

"Sir, we don't have much choice. He is, after all, our only contact with the gang. We have to continue to trust him, even knowing that he is, at the very least, a bit compromised."

Mrs. Che agreed.

"Yes, Inspector Chang. But, I think we also need to keep a presence at the hotel to monitor Mr. Jennings' activities and also as a backup for him. When I was there I ascertained that several positions as maid are available and—." Mrs. Che realizes that her words have touched upon a still raw and exposed nerve in the office. She is fast to apologize:

"I'm sorry, sir, but...well, we do have to keep our eyes on the investigation."

Chang nods in agreement;

"It's okay, Mrs. Che. Go on, please."

"Well, as I said, I think I should obtain employment there as a maid and continue Mrs. Wong's undercover assignment."

Chang and Detective Liao are silent for a long while. Then Jacob heard Chang yanks open one of his desk drawers where he keeps side arms.

"Mrs. Che, that sounds like an excellent idea. I want you to keep this small nine-millimeter with you just in case. I think had I not instructed Mrs. Wong to remain weapon-free, she might have been able to defend herself. I don't want to hear of another of my people jumping out of some damned hotel window."

"Thank you, sir." Mrs. Che slipped the side arm into her purse.

"Liao, would you please get General Syongrui on the phone? I need to discuss the amount of weaponry the gang's requesting and see what we can work out."

"Yes sir." Liao picked up the phone and dialed.

"In the meantime, Mrs. Che, you secure that position at the hotel, and let us see what develops from there. Make yourself known to Jennings at your earliest convenience, and of course, let no one see you do it."

"Yes, sir."

Chang leans back in his chair,

"Okay, we're stirring the pot, let's see what rises to the top."

CHAPTER 27

MRS. CHE
ON BOARD

A few days after the death of undercover policewoman Mrs. Wong, Jacob is speaking with Jun Lao-Tzu, a new manager of his hotel who left a note at his door asking Jacob to please come to speak with him about the death of the employee Mrs. Wong

The hotel manager Jun Lao-Tzu apologizes for the horrible occurrence and asked if Jacob wanted another room, in view of what has happened in his present one. The manager goes on to reassure Jacob that, in case he is at all concerned, the investigating police did not in any manner suggest that anyone in the hotel, including the occupant of the room, have anything to do with her suicide. He also says that he will reduce Jacob's room charges by fifteen percent and twenty percent if he decides to keep he same room.

"Well, I thank you for that, Mr. Jun Lao-Tzu, but I am curious as to how the maid chose my room to do this to herself. I mean, was she …?"

Someone is knocking on the manager's door.

"Excuse me, sir." The manager opened his door and Jacob is surprised to see Mrs. Che at the door. She smiled demurely at the manager.

"Please excuse me, sir, but are you Mr. Jun Lao-Tzu?"

Jun Lao-Tzu took a quick moment to assess her shape.

"Yes. What can I do for you, please?"

"I have been sent to you by the employment agency to apply for the position of maid."

He smiles widely.

"Oh, yes. Please come in." He turned to Jacob,

"Sir, if you will ex—"

Jacob shakes his hand and beat him to the punch.

"If you don't mind, I'd like to wait. I have a few questions for you."

Being attracted to Mrs. Che, Jun Lao-Tzu is eager to get rid of Jacob, but he knows that subtlety is an issue here. He gestures for Mrs. Che to be seated at his desk, and Jacob sits in a chair facing them. The manager glances uncomfortably at Jacob and then began his interview of Mrs. Che who hands him a completed employment application. She crosses her legs, letting her dress ride a bit higher than she ordinarily would, knowing that Jun Lao-Tzu's eyes are locked and leering.

His lecherous gaze moved up and down her body with the speed and fidelity of a laser, pausing for a long moment at her breasts then on down to Mrs. Che's well-formed thighs and slightly muscular legs. She uncrossed them and sat straighter in the chair.

Lao-Tzu clears his throat and returns to glancing over her application.

"Well, Mrs. Che, I think you are going to enjoy working here. We are like family. This gentleman is one of our guests, and he and I are having a pleasant discussion, but business before pleasure."

He pressed an intercom button and spoke in Mandarin. After several minutes an older woman, slightly bent, entered the room, carrying folded sheets over her arm.

"Mrs. Lo Chen, this is our new employee, Mrs. Che. I want you to please introduce her to the staff and see to it that she has a clear understanding of her duties here at the hotel. She is to begin work immediately. That is, if it's okay with you, Mrs. Che."

Mrs. Che smiled, stood and bowed.

"Yes, sir. It is quite agreeable. And thank you for the position."

He lit a cigarette and let his eyes rest on her breasts, knowing that she is looking at him but unaware that Jacob is watching him too.

Mrs. Che follows the older woman from Jun Lao-Tzu's office, glancing back at the manager with a seductive smile. Their grins met. He let his tongue wash gently across his thin mouth for her. She smiled again and turned away grabbing the doorknob of his office door. Jun Lao-Tzu held up his hand and gave Mrs. Che a sly wink.

"Oh, you can leave the door open, Mrs. Che."

She returned his smile but she smoothly closed the office door behind her.

"Yes, sir."

Jun Lao-Tzu laughed and then quickly stood and walked to his office door. But then he remembered that Jacob is waiting for him and he looked at him apologetically.

"Sir, I will have to speak with you at another time. First, I forgot that it is essential that I make sure the security staff know there is a new employee."

He steps from his office and waits for Jacob to follow him. Mrs. Lo Chen and Mrs. Che are both farther down the hall and have just turned the corner so they did not see Jun Lao-Tzu and Jacob coming behind them.

When Mrs. Lo Chen she sees the manager approach she hurriedly whispers to Mrs. Che:

"...Please be careful. He is new manager here. When maid kill herself, they fired old manager and hire Jun Lao-Tzu. He has already been with two women here so quick. He seems very reckless."

Then, reaching the end of the hall and the second floor maids quarters and seeing the manager and Jacob coming, the older maid walks quickly ahead of Mrs. Che to the door labeled: **Laundry Staff** and holds it open for her.

Before she enters the room Mrs. Che glances back at the manager who is watching her.

Jun Lao-Tzu turns to Jacob and apologizes:

"I'm sorry sir, but only employees of the hotel are allowed beyond this point. It is a matter of insurance." He extends his hand to Jacob. "But you and I will speak again."

He hurries down the hall towards the employees' entrance before Jacob could answer him.

Later that evening, Ginger and Jacob are strolling alongside a motionless a peaceful NinShung River Park Lake. Ginger senses that something is bothering him and she continues glancing at him without speaking.

He begins blankly perusing the food wares of the vendors along the way. It is very warm, and he decides to look for someone selling ice treats. Finally, she nudged him hard in the ribs.

"Ow! What was that for? What did I do?" He asked.

She pouted, stopped, folded her arms and glared at him.

He has not a clue.

"What?"

"You say you love me, huh?"

He pulled her to him.

"Yes, I do. Don't you believe me?"

"Then how come you never hold my hand anymore when we walking along places? You don't love me."

"I do." He took her hand.

"Humph." She pouted more.

He bent and kissed her hand and then kissed her. She giggled and leaned against him and pursed her lips for the next kiss.

"Ginger, you want some ice cream?"

She shook her head, mumbling:

"… I got me a crazy man."

"Now what did I do?"

"I wait for a kiss, and you looking for ice cream."

He kissed her hard and long.

"Don't you want something cold? It's real warm tonight."

"Nope. What I want is right here leaning against me and me against him." She looked around. "Come on, let's go sit on the bench."

The park is alive as always with some adults fishing for carp with bamboo poles and dozens of children playing, running back and forth, some of them screaming at the top of their lungs, paying scant attention to Jacob and Ginger.

"Ginger, did you like the movie we just saw?"

He held her close and playfully pressed his mouth against her nose.

"Yes, but too much speaking. I think maybe movies need more kissing and not so much speaking. It's not like you and me. We do a lotta kissing and not so much talk. Huh?"

"Right."

Ginger pouted and folded her arms, turning from him.

"Maybe we don't talk much 'cause you got nothin' to say to me about love, maybe. An' at your room you all the time reading that crazy book. What chu call it?"

"The Cabala. It's not a crazy book."

"But you say it's black magic."

"No, I said it's mysticism."

"That's not black magic?"

"No, it's…well, it's a mystical interpretation of some religious areas of the Bible."

"And your Bible ain't magic, you think? Never mind, Jake With Secrets. But when you gonna finish reading it?"

"Oh, I finished reading it long ago. At this point I've reread it many times, so I guess you could say that now I'm studying it. Trying to learn more about what I've already read. I've read other books on it, but I always seem to come back to this one."

She stared at him with a slight frown.

"Yeah, you a crazy man."

They laugh and begin kissing. A little girl came up to them and begins teasing the kissing couple. Ginger looks at Jacob and begins laughing at the girl teasing them in Mandarin.

"She is asking us when we are getting married, Jake With Secrets."

Jacob began singing.

'I'm getting married in the morning,

Ding dong! The bells are going to chime,

Pull out the stopper,

Let's have a whopper!

But get me to the church on time.'

Ginger and the little girl are completely perplexed, and they both stared at him as though he has lost his mind then suddenly they both squealed with delight.

"Now I know you really are a crazy man."

He slipped his hand around her waist.

"I'm crazy about you."

He kissed her long and deep. The little girl began jumping up and down and giggling and clapping her hands together wildly, laughing and screaming until her father, who is fishing, called her away. Ginger and Jacob remained locked together.

PROMISES MADE

Jacob is positive he heard a noise. He cut off the shower, stepped from the tub and listened for the sound again. There is no repeat sound but he definitely sensed a presence in his large hotel room. But Ginger left him a few hours earlier so there should have been no one in his room but him.

He snapped off the bathroom light and stands at the bathroom doorway staring into his dark room even though he left the lights on in it before he climbed into the shower minutes ago. He stealthily feels for the light switch at the edge of the wall near the bathroom door as his eyes try acclimating themselves to the darkened room.

Someone grabbed his hand.

"Boo!" A giggling Ginger is standing against the side of the wall at the light switch.

"Ginger? I didn't know you were coming back so soon." He hugged her but she is apparently preoccupied. "Ginger, what's wrong?"

"Jake With Secrets, do you really love me?"

"Yes, I do, Ginger."

"And you mean it when you say you take me to America with you? You really gonna marry me?"

"Yes, I mean it."

"We gonna take my sister with us, too?"

"Well…."

"She has money. She'll pay her own way. You get her a visa, say she's your maid. I'll be your wife. She'll be your maid. We all have big fun together." She pointed to two suitcases. "I got my bags with me this time. I just bought these on sale. I'm gonna stay here with you from now on. Delilah says it's better for both of us if I stay with you. The gang, well, I don't think they like me a lot no more; especially Chewy."

"Great." He kissed her, but this concerned him greatly and it put an entirely different twist on things. He is going to have to sort this out. But Ginger's hands are roaming over his naked, partly wet body, and he is losing his focus.

Her fingers always feel like flower pedals against his flesh. He picks her up and carried her to the bed where he slides her short skirt up and slipped his hands between her thighs and pulled her body closer. She opens her legs and he presses his mouth against her moist panties. She yanks them off and repositions her legs draping them over his shoulders and letting her feet slip down to the small of his back.

Jacob took a really long inhalation of her female fragrance, sweet, young, and delicious, and his head swirled. He pushes himself lower between her legs until he is in position for his mouth to slide smoothly over her wet, glass smooth, fur surrounded vulva.

Her body tensed for a moment then it relaxed and she wiggled under him on her back, using her feet against his back to compel his face even closer while both her hands gripped the bed sheet as his tongue begins flicking over and around the outside of her orifice and worming its way about inside her.

He knows that soon this foraging will cause her liquids to surge and coat the trembling red seeker that is his tongue. And sure enough, after a few minutes, the gift of her precious, milky nectar relinquished its rich, opaque coating over his lips becoming a glistening presence and Jacob moaned and spread itself over his red, squirming cavern visitor bathing in the exotic sensation of being lost in the exquisite, flowing aromatic wonder of Ginger's young, fluid womanhood.

And then jealous, merciless dreams overtook her, refusing to allow the sensations from such a paradisal visitation to linger except for a replication of the mellifluous tonality of her scream retrieved here some area of her fleshy cache where such pleasant things are continued ad infinitum until tender moments of need.

But now, awake and gratefully in love and turned siren, she lovingly toys with the object of such precious deposit by gently squeezing the tip of her love prey's nose as a prelude to a forthcoming, though yet distant, final and distinct declaration of her loves' entire intention, cooing:

"Jake With Secrets, I have something to give to you."

Jacob stirs awake with a smile that is immediately smothered by Ginger's soft, generous mouth. She pulled out his Rolex watch and his gold necklace and two rings." She shrugged. "I stole this stuff back from Chewy. He's gonna be real mad but it's okay with me. I don't have the money I took from you because he spent it all. I didn't spend any of it."

He kissed her hands and gently took the items from her. Then there is just the hint of threat in Jacob's tone.

"Is Chewy going to try to hurt you?"

"No, because I'm stayin' here with you. Besides, he knows my sister would kill him and I think, in some kinda way, he's kinda scared of you,

I think. But he ain't no kinda coward though but there's something about you that kinda bothers him; something about you he's not too sure about. Anyway, he knows I can do things to him. I know things."

"As small as you are? What kind of things do you know? Karate? Judo?" She shrugged.

"Things."

He laughed. Now she has her usual coquettish look that shows when she is ready to act silly and playful with him. That is the Ginger he knew to be simply irresistible. He grabbed her and kissed her hard. The shock of it took her breath away for a moment. She pulls her face back and looks at him as if she is seeing him for the first time. She uses her hand to fan herself.

"Wow!" She is genuinely and pleasantly surprised. "That was really nice. Where'd that come from? It ain't my birthday, is it?" They both laughed.

"That's how I feel about you. I don't know where it all came from, but it's there and it's real."

"I got something to tell you." She suddenly seemed a bit unhappy again.

"Okay. What is it you want to tell me?"

"I think maybe Baofung is thinking about killing you."

The expression on her face is apologetic. Her hand finds his face and caresses it. Her eyes search his features as if looking for some sort of response, but nothing registers on his face.

"Why do you think that? He and I got along fine at my meeting with him at his home office. He even said he saw something around me."

"Yeah, and when you met with Dr. Cheung, he saw something too, but he ain't like what he saw an' Baofung neither. First, Dr. Cheung said he saw something he don't trust, and he tell that to Baofung and he asked Baofung to meet with you to see if he feels the same. He said he felt the same strange thing around you or inside you or something. And then one time Chewy and Jub Jub went to your hotel to search your room to see if they can find if you real hustler or not. But Chewy say they only find your books. Chewy say you got a purple book what's got all the pages glued together. He couldn't even open it."

Jacob knew that is his *Book of Skins* prayed shut by his grandmother so that only he is able to open it.

"Yeah, he's right. I accidentally glued it shut."

She looked at him curiously.

"What? Anyway Chewy got real interested in your Jew book."

"The Cabala?"

"Uh-huh. Chewy say that it's a book of magic and it's for Jews, so he says you must be a Jew. But Jub Jub say he never heard of no black Jewish hustler."

Jacob saw that it is all making some sort of sense now. Chewy and Jub Jub Tai has been in his room. Mrs. Wong must have caught them or she might have been looking for notes for Chang when they caught her. He and Jub Jub Tai could have roughed her up, and then to cover themselves maybe they dumped her out his window. And now they wanted to kill him. Have they figured a connection? Has Mrs. Wong told them anything?

"They also see that your name's not Jake, it's Jacob. So, now Chewy is really confused. He gets mad, and he says you lie to him. He says your name is Jacob, and you're a Jew. He calls you Jacob The Jew."

"Yeah, but why did they—"

Ginger interrupted him:

"He now says we all gonna call you Jacob The Jew. He tells everybody that's your real name now. No more play. He says you're Jacob The Jew. But that name is okay with me. I like it. Then when Baofung hears about this he says Jacob The Jew is a strange man and a real danger to *The Chinese Blood*. And Chewy says yes he knows that."

"Ginger, why did they kill the maid in my room?"

"Huh?"

"Why did Chewy and Jub Jub kill Mrs. Wong, the maid?"

"The maid? Your maid is dead? They ain't killed your maid. I wish I killed her. I hated the bitch. But I didn't kill her either."

"You said they were in my room. And the maid fell out of the window in my room—fell or maybe got pushed or thrown out of it."

"No, they just go to your room to look for stuff on you not to kill some ol' ugly maid. Why would they wanna kill some stupid ol' maid?"

"I don't know. It just all seems strange."

"But I'm pretty sure Baofung's ready to kill you, though."

"But why?"

"Because everybody is really confused about you now and they don't know what to do with you. They see your stuff for magic in that book. But I still think Baofung kinda thinks maybe you a Voodoo man, but he don't know what kinda Voodoo man you are. I think maybe Baofung might be a little nervous about your magic." She giggled and hugged him. "Has Jacob The Jew got magic? You got Voodoo maybe? Is your book Voodoo?"

Jacob is still pondering the death of Mrs. Wong.

"No." "Ginger, if *The Chinese Blood* didn't kill Mrs. Wong then who did? And why?"

"Why you askin' me? How do I know? Anyway, like I was sayin', nobody knows if you a real hustler, or if you—well, they know you not the police. Hong Kong don't have no black police, but Chewy say that there also ain't no such thing as a black Jewish hustler neither. So he says maybe you CIA. But Baofung says no such thing as a black Voodoo CIA man. So don't nobody agree what you are, but they agree you a Jew and a danger to *The Chinese Blood*. So, now everybody will call you Jacob The Jew until they figure out what else you might be."

"What about the gun deal? Did anybody mention the gun deal we talked about? Baofung gave me an order for a lot of guns. Is he still going through with it? Is the gang still on board with that?"

Ginger shrugged.

"I don't know. They don't talk around me so much now. And my sister don't want me around the gang unless she's with me. Chewy say he thinks you and me are really in love, so he thinks I know what you are and won't tell because I love you. Now everybody looks at me funny. So my sister says to me to leave, to go to you and stay here, so I buy suitcases and now I stay here." She held Jacob close to her and whispered: "…But Delilah says to be careful, 'cause Baofung might start using his magic on us."

Jacob wondered if the shadow he saw in Chang's office has anything to do with Baofung.

"Ginger, I thought I saw a person's shadow moving along a wall."

"A shadow? Where?" She sat up on the bed and looked around the room.

"In an office. The shape looked like a woman's shadow. But it was moving on its own."

Ginger gave that some thought then she nodded.

"Then you have seen an immature *shadow deschong*, a creature created by a sorcerer, and it is surely the work of Baofung," she said firmly. "It starts off as a shadow form, and later it matures into something that has eyes, ears and a mouth, but is still a shadow. Only the person it is meant for can see it until it has completely matured in form; when it is fully formed, anyone can see her. Until that time, it is a spy. After it grows eyes and ears, it is able to give reports to its master about what you and other people say."

"Mature form?"

"Yes. When a *shadow deschong* comes off the wall and is a full, three dimensional entity, what is known as a *Deschong*. No longer is it a *shadow*, it is a *deschong*; a living thing that is almost human. And if given he proper amount of time for all its features to be complete, it is undetectable by any human being. But, if it is a renegade deschong, it is eager to get free of the wall and will come off before letting its human features to form fully."

Jacob shook his head.

"That sounds kind of scary."

"Yes, she is. She can be used to kidnap a person or murder someone in her fully physical form off the wall. She can also force a human into becoming a shadow and take him into the two dimensional world she temporarily lives in."

Jacob finds this all really peculiar and he wants to know more:

"So she can't force you onto the wall until she is exactly like any other human with every human feature fully duplicated. Then it is able to physically act against either the person it is sent to harm or the person it wants to…well, I guess kidnap; pull onto the wall to live with her."

Ginger frowned briefly at him and then continued:

"Yes. It sounds weird but she can't make you two dimensional until she herself is three dimensional. The *shadow deschong* dies after her assignment is finished unless her master has further need of her; she can live as long as her sorcerer has need of her abilities but then she is to be sent to serve the Mistress of Hell.

He is turning the name over in his thoughts.

"Ginger, is the *Deschong* always a woman? Can it ever be a man?

She shook her head:

"Never a man. Always it is a female. But I do not know why. I do not know a lot about them. But I do know that the moment she is about to kill someone she has a disagreeable body odor, bad enough to cause a person to grow weak."

Jacob is intrigued:

"…My God."

"A sorcerer will usually makes his *shadow deschong* from one of his students; so there is a supposed loyalty. Baofung has such a school in Japan and his students are women of all ages, never more than four students at a time and they are always females. His students are called 'The Dark Ones,' because of the powers he gives them through the teaching of very *Dark* magic. His *Dark school* is whispered about even in my village when I was a child in the mountains."

Jacob is entranced.

"… The deschong is a perfect zombie."

"No she is not a zombie." She thinks about it and then shrugs. "The *Deschong* is quite complication."

Jacob is curious.

"Could a *Shadow deschong* find me in the States?"

Ginger almost chuckled her response:

"If you have been marked, it can find you anywhere once the sorcerer 'marks' you. He does this by giving the person a 'Divining' potion in something to eat or drink. Once it is swallowed, the human being becomes like a beacon. *The shadow deschong* follows the scent of you. She will find you no matter where you go."

"Well, I ate and drank with Baofung."

Ginger shrugged.

"Then you have been marked by Baofung. The potion is in that drink or maybe even it could have been in the food. That is how the *Shadow deschong* found you." She hugged him. "I think I need to gather some leaves from some plants and a tree there and make you a tea for protection against Baofung's *shadow deschong* even though it has not become dangerous to you yet. But who knows what will happen?"

"What is she going to do to me?"

Ginger shrugs.

"I am not sure. just how much this tea I am going to make will protect you but . But we will start with the tea and then we will move on to some Asian magic that I will teach you." She hugged him. "I do not want my Jacob the Jew to ever be harmed." She looks at him. "I will destroy whoever tries to harm you. Such is my love for you."

Sometimes love entails visiting a wooded area in the dead of night with the adjacent park mostly deserted with no children playing and no lovers other than Jacob and Ginger are there expressly because of these conditions: darkness, emptiness and no children.

But this time Ginger and Jacob are there to forage for the plants she needs to ward off attacks from Baofung. As she and Jacob walk through the weeds, she points out different low-hanging trees and plants and describing the bushes and trees they are looking for and the special powers and effects they produce for the user.

She crouched to pick a plant:

"You see, these plants we call 'olanjola,' and we use them to calm the nerves. The leaves from this tree are used for creating a low serenity, a kind of Nirvana. Branches from these low-lying bushes are called 'jaosing' and must be boiled, because if they are eaten and not boiled, they are poisonous and will make you very, very sick before killing you. But when they are boiled and consumed as a tea, they gain in strength and lose their toxicity. Is that the right word?"

"Yes, it surely is Ginger."

"Once boiled, they will remain in your body but only to fight off negative things inside you. These branches will kill whatever Baofung has placed inside you through the brandy you drank. Once they kill what they need to kill, they will leave your body. But the *shadow deschong* will still know and be able to find you."

"You're sure these plants won't kill me?"

Ginger places her hands on her hips like an exasperated mother and then reaches out and pinches his nose. That reminded him of what his grandmother Elizabeth always playfully did to his grandfather Paul and sometimes with him.

"No, they won't kill you, but I will if you don't stop being such a baby." She kneels on the dirt and takes out a butter knife from the hot el to use as a spade digging several inches beneath the soil to rip loose a wide plant with a very thick root. She holds it up to him:

"Now this root is called 'episochong,' and it is extremely poisonous. There is nothing you can do to make it not be excepting to use it with the other plant that I have explained to you. I guess one poison gets rid of the other's poison but they are still both very poisonous. Does that make sense to you?"

"Actually, it does, Ginger. Yes."

"If it is given to someone without the other there is no cure for it. I cannot explain to you how this one works with the others, but it works when you use the two together in the same tea."

"Is it that you may not explain or that you don't know?"

"Yes, I know, but I am not allowed to tell you. I have already told you a few things that perhaps I should not have told. But I can tell you that when I was born our village holy man saw that I was chosen to be of the faith of magic and needed to be taught by him which is the only way to be guided into the faith of magic. Among some of the sorcery I learned is the Left-Handed Path, something I have seen Baofung use; it is a very deadly sorcery."

"What's the Left-Handed Path?"

"It is a very strong form of Chinese sorcery and can be used against another sorcerer but one has to be very careful that she is doing the right thing because while it is powerful it also most dangerous. My Shaman warned me never to use either one unless to save my life or a loved one against some powerful sorcerer. But it is not as strong or as frightening as *Guman Thong*; I have been warned never to use that magic for any purpose, no matter what. Baofung uses the Tao of the Left sorcery as one kind of magic but even he does not use the *Guman Thong*. But he has so many spells, rituals and magic that he can use; he does not need to resort to using the *Guman Thong*. Does Jacob The Jew think he could ever believe in magic and sorcery? Ah, but I know Americans do not believe in such things. Am I right?"

"Well, much like you I too have been taught certain magic when I was a child, but by my grandmother."

"Is that true? Then perhaps you and I are well-suited and meant to be. Maybe that is what has happened with us, why we are drawn to each other. Then we must talk. But for now, we must finish our work here in the park. What we're gathering here have things in them that ward off or at least fight against certain kinds of magic. Fighting against the *shadow deschong* is difficult. They have no real strength, and their power is much like most ghosts' powers. Their powers are mostly 'ghost' powers, nothing that is physical unless they have taken human form and even then their strength is in spells and magic."

"Okay." He is looking at the dense shrubbery. "But isn't reaching into these thick bushes for things in the dark kind of dangerous? I mean, how can we tell what we're grabbing hold of? I can't tell where my hand is going."

"Oh, don't worry little one." She giggled. "I will never have you do anything that will harm you. So, I will pick the leaves from the bushes and ground and you can pick from the trees. Is that better, my little frightened baby?"

"Well, yes, but I don't want you doing anything dangerous either."

"Hush. Come, let's hurry."

For the next hour they harvest the necessary leaves and plants for the tea Ginger is to brew for him. But even performing the serious business of leaf and root gathering for the preparation of defensive teas, Ginger and Jacob find time to playfully wrestle each other and for her to cavort and frolic about; she even manages to get Jacob to mimic some of her silliness.

But once back at his hotel room, Ginger assumes a serious role and begins preparing the tea. There is one root she dug up that she has not touched, and he is curious that she has not used it.

"What about that root? Are you not going to use it?"

"No. Not now. Not yet. We do not have to be worried about *a shadow deschong* now and that root is for the *Deschong, the matured shadow deschong.* Here, eat these three leaves." She took out some more leaves, but different ones, and rinsed them and gave them to him.

Jacob looked at the leaves curiously:

"What are these?"

"It will help slow Baofung's magic in case he decides to try and harm you. Sooner or later his magic may become violent. Then I will have to use my own magic against him to protect you." She cupped his face in her hands. "I will never allow anyone to harm you."

"I love you, Ginger" He wondered if one day he might have to use his magic to protect her. But he also wondered if his magic would work in Hong Kong since it did not overwhelm Desirlee in Tokyo.

She wiped some of the sweat from his face.

"But when Baofung sees that I am using magic to help you, then he will become my sworn enemy, and eventually he will try to destroy me too. Do not be fooled by his charming manner. He is truly an evil person. There are times he even smells of this evil."

Jacob holds her:

"We will fight against his magic together."

Ginger kisses him but gets back to the business at hand:

"Maybe I shouldn't but I am going to explain the episochong root to you. That is the one I should never speak about to anyone who is not in the faith. But since you have told me your grandmother taught you magic since you were a child, then you are in the faith and I am allowed to speak of it to you."

Jacob listened closely as Ginger spoke:

"The episochong root is the means of opening the mind to be able to detect any strange thing that is in it including cancers of the body and brain. But what is most important is it sees what *Dark* magic the person is surrounded by and produces an aura to protect the person. But even though it does not work against a sorcerer and his *Deschong* it will keep the *Shadow Deschong* from making you sick or crazy. But she is too late for crazy with you." She giggles and kisses him. "You already got a head start on crazy before the *shadow deschong* got here." They burst out in loud laughter. After more kissing, she cuddled up to him. "There are a few other things it can do, but we will speak of those later."

"I wonder if the gang is going to keep their word about our gun deal. Because if they have Baofung doing his magic against me, then I guess maybe it's off. They promised to show me the *cherry berry* because they want to use it as a barter, to trade with instead of just all cash."

"They're not gonna show you the *cherry berry*."

"Ginger, what makes you say that?"

She shrugged.

"Nobody knows what that thing looks like—only Dr. Cheung and Baofung. Nobody in the gang ever sees it."

"Why is it so popular? What kind of drug is it?"

"We only know it's a real big, big seller but just to certain people in your country. Some people in New York always wanting it. A lot of it."

"If it is such a big seller, then why don't they sell it here in Hong Kong?"

She shrugged again.

"Nobody wants problems with Inspector Chang, and if they start selling it here in Hong Kong then it will give Chang full power to go after whoever is doing it. Nobody in the gang wants that. Inspector Chang is a thug police. He's so much thug he almost ain't a cop."

"Chang?"

"He's a police inspector. Chang's a crazy man. Like you. But he's crazy crazy!"

"Ginger are you telling me that nobody—nobody has seen this drug, and yet it's being shipped to other countries right under the noses of the authorities?"

She stared at him for a long moment before shrugging her shoulders.

"I dunno how he does it but yes it has only been seen by Dr. Cheung and Baofung. They say that even *The Chinese Blood* gangs in your country who deliver it never sees it. All they do is they go to where Dr. Cheung has it stored in his warehouses where it is already packaged and they make pickups and they deliver it. Dr. Cheung tells authorities that the warehouses are his research buildings so that explains all the exporting he does to U.S. I hear he's maybe gonna expand. Have more gangs deliver drug and maybe to other countries. But no Asian countries."

"No Asian countries?"

"No."

This is information Jacob needs to hear and be able to report back to Chang and he is sure that will ease some of the tension between him, Chang and his staff.

"So you don't think they're going to show me the drug."

"Well, nobody ever really trusted you, baby, 'cause Chewy always say from first time he met you that you're too showy. He thinks that maybe you not too smart and that they can fool you and use you to get stuff. Now he don't know what chu are. Maybe they gonna show it to you, but you ain't gonna live to go tell nobody."

"Do you think they might still want the guns?"

Ginger became irritated.

"What's the mattah with you? You really that crazy? I just said that maybe they're going to kill you and me, and you still think about guns? You that greedy? You think you gonna outsmart them? They probably going to take the guns and kill you? Or get Baofung to make you like a zero person. Like a zombie who just sit and stare into space unless he tells you to do something. I have seen him do that to a man. Baofung is really a dangerous sorcerer."

He believed her.

"Ginger, you're right. I've got to take time and try to figure this out."

"My magic's strong enough, I think, to maybe kill Baofung, but I don't want to kill nobody." She placed her arms around his waist. "You got nobody but me on your side, Jacob The Jew. Nobody got your back but me, and I got only you an' my sister. Maybe you can just forget the guns and marry me, and we jus' go to America with my sister."

At this point Jacob wishes he could forget everything except Ginger. His emotions are being ripped apart by this sudden and unexpected confession of truth from Ginger. Now he is torn between his duty and the entanglement of being in love with her.

Ginger is looking around the room.

"Where is your stupid microwave? I have made some tea from the leaves I gave you to chew before." While waiting for the water to boil, she pressed her face against his chest. "But I want Jacob The Jew to be more truthful with me. If we are getting married, we don't need secrets." She kissed him. "Besides, I have a right to know who I'm risking my life for. But no matter what you are, I love you even if you are a Voodoo Jew."

He laughed and kissed her.

"Ginger, I'm going to trust you, and if you betray me it will mean my life. The gang will kill me."

She shrugged.

"They are already fixing to kill you anyway."

He looks into her eyes:

"I'm a police officer and I'm working with Inspector Chang on the investigation into the gang's *cherry berry* drug."

Ginger's eyes stopped dancing and widened. Her breath halted somewhere near the center of her throat.

"Oh my God! Now Hong Kong got a black cop?'

Ginger jumps up from bed and starts walking around Jacob's hotel room in complete shock. She did not know what to make of what he said to her and she keeps walking back and forth with her hand over her mouth and shaking her head. she stopped and looked at him:

"You really a cop?"

"Yes and I'm working with Own Chang and the Hong Kong police in the investigation of *cherry berry*."

"But when did Hong Kong get black cops?"

He laughed. How much more should he tell her? There is not much more to tell her. In a couple of sentences he has already told her everything. He dreaded thinking that Ginger is putting on an act, doing what Chewy has told her to do; there is always that possibility.

"No, I'm Not a Hong Kong cop, I'm an American police officer, Ginger, serving in the army now and assigned to Military Intelligence. I am here on loan to help in the investigation of the *cherry berry* drug because of my civilian investigative background and languages."

"You a soldier too? How many things can you be before you just explode or somethin'?"

"Sometimes I wonder myself."

The moment he divulged that information, something in him felt greatly relieved but he also hoped that no one is listening other than Ginger. He only just remembered now that Chang warned him that he should turn the radio up loud when talking about anything confidential. But it far too late to be concerned about that now.

"And I have been raised in magic. My entire life has been learning magic and how to use it. He paused. He knows he has to become a lot more familiar with Chinese sorcery to be able to use his magic against it effectively. Ginger walks to the window and looks out.

He knows that this is an awful lot for her to digest, and she is probably having some difficulty processing what he has told her. He pressed himself against her back. Ginger turned her head and their lips met softly.

He is caught up in deep concerns about their current status with *The Chinese Blood*, thinking it has always been Chewy's plan to get rid of him as inconspicuously as possible after stealing the weaponry he is going to deliver to them.

Ginger turned around and looked at him.

"You really a cop?"

"Yeah."

"A Hong Kong cop?"

He laughed.

"No, not a Hong Kong cop Ginger. I told you that I'm an American cop and a soldier in the US Army Military Intelligence on loan to Inspector Chang who thinks that *The Chinese Blood* gang is responsible for exporting and manufacturing the *cherry berry.*"

She shook her head.

"It's Dr. Cheung and Baofung's *cherry berry* drug not *The Chinese Blood*. And Dr. Cheung and Baofung they keep all the money from it. The doctor wants to build a thug army. I don't know what that means though. Like I already told you, *The Chinese Blood* gangs in New York deliver it to special customers and they collect the payment in gold or sometimes diamonds and sometimes cash but mostly diamonds and gold. But now Dr. Cheung wanna go mega, I think. I dunno."

"So how does he pay the gang? Gold or diamonds or cash?"

"I jus' tol' you he ain't paid them nothing yet. Not really. He tells them that they gonna work something out later. They say he's gonna use Asian gangs to deliver the drug." She takes a sip of the tea and has him drink more of it. "Asians ain't got no fear. But he kinda got his eye on a few American gangs he thinks is almost as bad as us." She shrugged. "I dunno about that, though. Anyway, the police already know that. How come you don't know? You a cop, ain't chu?"

"We do know, we just don't know what the gangs are getting ready to do; or why they're converging in Tokyo."

"I just told you, the *cherry berry*."

"But what about the *cherry berry*? What is the meeting for? To discuss what? And why Tokyo?"

She shook her head.

"I dunno how come you don't listen so good. Didn't I already just tell you Dr. Cheung wants to go mega and he's maybe gonna have a whole lotta gangs doing the deliveries in a whole lotta cities? My sister Delilah say she overheard Chewy and Dr. Cheung talking about it. Dr. Cheung has contacted some gangs, big gangs, and told all of them to gather other Asian gangs who practice magic, who practice occult and they gotta do something but she won't know what it is they gotta do for Dr. Cheung for him to choose which gangs to use."

"And *The Chinese Blood* trusts the doctor?"

Her expression grew serious.

"*The Chinese Blood* got crazy people. Dr. Cheung knows not to betray them. They'd kill him. The only one they scared of is Baofung. But I think if they have to…they might try to kill him too. But they really scared of his magic."

"Do you think the gang has stopped trusting me?"

She threw her hands up at the ceiling with an exasperated groan.

"Jacob The Jew, how many times I gotta tell you that nobody never did trust you in the first place? Chewy liked you and he is very strong in gang but he didn't trust you. At first, he thinks you silly. He says you like bragging. He says you too flashy." Then she remembered something and she leaned close to him. "I forgot to tell you this: you remember when you met with Baofung?"

"Yeah. Why?"

"You said the wrong thing. You ask him if gang wants to buy helmets—then he knew you not a real gun dealer. Gun dealers don't sell no stupid helmets, Jacob The Jew. That is a big boo boo."

"Oh."

"Chewy say you sound like you used to be some army quartermaster or somethin' talkin' about helmets. But they still don't know what you are. You a black man, so they think if anything, maybe you CIA, so I think maybe they gonna wait to get guns from you, then they let Baofung kill you. But maybe they gonna keep getting guns from you as long as they can."

"Ginger, who's the leader of *The Chinese Blood?*"

She shrugged.

"Everybody. Nobody."

"Huh?

"What difference does it make?" She pointed to the cups of tea they are drinking. "Drink the tea. You're gonna need strength to do what you must do to help me with my magic against Baofung, because it might become real strong and if it does then since he's a sorcerer, I might have to try to use *Guman Thong.*"

He sipped more of the tea wondering what his part in this ritual of hers is going to be. Whatever it is, he knows he is probably not going to like it, but he has a feeling that if he did not follow her instructions, he is going to be facing some problems that he will have no idea how to deal with.

"What do I have to do?"

"Something that will be scary for you." She eased him onto a chair in the kitchen area and sat on his lap. Pressing her face against the side of his neck, she murmurs: "...A few scary things. Calm down and I'll show my scared little baby tomorrow." She gets up and pulls him towards the bed.

"Now come on to bed so I can snuggle." She jumped in bed, pulling him with her.

He happily wrapped his arms and legs around her and she did the same and in a moment, they are both sleeping.

Someone is knocking on the door. Jacob glances at the hotel clock and could not believe the hour is the next morning. He would have been willing to swear that they have only been sleeping for maybe as much as ten minutes but it is the next day.

The knocking stopped but then there are keys fumbling in the lock to his door. So now someone is trying to sneak into his room but the door is refusing to have any part in such a clandestine business as burglary and it warns Jacob with loud creaking. But burglars don't generally creak. Not loudly. Jacob is out of bed quietly stealing to the door. But now a more proper manner is resumed by the intruder and the foolish person knocks once again gently on the proud wood, but alas this time it only serves to wake Ginger who so abruptly pops up she almost pops herself out of bed. Such curiosity. Her eyes are stretched unnaturally wide. So what is there to do now but to wait for Jacob to initiate the theatre bond to follow when he opens the silly door that is hiding his morning's entertainment on its opposite side and say good morning to:

Mrs. Che bowing and smiling at them while just behind her is her fast approaching trainer, Mrs. Lo Chen but who by now is just too late to stop the intrusion

"Good morning sir and Miss." Mrs. Che said quickly. "I am a new maid being trained.

Ginger's eyes rolled up in her head. She sucked her teeth loudly, sighed and threw her hands up toward the ceiling and jumped out of bed. She walked close to Mrs. Che and narrowed her eyes glaring at her and said

"Aw, hell, here I go again with another old grandma hoe on dick patrol! I guess I'm gonna have to shove a damn GPS up this one's ass so she can be able to find a room other than this one to clean." Ginger turned from her, cussing lowly, and walked back to the bed and climbed beneath the covers. Then she sat up on the bed and said: "Maybe we should just get another bed for the damn horny maids this hotel's got."

Mrs. Che's trainer, Mrs. Lo Chen grabbed Mrs. Che's arm and stepped in front of her, speaking impatiently to her in loud Mandarin while wagging a finger in Mrs. Che's face. Then she switched to English:

"We do not have conversations of introduction with our guests, Mrs. Che. And we only clean the rooms that have left a card on the door as I have spoken to you of before. You must pay better attention asking for the room to be cleared." She pointed to Jacob's door. "There is no such card here." Mrs. Lo Chen turned back to Jacob and bowed. "Sorry for her intrusive impudence, sir. Please forgive us."

"Oh, it's okay." Jacob said, with a quick glance over at a fuming Ginger who is sitting up on the bed with her arms locked together.

"We do not wish to disturb you any further. We will return at another time." She abruptly turned and grabbed Mrs. Che by the arm and gestured. "We go to another room."

Ginger plops back on the bed and throws her hands up in the air: "Wonderful."

Ginger climbed beneath the covers, burying her head beneath. Mrs. Che pushed her cart away and down the hall to a room with a note to clean the room hanging on the doorknob. Jacob watched them take in clean sheets and prepare to clean the room.

He closed the door.

CHAPTER 28

CUTTING TO
THE CHASE

Afternoon. Jacob's room is cool, but the temperature outside is unseasonably warm. He and Ginger stand at the hotel window staring down at the people on the street, most of whom are either standing in the sparse shade or wasting no time seeking some shelter from the overbearing sun.

Jacob slipped his arm around Ginger's petite waist and gently pulled her to him. He kissed her and after a moment they turned away from the window, moving their bodies to the rhythm of the tune the radio in his room is playing. He whispered in her ear:

"...Ginger, try not to worry."

But she is worried, and it shows clearly on her face. It has been a few days now that she has officially move in with Jacob as her sister has suggested, and she has not heard from her or any of the gang. In fact, no one from the gang has contacted either of them. It has also been a while since he has communicated with Chang because he has nothing to report to him.

"Maybe I should go to the gang to see that my sister is safe. I do not think they will harm me as long as she is alive." Ginger wondered. "Why is Jacob The Jew not worried?"

"I am worried. But what can I do? I have to wait for Chewy to call me, and I am not going to let you go to the gang alone."

"Yes, maybe you are right. They don't trust me a lot. Too many things happening together. Maybe when they get the guns from you, then they maybe gonna kill you and me together. Maybe they're gonna kill us both anyway, even without the guns. Probably now they are figuring out who to kill first. But I really think Chewy's really kinda scared you might be CIA so he might not be so eager to have you dead."

"Ginger you've gotta stop worrying about us being killed, even though you just might be right." He rubbed his stomach. "I'm hungry. How about you? Maybe we can order some pizza."

She shakes her head.

"No, let's wait. You should drink more of the special tea I made for you."

A song that she liked drifted from the radio, and she began dancing around the room like a ballerina something she has the perfect body for, he thought. She is an absolute delight to watch, a lithe, beautiful young woman who, despite her gang background and her difficult childhood, seemed, at times, so innocent in thought and in person. He has watched her play with a million different hairstyles earlier. She is angry that none of them is what she wanted, angrier still that she has no idea of what she wanted to begin with.

But Jacob knows that compelling innocence is due to Ginger's youth and one of the most appealing things about her. While she is still mature beyond her years something that may have been necessitated due to the demands her life has placed upon her in many ways. He knows that, thanks to her sister, Ginger has followed a path laid out by her has elevated her status within a certain stratum of society. However he feels that she constantly fantasizes cosmically of other levels she desires to reach and possibly reside; but she is puzzled that those enigmatic societal positions are perhaps positioned at unattainable heights levels.

Still she dreams such an achievement is within her reach though by some indefinite means and yet she knows that it is within the power of her mind to grasp, when it arrives, the first opportunity sighting the ability to leap quantum distances beyond this current leaking of life.

The music on the radio slows and Ginger jumps up began doing sultry, sexy movements that he knows is what she calls, "my irresistible sex dance," but she always made it clear to him that 'this dance is only for you and never anybody else,' and he knows that it is strictly tailored by her for his visual pleasure and enticement; her thin but still generous and perfectly shaped hips slowly, sensuously grind the air, pumping as her hands slide over her own body and fingers beckoning Jacob to come and join her, reaching out to him like some siren beckoning him to become one with her with no danger of rocks.

And like any other love-doomed sailor hearing the irresistible song of the Siren, Jacob floats to her, his body undulating in rhythm with the music and locked in timing with her gyrations and irresistible movements. Melting against her and her flesh dissolves into his, their bodies swaying like a single flower caught in some invisible but so gentle breeze that neither of them truly understand but are equally lost in. They can see only each other, and soon their visions are blurred by mutual sweating and increasing lust.

Her arms slip around his waist just before his hands gripped her shoulders and almost desperately pulls her face against his. Her satiny-soft mouth spreads wide and eager against his all-engulfing mouth. He lifts her and almost runs to the bed with her and the moment their bodies touched the mattress…

The phone rings.

Neither of them moved although the ring is something they'd been waiting for but neither of them wanted it at this moment. Not now. No, not now. They both lie there trying to wish away the foul sounding intrusion from the stupid, clamoring instrument producing the annoyance.

Sitting up they continue to hold onto each other almost as though their combined wishes carry the power to make the rude, intrusive thing answer itself. But, of course, such a wish falls on indifferent, relentlessly ringing ears. And so, it does not.

Ginger releases an exasperated whoosh of air and lets go of Jacob. Her shoulders slumped and she collapsed back on the bed, sucked her teeth, snatched the hem of her shorty nightgown back down to an almost "maiden" height and turns her back, growling some indecipherable utterance to Jacob who grumpily reaches for the persistently noisy black monster.

"Yeah, hello."

Nothing.

"Hello?"

Something.

"… No. Yeah, okay. Thanks." He hung up.

Not that she really cared at this moment, but:

"Who is that?"

"Room service. They want to know if we want to order food. They're about to close and since we always order, they wanted to make sure we are taken care of."

Ginger lays back on the bed. She is looking questioningly at Jacob and he thinks he knows precisely what she is thinking, and he thinks it is the identical thing that is repeating itself in his thoughts:

Is this the way to allow such a special moment to pass—letting a food inquiry derail the romance express jet, to let it just be thrown away, tossed aside, done away with so crudely, with disdain while you just stand there as though having forgotten where passion resides? Not afraid to try resurrecting old phantoms for fear of commitment I hope. Time to be practical and get back to thinking about guns, is it?

He tries to smile but she is having none of it until she gathered herself a calm decorum that floats by her. Yes, it really is time to be practical. They both wanted Chewy or someone from the gang to call them. She needed to get word that her sister is okay and time to prepare herself mentally for the tasking sorcery she felt she needed to do to protect the man she so deeply loved.

316

Jacob is hoping that the reason for Chewy's absence is that the gang is trying to figure out where to have the delivery of the rifles made and making arrangements for the drug to be present for his examination. He watched Ginger pour them more tea.

"So, you said you don't think they're going to show me the *cherry berry* when I deliver the guns?"

"I dunno." She obviously is not interested in talking any longer about whether or not they will show him the drug.

"I don't think they'll want to kill me if they think I can get more of the weapons for them, especially if they can barter with their product and not have to pay out so much cash."

She locks her hands on her hips.

"Jacob The Jew whatta you know about Chinese thug people? You an American cop! You don't know Chinese thug life! *The Chinese Blood* are dangerous people, and smart! Not just street thugs! Maybe by now they already know you're a cop! If they know that, then that means you're a dead man, and I'm a dead woman! You have to get me and my sister to America. So forget about the guns, and let's get out of here. Out of the country!" Ginger sits on the edge of the bed and angrily folds her arms.

"Ginger, I—" Jacob's eyes are fixed on something behind her.

She notices and turns around, but she sees nothing and turns back to Jacob.

"What? You see something?"

"Yeah. That shadow thing is back."

She glances around the room again and kept looking but sees nothing but the usual things in his room. She lightly slaps herself on the side of her head.

"Why am I looking when I know I can't see 'it?' It is time we do what we have to do to stop Baofung. I do not think it always appears that she wants to harm you, this *deschong*. But they can be a puzzle, a contradiction. She may pretend to pretend to love you to discover your weakness, the simpler to destroy a person. And that is when she can attack you and then it would be easier for her to destroy you. But then, I do not really know the *deschong*. And that is when he can attack you and then it would be easy for him to turn you into something that just sits and waits for him to speak to it. And I am sure that soon his magic will turn more dangerous for one of us. There is only one way to be sure to stop a sorcerer, and that is *Guman Thong*, a most powerful magic. I have told you of this before. We have to attack Baofung now whole he does not expect us to; and the only real weapon against him is the Guman Thong."

"But you said you've been warned to never use the *Guman Thong*! Besides, the *shadow deschong* can't harm me. You said so. So why not just keep working on trying to get rid of it? If you go to extreme magic, because maybe then Baofung and your shaman will know it's you."

"Even with the little I am doing now, it is only a matter of time before Baofung will be able to 'taste' my presence. And if we get rid of the *shadow deschong* then he will know I am the one who did it but it does not matter at that point. And you need to remember the *shadow deschong* will soon grow eyes and a mouth as well as ears and something very close to a face. It will then report to Baofung everything you say and do. Even when you do not see it is here in this room with you, watching and waiting."

"But it isn't doing anything to either one of us. How do we know who she's after? Is it possible that she is after you and not me?"

"Yes, for now it is almost harmless. But maybe he did not create it to remain harmless. Do not think it always appears to you only for the reason of frightening you. It always searches for a person's weaknesses, which soon become very clear to it. It is not impossible that it may find a way to harm you while it is still a shadow if they can do such a thing. It depends, I think, on what Baofung wants it to do. But even so it is never deadly as a *shadow deschong* unless it is ever able to get out of the shadows and off the wall as a human."

"You don't think?"

Ginger clasped her hands around her arms and gave Jacob a rather exasperated look.

"Jacob The Jew, maybe you do not understand the things I have told you. I do not make *shadow deschongs,* and I do not know very much about everything to do with them."

Jacob is still bothered.

"I know. It's just that it's such a curious thing, this *shadow deschong.* In our case, it is not impossible that she may be assigned to me and not you or you and not me."

"Well, yes, to you or me. But to Chinese who have studied..." she shrugged, "we kind of have an understanding of why this thing works but not always how and not always what makes it work, what lets it do what it does or what it is empowered to do. But we must concentrate on Baofung's *shadow deschong*; it does not matter who she's assigned to; she is her for no good for one of us. I do not think it will take him too much longer to discover who is doing the magic against him, maybe three or four more days, maybe longer before he knows it is me. If he already knows then the *shadow deschong* is here for me because once he knows I am doing magic to help you, then he will begin to work his magic on both of us. He will likely decide to kill us both."

Jacob never thought of that possibility.

"So, actually, she could be here for both of us."

"That possibility is not impossible. He will surely want to kill me for such a betrayal. If that happens he will probably make me just disappear somewhere...somehow. I don't know what he'll do with you."

"He will make you disappear?"

She locked her fists against her thin hips.

"Well I don't mean he will make me go up in a puff of smoke and vanish like the stupid magicians do on stage. Chinese magic is not silly magic. It is serious and it can be used to be deadly. Maybe like the magic you have been taught by your grandmother. He will not take the chance for my sister to know what happened to me. Not right away anyway unless he is going to kill her too.

"Really/ Do you think he's trying to harm her, then?"

"No. She is very strong in the gang, almost as much as maybe Chewy, and can influence them if Baofung kills me. She and Chew would maybe be fighting for control of the gang. And Baofung will never do anything as important as taking the life of a gang member without the approval of everyone first. He would prefer to wait, but if I am working magic against him, then he will only wait for so long before he attacks me with his own magic and the gang will see it as justice. He knows that he must stop me as quickly as he can." She looked at Jacob and held his hand. "That is why we must do the *Guman Thong*."

Chill bumps are dancing across Jacob's body as he listens to Ginger and watches the *shadow deschong* dart around the walls of his room. He held his Moor's head and felt it vibrate against his fingers.

"How do we do this special magic you're talking about?"

"First we must find a graveyard."

Jacob did not like the sound of that even though some of the magic incantations his grandmother taught him required that they visit a graveyard to retrieve certain objects. And some of the incantations she taught him were performed by them in a graveyard.

Ginger suggested:

"There is a graveyard at Quixnon Hospital in Suir Qxin province. We can go there. There is where the poor people are buried and many young girls go there for abortions or to have their babies and leave them there for adoption."

She thought about it. "It is a sadness, but I think everyone in Hong Kong knows of that place. It has a very old graveyard; very old. It may be suitable. But we need to find a newly buried infant or at least one that is not too old."

He did not like the sound of that:

"A baby?"

She is fixing her hair:

"Yes."

"A baby?"

She stops and turns to look at him.

"Why do you keep saying that? Yes, a baby."

"But what are we going to do with a baby?"

"It is necessary for the spell. When we get to a graveyard I will read the graves to find a pregnant mother buried. If we can find such a grave and in that way we hope to find a child is maybe recently deceased; or at least one that is well preserved inside its mother; one that will not turn to powder once it is touched. The newer the better."

Jacob is staring at her as though he misunderstood what she just said. He is sure that he must have missed something in the conversation. But he loses his train of thought when he watches Ginger stretch out across the bed. Then she curled up on her side and slapped her hand against the space behind her on the mattress.

"Come, Jacob The Jew... sleepy time. Maybe tomorrow we can go to Quixnon Hospital."

He gently lay next to her, slipping his arm over her breasts. Ginger turned and kissed him gently, then she turned around to look at him and secured his arm over her, whispering:

"I love you, Jacob The Jew."

"And I love you more, Ginger."

As they held each other, Jacob wonders about the baby that Ginger has in mind for casting a spell against Baofung. He knows some items gotten for certain spells can be unpleasant, but...babies? He wondered...just how many more profound dilemmas lie ahead?

CHAPTER 29

GINGER
MOVES IN

The next morning the hotel phone rang with the startling suddenness and intensity of an air-raid siren, jarring Jacob and Ginger
awake. He sat up and glanced at Ginger who is stirring but could not quite
wake from her sound sleep. He sighs and reaches over her and picks up the
phone. It is a voice he wanted to hear:

"Yo, Jacob The Jew. What's up, my man? You sound like I woke you.
It's already seven in the mornin.'"

"Chewy? Seven in the morning?"

"Where's the merchandise you supposed to be gettin' for us, my
man? Long time no hear."

"Chewy?"

Jacob turned and looked at Ginger, who is starting to sit up after
hearing Chewy's name. She wipes at her eyes and turns to Jacob. He holds
the phone out for her, and she is able to distinguish Chewy's maniacal
laughter. She looked at Jacob, waved off the phone, and shook her head,
indicating that she did not want to speak with him. But Jacob is really glad
to hear from him.

"Chewy?" Jacob asked again.

"Yo, come on, my man. Who else would it be? I see you got my little
Ginger snap under your wing in there now, huh?"

"Chewy I haven't heard from you in so long I almost forgot what your voice sounded like." Jacob laughed, but it is brief and insincere. "I thought maybe you guys decided against our deal." He belched out a brief and insincere laugh.

Chewy waited a minute and Jacob knew he is probably digesting the meaning of Jacob's brief laugh and non-committal answer as to Ginger's whereabouts he just got from Jacob.

"Jacob The Jew come on now. Why would we do that? We been giving you and your girl Ginger some time to finish your honeymoon. Now I know Baofung done told you your people gotta deliver the goods first. Of course, you gonna get paid for whatever we get from you in cash even though you ain't givin' us a price yet. But once you bring the sample goods then we'll see what kinda quality your product is. After that, we give you a final count on how many of everything we want, you give us a price and we figure so much cash and the rest in barter. But we gotta like the stuff you bring and just to make sure you can get as much as we want, you gotta bring us half the order or somethin' real close to it for us to look at. My people might even up the ante. I dunno. They don't tell me everything." *shadow deschong*

"Well, I guess I'll ..."

"Yeah, you can do it. An' like I said, we got our product here waiting for you to check out later. We even gonna have a demonstration to show you how good it is. You know how it goes. You show us yours, and we'll show you ours."

Jacob hears another voice behind Chewy in the background. Chew muffled the phone and seconds later came back to Jacob:

"Hold on, my man." Whomever Chewy is having a conversation with it is clear that they are in disagreement. When he returned to the phone, his voice lost its energy and is slower and more serious.

"Listen, my man, we gotta see the stuff 'cause we got two other possibilities, and we to see it like yesterday. We're getting ready to bust a move that we've been blueprinting. That's how come you ain't hear from me."

"Oh. I'm glad to hear that there's no problem between us."

"Sure, things with you an' me is still cool an' the gang, my man."

"Well, I have to talk to my people again to see if they'll come up with good samples of everything you wanna order. Okay?"

"Yeah." A slight pause. "So how's Ginger? She there?"

Jacob looks at her.

"Ginger? Yeah, she's here." Ginger again waved away the phone. "But, she's sleeping."

"Yeah, well, tell her that Delilah is kinda worried, you know? Tell her Delilah wants to see her."

"Yeah, okay, I will. Listen, if I can get the merchandise, where do I have it delivered? And when?"

"We got a warehouse. I'll give you the info when you let me know what's what. Okay?"

No response from Jacob. Chewy spoke louder:

"Hello? Yo', is Jacob The Jew still there?"

Jacob is staring at the *shadow deschong* moving along his hotel room wall. It has grown a woman's lips "painted" a very bright orange yet no nose or ears but quite a voluptuous body. Jacob points to it for Ginger but she cannot see it.

Jacob thought that it seems to be trying to free itself from the wall, really struggling to do so by moving back and forth, pushing against the wall, repositioning itself on another wall, and trying even harder to free itself, but to no avail. Then it stopped its struggle and turns to Jacob. He looked at its beginning of eyes and the two slits of deep orange are locked on him.

Jacob has considered using some of the incantations he learned from his grandmother to get try getting rid of the shadow but since it has been no problem, he chose not to do that. At this point, it is not much more than a nuisance to him.

He points to the but Ginger sees nothing, although she looks everywhere for it. She goes to the wall touching it and chanting lowly. She picked up a cup of old tea that she has made for him and took in a mouthful. Here and there, wherever he points she spits on the wall and follows up with more very low chanting.

Ginger continues going to each spot that Jacob points out to her, repeating the same chanting and spitting, and soon the shadow is gone. He gave Ginger the okay signal with his thumb and forefinger making a circle. Ginger smiles and plops across the bed.

Chewy is hollering on the phone for Jacob to say something.

"Hey, did Jacob The Jew run outta words, or what? You still there? Talk to me, my man. What're you doin', tryin' to remember some of the magic outta your Jewish book?"

Jub Jub Tai interjected over the phone:

"Yo there, magic man. Ginger ain't tol' you yet, huh? That American Jew Voodoo magic shit don't work over here! Even I know that some magic can't cross big waters."

Jacob heard Chewy muffle the phone and he is sure that he is chastising Jub Jub about what he said.

"Sorry, Chewy. I kinda fell asleep. This is too early for me to talk to my people to get you a price for just the samples."

Chewy's voice turned a bit sour:

"Yo, you ain't listenin', my man. Forget the price. We got what we got an' if that ain't enough then take your shit back where it came from. I don't need you to get me no price—get me the fuckin' merchandise! It don't matter what you chargin', we only got what we got. It is what it is. If it ain't enough along with our barter then the deal is off, that's all, with no hard feelings."

The shadow returned, but this time it quickly flitted and darted along the wall and, hugging it, ran along the wall into the bathroom. Ginger is still hugging him and gesturing for Jacob to hang up the phone. He continued listening to Chewy:

"Yeah, so I'll get back to you tomorrow. Stay close to the phone." Chewy hung up.

Immediately Jacob hangs up the phone and turns to Ginger.

"Ginger, this time the *shadow deschong* has something like eyes, but they are like orange slits! Not only that, but it looked as though she is trying her very best to climb off the wall. She went away after your chants chased her, but then she just came back and went into the bathroom."

Ginger looks in the bathroom.

"I think she developed a hatred for you for some reason and wants to harm you. And from what you are describing to me, she may be getting stronger and trying to enter our world by pulling herself off the walls to attack you. But that does not make sense. Baofung wants it to attack you, so why is it trying to free itself instead of waiting until Baofung lets her form fully. Then she will be able to leave the wall at will and go back to being a shadow at will. Ginger shrugged and asked, "What did Chewy say to you?"

"He says the deal is still on, that he'll call me tomorrow. He says your sister is concerned about you." But Ginger is still looking at the blank wall.

Ginger holds his face between her hands.

"My sister has heard from me and she knows I am well. She is only pretending with them. Do not worry." She examined the blank walls again, slipping her arm around Jacob. "I believe I can defeat the magic Baofung is using against you so far, but it will be a most lamentable procedure with the infant. But we will have no choice soon; it is clear now that he has… what is that phrase Americans say? 'He has fired the first shot.' Soon we will return his fire, but it will be almost impossible without the Guman Thong. But, even after we acquire the infant, I must wait until the Guman Thong reveals itself to me for permission to use it."

"Okay." He held her close. "We'll see."

He held her close, hoping that she would calm down and go back to sleep. He knew, however, that sleep is not something that he will be doing for the rest of this morning. It is impossible to get the image of the eerie vision of the *shadow deschong* out of his mind. It's partial face and incomplete set of orange eyes and how they manage to lock themselves on him is unsettling. The thing most disconcerting to him is the fact that the *shadow deschong* is…

...now off the wall and standing in the center of the bathroom doorway.

CHAPTER 30

INSPECTOR OWEN CHANG'S ARMY

Commander Zhengzhong Zixin, the police chief in charge of Owen Chang's Special Police Operations Task Force, is a very tall, wiry man about forty with piercing dark brown eyes and broad shoulders, and like Chang he has a crew cut hairstyle. His face is thin to the point of being gaunt. His hand gave a grip that is rock hard and unyielding, not overshadowed by his voice, thick and deep like distant, rolling thunder, commanding attention when he spoke which is always with authority.

It is late evening and Jacob is in Inspector Owen Chang's office and has just been introduced to Commander Zixin and General Xien Syongruis by Chang. The men, except for Chang, are tense and on the edge because Chang has never called them in for an immediate last minute impromptu meeting.

Police Headquarters is being manned by its usual exterior late hour skeleton staff; but the far rear of the main building, where Inspector Chang's office is located is not patrolled and the only officer is on duty outside at the building's entrance. While it is the main structure on the compound, it is strictly used by police executive staff overseeing a few of the special training classes that are given to police officers who will be doing special political assignments to do with political figures, assignment; they are working in a covert department that does not exist.

"To begin with, gentlemen, Detective Liao and Mrs. Che, both of whom work for this department and are implicitly trusted by me are out of this loop; this at the request of lieutenant Jennings here who suspects there may be a leak somewhere in this building; and so, if not specifically needed for this operation, the fewer involved the better."

General Syongrui agrees:

"I think that's a good idea. The fewer the better. Actually in fact, neither of the ladies will be needed on this raid and so there is no practical reason for them to be included in the planning of such an important move."

Owen Chang nods:

"Now, as for our operation, once we get the sample of army weaponry to the gang, we follow them by means of a tracking device planted in several of the weapons and the trucks to the location they are delivering them." Chang looks at Jacob. "Jennings, if they discover that the weapons don't fire, your reply is going to be that your people are willing to show the weapons as proof that they can produce them. But they want to be met halfway which means show us what you are going to barter with because it is too difficult and very dangerous getting the amount of weapons they want. You'll tell them that they want the very latest in army weaponry and even getting these samples is almost impossible; they will have to show you their barter product."

Jacob is in agreement:

"Yes sir."

"But that conversation is only you are playing for time because we will be right behind him ready to break in, arrest everybody and get the drug. This way, in case the raid fails to turn up the *cherry berry*, it will, at the very least, catch the doctor with reported stolen army weaponry on his property. I'll say that a paid informer sold me the information on this weapons deal; and after weeks of surveillance, I found the information to have merit. So, along with General Syongruis and his soldiers and our special operations officers with Commander Zixin here we raided the location for the weapons. We had no idea that the illegal drug, *cherry berry* would also be on the property."

General Syongruis nods after thinking over what Chang has just said:

"We certainly will have him on the weapons bust if nothing else. But let's hope we find the *cherry berry* too because this raid is really big and it's going to bring out all the heavy political machinery that Cheung has both here and abroad. But, at any rate, I have the weaponry you've requested of me so everything is a go." He shook hands with Chang.

Commander. Zixin is on board:

"This sounds as though we're going to be making history. Fantastic sir." He said to Chang.

Inspector Chang poured a small glass of whisky for everyone at the table and they all toasted to success on this very ambitious mission.

"Oh, by the way, Jennings. When we say no one is to know, remember to include that young lady, Ginger, on our list, won't you?"

That stung Jacob because he has not considered keeping this from Ginger. He trusted her completely; but then too, he has to admit, no more than Chang trusts Mrs. Che and Detective Liao.

"Jennings? Did you hear me?" Chang is waiting for a confirmation from Jacob.

Jacob snaps out of his reflections:

"Oh, yes, sir. There is no doubt that she is on that list."

Chang gave Jacob a flash of a smile, as though he has read his thoughts. He claps his hands together and stands:

"Now if there's no other business, let's end this and remember our next conference is tomorrow at this hour."

The rest of the meeting is pretty much going over the last meeting's details about how the trucks holding the weapons would all be equipped with devices that emit signals that Chang will be able to follow. Details are gone over again and again to assure that absolutely nothing is being overlooked. The meeting, as usual, lasts until the late hours of the next morning. Now, allow me to lead you out of the building."

As they are all walking down the hall, Jacob begins experiencing the actual physicality of someone or something walking alongside him and pressing against him from the back. Then he has the sensation of there being someone on either side of him, even though he is at the rear with no one near him. Then the invisible entities on either side begin elbowing and fidgeting against him in an attempt to try and gain more space for themselves, something one might experience in a crowded elevator of rude riders. This strangeness ceased the moment they all stepped outdoors.

Later that evening, when Jacob arrived at his hotel room, Ginger is waiting up for him and eager to hear about the meeting. But Jacob is quiet. Ginger is smiling at him demurely, and he knew she is on tenterhooks eagerly awaiting to hear what he has to say.

Instead he made small talk, slipped out of his clothing and into the shower. When he came back into the bedroom, Ginger has a peculiar expression on her face that let him know that she knew he was holding back something from her that was important; but nothing he felt he could trust he with, perhaps; that he was avoiding speaking about what happened at the meeting with Chang. He returned her smile but there is nothing he can report to her. He slipped out of his clothes and sat on the bed remarking:

"Man, I am so tired. I really need sleep badly. And my head is really killing me."

He saw that she is still going to wait. It seemed clear to him that she wanted to know something, but she refused to ask him. She is just going to wait. Ah, but he recognized the old Japanese torture trick, Chinese version.

He wanted to reach for a cigarette, but that would have been so Humphrey Bogart-ish and far too cavalier for this moment. Besides that, he did not smoke. He attempted to conjure up another smile for her, but it is too late, she knew better and before his grin reached fruition she slid her slender fingers up his bare leg and squeezed his thigh.

Geneva Convention violation. She drew closer and blew her hot breath against his mouth while squeezing his inner thigh. Her tongue slid across and over his mouth, wetting it. The better to commence interrogation. Name, rank, and serial number only. She pulled her face back from his and smiled.

"You okay, baby? Man, that must have been some meeting. What happened?"

"I'm okay. Nothing happened, not really." He lied.

She knows he is holding something back. She leaned over and pressed her face against his groin, taking him into her mouth. His body exploded with electrical ecstasy ripping back and forth from the tips of his toes to what felt like a cartoon character's exploding eyeballs and back again.

His body convulsed and he gripped the edge of the small kitchen table, knowing he is about to break to give in and tell her of the secret raid coming up. *Aw, hell. Here's the secrets baby. Hey, General, gimme your damn briefcase. Here's some more secrets darling just in case you run outta secrets. If you need me to I'll even get them notarized for you. Just, whatever you do, don't stop this unbearable Chinese torture.*

But she did. Ginger's mouth ceased sliding up and down over him there and instead, her lips released him and she sat up looking at him with a small coquettish pout. She turned from him, deepening her pout. She sucked her teeth loudly.

"Okay. If you say so. Whatever." Her voice sounded as though she may have been about to cry.

Jacob touches her but when she turns to him he is met with a sweet, young face turned to solid stone. She lays her head on the side of his neck and sobbed:

"You don't love me. I tell Jacob The Jew everything, but you pick and choose. How can you love me like that? Anyway, maybe I already know."

"What?"

"What I already know is that your love for me is just inches," she made a very small measurement with two fingers, "but my love for you can bend numbers, make them explode." She began weeping piteously. "And I don't even know why I love you like this when you think I am just a play toy." She curls up on the bed.

He put his arms around Ginger and holds her. Short tremors ripple across her soft flesh. He kissed her shoulders and tries to wipe away her tears, but there are too many of them, and so he presses the side of his face against hers.

She gently moved him away.

"I tell you everything I know, but you don't trust me to speak. Why? I know you told me about your meeting with the police inspector. I know the police going to arrest some gang people probably. How come you scared to let me know what I already know?" She sits up on the bed and crosses her arms defiantly.

Jacob gets up and began pacing the room for a few minutes then he sits next to her, takes a deep breath and let it out slowly. All the while they looked into each other's eyes and her crying diminishes to a sniffle. She stares at him and shrugs.

"I guess I will sit by my altar and pray that one day you will be all the way truthful to me. And that I will live to see that day."

He just could not handle her being unhappy. He loved her too much.

"Chang is making plans to pull a raid when I deliver the guns to *The Chinese Blood*."

She grabbed his arm.

"You must not shoot my sister. You must not nine millimeter Delilah!" She pointed her finger at him. You hurt my sister an' we don't get married." She sat up on the bed and folded her arms. "You hurt my sister and maybe I *Guman Thong* you."

He has no answer for that.

She grabbed his arm. "Jacob The Jew must promise me that you will not shoot my sister! Tell me!"

"Of course I won't shoot your sister, Ginger. There really should not be any shooting at all. I am not going to shoot anybody."

She waves her finger.

"Oh, yes, there will be shooting, maybe much shooting. *The Chinese Blood* will fight. They have no fear of police or anybody else." She thinks about it for a minute. "Are you going to shoot Chewy?"

"Ginger, I'm not going to shoot anyone."

"Or maybe shoot Dr. Cheung?"

"No."

"Baofung?"

He hesitated before answering.

"Ginger, will your magic kill Baofung?"

She shrugged.

"Maybe yes. Maybe no. But your nine-millimeter will."

"Yeah."

"Anyway I will pray you are safe. I have not had time to teach you enough Asian magic to keep you alive maybe."

They both looked at the tiny altar Ginger has built in a corner of the room with the small doll and items of food, a candy bar, milk, cookies, and an apple.

Jacob finds the altar fascinating and at the same time kind of eerie. From the long talks he and Ginger have shared about magic, he has come to know that there is a lot more to Chinese magic than he would ever have believed. He knew it would be wonderful to add it to his repertoire of magic. He promised to teach Ginger some Western magic; together the two of them will represent great firepower in new and old world magic.

"Jacob The Jew, do you really love me? We are really to be married?"

"Yes, I do, and yes, we're going to be married. Ginger." He held her face between his hands. "I truly love you."

"Yes?"

"There is something I have been wanting to tell you."

The shadow came off the wall last night and it was standing in the bathroom doorway watching me, or us."

She stared at Jacob for a long time then slowly nodded. She went to her altar and lit a candle and motions for him to sit next to her on the floor.

"But how could that happen?" She looked around the hotel room. "Why would she want to separate herself from the wall before her time to do so?" Ginger is staring at Jacob. "Unless she..."

He feels a chill at her unsaid words.

"Ginger, what is it?

She holds his hand.

"At first I thought the shadow wanted to harm you, but she is off the wall and is not fully formed. She has turned renegade. But to what purpose? The *shadow deschong* is sent here to harm you but I think she has developed feelings for you. She wants to take you back with her."

"What?"

"Yes. But, I think this one could also be thinking of hiding with you from Baofung and living as a human. I don't really know which, but I am sure that she has forced herself from the wall and shadows to pursue you."

"But, Ginger, how could you possibly know that? How could you know such a thing."

"You said she is standing in the bathroom doorway watching you or us. She would never have any interest in me unless to harm me; the same as she should have in you. But, she is watching you the way a bashful admirer coyly watches the person she hopes to one day have. She is a woman made from a woman only. Love is love even for the life form being what it is."

Ginger rushed over to her altar and lit thirteen candles, murmuring a prayer as she set each candle aflame. She looked up at Jacob, saying:

"No, this must not happen. It is time that I teach you some of the ways of deep Chinese magic. And we must begin right away. First I want to teach you to repel her. And then I must go to the mountains of my village to seek my Shaman."

Jacob is confused"

"Your Shaman?"

"Yes. I have to get permission from him to perform the Guman Thong. Otherwise it is a most unwise sacrilege."

"But Ginger I thought you were already trying to do it before when you said we have to go to a graveyard and get a baby. You didn't have to ask permission for doing that?"

"No. I wanted to see where a baby is available. That way, when I perform the ritual, we will not have to go searching." She is busying herself at her small altar with her mind is ambivalent and wandering between the right prayer that goes with the *protective* spell she is creating for Jacob and vacillating to…

…whatever it is that Jacob has not told her about the meeting.

CHAPTER 31

FIRST COME,
FIRST UNDONE

Inspector Chang has called a second midnight meeting and Jacob arrived an hour early, at eleven and as usual he parked outside the compound and walks in. The area has the usual personnel: two jeeps with four armed police officers are patrolling the grounds and the perimeter with the officers on duty at the electrified gate entrance to the main building on the rear grounds.

Strangely, Jacob did not recognize any of the officers on duty, though he is sure that at least a couple of faces should be familiar to him; but they are not. And his Moor's head pendant is vibrating strongly.

Walking to the headquarters building, he sees there are lights inside some of the buildings being manned by the usual skeleton personnel some of whom are officers bringing in criminal perpetrators while others attended to clerical duties.

The officer on duty at the door to headquarters is also not one he has seen before. What strikes Jacob as peculiar is the officer's uniform; it is unkempt, almost looks soiled; a stark contrast to the usual appearance of the officers' uniform which are always perfect neat, smooth to the point of seeming to have been painted on them. The officers he walked past are wearing uniforms that look as though they may have slept in them.

Finally the officer at the door returns Jacob's identification card and steps aside. Jacob took a took a deep breath, inserts his card and after the lock clicked, he walks through the door and into the building.

Inside, the glass enclosed offices are, of course empty since this building is never used other than the hours of seven am until seven pm. But there is a different feeling this night and he is acutely aware of his Moor's head pendant warning him of evil thereabouts. For some obscure reason, the office areas feel...occupied.

He warily makes his way along the narrow hall through the twisting corridors and their swinging doors listening for sounds though he has absolutely no idea what sounds he could expect. But a familiar sound freezes him in place compelling him to listen closely to a hollow reverberating sniffling; a lamentable weeping of a young child that he senses is lost in a darkness but somewhere infinitely farther than the darkness of the halls.

He waited to hear the sound again so that he could determine where the crying is coming from but it seems to be sounding from every direction at the same time; the weeping even seems to be dripping from the high ceiling in the hallway.

And then there comes abrupt silence. After a few minutes of no further sound, Jacob walks slowly on with trepidation but he is suddenly inexplicably filled with a deep sensation of the deepest throbbing of melancholy.

He thought of what Ginger said to him after teaching him his first lesson in sorcery but now her voice was that of a child reverberating through the halls but in an eerie kind of whisper that is warning him:

"Jacob the Jew...my magic may open your mind; you may see things, spirits, especially the melancholy dead...I think Baofung wants to kill you. He may even send spirits and ghosts to replace t hose around you; they will look the same but they will not look the same."

A grinning, ashen face peeks at him from around the edge of the corridor several feet down the hall. Jacob whispers a phrase Ginger taught him:

"...Derumb sennobils santur alvoirme."

A look of shock registers on the features of the ashen face and the disembodied head falls to the floor, tumbling a few feet and coming to rest looking up at him with a sadistic grin.

Then there is disquieting silence. But as quickly as it had begun, it changed in some way that he did not understand. He waited several minutes listening for any sound before allowing himself to take a deep breath of relief.

Using the key Chief Inspector Chang gave him, Jacob opens the office and enters. Turning on the light, he glances around and, satisfied that he is alone, he makes tea and sits at the table sipping it and although he feels a slight chill in the air, he leans back in his chair and finds something resembling sleep until …

Chang and Zixin's chuckling voices woke him and Jacob sat up in his chair and collected himself. Zixin smiled at him but Chang is wondering:

"Jennings you obviously got here early, but what are you doing sleeping? Are you okay?"

Jacob looked around.

"Yes, I'm fine. I'm okay." He looks around the office again.

But Chang is not at all convinced that Jacob is okay and he knows that something has happened but he cannot imagine what.

"Listen Jennings…just what happened with you here tonight? You look…I dunno, shaken up or something. You sure you're okay?"

"Listen, sir, you're both going to think I've lost it but…earlier out there in the hall I had a very unusual experience and I guess it kind of unnerved me. I was accosted by some people."

Chang and Zixin looked concerned. Chang put down his cup of tea and glance through his open office door. He went to the door and glanced around outside before carefully closing it and returning to the table.

"What kind of people, Jennings? How could anybody possibly get into headquarters?"

Jacob reached for the teapot but. Zixin grabbed it first and filled Jacob's cup. He also is a bit anxious to hear what Jacob has to say about being his confrontation in the hall. He is concerned:

"Are you okay? You weren't hurt?"

Jacob shook his head and took the cup of tea from Zixin:

"No, I'm okay. But it is a really unusual kind of thing. Outside in the hall, I...well there are..." He is reticent to continue. But it appears that Chand knew what may have happened and he finished he sentence for Jacob:

"Dead people? Ghosts? You have visions of the dead?"

He is surprised that Chang knows what happened and it greatly relieved him. He relaxed and told the story:

"Yes, and I'm sure it has to do with the magazine article that Mrs. Che gave me to read during our car ride."

Chang lit a cigar.

"Maybe not, Jennings." He looked at Zixin and shrugged. "I don't usually find an opportunity or the occasion to talk about the dead but... well yours is not the first time someone has bad experiences with the souls of the dead that apparently are still on the premises. My superiors have urged me to discourage talk about some of the things our people here at headquarters have seen, but... anyway it's been some time since any incidents here."

"Ginger told me that Baofung might send things to harm me including something that's called a *shadow deschong*. But she's using her magic against him to protect me." But he is curious about what other people have seen in the building. "Sir, what have other people seen here?"

Chang took a long sip of tea and leaned back in his chair:

"Well these buildings were not always Police Headquarters building. By that I mean we did not construct these buildings, they were built hundreds of years ago during the medieval times and is called Du Lam. It used to be a scary place called, Du Lam. A prison, of sorts. During that period, acts of cruelty abound. Some prisoners of warlord Ju-Guang Lee were chained to the wall and benches, and some, for amusement, were allowed to run about looking for a means of escape or stealing a crumb of food; when Lee or one of his soldiers tired of raping or beating a prisoner, he killed him or her."

Jacob nods his head:

"Yes, I read some things about these buildings but I never knew that."

Chan went on:

"It is written that the caveat is that the dead prisoner is to be drained of blood that is to be given to Ju-Guang Lee to drink; this blood allegedly keeps him alive, strong and one of the rulers in the underworld once he dies. In life he is truly a great Samurai and greatly feared. It's written that he is all of seven feet tall and always gayly attired in the most beautiful combat gear to be made. I think the reason you are 'visited' is due to Ginger using sorcery against Baofung. Do you know what kind of magic Ginger is using?"

"I don't know what kind only that it's sorcery."

"She might be using the 'Left-Handed Path' one of the things that, as a child being taught by a shaman, she may have been shown that magic but not taught how to use it; the 'Left Handed Path' magic is said to be very evil and I think it carries the possibility to turn back against its user, too. But it is believed to be a very angry and a very dangerous magic."

Jacob could not understand how Chang knew about Ginger and magic.

"You know about her studying with a shaman as a child?"

"My office has *The Chinese Blood* on our map for some time now. Detective Liao and Mrs. Che are a formidable team in researching gangs as a unit and individually. They found that Ginger is chosen to be taught sorcery and magic by a Shaman much more powerful than even Baofung is reputed to be. We are not able to find out specifically which magic she has been taught, but we know that one form of sorcery is 'Work of The Left Hand', a most insidious form of magic."

Jacob is stunned by what he is hearing. He does not know what to say.

"I see."

Chung continues:

"Ginger and her sister are at the forefront of the gang so we chose to delve into her background in detail. But we have similar information on Chewy, Jub Jub Tai and several other members of the gang whom we believe are using black magic or studying it and they are also prominent gang members."

"Yes sir. As I told you earlier, I've seen their violent side and they don't need black magic, believe me."

"Now, Ginger obviously loves you and believes you love her otherwise she would never use sorcery to protect you, not against a sorcerer as powerful as Baofung is reputed to be. I recommend that you might want to do some research on Chinese sorcery to give you a general idea as to what you're possibly going to be dealing with. It can be very interesting."

"Yes sir. I believe I will do that."|

"For instance, did you know that in eighteenth-century China sorcerers are roaming the land cutting off men's 'queues,' braids worn by royal decree. Actually, after the Manchu's conquest of China, the Manchu hairstyle became mandatory. A man caught wearing the queue hairstyle would be executed, the penalty for treason; it is considered to be treason if a man wore a queue hairstyle. It is thought that by doing so, the sorcerers are stealing the men's souls. That is what Chop Chop Chewy believes he is doing when he carves his initials in the flesh of others."

"Is that a fact?"

"I say that only to illustrate that the Chinese are a proud and brave race. But we are also lovers of adventure. And I am hoping Ginger succeeds in defeating Baofung because with him gone, it may be the end of the *cherry berry;* as well the same with Cheung out of the way."

Chang handed him a "baby" nine-millimeter side arm identical to the one he has given Mrs. Che.

"Bury this deep somewhere on your person. I feel the time is close and sometimes things don't go as planned and if we don't reach you in a timely fashion, I don't want you facing Cheung and his group with empty hand, wishing."

Jacob took the weapon and smiled. He also is not fond of simply...

....Wishing.

CHAPTER 32

I DON'T THINK SO

Sunday. Jacob is moving his car to the shady side of the hotel's parking lot so its interior will not be so piping hot if he has to use the car in the daytime. Ordinarily he would just let the top down of the convertible but in case of rain he knew he should leave it up. Glancing around the area and wiping away sudden sweat from the stunning heat, he hopes that Chewy does not call him for the shipment of guns any time soon, not during this heat. The temperature this day is too hot to bear and he briskly returns to the cool of the hotel lobby and stands in the for a long moment indulging himself in it.

His encounter with the spirits and ghosts at Police Headquarters comes to his mind as he enters his hotel room just as the hotel phone next to a gently snoring Ginger begins ringing. He stopped for a moment to smile at her then picks up the phone. It stops ringing before he could answer it. He stood there waiting for it to resume ringing but since it did not, he undressed and stretched out on the bed next to Ginger; she stirred and slipped her arm around his neck and nestled her head there and quickly returned to her snoring.

He bends down and kisses her on the forehead, awakening a sullen Ginger who makes no effort to acknowledge him. She just lay staring vacuously at the side of his neck. Then with an ever so slight crane of her head she fixes her gaze on a large black fly moving busily about on the black beige ceiling above the bed.

The buzzing fly takes no notice of the huge spider stealthily approaching it. When the spider is within half an inch or so from the fly doing its hectic search—it grabbed the flitting insect and within seconds wound a silken coffin around it suspending it from the ceiling by a short web; then it scurries away.

Jacob startled Ginger when he touched the side of her cheek.

"Morning Ginger."

She tries to smile at him but she has not been herself for some time now, spending almost every waking hour at her altar or looking in the mirror. Often he found her asleep at her altar presumably after having prayed most of the night or morning. She snuggled closer to him and closed her eyes, but not to sleep, just for the warmth of comfort she always felt when close to him.

He gently stroked her cheek while taking a note that nothing about her features has really improved; the most peculiar thing is happening to her and they both knew it is the work of Baofung: Ginger is aging, more and more each day and her energy level is at almost zero; she dragged about the hotel room sometimes almost as though drugged. It has been three days since her last meal. She worked hard at her spell removal prayers but none of them worked and yet she relentlessly prayed. But she is getting weaker, he thought.

He noticed she has lost weight, but she has always been slender, so it is difficult to tell how much. He wanted to speak to her about his concerns but he knows of no way to broach such a precarious subject as weight with any female, let alone one he loved.

He worries that she has spent an inordinate number of hours chanting special prayers that he assumed are against Baofung's magic with no results and he wanted to try his spells; one in particular is an "aging spell" likely similar to the one Baofung is using against her but he thought to do it in reverse as he has been taught. There seemed to be not many alternatives since Ginger has earlier gone to the mountains in Hong Kong for permission from her shaman to use the Guman Thong to defeat Baofung. Unfortunately he refused her permission.

The phone rang again. He untangled himself from her and lazily got up and answered it.

"Hello?"

"Yo, Jacob The Jew! What's up my man?"

"Chewy."

"Yeah, it's me, Chop Chop, waitin' on them bang bangs. What's up with that? We doin' somethin' here or what?"

"I've been waiting to hear from you."

"Okay, so listen. I'm gonna give you an address. Ginger knows where it is an' how to get there. I need you to get me that package right now. It takes two hours to get there."

"Right now? Listen, I've got to get hold of my people first and see if the weapons are packed. And is this place safe? No police around?" Jacob heard some really low snickering on Chewy's end, then a very long pause.

"What was that you asked me?"

"This two-hour-trip place. Is it cool?"

"It's one of our warehouses." Chewy snorted a short laugh. "Why, you worried? Is Jacob The Jew scared of the police? I don't think Jacob The Jew is scared of the police." Chewy is laughing, but not his usual, insane kind of laugh. This laugh is far more controlled and sinister sounding.

"Just being careful, Chewy, that's all."

"Yeah, whatever. The place is 17 DinSulo Shantung. I'll call you in a couple of hours and tell you what time we'll be there and what time you should leave. 17 DinSulo Shantung. Got it? I'm out." Chewy hung up.

Jacob came over to the bed and lay down next to Ginger. She looked at the address that he has written down .He slid the phone onto the base and thought about it for a moment.

Ginger was half awake when the phone rang but when she hears Jacob repeat the address to himself she woke fully and warned him:

"They fixin' you a trap! That's a trap." She climbed out of bed and grabbed the paper he has just written the address on and read it, warning him again: "No! You go here then for sure you'll die!" She threw the slip of paper to the floor. Her grasp on grammar sometimes slipped when Ginger is really angry. "I'm not going there!"

"Why?"

"I jus' told you—it's a trap! If I go with you, then I die, too!" She slapped her hands together. "I don't wanna die! I ain't no hero! If Jacob The Jew wanna be a hero—then you go!" She turned her back to him and began crying. "Baofung is already killin' me."

"So, you're saying this address is a phony?"

She pointed to the paper on the floor.

"The way to that address is top of a mountain. High mountain. Small road. An' near the top of the mountain it turns to a one-way road that is not wide for maybe a few hundred yards straight. I know how they think. They gonna hide and shoot you there on the road. Then they take the guns. When they attack, you can't back up. One way only." She approximated with her slender fingers. "No room to turn around and run. It's a death road. You drive forward fast on this road and you're gonna be a dead man. Too narrow. Everybody walks on this road. No cars, maybe one or two every few months but even then sometimes they go over the side. Dead men. But you're gonna be a dead man alone. I'm staying here."

Jacob has to think about this. If he tries to call this off they would only come up with a more ingenious way of killing him for the guns if that truly is their intent. Ginger begins to move anxiously about the hotel room, holding her arms close to her chest. She scrutinized the setting on the thermostat, twisted its dial, and looked at him.

"You're not cold?"

"No, kinda warm, really. Are you cold?" He went to her and rubbed her arm. "Yeah, you do feel kind of cool. You got a fever?"

"No." She moved away.

He thought he understood something of her anxiety, what with the sorcery and the disquiet that he assumed accompanied it. But it is true that she is visibly aging.

Ginger hugged him.

"What is it baby?"

"I'm dying. Baofung is attacking me. She walked over to a mirror on the dresser and stared at herself. "Look at me." She turned to look at him and shook her head slowly. Her smile is sad. "Jacob The Jew sees…but he won't speak. I have only a single defense left to use. But, it is so horrible."

Jacob has a terrible premonition that she is contemplating something that is going to draw him deeper into this quagmire of painful complications resulting from the mystic war between her and Baofung. But she is doing this magic for him so how could he not support her? He wanted to do something to protect her, but what could he do?

"Jacob The Jew…I am only nineteen, but my face seeks to be my mother's. Can you not see that I am withering more every day?" Ginger clenched her fist and screamed at him, "Why are you so blind? Look at me! Baofung knows I am defending you, and he is taking my youth. My life!" She walked to her altar and fell to her knees in prayer.

Jacob carefully approached her, not wanting to interrupt her prayers. He knelt next to her and gently pulled her to him. She felt so fragile now, thinner than before, almost wafer-like. It occurred to Jacob that she might have underestimated Baofung's power. He wanted to use his magic or combine his magic with some of the Chinese magic Ginger has been teaching him but he has no clue as to how to do that and he did not want to stress her out any more due to the state of her condition. Besides that, she pretty much told him that western is magic almost powerless against Asian magic.

Ginger twists in his arms and looks up at him.

"Baofung's magic is going to kill me. I am growing old."

"We'll beat him, Ginger. There has to be a way, but you've got to come up with it because I don't know of any way of dealing with Asian sorcerers and by the time I figure out a way, he can damage you even more. How do we get to him? There has to be a way to physically stop him."

She shook her head.

"Only the *Guman Thong* can stop him. But my shaman forbids it."

"Ginger, at our last meeting Inspector Chang said something and I'm thinking that maybe since Baofung is attacking you, then why don't you attack Dr. Cheung? Maybe that will stop him. Maybe not kill him but make him just… I don't know, just maybe go away."

Ginger sucked her teeth and shook her head.

"I do not do. 'wandering' magic." She dismissed the idea.

Jacob thought about the myriad of problems he is entangled in, the most convoluted of which is their love, which is threatening to cause her demise. He kissed Ginger. He has to protect her. He shuddered thinking that maybe he is all too capable of doing something desperate, something illegal if it meant saving her.

He cradled her in his arms, gently rubbing his fingers over the soft flesh of her sallow cheek. He waited several minutes longer then he stretches her out on the bed and covers her with a sheet. He could not put it off any longer, he has to notify Inspector Chang about the location for delivery, but he also has to tell him of the danger Ginger has warned him about.

If the road actually is as narrow as Ginger said, then Chang is going to have to make plans to thwart any hijacking or assassination attempts on that road. Chang's backup would have to be by air, a couple of helicopters maybe. He smiled. The image pleased him. He reached for his cell phone and … wait a minute. He looked at Ginger who has fallen asleep.

Did she say nineteen?

CHAPTER 33

CORPO SECO

Chang told Jacob that it is going to be impossible to get the weaponry together that fast, that more time is needed and that he is going to have to tell Chewy that. Hours passed and Chewy never contacted Jacob and Ginger again and so they waited until...

The hotel phone rang causing both of them to start.

Jacob snatched up the phone.

"Hello!"

"Yo, Jacob The Jew sounds upset."

"Chewy? I'm glad you finally called."

"I need you to be ready to pull out in one hour." Chewy's voice is demanding. "One hour."

"Chewy, my people canceled!" But Jacob is speaking to a dial tone. Chewy already hung up. He dropped the phone on the cradle.

"That was Chewy. He wants us to leave in an hour." He held Ginger's hand. "I've gotta call Chang."

Ginger shook her head.

"If you leave with Chewy, I won't be here when you return."

He has the phone at his ear, but he is looking at her.

"Ginger, what're you talking about? Where are you going to be?"

"With my ancestors..." is her wry response.

"With your—"

Chang is on the line.

"Chang here."

"They want us to leave in one hour."

Chang's response is curt, impatient:

"Jennings I've already told you that's impossible! Listen, I'm in a meeting with General Syongrui, and I can't talk now." Chang hung up.

Jacob slipped the cell back into his pocket and slumped forward staring down at his feet on the floor. He jumps when Ginger's cool hand slides up his back.

"Jacob The Jew is anxious." She kisses him, and they remain embraced for a long moment.

He smooths her hair.

"No more talk about you dying, okay?"

She just stared into his eyes and then buried her face against his chest, cooing a light, almost childlike murmur, and she pulled him closer.

The phone rang. He grabbed it.

"Yeah, hello." He turned to look at Ginger, who is watching him. "Who is this?"

"Who else would be calling you clown? I got some bad news. Everybody here canceled on me. I'll get chu a new date. Not to worry." Chewy hung up.

Jacob hung up the phone and let out a deep breath. He plopped down on the bed.

"Chewy canceled."

"Good.

"I have to call the inspector." He dialed Chang but this time remembered to turn the radio to a loud decibel before speaking: "Sir, the meeting has been cancelled."

Chang sounded relieved:

"That is really good!"

"He's going to call me with a new—!"

Again Jacob is talking to a dial tone. Jacob sighed, turned down the radio and hung up.

"What the hell. Everybody's hanging up on me."

There is a tremendous crashing sound in the bathroom. He and Ginger look at each other, unable to imagine what could be the source of such a noise. The bathroom door opened slowly and a young woman is standing there, naked with an almost opaque orange smoke swirling over her body. She is smiling at him with orange lips appearing to be paint over her dark form. Her eyes are also completely orange but deeply sunken, and only a hint of a nose, more space there than anything else.

He cannot believe what he is seeing. The *shadow deschong* hisses at Ginger but turns to Jacob:

"Simple thing. Come." She stood there beckoning to him and grinning widely as takes staggering, halting steps towards him, then, after seeing Ginger come to stand next to him, the *shadow deschong* is now furious and she screams at him: "Come here! Why *shadow deschong* do you not love me as I do you? You stupid thing!"

Ginger also can hardly believe what she is seeing. She knows about the *shadow deschong* but has never seen one until now. She murmurs:

"…Oh, my God. The has come off the wall."

The *shadow deschong* hisses at her but continues to advance on Jacob.

Jacob squeezed his Moor's head, letting its tongue pierce his finger so that he is now able to summon being from the Dark. He raises his hand high and commands:

"Corpo Seco, rise! Be before me here!"

A whooshing noise and a curtain of green flames flashes between the *shadow deschong* and Jacob, separating them. A horrible looking man rises from the flames, his face is half melted away.

Jacob knows the demon he has summoned is **Corpo Seco**, who, in Brazilian lore is a man so evil that even Satan gave back his soul, refusing to keep him.

Ginger recognizes him and warns Jacob that:

"Jacob, do you know who you have called upon? This thing, this Corpo Seco is so vile a creature that neither the earth nor Satan could abide him. The earth would not even rot his flesh or allow him to remain in it and doomed him to walk the earth until Judgment Day much like Ju-Guang Lee; Jacob knew that neither of these spirits could be fully trusted." She backs away, but holds onto Jacob, frowning at the sight of Corpo Seco. She has seen him before and yet she does not remember Corpo Seco is so short; maybe, she estimates to herself. She smiled, appreciating the humor of a monster with Seco's reputation being only five feet in height.

He is short, a bit less than five feet in height, and his naked body appears tubercular, ever so far beyond fragile; it is skeletal and gray and now the entire room smells of the grave.

Seeing Ginger is a delight to him and he turns from starting to deal with the *shadow deschong* to creeping toward Ginger with a lecherous grin. Jacob, seeing intention steps between them. Corpo Seco easily shoves him aside and reaches for Ginger. But Jacob yanked Ginger behind him again and demanded that the creature do as he has been told.

"Return the she creature to the shadows of her wall! I have charged you, Corpo Seco!" He did not obey. But when Jacob spoke that command in Latin, the words froze the demon where he stood: "non revertetur per viventem in obumbratio eius de muro, praeceperam tibi."

Corpo Seco, struggles against it, but he turns on the *shadow deschong* but he struggles to make one more attempt to raise his hand against Jacob who speaks first:

"Flames of purity—rise! Find us among the decadence!"

The floor trembles and quakes terribly as the hotel's lights blink erratically then all is dark. After a moment, a figure appears that is surrounded by a flashing orange flame engulfing his body.

Ginger is still standing at Jacob's side, but she gasps, amazed at his powers. They hold hands and standing side by side they recite their separate prayers against evil.

Jacob sweeps his hands wide and high, thick sheet of white flames erupted from the floor, wiped out the green flames that preceded Corpo Seco, then they surrounded the *shadow deschong* and Corpo Seco, vanquishing them both. Only Ginger and Jacob remain in the room.

For a long time Ginger cannot help but smile at Jacob in admiration of his powers with magic. But is amazed that even Corpo Seco has the ability to resist his summoner at such length. He tells her:

"One of the things my grandmother told me to remember is that demons change residences in the Dark the way humans do on earth. Sometimes they may move to...well, let's say to bad neighborhoods and they change. She taught me never to believe a demon will obey you completely or not decide to turn on you. Maybe my mistake is in calling on one of the worst demons I could summon with Corpo Seco."

Ginger squeezed her arms around him.

"Yes, even I know about Corpo Seco. He has always been the evilest of all things vile." She smiles at him. "I think the things I teach you and maybe the things you teach me, then our magic will be so much more powerful. But there is no doubt that together, we are just wonderful!" She squealed with delight and dragged him to the bathroom. "Come! We shower and then we..." she giggled with such enthusiasm that it caused Jacob to begin giggling.

CHAPTER 34

AD NOCTUM
(INTO NIGHT)

Days later the night has become thick and humid. Although Ginger's shaman has refused her permission to use the dreaded Guman Thong to destroy Baofung, she is going against him and is beginning to assemble the necessary items to fulfill the requirements for performing the ritual for Guman Thong.

Now she and Jacob stand sweating in the shadows of an alley at the rear of a nearly deserted street at the end of which is a home for unwed mothers. The humidity, heat, and smells of what Jacob hoped are rotting foods in the alley are almost causing him to add his stomach contents to the stewing alley garbage.

Ginger points to the rear of a small building that has pots and pans hanging from nails on its side. There are many large pots in the rear yard on the grass, some of them holding an overflow of soiled linen, others with lids on them have secret contents.

"First we will go there, to the rear of that house. It is the one for the unwed mothers. I am hoping their basement window is open. I think they have fetuses in there yet to be buried or perhaps sold or donated to medical people for research. But, whatever, that is where they keep them until they get rid of them and if they are not sold or donated, they are often simply burned, but I do not think they are ever given their own grave; mostly I think they sell them or the doctors take them. Sometimes the mothers have a change of heart and they leave with their babies in their arms."

"Ginger are you sure that you want to go against your own shaman? There must be some kind of punishment for you if you do this, isn't there?"

Ginger's features are blank and she nodded slowly as though thinking over each nod. Her monosyllabic answer sounded eerie and gave Jacob chills:

"…Yes." She muttered, fondling the special sacrificial knife that purloined from her shaman she during her from her visit to him when she went overnight to Hong Kong to ask him for permission to perform the Guman Thong. He advised her to stop attempting to destroy Baofung and instead simply engage him in sorcery combat; he noted to her she is a most competent young maiden sorceress and capable of defending herself.

Jacob looked at the knife Ginger is holding and he commented;

"That knife is really beautiful. Is it gold?"

"Yes, it is. It is the only knife that can be used to sever the umbilical cord for live retrieval or it is used to open the mother and extract the baby; and this is usually done with a buried mother who is still carrying her child. It depends on which is the most opportune for us."

"But how can you do that if the baby is in that basement, meaning it has already been born?"

"I do not want the fetus that is born, but I need to see the records of the mothers who are patients and still carrying their babies or grave numbers of those who are buried with their babies; mothers who very often attempt to give themselves abortions and end up dying here. They will not bury a child alone but will bury the mother and child if she is still with child and dies in such a state."

No matter how much she changed the scenario, Jacob felt badly about this mission but knows that he must do what is necessary to help Ginger defeat Baofung. He wishes the task to help her accomplish this goal was not so gory.

Ginger came out of her crouch and grabbed his hand:

"Come."

They slither through the alley heading in the direction of the unwed mothers' facility, through an alley that reeks of garlic, ginger, old fish, and spoiled meat. Jacob shifts uneasily as a rat scrambled over his feet. This is just insane, he is thinking. Then, like a cat having sighted an oblivious mouse, Ginger let go of him and quickly edged nearer the cellar window. He sank deeper, preferring to remain hidden in the shadows behind her, not wanting to follow her inside. Even taking a deep breath failed to calm him. He is overjoyed to see a woman walk out of the basement, empty a large bowl of liquid onto the grass and return to the basement room. Ginger, exasperated, turned to him.

"We must wait until she leaves." She sucked her teeth loudly. "Damnit."

But something is wrong. Ginger looked at Jacob with a panicked expression. She leaned against him and slowly began sagging but Jacob grabbed her just as she collapsed completely.

"Ginger! What's wrong? What's happening to you?"

She managed to get out the words:

"…Ambulance. Please." She uttered hoarsely and dropped the blade. Jacob picked it up and shoved it in his pant waist.

"How do I get one?" He carried her from the alley to the front of the building and began fumbling for his phone, hollering to the people standing around:

"Ambulance! Doctor! Doctor!"

After a moment, a middle aged woman ran from the unwed mothers' home over to where Jacob is kneeling and holding Ginger. He looked at her with desperation as she bent over to them.

"Are you a doctor, Miss?"

She nodded.

"Yes. Is she American?"

"No, she's Chinese."

The doctor, examining Ginger, shook her head impatiently.

"No! You! American?"

"Yes. I'm American."

"Wife?"

"Wife? No, she's my girlfriend."

The doctor stopped examining Ginger and took a long at Jacob then back to examining Ginger.

"Is she pregnant?"

"No, just sick. She's just sick."

The doctor touched Gingers stomach but immediately drew her hands back as though she has just been burned.

She took Jacob's phone and dialed, taking a moment to say to Jacob:

"There is a demon scratching at her stomach." She presses her mouth to the phone and begins speaking in Chinese but is stopped by Ginger touching Jacob's face, moaning the words:

"...Jacob the Jew is loved by this one." Ginger then lapses into an unconscious state as a crowd gathers around them.

It isn't long before an ambulance arrives and the doctor speaks to the drivers and directs them to take them all to the local clinic. On the way to the clinic, the doctor questions Jacob about his relationship to Ginger. She determines that though Ginger and Jacob are serious lovers he knows next to nothing about her personal history. She says that he is not going to be very much help at the clinic where they will want to know her personal history, especially if she is on any medications. But she says that he will be able to get word about what's wrong with her from either her or the clinic administrator. But that he will have to go home and wait to hear from someone. He is glad the clinic is not far from where he parked his car and not too far from his hotel.

He is assured by the female doctor that accompanied them to the clinic that either she would call him at his hotel or Ginger would call. At the very least, she assured him that it may be a representative of the clinic would give him word on Ginger's condition. But he needed to go home and wait to hear.

After checking Ginger into the clinic, and speaking a bit more with the doctor, he left the clinic after giving his personal information to them. He asked several times if he would be allowed to wait in the emergency area to find out what is wrong, but they showed him how packed it already is and they need the space for those who are seriously ill. After making sure Ginger has been admitted into the clinic, he asked again if he would be allowed to wait in the emergency area to find out what is wrong, but they showed him how packed it already is and they need the space for those who are seriously ill. He could see that he has no choice but to go back to his hotel and wait. So, he checked again to make certain he has left his personal contact information and left for his hotel.

When he reached his hotel he contacted inspector Chang who immediately warned him that: "Under no circumstance should you let Chewy or any member of *The Chinese Blood* know about this; even her sister."

He agreed not to do that even though he hardly needed to be told that. He's glad that he remembered to get the phone number and name of the clinic she has been admitted to and also Ginger's room and phone number. Now he can only wait for the phone to ring, hoping the call will be from Ginger and not Chewy. From this point on, he can only desperately wait for a call from Ginger and not Chewy. He stretched out in a chair at the phone and closed his eyes.

When he again opened his eyes it was ten o'clock in the morning. He groggily got himself together and dialed the clinic for an update on Ginger's condition. But he was told that there are several patients named Ginger and that he would have to know he given name, the first and last given name.

He hung up the phone. He has no way of getting that kind of information unless to contact Delilah, but that was impossible since he has no idea where she is. Now, all he could do is wait.

He is thinking that if he does not hear from either Ginger or the clinic soon he is going to return there and if he to do it, then he planned on searching the wards until he was able to find her.

The phone rang. Jacob snatched the receiver, hoping it is Ginger on the other end.

"Hello?"

"Hey, Jacob, my man, you sound sad. You okay?"

"Yeah, Chewy, I'm okay."

"Something wrong?"

"Looks like something's always wrong lately."

"Well, I got good news, my man. I got us a new location, and that means you ain't gotta go up that tricky mountain trail with that merchandise. How many trucks we got?"

"I don't really know how many trucks there are, Chewy. Is that important? I've got the goods. Isn't that enough?"

"Man, somebody sounds touchy this morning. Okay, I guess I can count 'em myself, 'cause I'm gonna be riding up front in the lead truck with you. You and me are gonna be together again; just like in a song."

There is a long, deafening silence. At this point Jacob did not really care about the guns or Chewy stupid sense of humor and he did not care to continue speaking to Chewy. He is at his wit's end about Ginger, but he knew this is not the time to lose it. Jacob dully asked:

"What's the new address, Chewy and when do we leave?"

"I'll tell you the new address and we leave when we leave. So, just have the merchandise on the ready so there won't be no problem when I call you again and say, let's go." Chewy hung up the phone.

The moment Jacob replaced the phone in its cradle, it rang again and he grabbed the receiver.

"Yeah what is it now?"

Ginger purred over the phone:

"… I miss Jacob The Jew."

"Ginger! Oh, my God! I was so worried! How are you? Are you okay? They made me leave the clinic, since I wasn't related to you and didn't know your last name or other information, but I tried to stay. I tried to stay with you, but they started talking in Mandarin about getting security to escort me out, so I just left. I didn't want to make problems for you in there. How are you?"

"Better, I think. I am not worse. I do not know when I will be released because they do not know what is wrong with me and they are still running tests. But there is a female doctor who is a very pleasant woman. She speaks highly of you. She is burning religious incents in my room. Curious. Anyway, I will need you to take care of that other matter for me and bring it to our room. But you will have to do it alone. I will call you again and tell you what must be done and how you can do it. You have my religious item, I hope."

"Yeah, yeah, it's in the trunk of my car now."

"You are my love, Jacob The Jew."

"And Ginger you are mine."

Jacob is feeling like a schoolboy in love. But that is short-lived when he realized what he has just agreed to do.

Ginger spoke in hushed tones:

"…I believe that they know what is wrong with me, but they will never admit to it. They know it is someone's magic. They have given me medications and vitamin drips and liquids that will refresh my body, but that will only prolong what is going to happen if you do not do what is needed to be done."

"I'm glad you called."

"They do not want patients to use the telephones and they are moving me to maybe a public ward so it will be hard for me to reach you after this call. The female doctor who said she accompanied me to the clinic arranged for me to make this call. She says that I require complete bed rest and no more telephone calls. I must go now. A doctor is here and he's about to enter my room. Everyone here wears masks. Oh, he has a needle and I do not like needles. I will speak to you when I can. Please be ready to do what you need to do."

"I will."

"Oh!"

"Ginger what's wrong?"

"This doctor is—!".

"Ginger what is it? What about your doctor?"

"It's Ba—" The phone clicked off

A dead phone.

Jacob knows that if he goes to the clinic the staff would never allow him anywhere near Ginger. The only thing he can do at this point to help her is to do what she once explained to him. But first, he needed to call Chang to get ready for the latest changes from Chewy about the weapons.

Chang is not thrilled to hear Jacob tell him that there has been yet another change:

"Okay, Jennings, let's hear about this latest change Chewy's made."

"Chewy said his people changed up on him and he'll call and let me know the new time and new place for delivery. And he says he's going to be riding in the first truck with me. By the way, he wonders how many trucks we're going to have."

Chang thought it over.

"So, he not only changed the time, but he also changed the place for the delivery."

"Yes, sir."

Jacob hears Chang puffing on his cigar, a sign that he is thinking about something.

"The gang's playing games and the more I think of it, the more I don't like Chewy riding in the lead truck with you. What the hell is that about?"

"No idea, sir."

Chang's voice registered anger:

"I think we can be sure that they're going to keep changing the time, if not the locations, for delivery, sir. Anyway we are going to have a lot of trucks as we can manage because that means we'll have more officers and soldiers for our raid. We will spread out the weapons in the trucks. Supposedly they'll be riding in the trucks as guards for the army property; standard procedure we'll tell them. It's something the army does in case of attempted hijacking, they will only succeed in getting a small part of the entire shipment unless they're able to hijack every truck. Whatever, we've got the trucks and their payload all waiting here at headquarters."

Jacob understands.

"Makes sense to me, sir. But, sir, is it possible they're stalling for time? Once they give us an address they know that Ginger knows immediately whether there is something wrong or not. I figure now, with her out the mix, they can give us an address and we won't know one way or another what the gang is thinking."

"You may have something there, Jennings. Are you thinking that may be why she's suddenly so sick?"

"Yes, sir, but they don't know that she is out of commission, and they have no way of finding out. So, it doesn't make sense, I guess."

"But it might also mean that they know that we've silenced out link here at headquarters if there is such a link by keeping this raid between just you, Commander Zixin, me and General Syongrui. So we're sealed and they retaliate by maybe sealing their 'leak' which would be Ginger?"

Jacob knew it is all very logical and it all seems to fit perfectly into place; and he does not care for the fact that he has just unwittingly woven a web that ensnared Ginger into a logical position of guilt."

Chang's voice jolted him back to their conversation:

"But that can't be since you certainly did not tell Ginger about the coming raid. Isn't that correct, Jennings?"

Jacob choked up a bit.

"Sir it wouldn't make any difference since Chewy's changed the time and place for delivery so many times. Besides, she's really incommunicado while in the clinic and I can't reach her because they're moving her to a public ward. They surely won't allow me to see her so that puts her out of the picture for now."

Chang is silent for a while on his end.

"Yeah. I guess you're right, Jennings. Okay, Jennings. The general me and the commander will be spending nights here in case you get another call, a legitimate call for immediate tie ups for the weapons."

"That's great, sir."

Another long pause from Chang's end. Jacob hears him blow out a long puff of smoke:

"If you don't hear from them by tonight, we need a meeting at our usual midnight hour. Goodbye Jennings."

Chang hung up without giving Jacob a chance to respond.

CHAPTER 35

THE SHADOW
DESCHONG

Four days gone by. Jacob is racing behind the pulsating engine of a monstrous fire truck, both of them stretching ahead at a terrifying speed, on their way to a distant fire but the huge, wailing, red machine is in his way the motor in Jacob's jaguar roaring at four points over a 100 mph taking on this colossal energy force racing it to a distant fire though he is behind it at the moment on a highway that has only one lane going in one direction and the race has been going on for some indeterminate time but then an Asian fireman on the truck leans in an insane glare at Jacob and slaps him with his hand which is aflame from the burning white megaphone his scorched, blackened hand cannot release and tries to scream away the horrific pain drenching up from beneath his bowels as he presses the megaphone's button emitting a blasting, piercing siren scream noise of such power that it destroys Jacob's entire front car window along with his hearing swelling his heart to the limit of bursting and causing it to beat in a dramatic drum roll seconds from its conclusion and therefore its need to force Jacob to—.

Sit up in bed out of breath, wakened by the horrible sound of the hotel telephone ringing shrilly until he is able to put it out of its misery by Jacob sleepily snatching it off its cradle, jamming his mouth against its mouth and inquiring:

"Yeah—what?"

Whoever has been on the other end is no longer available or desiring to speak with him. He hung up and plopped back on the bed, taking deep breaths to try calm his racing heart.

He got up and sleepily walks to the window and looks out. It is night. His meeting with General Syongrui, Chang and Commander Zixin at Police Headquarters was three and a half days ago. And still no word from Ginger or Chewy.

He desperately wanted to see her, touch her .and hear her voice. The phone rang. He dragged over feeling drugged.

"Yo, Jacob The Jew, what's up, my man?"

"Chewy, listen, you've got to set up a definite time and place. My people are getting antsy with all your last minute changes."

"Is there going to be a problem getting your people to stick with our deal?"

"Well, not so far but there could be if you keep changing delivery times and places."

"I don't understand. I'm guessin' this ain't their first dance. They ought' understand how this shit works on something this huge. Man this is a big order, my man. We ain't nickel and dimin' here."

"No, but wouldn't you get nervous if I kept changing the dates and places for delivery?"

"We need that merchandise, my man. But if my people tell me to change, then I gotta tell you to change. Maybe my people might be watchin' your people. If they see or hear something that makes 'em suspicious, then they're gonna change up on you. You know how that security shit goes, man. If your people show funny or something, then we gotta back away. I mean, this order is heavy shit, my man. It's bad enough we throwin' bricks at the penitentiary as it is, but are you doin' something on your end to make my people worry?"

"No."

Some silence followed at both ends.

"Be ready to make delivery sometime early tomorrow morning. Stay in your room and be ready for my call. When I do call it's a good idea to have your trucks already at your hotel, my man. Tel you people that."

"Chewy if you're going to cancel—"

"Oh, and if you're worried about your girl, Ginger, she's under Dr. Cheung's care at his estate. A weird illness, but he is trying his best. He's gonna be takin' real special care of her while you and me is closin' our deal. She's a lot better now than when he picked her up at the clinic where you and our lady doctor dropped her off."

Jacob's blood chilled at the words: 'our lady doctor.'"

Chewy hung up the phone.

Jacob dropped the receiver on the cradle and dials Chang who scarcely answers before Jacob begins pouring information about the latest date to move the weapons. Jacob explained that:

"I have no idea what 'early' means, but this time he sounds more definite. He wants the trucks at the hotel an hour after he calls and who knows when that'll be? Listen, I'm coming to the office!" Jacob hung up.

Less than half an hour later, Jacob reaches Chang's office. Zixin and Inspector Chang and the general are lying on cots. He shook hands with Commander Zixin and General Syongrui. Chang springs up from his cot, jabbing his finger in Jacob's direction.

"Jennings I hope this one is real! Now you say they want them where, at the hotel?"

"At my hotel, yes sir. He did not demand that but I think, under the circumstances, it's better to have the merchandise ready and waiting."

Jacob nodded and then became morose as he turned away from them.

"They've got Ginger. They've got my girlfriend, Ginger. What're we going to do?"

Chang did not like that word:

"Your girlfriend?"

Chang is surprised that Jacob let that out. He has believed all along that Jacob has been compromised, but since it never seemed to be detrimental to the investigation he never really wanted to go deeply into the issue.

"We're going to have the weapons at your hotel at five in the morning. They're not going to want us there any sooner, I'm sure. If they do, then they'll have to wait." Chang knew he should inquire about Ginger. "Now what's this about Ginger?"

"She was kidnapped from the clinic. I'm sure it was the work of Dr. Cheung."

"Okay, well, I don't think we need to be too concerned about Ginger's safety. What would they gain by harming her now that they have her? I think that if anything they might see her as collateral. If things don't work out the way they want, they can make demands of you by using her. And Jennings, I hate to put it this way, but we are all expendable. Look, I'm sure that as a police officer yourself in civilian life and as a current army military intelligence man, you realize that the mission always comes first and certain risks and losses are inevitable. And you are not supposed to become really involved with her precisely because of this kind of situation. This situation as it exists can place you on the fence."

"Sir my mission without her total involvement would never have been possible in getting me as close to the gang as I am."

Commander Zixin saw the tension beginning to rise in the room, and he quickly made a suggestion:

"Sir, that was good thinking your contacting the General to bring the trucks here. Now, no matter what they ask for, we've got the goods waiting. I'm sure we all agree that things happen during covert assignments that are unforeseeable. Let's all of us just deal with the reality of the moment."

Chang knew he is right but he is staring at Jacob and it is clear that he does not really appreciate Jacob's relationship with Ginger. He shrugged and extended his hand to Jacob "The commander is right, Jennings." They shake hands vigorously and then hug. "I guess I'm just kind out of joint for wanting this guy so badly that I can taste it. You've really done some great work and you have gotten us a lot closer to the gang than we ever would have been able to do otherwise. I want to thank you for that."

"It's okay, sir. I think we're both at our wit's end."

Chang interrupted:

"And for what it's worth, Jennings, I'm sorry about your --about Ginger. Of course we'll do everything possible to insure her safety, but for now I need you at your hotel. And remember, we'll be there with the trucks and I'll be waiting downstairs at your hotel with the merchandise to follow your trail with my men. We have five trucks and every man on those trucks is either a police officer or one of General Syongrui's soldiers. They'll all be wearing Chinese Army uniforms as should be any group of men with army weapons here."

"Good to know, sir."

"They haven't been apprised of the situation here, but we will let them know now since it is about to...what is that American expression? Jump off."

Jacob laughed.

"Yes, sir. It's about to jump off."

Chang walked Jacob back to his car outside the compound, apologizing again during their walk for his rude temperament and things are as usual between them after that.

On his drive back to his hotel, Jacob's head is spinning and once he arrived at his room he welcomed the sight of his bed, though he tossed and turned before he fell into another fitful sleep, a restless dozing that did not last. At first he thought it is something in his strange dreams that is continually troubling him into waking and he realizes it is not dreams but reality in terms of being responsible for too many overwhelming things at the same time; Ginger facing imminent death at the hands of Baofung who now holds her prisoner, weapons being available for the gang to inspect; the safe return of said weapons, having knowingly corrupted the investigation by developing romantic involvement with a suspect; withholding that fact from the person for whom he is working.

But this time what wakes him is a woman screaming and he wearily forces himself to sit up on his bed. As he tries to clear away the cobwebs of his difficult sleep the screams change to a woman's continuous almost sensuous moaning. He looked around his dark room but seeing nothing in the shadows. He turns on the light.

The sight of the *shadow deschong* who is again off the wall is now perched above his head on his bed's headboard locked him in place. Her head is a fluttering wisp of black flames that dissipates then reforms itself into a human head with ashen white nostrils and mouth. Its orange widened as she leans her head forward and screams again, but this time with an intensity that is ear shattering. He clamps his hands over his ears, drops to his knees. But struggling mightily, he gets to his feet and snatches open his room door. When he starts to rush out there are people in the hall.

Several maids are gathered together and standing in the hall staring at his room, all of them terrified by the sounds of the screaming *shadow deschong in* his room. One creeps up to him and hands him a lighted white candle, and another gives him a white crucifix. Then they all rush away making Signs of the Cross and taking furtive glances back at his room as they quickly exited through an emergency stairway door.

Jacob's mind races through different conjures. He surely does not want to chance conjuring Corpo Seco again knowing he could not be completely trusted to do what he is ordered to do without creating complications.

The *shadow deschong* stops screaming and begins moving towards him. Her body is now a silhouette of orange smoke with intermittent white flames flaring, but clearly retaining the form of a shapely woman. As she reaches to within a few feet of him, her tongue flicks out, orange and forked.

He twists his fist against his palm:

"Sic! Sic! Sic!"

Immediately the din of a pack of invisible dogs snarling, snapping their teeth, and barking fill the hall Invisible growling demon canines began attacking the *shadow deschong,* pushing her back, and in less than an instant she folds back onto the hall wall as a shadow.

But then the barking dogs, though still invisible, apparently joined her on the wall, their shadows now clearly seen and they chase the *shadow deschong* fled along at a flashing speed back and forth on the hallway walls until she, the dogs and the sound of their pursuit all disappear.

The hall is plunged into silence and Jacob returns to his room and places the candle and crucifix on the table near the phone and waits, almost expecting the *shadow deschong* to return. After the passing of several moments …

…she does.

Apparently the *shadow deschong* has managed to defeat or somehow evade the hellhounds and now is standing in the middle of his hotel room glaring at him and once again slowly walking his way.

But this time the closer she is to him he feels a building electrical current coming in pulsating throbs in the air. He is startled by the sound of her voice:

"You stupid human! I have separated myself from this wall and my master for you! And you reject me!" Her entire form began wavering and the barking dogs have returned somewhere in the near distance and immediately she is back on the wall. After a warning to him:

"Do not think it is over. It is not over."

…And she is gone.

CHAPTER 36

OKAY,
LET'S DO THIS

2:30 a.m. Again with the hotel phone. Jacob placed his hand on the phone, wondering if it is Ginger or Chang or Chewy. At this point he is so mentally exhausted that it did not really matter who he has to speak with.

With a resigned sigh, he picks up the phone and hearing the voice, once again his heart began racing:

"Yo, Jacob the Jew. It's Chewy." He listened to the insane laugh. "Holler at your boy, fool+-."

"Hello Chewy." Jacob's voice belied the exuberance he felt inside despite himself. "What's up?"

"I see your trucks. Come on down and let's roll, man! Your people sure sent a lotta soldier boys with them trucks. I hope they didn't make a mistake and pack gold in all them cases instead o' bang-bangs."

"It's army. That's how they do things when It comes to this kind of merchandise. They wanna make sure nothing funny takes place."

"Yeah. You ready to roll?"

"I'm ready."

"Well come on down and let's be outta here, my man."

Jacob hung up the phone and someone banged on his door. He opens the door to a grinning Jub Jub Tai.

"Chewy says for me to come up an help you in case you needed to pack up some of Ginger's clothes or somethin." He stops grinning and walks in, brushing Jacob aside and surveying the room. He turns around to Jacob. "Put your shirt on an' let's slide, yo."

Jacob does not have the energy to argue or make any smart remarks in retort so he slipped on dungarees and a light jacket and silk shirt and tennis shoes and is ready to go.

On the elevator, Jub Jub moves close to the female operator and patted her on the behind. The woman flushed and said:

"Please don't do that, sir."

He pressed his mouth against the side of her neck and murmured:

"...How much you speak for 'short-time?' Huh?" His hand is fondling her behind.

The woman is on the verge of tears but the elevator doors slide open sparing her any further humiliation. Walking out behind Jacob, Jub Jub turns back to her:

"Keep that pussy down there warm for me. I'll be back an' I like it when a bitch cries for me." He laughed and sauntered on behind Jacob who is standing and waiting for him.

Outside Chewy gestures for Jacob to climb in behind him in the lead truck. He moves over against the driver to make room for Jacob to sit next to him.

The driver remains stoic, staring ahead waiting for orders from someone to move out. All of Inspector Chang's undercover officers and General Syongrui's soldiers are dressed in army fatigue clothing.

Chewy leans over and nudges the driver.

"Yo, let's go, driver."

The vehicle's motor sounded as though it is struggling to turn over, but finally it does and it is a hoarse roar that launches it in an almost violent jump forward. The driver stomps on the clutch and shoves the gear stick into the next position and the truck moves along a bit more smoothly.

Once the vehicle is moving, the driver yanks on the gear shift and the truck complains but finally allows itself to be forced into the last gear and so moved smoothly onward.

None of the driver's struggling with the gears has escaped Chewy's notice even though he keeps looking in the side-view mirrors at the other army trucks behind them. Jacob thought he might have been studying them, looking for some error, some mistake. After moving along for half an hour, Chewy looks at the driver and grins.

"Yo, man. You look like you ain't used to drivin' this big boy. For a minute there I thought this old monster truck was gonna explode before you located them gears. What's up with that, soldier boy?"

"Sorry, sir." Is the driver's response. I'm a clerk typist not a driver. I'm not a gear driver."

Chewy stares at him for a length of time and then he asks him the same question he has already asked Jacob:

"Five trucks, huh? How come so many trucks an' soldier boys, my man?"

"I don't know, sir. I just follow orders."

"Yeah, yeah, well keep rollin', dude! Follow that order." Chewy turned to Jacob. "Is Jacob The Jew havin' fun yet?"

Jacob did not like the fact that someone as unpredictable as Chewy is in charge. He also did not like the fact that Chewy has told his enforcer Jub Jub Tai to ride shotgun on the last truck; Jacob knows that move is being done to make sure that someone is on the lookout to make sure they are not being followed."

Chewy laughs at the nervous driver:

"Yeah, well, anyway, these trucks ain't no joke. They're the real deal." Chewy seemed to be thinking out loud, calculating something. "Yo, driver, what's the name of this truck? What's it called?"

The driver robotically responded:

"We call it deuce and a quarter, sir."

Chewy grinned at him.

"Yeah, you do." He turned back to Jacob.

"Jacob The Jew. Whassup? How you feelin'? You don't look happy."

"I was thinking about Ginger."

"Oh." Chewy snorted a short laugh and poked the driver in the ribs. "You hear that, driver? He's worried about his little Ginger flower. Ain't that sweet? It's givin' me diabetes." Chewy erupted in raucous laughter, phony, loud, and continuous. During his laughter, he is keeping furtive eyes on the driver and the side view mirrors.

"So what's up, my man? How do you like wearin' that army uniform?" Chewy asked the driver. "It sure don't look so comfy."

The driver continues staring at the road ahead when he answered:

"It's not bad, sir. Got no choice."

After a moment, Chewy appeared to like the answer and laughed even louder than before but ended it abruptly and nudged Jacob hard in the ribs.

"Your boy here gave me a good answer, huh?"

Jacob knew that Chewy is always at the edge of being violent, but he is acting more combative than usual. He wondered if the gang has concluded that he and Ginger have betrayed them to police authorities, because if they have that means he and Ginger are marked for death by them. Chewy slapped the top of the driver's leg really hard.

"Yeah, looks like your driver here is... what's that word you Americans like to use? Oh, yeah. Noncommittal." Chewy pointed ahead.

"Slow down and turn left at that sign and get onto the side road. Then you lookin' for a one-lane dirt road. When you see it—get on it." Chewy's demeanor turned sinister. "You got me?"

"Yes, sir."

The driver turned onto a dirt road. Chewy glances out the window at the other trucks behind them to make sure they are following his lead. The moment all the trucks are traveling on the single-lane dirt road that lead through a dense forest.

Jacob has a very strong feeling of déjà vu. He closes his eyes and revisits the memory of traveling through this forest. Although they took a different route to reach the woods before, Jacob sees now that there is no doubt that it is the same woods they traversed before and that they are probably heading for Cheung's estate again.

Chewy tapped the steering wheel.

"Yo, hold up my man." He jumps out with a pair of field glasses to check the convoy, especially interested, it seems, in the rear truck. Jacob knew this is to check to see if anyone is following even though he has assigned Jub Jub to do that.

Chewy climbs back in and the truck bolts forward and again they are on the move. After several minutes they are deep into the forest blasting down the irregular dirt road, rushing along between its dense, irregular vegetation and deep holes in the dirt path which caused the truck, when it is attempting dodge the deep pits to bump up and down and shifting heavily from side to side, threatening to turn over on its side.

Chewy is laughing:

"Damn. Good thing we ain't carryin' no nitro, huh?" He yanked out a nine millimeter and pressed it against the driver's temple.

"We movin' too slow. How come you driving so slow, my man? Speed it up and speed it up now!"

The driver presses the accelerator and the truck jerks forward at a much faster clip of speed. Far too fast, Jacob is thinking. At this speed the driver is not going to be able to miss some of the holes in the road, not to mention some of the large rocks.

Jacob tries reasoning with Chewy:

"Chewy, we're going too fast. If we hit a really deep hole or one of those big rocks we've been barely missing, then this truck is gonna be a pile of bent metal."

"Shut up an' let this soldier boy drive."

After they traveled deeper into the forest for several minutes, the forest dirt road seemed to begin to smooth out until eventually the dirt road was completely smooth and barren of rocks and irregularities in its structure.

"Alright! There they are!"

Ahead of them on the side of the road is a very large truck with "FISH" printed on its side and a large group of young Asian men, all of them bearing arms, are standing beside it.

"Now what, Chewy? What's with the truck over there?"

Chewy reaches over Jacob and yanks the forty-five pistol from the driver's hip holster and shoves him against the door.

"Get out! Come on, get out!" The driver climbs down from the truck and Chewy pushes Jacob out the passenger side seat door. He climbs out behind him and when all the trucks catch up to them, Jub Jub runs up to the fish truck. He waves his hand at the men next to the fish wagon.

"Let's go! Open up an' lets' rock!"

A second horde of armed young men and women pour from the rear of the large fish vehicle and a third from behind the underbrush all the way down as far as to several yards beyond the last truck in the convoy. Most of them emerge armed with pistols and rifles, a few carry bats. Chewy turns to Jub Jub Tai.

"That's right, Jub Jub, get 'em moving!"

Jub Jub Tai yelled in Cantonese and English for the gang members to take over the trucks and for them to make sure to disarm all the soldiers, including their walkie talkies and have them load all weaponry from five trucks into the Fish truck.

While the transferring of weaponry is going on, Jub Jub Tai posts a few other gang members are posted to keep a watchful eye on the back road to make sure no one is coming up behind them, with the orders to:

"If you see somebody is followin' us, then light 'em the hell up! Ain't supposed to be nobody on this road but us tonight! An' you all know what the police look like! Now, move!"

But Jacob is thinking that the forest makes it easier for Chang and his team to remain hidden from them because of the heavy forest foliage and there are so many twists and turns in the road and different paths to take though not all of them can possibly lead out of the woods, he imagined.

This whole operation would have been effective for Chang with the army trucks, but who knew Chewy was going to change trucks? Now, Jacob has no idea how Chang is going to find him. He'll find the truck because it looks as though Chewy is going to abandon them right here. And now that they are transferring the weapons to their private truck, there would be no more signal for Chang and his people to follow.

Jacob remembers about something Ginger told him about the gang a long time ago: "…They're not stupid." And she is right. This is a smart and unexpected move by them.

When the transfers are done, Job Jub Tai directs the gang members to have the soldiers crawl headfirst into and beneath the deep, heavy undergrowth and to not stop crawling.

"The first one to stop crawling, or to turn around," Chewy warned them, "gets to have the honor of getting' every one of you shot dead. Crawl and keep crawlin' 'til you reach China." Both he and Jub Jub loved that line and they roared out loud continuous laughter until Chewy abruptly spun around and pointed to the trucks.

"Alright, crash two of those trucks into each other so that they block the road. Then yank the flatten all the tires on all the trucks. Hurry up, we need to be outta here!"

The gang members and Jub Jub climbed into the trucks and he and the other members carried out Chewy's orders for disabling the army trucks. When they finished, they climbed into the rear of the Fish truck with the weapons.

Jub Jub secures the outside lock on the door and then he joins Chewy and Jacob in the cab of the remaining army truck. Jacob's heart starts racing. He cannot believe that Chewy is keeping on of the army trucks. He could think of no better mistake Chewy could have made not realizing that he is leaving a truck with a signal source, that is until Chewy says:

"Oh," Chewy looks at Jacob and says: Jacob, my man, you almost let me forget. You naughty boy." Chewy hollers out for his men to: "An' crash them other army trucks into each other near the other two, to help block the road more and yank out all the distributers. It'll take them forever to free up enough road to try following us." Chewy looks at Jacob and grins; "Not that anybody would ever do somethin' like that. Right, my man? I mean, your people would never do that, now would they" He slaps Jacob on the shoulder.

Jub Jub saluted and hollered to Chewy:

"Done and will be done, my General!"

Jub Jub joins the others with the orders from Chewy and when they have finally finished with the disabling of the trucks, Jub Jub climbs behind the wheel of the army truck, Chewy and Jacob join him in the front seat and they leave as Chewy says:

"Four trucks out of commission and one truck ready to complete the mission." Chewy slaps Jub Jub five and says:

"Very good, my man. Now, home James."

Jub Jub floors the accelerator and the Fish truck trembles, threatening to choke off unless he eases up and allows time for the clutch to engage properly. He does and they lurch forward the huge motor roaring loudly.

Chewy again checks the rear view mirrors and seeing no one behind them, he leans back in the seat and relaxes, slipping his weapon back into his pocket.

Jacob knew this move with the trucks is, at the very least, problematic.

"Chewy, what's going on? Why are you doing this? Those trucks are army property. You can't just leave them there on the road like that."

Ignoring Jacob, Chewy slaps Jub Jub Tai 'five.'

"My man. Great job!" Then he turns a serious face to Jacob. "The trucks? Oh, I have a feeling that they'll be found." He laughed briefly. "Besides, didn't we leave a bunch of soldiers with them? Sooner or later they're going to realize that it's safe to turn around and to back to their trucks."

Jacob leans back in the seat and stares ahead. This time he gives Chewy credit for obviously giving this operation a great deal of thought and planning it well. Unfortunately for Jacob, it looks as though Chewy's plan is going to work. Jacob wonders if Chang has planned on something like this, even though it is never brought up at their meetings.

If Chang has made no provisions for the unexpected, then Jacob knows that this time he is definitely not going to be allowed to leave Cheung's estate alive. It is going to be a very uncomfortable time once they reach the doctor's estate.

The truck finally breaks free of the forest and is rushing along streets profuse with civilian pedestrians, vehicular traffic and numerous vendors plying their trades. This time Chewy does not scream at them from the truck and instead he stares straight ahead as though lost in pleasant thoughts.

Jacob is wondering could it be that three experienced minds, Chang, Commander Zixin and General Syongrui could possibly have overlooked taking into account the unexpected.

Obviously Chewy has given this a lot of thought, but there is usually something that is overlooked in the best of plans; and Jacob knows that Chewy has let something go unchecked and surprisingly so.

Half an hour later Chang's three emergency vehicular trucks and General Syongrui's army vehicle convoy pull to a slow stop at the abandoned army trucks. The soldiers who were hijacked are returning, drifting back to the trucks and milling around the damaged vehicles. They dread having to explain to Chang who, along with Commander Zixin is walking over to them

Chang looks at Zixin.

"I guess we can see what happened here."

Zixin sighed and nodded.

"Looks like the gang crashed the trucks into each other. From the looks of it, they flattened the tires of these trucks and then hijacked the weaponry and Jennings. And it's going to take us forever to clear this mess and to get going again."

One of the soldiers speaks to Chang and Zixin about how were caught off guard:

"Sir, they had armed people hidden in the bushes and in a truck that is blocking the path there, and some even came out of the woods. They hit us before we could get our bearings. They took our cell phones, our walkie-talkies, and our weapons, and they forced us to load all the weaponry onto other trucks and left these here to block the path."

Commander Zixin says to the men:

"We've got to move these trucks. We're losing precious time. Let's go!" And then to Chang: "Thank God you thought to set that tracking device in the cell phone you gave Jennings in case the gang found the one on the trucks. Not to mention the one you put in the weapon you gave him. But we don't have that long before the signal will be too weak to follow. We're going to have to use our vehicles to clear the road of the trucks."

Chang is staring at the army trucks crashed together and blocking the forest path.

"This is a smart move by the gang. This path is so narrow it's only fit for one-lane travel. If a person takes the wrong path, you might meet someone coming the opposite way and be forced to back up. Chewy knows the right path to take and thankfully since he blocked that road, we have to assume he took that road; one flaw so far in his plan."

Chang watches the men busy themselves moving the trucks from the road. He surveys the area.

"It's going to be hard getting our huge army emergency trucks through the tight squeeze of this forest road and all these damned close trees. This road is probably only used by farmers and their cattle, sir. I think the only other traveler a person would run into by taking the wrong road would be someone moving their herds of livestock. Of course that would be just as bad as backing up. It would take an inordinate amount of time if the person is in a hurry. But I think the soldiers have experience in using winches."

Zixin sees a problem approaching:

"Speaking of the army, here comes the general, sir."

Chang turns and sees General Syongrui's truck at head of the convoy jerk to a sudden stop. Even from where they stood, Chang could hear him cussing. Syongrui is staring at his wrecked trucks as he slowly approaches them, suddenly turning his glare to Chang.

Chang knows he is rightfully furious because of the hijacking and the weapons gone. He knows his friend General Syongrui is taking a really huge chance just helping him, but if these weapons are lost, for such a large and unauthorized amount of rifles and army weaponry will mean the end of the general's position and a likely court martial and possible even jail time.

Chang watches the general bang his fist against the palm of his hand as he angrily stomps the ground in approaching him and Chang imagines that it is almost as though he can feel the earth cracking and trembling beneath each of General Syongrui's steps.

For just a second Chang freezes because he could swear that, when the general snatches off his helmet, Chang is positive that he sees General Syongrui's gray hair spouting steam.

Syongrui's anger appears equal in power and fury to the full wrath of a violent runaway locomotive out of control at full throttle. The general's hand is locked around the grip of his sidearm 45 pistol as he storms towards Chang who's body stiffens; and he said lowly to Zixin:

"… Commander, maybe you'd better stand aside. I think he's gonna shoot me."

CHAPTER 37

FIND ME
AN EXIT

Chewy and Jub Jub Tai began laughing hysterically at how they have outsmarted any possible followers. Chewy signaled for Jub Jub to slow down. He grinned at Jacob and is expecting some reaction or question. But getting none, he snorted a brief and humorless giggle and looked out the front window. After a few minutes he gestured toward the scenery.

"Does Jacob The Jew recognize?"

"Yeah." Jacob said.

Jacob knows precisely where they are heading. Sadly, again he is going to be on his own. He did not see any way for Chang and his backup soldiers and police officers to find him because there was going to be too much distance between them by the time Chang's crew straightened out the crashed and disabled army trucks. Even if they managed to get past the forest blockade Chewy has created, how could they possibly find him after that? Tracking devices only work for limited distances and he knew that.

Chewy's truck turned onto the lane leading to Cheung's wrought-iron gate guarding and surrounding his estate. After being buzzed in the Fish truck drove past the fencing and onto the estate but this time continuing on to the rear of the buildings and into a grove of trees at the rear of the buildings. After a moment, the truck reaches a clearing where another low building stands.

Chewy proudly said:

"Jacob The Jew, welcome to the medical facilities of Dr. Cheung."

When their truck approaches the side wall of one of the buildings it stops at the bricked edifice and Chewy pulls out his cell phone and dials a number. After a moment, the side of the building lifted up like a garage door allowing them entrance to the rather large, wide space facility.

After several minutes, all the trucks are inside and parked in separate stalls. Chewy, Jub Jub Tai and Jacob disembarked. Chewy is smiling broadly at Jacob as the gang assembles in the warehouse awaiting further orders from Chewy.

"Jacob The Jew seems puzzled, or maybe he is awestruck the gang's got this kinda facility. Yo, we do be connected, bro." For the first time Chewy's laugh seemed normal.

"Chewy, this is not the way to do business," Jacob weakly objected. "It isn't right."

"Sure it is. You and me already know everybody can't be trustin' everybody. You an' me, we got too many people for everybody to be trustin' everybody. We gonna check out the merchandise, an' if we like it, then we'll keep it. Of course, I got a feeling we're gonna keep it either way." This time his laugh returned to its usual maniacal pitch.

Inside Dr. Cheung's home, Chewy and Jub Jub Tai quickly ushered Jacob into a large room. He is surprised to see Delilah seated at a long table inside the room. She smiled at Jacob and rose as Chewy greets her with a kiss.

"Delilah, baby, guess who's comin' to dinner?"

Delilah casually approached Jacob and gives him a long and wet kiss, her arms encircling his neck. With some hesitation, he accepts her kiss sensing there is a reason for it. Delilah let her mouth brush against Jacob's ear, hurriedly whispering:

"Now that they have you they are going to kill my sister because Baofung knows she was working sorcery against him. She almost killed him but she didn't know it and I couldn't get to her to let her know. If they hurt Ginger, I will kill them one by one until I am stopped. But I will begin with Baofung. they're gonna do something strange to you with the *cherry berry*, but I don't know what that is."

She turned around to Chewy who is talking to Jub Jub about something and paying little attention to them. Delilah kissed Jacob and then again pressed her mouth against his ear as they hugged. She whispered "... I'll try to help both of you but my sister I must help first. She spun quickly around to grin at Chewy. "This 'butterfly' boy still needs some kissing lessons." She pecked Jacob on the mouth with her pursed lips then spun around again and slinked back to Chewy and locked her arms around his waist, grinning vacuously at Jacob.

Something is moving in his pocket. His cell phone has begun vibrating. Chang is trying to reach him and Chewy is watching him and slowly walking his way. He surely could not answer the phone and if Chewy is getting ready to start a fight with him then that may mean they know who he is and it is going to be an all-out war with Ginger's life in the lurch. Chewy grins and stands close to Jacob.

"Jacob The Jew, how come you acting so nervous all of a sudden? You okay?"

Jacob shuffled his feet.

"I'm fine, just a little—"

A young Chinese girl rushed into the room and over to Chewy. She whispers in his ear then quickly exits the room. Chewy's expression becomes serious. He slowly pulls a knife from his pocket and moves even closer to Jacob.

Jacob backed up until he is against a wall. Chewy snatches him by his shirt and pulls him close, his knife only inches from Jacob's face. Just as Jacob prepares to strike him, Chewy explained his move.

"Looks like Dr. Cheung's has summoned you. Too bad he wants you in one piece. There's something about you, Jacob the Jew, that's always smelled funny to me. But they say nothing is proved against the black Jew yet." He tapped his knife blade against Jacob's chest. "I say let me use this and it will be proven." He lowered his knife and returned it to his pocket. "Come on, it's time for your doctor's visit."

Chewy leads Jacob from the room and motioned to Delilah.

"Come on with us, baby. Oh, and Delilah, you should see the beautiful guns and army stuff that Jacob gave us." Chewy began his wild laughing. "And Dr. Cheung's got a beautiful gift for him, an' he's gonna give it to 'im tonight, too." He bursts into insane laughter, doubling over in pain, he takes a moment to try and catch his breath.

Delilah took this opportunity to again hurriedly whisper to Jacob.

"...They keep moving my sister from room to room over and over so I am unable to find her. Whenever I think I know where she is then they move her again. But Chewy and Jub Jub know."

She steps away as Chewy straightens from laughing and glances back at her. They all continued walking down the long hallway stopping at a golden colored door where Chewy knocks and waits.

Delila whispers from the side of her mouth, never taking her eyes off Chewy:

"... If they show you the *cherry berry*, you will never be allowed to leave with the secret. Do not ask to see it. But I do not think you will have a choice. Be prepared to fight for your life. Be very careful of Chewy. He is a very crazy and dangerous person. He kind of likes you but not that much."

Chewy turns around to Delilah and asks her:

"What did you just say, babe?"

Before she could answer, he turns back around to a muffled voice coming from the other side of the door. Chewy opens the door and gestures for Jacob to go ahead of him as he looks prolongedly at Delilah. Jub Jub remains in the hall, waiting.

Inside the room Cheung is wearing a black flowing robe with large grey pearl buttons down the middle and a wide choke of grey pearls. He is standing in front of a wide, black desk. On one of two round tables in the room there is a golden fruit bowl, the center of which stands a large, metal, golden pineapple surrounded by fresh apples, pears, grapes, and oranges.

Cheung bows to Jacob, who returns his bow as the cell phone in his pocket started to vibrate again

"Thank you, Chewy." He waves him from the room, "Oh, and please wait at the entrance and ensure that no one disturbs us."

"Of course, doctor." He bows and leaves.

Cheung gestured for Jacob to sit at the table with the fruit.

"Please be seated."

"Thank you, Dr. Cheung."

Jacob sits at the small table and Cheung places a small medical packet on the table and sits facing him. Jacob is curious about the pouch but he assumes that he is going to find out anyway and he has the vague notion that it is going to be something unpleasant. Cheung extends his hand to him.

"How nice to see you once again, Jacob The Jew. But why don't you and I get down to business immediately, sir, since we have the merchandise you promised to deliver and I have been told that it is top quality. I thank you for that. Now we will deliver our promise to you."

He pushed the packet toward Jacob.

"This is what I call: 'the Chief Inspector Owen Chang hysteria packet.'" He reached into the medical packet and took out a plastic pouch of blood. Jacob stared at it but has no idea what it all meant.

"I don't understand. That looks like a pouch of blood."

"Yes, this is my creation. This is a synthetic blood that has somehow been given the name of, *cherry berry*. Somewhere along the way someone nicknamed it and I feel it is as good a name as any; perhaps a bit crude considering what it represents, but what's in a name, eh?"

Jacob is stunned. He picked up the packet and examines it.

"So, this is the *cherry berry* everyone is looking for?" He said it before he realized the terrible blunder he has just made.

Cheung grows a very broad smile and intertwines his fingers.

"Oh? Are there a lot of people seeking this product? How interesting."

"Well, the word on the street is that the name is an enigma, something that people talk about but no one has any real knowledge of. It's more like a myth, I imagine, than anything else. And you know people always want to either prove or disprove myths."

Cheung simply stares vacantly at him for a moment before saying:

"Then allow me to elucidate *cherry berry* for you. Some of this blood's properties have great benefits for those for whom I created it." Cheung sounded like a proud father, "But unfortunately, as is often the case with any new advance in science, and something inherent in all experimental medicine, one should use caution when availing themselves of this product as there maybe aftereffects. Some of its properties are a bit unstable, and certain patients may experience unpredictable and rather unpleasant reactions to it; especially if they abuse it. In fact, it could pose certain issues even for my clients who use it properly. But it has such marvelous benefits for them so as to, at least in my mind, outweigh the few difficulties it presents."

Jacob touches the pouch again.

"What kind of benefits does it offer and if this is only a new synthetic blood then why is it being kept under wraps in such a clandestine manner? I would imagine you'd be lauded for this discovery."

"Discovery? No, that is a word fraught with luck, chance, serendipity, accidental and happenstance. This is the result of brilliant research. My product is the result of years of relentless research and what I refer to as an esoteric science. At any rate, as of now, donated blood has a shelf life of forty-two days and must be refrigerated, but as I said, this blood does not require refrigeration and has an unlimited shelf life."

Jacob is fascinated by what seems Cheung's knowledge of blood, but then remembers that he is, after all, a research scientist involved in that kind of research and a medical doctor.

Cheung continues:

"Your American army wants to use dried plasma that can easily be reconstituted with water for use in combat situations where blood for transfusions is not readily available. In fact, in the year 2014 dried plasma is credited with saving the life of one of your critically wounded army rangers. My product is plasma-like and able to be used across the board for my clients regardless of their blood types and not cause immunologic reaction and a perfect replacement for plasma. Ordinarily. Sadly, one of its deficiencies is creating red blood cells that reach full-capacity oxygen transport the way the 14 million pints of transfused blood used every year does; so that is unfortunate. But just imagine the possibilities for combat once it is refined. That is, if I choose to allow it to be used for such a despicable thing as war. Of course with my clients the blood type is a non-issue and that is not a criterion for its creation. A wonderful unforeseen benefit is that it also cleanses the blood of any deficiencies or diseases."

"Would it cleanse the blood of cancer, Dr. Cheung?"

"My clients are unaffected by cancer and other human diseases, but, yes it is capable of doing precisely that. Still, this blood does pose unfortunate side effects for them but especially for unauthorized users."

"So, I guess that means you still have more research to do, more trials to make it totally compatible with human blood. Blood banks and other similar facilities would never accept this synthetic blood you've come up with."

"Well without really close examination and thorough testing, it is impossible to tell the difference between my product and real blood. But at present, there are many thriving communities begging for more than I am able to provide at the moment, but only for the moment. I am in the midst of expanding. I plan on being able to organize communities of gangs to make drug deliveries to my special customers. With gangs making deliveries, no street thugs are likely to try and take the *cherry berry* or the money from them. And with all the gangs involved being exceptionally well compensated for such a simple task, there is no danger of thievery. Besides, no one knows what the new 'drug' looks like, or what it is and how to use it except for my clients." He smiled at Jacob. "And you're certainly not going to tell anyone."

Jacob understands clearly the meaning of Cheung's last statement.

"No, sir, of course not. This sounds too important to allow such leaks."

"Oh, they know they're delivering blood, but that is all they know. I'm sure they may all guess that the drug is hidden somewhere in the shipment but never would they think it's in the actual blood itself."

Jacob marvels at the simplicity of such an intricate and well-conceived crime network. It seems to be perfect. How is Cheung going to be stopped? Especially since maybe only Cheung and Baofung know what the *cherry berry* actually is.

"Doctor, this all sounds foolproof. But what happens when the drug cartels see the overwhelming popularity of your drug? You don't think they're going to let you operate alone and wipe out their businesses, do you? I'm sure someone will come up with a duplicate drug or the cartels will find a way to wipe it or you out of the market."

"Oh my dear sir, as far as replication is concerned, that can never happen, since my associate Mr. Baofung and I are the only ones who know the necessary ingredients. Even if the blood is analyzed some of the ingredients and the processing of the blood will never be determined. Mr. Baofung has kept the roots and flowers he uses secret even from me, and I have not shared with him certain chemical ingredients I have included in the blood. And if the police intercept a delivery, it is only blood, and there is no law against having pouches of blood. Especially when the deliveries are being made for a doctor with complete political immunity to provide medical care for clients with special hemophiliac needs in other countries. As far as any competitors are concerned, they will be, believe me, quite easily vanquished."

"But I still don't get it. Synthetic blood? If you've created a new synthetic blood, with significantly greater qualities. Why do you hide it? What's your plan for the future?"

"Well, I am entertaining the possibility of integrating it into America's blood supply system. Gratis." He laughed.

"But you can't do that! Your product isn't proven! Why you might end up poisoning hundreds of thousands of people in one country alone! You said that the blood is unstable. Unproven. It might be toxic to humans until you work it out!"

Now the word "human" struck Jacob as being incongruous with conversation concerning this product; and he realized that Cheung has used it in an unusual way in describing his clients' immunity to "human diseases." Is the doctor misspeaking then or not? "Wait a minute. You said that humans have bad reactions to it. I don't get that part. If you create a blood for humans, then how is it that it works for some and not for others? I mean you obviously have a large clientele for it, so what makes the other humans not susceptible to negative aftereffects of the blood?"

"Well, that is something I hope to find out tonight."

Jacob certainly did not like the sound of that. He sat up in his chair.

"But just imagine the havoc that would ensue if I were to integrate this blood into the blood system of some unsuspecting city or country. Think of me having people positioned in several countries ready to do precisely that at my command. Countries would give me whatever I demanded. I could control entire countries without a moment's violence and shedding an ounce of blood. No pun intended."

"You wouldn't do that."

"Oh, you silly person, but of course I would. I am working now at refining it to be even more undetectable but no less effective. But I do need more volunteers to work out any negative effects the blood may offer with certain dosages and certain people. At any rate, that is not in the immediate future. I have other plans at the moment for this product. I am thinking of assembling an army as an addendum to my synthetic blood that will give me the power of absolute takeover. They are the ones for whom I have created this blood. I have increased the efficacy of each pouch, assuring that each one will allow four doses instead of the usual two."

Jacob is seeing the genius in the doctor but also a genius hat has been overtaken by greed for omnipotent power. He listens to Cheung continue:

"My blood product is one hundred percent addictive after the first dose. But it is an addiction that affects users differently. So far, one section of my clients when they choose to withdraw from the *cherry berry* do not die but they become lethargic and eventually fall into a state of estivation leading some to a state of comatose.

"No current client can overdose on it, even by using the entire pouch at one time but it is surely totally addictive to them. But neither will the client be able to increase the potency of a dose by doubling or tripling their doses. It will still supply only a single euphoria per dose at the same level but never more. And I will know the precise amount each of my clients has purchased and therefore know when they will need more. A certain period of time must elapse before the next does becomes effective. If a client has entered a state of suspension, then the body does not require the *cherry berry* but only for a certain period of time before it will demand it. And, of course, once it is used there is no turning back. It causes complete, total and overwhelming dependency. If I deprive my clients of my product the result will be severe predation." He touched Jacob's hand. "Who knows but that soon, perhaps, much of the human race will follow in suit on some level of *cherry berry* participation and find a means of achieving its benefits." He picked up the pouch of blood placed it back in the medical packet. "In the meantime … it is a very complicated item, this *cherry berry*." Cheung held the pouch in his hand as though guessing its weight.

Jacob is weighing Cheung's words.

"Dr. Cheung, though I question your product's dependency aspect, it is quite obvious that you've created some kind of new synthetic blood for hemophiliacs with some unproven properties but with proven unimaginably wonderful benefits for storage which means also for lengthy transportation with no need for refrigeration; a marvelous advance for hemophilia. I assume that hemophiliacs are your clients, am I correct and that it somehow works for a chosen section of them?"

Cheung shook his head.

"No."

Jacob did not expect that answer from him.

"But, then who are you clients?"

Cheung held up the pouch of blood and then he gingerly set it down again. He studies Jacob's features for a long moment then leans back in his chair and smiles at him.

Jacob is about to repeat his question, but the doctor's smile vanishes and he leans forward quickly and says:

"Vampires."

Jacob almost stops breathing. When he gathers himself he grins.

"Yeah. Right. Uh, you did say vampires, didn't you doctor?"

"I did. The creatures of so many legends."

"Dr. Cheung, you don't really expect me to believe that you've first of all even been able to find vampires abut also that you've come up with a synthetic blood for them?"

"No, I don't expect you to believe. And that is the wonderful part. Who would believe you if you told them?"

"But, why would you create a blood for vampires, even if there are such creatures?"

"The initial reason for this blood is, in a sense, mimicking humans who stock up on wood for the coming winter, or on food and water when a bad storm is predicted. The client would want to be able to have a substantial supply of blood available that totally satisfied their blood need over a prolonged period of time. They wanted a blood supply on hand that would not necessitate his people to have to hunt so often for their daily sustenance. I came up with such an item that, quite by accident, also offers a five-hour euphoria, a truly supreme ecstasy unlike any other for the intended users. But there are contraindications."

"A synthetic get-high, lifesaving elixir for vampires. I have to admit it's quaint if not totally and insanely unique."

"It is also, by the way, sir, not illegal. So if the good Inspector of Police Owen Chang were to find my product and prove its existence, what could I possible be prosecuted for? I am, after all, a blood research scientist and it is a synthetic product of my own creation. What have I done that is illegal? He can never prove that it is a product for sale; rumors, only rumors."

Jacob gives that a lot of thought:

"Actually, if what you're saying is true, then you're right. But then why are going through all this trouble? You can't be prosecuted for your experiments even if they are for…vampires."

Dr. Cheung smiles and picks up his packet of blood, examining it:

"Because I cannot afford for my product to be confiscated by the Medical Ethics Board. It would take them years to clear me for further research if they were to do so; and that is not likely to happen since I cannot provide them with a list of all the properties of my product that means I'd have to go underground to continue my work. No, such a move would make my continued research impossible."

"Why can't you list your ingredients?"

"Because certain of the properties are known to be poisonous to man. They'd find that out after very long research and experiments. Then they'd find that the cherry berry is not fit to be used as a blood product in any sense of the meaning. I can be prosecuted along the way for creating a known deadly substance for unknown personal reasons. Public hysteria might declare that I am a germ warfare terrorist. I would be jailed eventually until I revealed my sponsor for my experiment. And that, of course, is quite impossible I assure you."

"In other words, my dear sir, I cannot be legally arrested for my cherry berry but by the time the boards and courts finish with me, I would be ruined, my properties confiscated and my reputation finished."

"Is that why you won't tell me who your real clients are or who your client is, Dr. Cheung? I get the feeling that you're just not ready to tell me who your clients are. I mean, this vampire business…"

"I promise you that after tonight you will be a true believer. There will be no doubt left in your mind. Tonight we will determine just how *cherry berry* affects humans. As for my sponsor, his name is Anston Reinsorth. After I administer the cherry berry to you I will see to it that he meets you.

I promise you that. Mr. Reinsorth comes from a very long line of vampires, a very old family of vampires."

"But why me, doctor? Why not someone off the street maybe even a volunteer?"

"Because *The Chinese Blood* can use your particular services, your contacts, your sources; and if this drug affects you the way I intend it to, you will be my servant; if that fails, then my associate Yongli Baofung will turn you into a personal zombie-like person for our use until I can perform more advanced experiments to improve my cherry berry to the point that it suits our purposes perfectly."

Jacob flinches at his cell phone vibrating in his pocket. He is thinking that the quietness of the room will cause the low sound of the phone to be heard by Cheung. He needs to engage the doctor in conversation to cover any sound from the humming.

"How many vampires are there, doctor?""

"Oh, there are too many colonies and vampire cells to even count found all in different countries. America has over one thousand such colonies according to my client Mr. Reinsorth and they are increasing. I would imagine that think that you've made the acquaintance of more than a few vampires here in Hong Kong without having the slightest suspicion."

"And since humans can't use this blood you have no problem with poisoning some with this synthetic blood?"

"Not really that simple. You see, I have no idea as to what effects, if any, this blood will actually have on humans. There is no doubt that some humans will be able to use this blood, but if not I need to know what happens to them but that will take different people. That way I can always attempt to remedy the aftereffects. But, then the aftereffects may be something that humans greatly benefit from, although these changes may prove to be not acceptable to others. You see, it is likely the person's physical appearance will be greatly changed. Thus, I am at the precipice this very evening of launching my first human trial."

Jacob is really curious about this *cherry berry*. It certainly is not anything he thought it might be.

"What happened with the experiments you said you already performed?"

"Well, the monkeys in one of my labs are given the blood orally. The euphoric effect lasted only an hour, and then they slept for three days. But when they are injected with it … the results were all well beyond human comprehension and they had to be destroyed. I need human trials to see if the effects will be similar with humans or what effect it does have on them. After all, I will eventually be dealing with humans and not monkeys in the long run. That's where Jacob The Jew comes in."

"They slept for three days you say?"

"Yes, but I believe it was more of a state of estivation, I'd say since they are perhaps more in a kind of torpor state but most are not conscious. Vampires once using my new blood, can also enter into states of estivation but for no longer than two months because then the bodily functions resume. Then they wake with an insane craving for the *cherry berry*. And they are able to come out of estivation and consume more *cherry berry* if it is available. If it is not available, they can resume states of estivation but for no more than an additional month but will nevertheless be beleaguered by an excruciating desperation for the *cherry berry*."

Jacob nods.

"Sort of withdrawal symptoms, I guess."

"Perhaps. After that period, If it is not available by then, well, then they will take to the streets and resume hunting their human prey but at a much higher level of hunger; more than three to four times as much blood is needed to replace the *cherry berry*. So, after a period of six months use, they are totally addicted to *cherry berry* and so human blood lasts them only for, perhaps, twelve hours thus the need for increased consumption of human blood."

"So, you're making addicts of the vampires."

"Now that I hear it spoken, I think that the word addiction is such a profane phrase. Do you agree? The fact is that human blood will no longer satisfy their hunger completely. Only *cherry berry* will do that once it has been used. The good thing is that they are never vulnerable when in estivation. They are always alert and able to respond to anyone attempting to harm them when they are in that state of dormancy."

"And being that it is essentially blood, I assume that *cherry berry* can only be administered orally?"

"Well, no, but that is the only way I recommend it to be done for the present. However, recently a few of the younger vampires from the colony, I guess you would consider them the more modern types of vampires by them injecting the blood although they are expressly directed never to do so. The results of their insolence resulted in aberrant behavior foreign to vampires. Those vampires who injected themselves, left the nest and wreaked havoc on the human population's farm stock animals. I believe it is the farm animals that the young renegades happened upon as opposed to humans. You see at that point their cravings are no longer simply for blood, but rather for pure violence. I imagine that eventually they would have turned on their own for their blood sustenance but my product is available within their colony, though their behavior is condemned. The colony would have been in danger of being discovered had those vampires come across humans and attacked them."

Jacob cannot help but be fascinated by listening to Cheung regale him with tales of his blood product, *cherry berry.*

"I see."

Cheung sees Jacob's fascination and he is happy to continue to tell him about the product.

"As it is, all colonies prefer to be thought of as myths and are very careful as to how they access human blood and they have mastered ways to do it safely with no possibility of being discovered; but those methods are becoming more and more difficult to accomplish. After all, there are police cameras almost everywhere and everyone has a cell phone that takes videos and photographs. Contrary to lore, vampires do show up when photographed. Those young vampires are warned that if such an incident occurred again, from anyone within the colony, the violators would be condemned to death and executed. But I decided to take a closer look at the vampire's injection and experiment on it with my monkeys."

"What happened to them?"

"Well, my next experiments were with the monkeys using *cherry berry*, they grew thicker bodies, some of them became badly stooped but oh so much more muscular and alive. They grew baboon teeth and attacked each other until only one remained alive, barely breathing. The peculiar thing is that the surviving one began to devour the dead but selected only the eyes and the bones, leaving the flesh behind."

"I see." Jacob's cell phone vibrated again and he flinched.

"I believe that Jacob The Jew is thinking of the colonies of vampires again. Am I correct, sir?"

"I guess." He did not feel like bandying words with the doctor at this point.

"Allow me to sum up by saying that there is only one thing left for me to do. And that, Jacob The Jew, is precisely where you come in. How wonderful of you to not only gift us with such wonderful weaponry but to also volunteer to advance my research. You see, after I give you the drug, we are going to place your precious Ginger in the room with you to see what happens. Come to think of it, I believe that I will do the first dose by injection—shoot straight for the old heart as some Americans say. And then much later, after you and I have toyed with this we might even try administering it intravenously; a far slower method but perhaps it will afford us more time to see different stages of reaction to *cherry berry* going through your system."

"I see."

"I am sure by now that you have determined, the *cherry berry* is mired in quantum complication."

When Cheung stops smiling, he abruptly stood and Jacob braced himself with a myriad of spells and magic moves raced through his mind in preparation for being attacked. The doctor claps his hands together smartly and immediately Chewy and Jub Jub Tai enter the room.

Dr. Cheung tells them to:

"Please show our guest to his room and since this may be his last night with us as a guest, please make sure that he has the most comfortable accommodations and if he is hungry, please see to it that he has dinner and refreshments. We wish him to have every comfort until later this evening when he meets our very special guest Mr. Welleck."

"I sure will, sir."

They exited the room. Jacob is disappointed to see that Delilah is nowhere to be seen in the hallway. Chewy shoved him along and growled:

"Come on, stop daydreaming', Jacob The Jew. Let's go."

Jub Jub Tai also shoves him then he walks around in front of him.

Jacob followed Chewy and Jub Jub Tai down the hall with Jub Jub Tai lead the way. He has the feeling that Chewy is hoping he will try something but Jacob knows that absolutely nothing can be gained by engaging them in combat at this time. Jacob knows that he is a prisoner, but not a stupid or defenseless one.

Chewy and Jub Jub Tai push Jacob into a very large room that, in keeping with the other parts of Cheung's estate, has a beautiful décor that he is sure easily rivals the lushest hotel suite in any country; it certainly put his present hotel room to shame.

The bed is lush with beautiful thick pillows, silk sheets, and a canopy that hearkens back to earlier days. There are two sinks with gold-bordered mirrors and gold-colored faucets that Jacob thinks might be real gold. Softly diffused recessed lighting from the ceiling served to warm the atmosphere of the room, bathing it in a deep, gentle orange. The rug is deep enough to sink into. A Chesterfield Sofa rested against a wall adjacent to a canopied bed covered with large pillows. An Edwardian chair sat at a vanity table near the bed. In the center of the room is a large round mahogany table with a wine decanter.

Jacob sits at the table and considers whether to drink the wine sitting there. He surely can use a drink now and he is sure that they are not going to poison him or give him some drug that might affect the *cherry berry* they are planning for him.

He checks his cell phone. There is no signal, which did not surprise him at all, still he attempted to call Chang, but it is to no avail. He could only wait for him to call again.

Someone knocked gently at the door and he heard the sound of a key being inserted into the lock. He braced himself, again his mind goes through a series of magic to use against anyone in case they come for him. He hoped nothing happened before he has a chance to meet Welleck. The door opened and Delilah steps inside the room and quickly pushes the door shut, but not before looking up and down the hall to make sure she is not seen. He is overjoyed to see her and hoped that she has some news about Ginger.

"I stole this key, and I cannot stay long. I found where they have my sister. As I said before they have been moving her from room to room to make sure that I don't find her. But I have one good friend who told me which room she is in."

"Is she still very sick?"

"She has recovered. Perhaps because Baofung has been too ill from her earlier spells to continue his revenge against her."

She places her hand on his.

"You must leave, even if you go without her. Do you know what they are going to do to you?"

"Yeah, they are going to use *cherry berry* on me to see what effect it has on a human who has been 'turned.' Then they want to use Ginger to see what I will do to her in such a state. Delilah, the doctor showed me the *cherry berry*. It's blood. That's the drug."

She looks at him with a blank expression.

"But how can blood be a drug?"

"It's made for—" He couldn't say it for fear of her thinking he is trying to deceive her. "It's just something certain people use to get high with lethargy and a euphoria. It's like smoking opium."

She makes a questioning face.

"They're smoking blood?"

"No, they're—Okay, listen. It's hard to believe, but the doctor said his clients are vampires."

She stared at him. At first she wanted to laugh. Then she became angry.

"What're you talking about? You sound like they already gave you the drug. You sound crazy."

"I'm telling you that he says that his clients are vampires and I actually believe him. This blood satiates their thirst for human blood."

She slowly begins backing away from him.

"Are you talking about bats? Vampire bats?"

"No. Vampires. Real vampires."

"You really not joking? Not lying? Vampires like in the movies?"

"It's what he told me. I don't know how it can be true, but I believe that there's truth here somewhere."

"What will happen to you then if they give the drug to you? Will you turn into a vampire bat?"

"I don't think so, but I don't know. Dr. Cheung doesn't know either, and he wants me to be his guinea pig."

His cell phone is buzzing again. He eagerly yanked the phone from his pocket.

"Inspector Chang—is that you?"

Delilah is shocked to hear Jacob is talking with the Police Inspector Owen Chang. Looking at the expression on her face, Jacob could see that Ginger has not told her anything about his police connections.

Chang is hollering:

"Jennings? I've been calling!"

"I know, but I couldn't answer. This is the first time I've been alone. I'm with Delilah, Ginger's sister."

"Jennings, we're out of the woods but we lost your signal twenty minutes ago. We cleared the trucks, but we've lost the signal. Where are you?"

"At Dr. Cheung's estate—and listen! I've seen the *cherry berry*!"

"Jennings never mind that now! You're breaking up badly! Where did you say you are?"

"I'm at Dr. Cheung's estate."

"How do we get there?"

"I can't tell you the way here, but I've got somebody here who can: Delilah. Ginger's sister." He offered her the cell phone, but she steps away from him.

"Jennings?" Chang's voice is surrounded by static and growing weaker. "My signal is dying! Jennings cut the phone off so you can conserve what's left of the battery life. Wait for me to call you again. I will call you every fifteen minutes. Make sure to keep the phone—" The phone is dead.

Jacob looks at Delilah, who is glaring at him in the worst accusatory way. Then she slowly advances on him, a bewildered look on her face.

You are with the police? Hong Kong's got a black cop?"

"No, I'm—"

"You betrayed my sister."

"No, I didn't."

"Chewy is right. You don't love her! But she thinks you do! You bastard! And I was going to help you! I must have been out of my mind!"

"No, Delilah, you don't understand. I do love Ginger. She knows about me, and I don't have time now to explain things to you. I've got to get out of here before they come for me!"

"I hope they kill you! They should let Chewy kill you! Take you apart in pieces. I should kill you!"

"Delilah, go to your sister and ask her. I'm telling you she knows about me. We don't have time to argue with each other. You have to believe me. If you tell them about me, they will just give me the drug sooner. If I die, then Ginger might die too because no one knows what kind of creature I might turn into and like I said before, they're going to have Ginger in the room with me!"

She walks slowly toward the door, keeping her eye on him, studying his features. She turns away slowly shaking her head as she grabs the door-knob. But before she opens the door she turns back to him.

"Okay." She is clearly trying to get her thoughts together. "I will ask my sister if you are lying, but I won't help you until I find out."

His cell phone begins buzzing again. He yanks out his phone: "Chang?"

"Jennings! No time! There is almost no phone signal now. How do I get to where you are?" Chang's voice sounded as though he is underwater.

Once again Jacob tries to give the cell phone to Delilah, and again she refuses. But this time she leaves the room. For a long moment Jacob stares at the closed door, hoping it would open again and that she will relent and give Chang the instructions to reach the estate. But the door remains closed.

"Chang?"

"Hurry up, Jennings!"

"Chang, I'm sorry, but—" The phone is nearly dead again.

Jacob slips the cell back into his pocket and sits at the table. He knows this is the end. There is nothing further that he can do or hope for at this point. He grabs the decanter of wine and hoists the bottle to his mouth. He resolves that when they came for him to use his gun first and then the strongest magic he can come up with. He is thinking about Ginger promising himself that if they harm her he will raze the entire estate with all the magic and creatures he can summon. And now that he thinks of it, this might be a perfect place to conjure Corpo Seco..

Half an hour later, Chewy, Jub Jub Tai and another gang member that Chewy called, Coo Coo, a squat, thick bodied, heavily muscled young man entered, followed by Cheung who is holding a hypodermic needle housed in a metal sheath. Jacob is sure that the hypo contains *cherry berry.*

"I have decided that it is not proper respect to ask my guest, Jacob The Jew, to wait any longer. I am sure that, with your intellectual curiosity are as anxious as I to see the outcome of the experiment I spoke of earlier with you."

Before Jacob could utter a magic chant, he remembers that he has the gun that Chang has given him but when he discretely reaches for it, Coo Coo jumps in the air and kicked him on the side of his face sending him backwards in a violent tumble landing him hard on the floor.

Coo Coo pins him to the floor while Cheung measured the solution in the hypo, squeezing out a few drops. Then he kneels next to him on the floor and prepares to push the needle into Jacob's forearm.

THE CAVALRY DOES NOT HAVE TO KNOCK

Jacob manages to twist away and shove Cheung, but Coo Coo snatches him and presses Jacob's back against the floor and presses his knee hard against Jacob's stomach, and Jub Jub locks his hand even tighter over Jacobs's mouth and strengthens his grip on his arms with a great deal more force to steady it for Cheung's needle.

Coo Coo and Jub Jub, still pressing Jacob to the floor, are laughing.

Jub Jub remarked:

"Jacob The Jew ain't got his little Ginger cookie to help him out now. He ain't got his little Ginger to save 'im." He leans his face close to Jacob's and hissed: "Not so tough without your little Ginger, huh, punk?"

Cheung holds the needle steady at Jacob's forearm, keeping it steady as he prepares to press the needle in Jacob's arm. Jacob's gun is still in his pocket but he cannot reach for it. Cheung paused before injecting the *cherry berry* to gloat:

"Jacob The Jew, I am surprised that you are being so terribly rude and uncooperative. After all, you and I have already discussed this procedure and we are all here on the brink of history. Just imagine the experience you are about to undergo. You will be the first man in history to metamorphose into something like the world has never seen or even imagined. You will be the toast of the town, a celebrity unlike any other in the annals of any country's history!"

Cheung slowly starts to press the needle into Jacob's vein when the room door explodes open as one of the gang members is slammed through it by an army uniformed police officer who rushes into the room holding a weapon pointed at Cheung.

There is great activity in the hall and many police officers and uniformed soldiers are rushing about with their weapons firing.

Cheung drops his hypo and jumped to his feet and motioned to Chewy nodded to Jub Jub and Coo Coo to grab the officer. Jub Jub Tai and Coo Coo released Jacob, got to their feet and Coo Coo grabbed the officer, quickly subduing him while Cheung exits the room through a door at the rear of the room. Chewy and Jub Jub follow behind him, but before he goes, Chewy calls out to Coo Coo:

"Coo Coo, finish him and help the others in the combat!" With that being said, he closed the door and Coo Coo does as he has been told. He rendered the officer unconscious with a punch. Before leaving the room, Coo Coo kicks Jacob hard in the side and runs from the room. Jacob who was just gathering his senses and getting to his feet collapse to the floor from the kick from Coo Coo who is now in the hall having joined the other members fighting Owen Chang's officers

Delilah rushes into the room and helps Jacob to his feet. She touches the side of his face where his jaw is swelling fast.

"Come. We must hurry! Your police are here! Some of them are in the hall gathering up gang members! Others are in the back fighting Cheung's security guards! "

She looked around the hall again and gave him the keys to a vehicle and she led him out the side door to a car parked a few yards away. Outside uniformed policemen and soldiers are everywhere approaching the other houses.

"You have to go! Now! I could not find Ginger. They moved her again, and even my friends in the gang don't know where she is! They all say that Chewy is thinking I may be a traitor too! He has told him I was whispering secrets to you in the all! I didn't think he was even noticing. I don't believe what you told me about the vampires. There's no such thing as vampires, but I believe the doctor told you that for his own evil purposes. He is a liar. I believe he told you that so that you still don't know what the *cherry berry* is and if you ever escaped, you would spread false stories about his drug. Now come get in the car, and I will open the gate. I have the code even though I think the gate has been destroyed by your police vehicles!" She held up a small black box with numbers on it. But he gave her the keys back.

"I'm not leaving without Ginger!"

Delilah is shocked.

"Nobody knows where she is! She could be dead!"

"I'm not leaving without her. She's my life Delilah."

She stares at him in utter disbelief. But she is really happy hearing what he said.

"Maybe you do love my sister for real. That is good. But no, take the car and leave!! I think they have already killed my sister! I must stay for my revenge. No reason for you to die, too. I am staying. I am going to kill Baofung and Dr. Cheung too. I don't know how many more I can get, but I am going to try to get them all in some way!"

"Ginger is dead? Do you—"

The startling sound of roaring motors filled the night air. Delilah and Jacob watched a huge black truck with a steel battering ram attached to its front crash into the gate, bending it. The lead police truck backs up and then lurches forward a second time. Part of the tall gate stands defiantly partly guarding access to the estate, but a third charge collapses it. Five police trucks roar through, followed by several army trucks and more uniformed officers on foot.

The second part of the convoy, five of Chang's unmarked police cars with their lights flashing rush in and still more cars and trucks come behind them. There are uniformed officers who have earlier stealthily gained access to the property by climbing the fence and they are herding hand-cuffed prisoners into an area on the side of the first building. Once those prisoners prostrate themselves on the lawn with their arms outstretched, a few officers are left behind to guard them while others resume the search for more gang members.

Cheung's security systems alarms are screaming, and together with the sirens from Chang's vehicles made it sound like a war zone, something that is intensified when General Syongrui's trucks arrive and crash through remaining gates and onto the grounds; different pitched sirens joining in the insane noise cacophony. Jacob is happy to see giant army trucks rumbling onto the property joining the other vehicles; a scene reminiscent of massive predatory animals throng to the attraction of a kill.

Chang, who is in the first wave invading the interior of the houses in front, runs from one of the rear doors to Jacob and Delilah.

"Jennings!" He gave a quick, disapproving glance at Delilah. "Where's our weaponry?"

"How'd you find me?" Jacob is overjoyed.

"When our phones went, I had no choice but to call Liao and she knew exactly where this place is. General Syongrui got hold of her at the office over his Army CB radio!

Jacob pointed to the back.

"There are warehouses back there that have faux building sides that open like garage doors but you need a code. That's where our weapons are."

Chang grinned.

"Yeah, I got the code."

Jacob is surprised as is Delilah. Jacob asked him:

"But…where'd you get the code?"

"Oh, I keep a universal building code for false walls. I keep it right behind the battering ram on the front of our emergency trucks." He started laughing.

Chang ran over to the first truck and speaks with General Syongrui and Commander Zixin. Then he stepped aside and waved the trucks through to the rear.

"I told General Syongrui and Commander Zixin about the phony wall on the warehouse. Syongrui's going to go get his trucks and weapons."

Chang looks at Delilah and smiles.

She returns his smile but then she steps away and prepares to go back inside the estate where the fighting is still going on but greatly diminished. and she steps away and smiles. She looked at Jacob and pointed to the building.

"I have to go back inside to find my sister. Be careful. There are many gang members inside hiding, some of them waiting to attack you and our men and they are all armed."

Chang wanted Delilah to know that she is not on the arrest list, neither is her sister:

"Delilah, I thank you for that information. And I want you to know that I've given you and your sister Ginger a 'Do not arrest' clearance in this raid. You can move about freely without being bothered by our men. Go look for your sister and we will take care of whatever we can take care of. Feel free to take some of my men with you if you feel you need them. But Jacob must remain with me. I cannot have an American involved in the possible shooting of Chinese citizens especially Dr. Cheung and his associates."

Delilah bows and smiles at Jacob:

"Yes, I understand."

Chang is reloading his weapon:

"After all, such an incident can be blown so completely out of proportion in light of this being an already unauthorized raid. Just imagine the press getting hold of it and saying that I used an American soldier trained in espionage in a terrorist raid on the respected Dr. Cheung's estate for the purpose of attempting to assassinate the good and honorable Dr. Cheung; and to murder innocent employees on his estate."

Delilah understood and she bowed to Chang.

"Thank you, Inspector and you are most correct." She kissed Jacob on the cheek and then ran back to the house.

A moment later, a horde of gang members poured from the side of the third building, only to be met by groups of armed soldiers and police officers rushing their way.

The gang, now seeing that they are not only caught in a crossfire but also greatly outnumbered and outgunned, surrender by stretching out on the ground to be handcuffed. Chang's men moved fast to accommodate them. After his officers secured the prisoners Chang pointed to the houses.

"I want every house on these grounds searched from top to bottom, basements included, secret walls, room—everything; inside you will find a woman named Delilah. Ask her about any secret walls or rooms. Above all—I want that *cherry berry*!" He turned to Jacob. "Jennings, by the way, you said you've seen it. Exactly what the hell is it that I'm looking for?"

Jacob hesitated, trying to come up with an answer that is not going to sound as ridiculous as it will, but…:

"They're hiding the *cherry berry* in pouches of blood, Inspector. Look for pouches of blood."

It took Chang a moment to fully register Jacob's statement. He wanted to ask for more information than that, but instead he turned to some of his men who are standing near.

"They've got it in pouches of blood! Spread the word fast! Pouches of blood! Find them! Pouches of blood! But don't open them! Just bring them to me!"

Every available officer and soldier poured into all of Cheung's buildings looking for the pouches of blood. There are the sounds of sporadic gunshots inside, but after a moment it is totally quiet. Chang turned back to Jacob.

"Jennings, you did say pouches of blood, didn't you?"

"Yes, sir, and I'll explain that later. Right now what say we join the General in the rear."

"Okay, let's go check on the general."

A few minutes later Jacob and Chang are standing at the rear of the estate. Their trucks have made short work of the secret wall. General Syongrui and his men have gathered up whatever gang members they found with the weapons and have them all lying on the floor, handcuffed, with his men standing guard.

Chang and Jacob are smiling as General Syongrui and Commander Zixin joined them. General Syongrui patted Chang on the back.

"Well, Owen, all's well that ends well. And can you imagine? These idiots were actually attempting to use my own weapons against me. I guess no one ever told them that rifles, even when you shove ammo in them, don't work so well without their firing pins. You see, Owen, I'm afraid I neglected to include them as part of the shipment. And when they began tossing our grenades at us, well damn me for being forgetful. It seems that I also mistakenly packed up practice grenades instead of the real ones. Well, at least the handles pop off and they emitted a tiny bit of smoke which caused us to laugh and miss a couple of shots."

General Syongrui is grinning and in a moment, Chang and Commander Zixin and Jacob are all screaming out raucous laughter.

Jacob, knowing what he is going to have to tell them about vampires, is the only one faking mirth.

Three and a half hours later, neither Cheung, Baofung Chop nor the gang members Chop Chewy, Jub Jub Tai or Coo Coo are anywhere to be found. Chang's officers and General Syongrui's soldiers have searched every room in every building twice, but there is no trace of any of them. Here and there in some rooms they find straggler gang members, whom they herded into the dining hall with the other prisoners being held, all of them laying on the floor in police restraints. from outside.

None of the officers or soldiers are able to find the location of any blood on the premises.

Chang cleared his throat for attention to speak to the captured gang members:

"Okay, boys and girls, let's see if we can make this simple. Who here is going to tell us where either the *cherry berry* is located, either that or give me Dr. Cheung's present location?"

No response.

He walked closer to the gang members on the floor.

"I see."

He spun to the side and kicked one of the seated prisoners in the side of his chest.

"Oh, I'm sorry. My foot slipped."

He reached down and brushed off the man's chest. Then he undid his manacles and snatched him to his feet. It is clear that the gang member are terrified of Chang.

"Please, Inspector, I have no knowledge of the *cherry berry*'s whereabouts. None of us do. We are not privileged with such information."

"Let's you and me have a private conference in one of these fine rooms." He looked at the seated group. "I will be having a private conference with several others of you seated here. But you'll have to wait your turn."

One of the young women called out to him.

"Inspector, in truth, none of us has ever seen it. Only Dr. Cheung and Baofung have seen it. We are not allowed to see it—none of us are."

"I'm afraid I find that difficult to believe." Chang really did believe them but he is hoping against hope that someone in the gang held at least a clue about the location of the new drug. "But since you have so much to say..." Chang shoved the standing gang member back onto the floor. Then he undid the young woman's handcuffs and yanked her to her feet. "You and I shall have a private conference, my fearless orator."

Jacob stopped him.

"Inspector, can we speak privately?"

For a moment Chang just looks at him as though he could not believe that Jacob is interrupting him. He leads Jacob and the others to a nearby room where they sat at a wide table.

"Okay, Jennings, you say you saw the drug. So, exactly what is this *cherry berry*? What does it look like and what does it do? What're we looking for here?"

"Sir, *cherry berry* is not actually a drug as such. It's a new synthetic blood."

"How can that be? Why would there be such secrecy over synthetic blood? What is it, a cheaper version or what?"

Jacob shifts uneasily on his seat.

"The product is not fit for human consumption and when I tell you who it's for, you're not going to believe me but I can only tell you what Dr. Cheung told me. And let me add that I believe him. This *cherry berry* is synthetic blood … for **vampires**."

Everyone at the table is staring at Jacob with expressions of total awe. After waiting a while, General Syongrui stands and shoves his finger at Jacob.

"If you think that's funny, lieutenant, then you're the only one at this table who does."

"That's the reason I didn't want to talk about it right away. I just didn't know how to broach this subject. But that's what he told me, sir."

General Syongrui walked over to where Chang is seated.

"Owen, am I to believe that I've put my neck and my career in a damn sling for you and this drug campaign you've been on, only to be told now that the drug is some damn blood for goddamn Dracula?" Syongrui is furious. "Because if that is the fact here, Owen—!" He let out a growl of great angst.

Jacob held up his hand:

"Look, let me pose something to everyone here. Let's suspend our disbelief. Let's say there are such things as vampires. The doctor is deadly serious when he said that this blood is for vampires. Real vampires? I don't know. There are cults that call themselves vampires, and they drink blood. But what I do know is that this blood of Chaung's is corrupt and way dangerous; yet it has enough of the properties of real blood to maybe go unnoticed if it is introduced into a human blood system. If it ever gets into any city or any country's main blood supply then we're talking mass death or, in this case, something much worse."

Syongrui demanded:

"What the hell can be worse than death, lieutenant?"

"Humans turned into creatures of some kind, I don't know, maybe driven insane or something.."

He did not want to go into the details that Dr. Cheung explained to him because it sounds too much like a horror movie and certainly not a believable one at that.

Chang abruptly walks out of the room and back to the dining hall. He addressed his men.

"I want photos of this entire place—each and every room. Search the premises again and this time pay particular attention for hidden rooms, passageways, false panels. Take pictures of the warehouse, the trucks with the weapons, and pose the gang members with their weapons next to them, the weapons they tried to kill you with. I want pictures of the gang members next to the trucks they stole from us. I want every damn thing possible put on visual record that incriminates them. I want photographs and videos! I want it to be that when a person looks at the photos and videos that there's no question about what took place. Understood?"

"Yes, sir."

"But before you do that, I want these prisoners secured in the rear of our trucks outside. Secure their chains to the posts in the trucks. Leave their dead where they dropped. Hurry up, and let's get this done."

Chang angrily returns to Jacob, Syongrui, and Zixin in the room, all of them are sitting with blank expressions on their faces. Chang sits facing them, then his shoulders slump, clearly evidencing that he is in a defeated frame of mind.

Commander Zixin shrugged.

"Well, I guess we might as well get ready to face some heat."

Jacob sighed and looked at the brighter side of it all:

"Yeah, but at least this time we've got the law on our side." He smiled at Chang. "At least this time, we can hit the doctor with stolen Army weaponry. He'll never be able to explain that."

Syongrui snorted:

"And neither can I. How am I going to explain how these men got these weapons? I requisitioned them on paper because I was so sure—no, I was absolutely positive that this raid would expose this dreaded drug and that having been done, then no one would even think about the army weaponry then."

Chang dropped his head.

"Oh no."

"So, how am I going to explain how my requisitioned weapons got into the hands of Hong Kong's most prominent doctor? And how am I going to explain why I requisitioned such a variety of the latest weaponry?"

Jacob stepped up in Chang's defense:

"I'm equally or more to blame for this mess because I got Chief Inspector Chang to believe that what Dr. Cheung and Baofung told me is true and that is that the *cherry berry* is going to be on the premises and I was going to be given a demonstration of its efficacy. I guess we are both so eager to get him and this dangerous drug that we—" then Jacob recalled, "actually, Dr. Cheung was about to inject me with the *cherry berry* to see what happens. So, this drug does have, obviously strange and unusual properties. We do have that."

Syongrui slams his fist on the table:

"Lieutenant have you forgotten that we don't have the goddamn drug!"

Chang held up his hand, smiling at Jacob.

"I won't have you take the blame here, Jennings. I'm the one who stepped on the cat's tail this time. Looks like I've spent most of my time doing that. I can't let you or anyone take responsibility that is mine." He looked at his friend General Syongrui. "I truly apologize to you, sir, for putting your career on the line with my haphazard operation that I have allowed to become more of a vendetta than anything else." He looked at his cigar. "But I was so sure of nailing him this time that I didn't look at the bottom line. Even if we got him with the drug and are able to identify it, it would all be thrown out in court without a search warrant, but I was really depending on 'Probable Cause' to make a case here. The main thing I guess that I really want is to find the drug and be able to identify it and stop its manufacture."

General Syongrui sighed and said:

"Well, the good part is that the weapons are mostly dummies, none of them are capable of functioning, including the grenades."

Chang walked over to his friend and locked his arm around General Syongrui.

"Yeah, and of course the good doctor is going to swear that he knows nothing about any guns. He'll say that we must have brought them with us onto his property to implicate him because I'm so desperate to arrest him that I'll try anything. Then he'll try to nail me for shooting up those thugs out there he calls security who tried to nail us first."

General Syongrui sighed. He smiled at Chang:

"Owen, for the over thirty years, all the way back to when you were one of my men in the Military Police—even then, even before you reentered civilian life and decided to become a cop, you've always been a defender of others. And I hope this little bit my men and I have done has helped you get close to achieving your mission against Dr. Cheung. And if you're after him, then he's damn sure guilty of doing something against the common people who depend on you for protection."

"Thank you, sir."

Syongrui looked at Jacob:

"But, gentlemen…please don't let that vampire stuff get out. And damnit, Chang. Even after all of this, I'd join you in this combat again! And be damned proud to do it because I know you and that doggone patriotic lance of yours is always going to be stabbing at windmills for the good of the people!"

Chang and Syongrui embrace.

"Thank you sir" Chang said. But he felt horribly empty, saying: "I feel as though I'm on television getting some award." "

Everyone laughed. Chang patted Syongrui on the shoulder. Syongrui says:

"Don't worry, I'm afraid we're all going to be on TV soon enough after this. Not to mention the newspapers."

Chang slaps his hand on the table.

"The doctor's got a 'safe room' somewhere on this property. That's where he and the drug are right now—at this very moment."

General Syongrui agrees:

"I'm sure that you're right but we have zero chance of finding it."

"Yeah, and I'm sure that Ginger's in there with him." Jacob lamented.

Chang sadly adds:

"If she's still living.

Jacob looks at him and knows that he is right. It is more than possible the gang may have already done away with her. Everyone stands and heads for the front door. Chang reassures the general that:

"We'll come up with a believable scenario for you later, sir for and explanation as to your involvement, and trust me it will be patriotic. Just give us a little time." Chang turns to Zixin and put his arm around him. "As for now I'm putting Commander Zixin in charge here to finish the search. And commander when you finish the cleanup, I'll be in my office. I need time to prepare a defense against the coming cries for my resignation from Dr. Cheung and his politicos. Come on, Jacob, let's get the hell out of here. Chang looks at Jacob and pats him on the shoulder.

"…Vampires. Well, it's not your fault that Dr. Cheung decided to have some fun with you. But of all damned things … vampires."

CHAPTER 38

HANDLING TRUTH
AND AFTERMATH

Three days after Owen Chang's raid, Police Headquarters is being inundated with calls from city politicians at the behest and defense of an outraged Dr. Cheung. Jacob and Zixin are sitting in Chang's office, in awe of the numerous calls from attorneys, politicians, local civic leaders and citizens all demanding the immediate release of every member of *The Chinese Blood* gang being held in police custody.

It feels to Jacob and Zixin that almost a majority of the people in Hong Kong are against Chang and demanding his resignation or dismissal. A multitude of people are demanding an investigation into the shooting deaths of gang members on the property of Dr. Cheung whose attorneys allege that Chang has engaged in "**questionable police tactics by the use of unauthorized and deadly force against members of *The Chinese Blood* employed by Dr. Cheung as armed security guards on his own estate.**"

Television news stations carried the story of the raid and Cheung demanding a public apology from Chang and calling for his resignation. Attorneys representing Cheung filed harassment and persecution charges against the inspector, including a cease-and-desist order.

Cheung's attorneys also subpoena Chang to appear before a newly convened Police Review Board for his conduct charging: "*...Breaching the private residences of Dr. Wo-Ling Cheung without a search warrant or* *legitimate reason to suppose a crime is being committed at the address and bringing stolen Army weaponry onto said property and alleging they were found there."*

A few television stations and one newspaper attempt a defense of Inspector Chang, citing how during Chang's ten years as a police officer and his current fifteen years as inspector, his objective has always been to take down criminals and eradicate crime.

Some elements of the media suggest that he has much success in bringing the criminal element to justice and instilling some sense of fear in those who would think to act contrary to lawful rules of conduct.

However, critics allege that, *"Chang has designed his lofty, puritanical goal to facilitate creating an image of himself that is larger than life: "As was the crime of Caesar, he desired to be king of all he surveyed. And by this brazen attack on such a revered person as Dr. Wo-Ling Cheung, it proved that Inspector Chang has placed himself above the very law he is supposed to represent."*

Jacob watched Liao come into Chang's office, bow to him and then she pours tea for everyone. Chang, who is reading the day's paper, slams the publication, cussing. When Liao handed him a cup of tea, he sighed and leaned back in his chair.

"Thank you, Detective Liao. What am I going to do without you?" He took a quick sip. "Well, it seems, according to Commissioner Kim Jeoling, with whom I have an appointment in a few minutes, that the good Dr. Cheung is now so terrified of me that he has been forced to leave Hong Kong and hide in the United States. Needless to say, this has upset a great many important people here in Hong Kong. Of course he has taken his consultant, Baofung, and a small assemblage of thug bodyguards from *The Chinese Blood,* who I am sure include Chop Chop Chewy, Jub Jub Tai, Geraldine Taipan, and that insane young man they call Coo-Coo who only recently finished doing five years on assault and attempted murder charges. One of my street sources who's remaining loyal tells me that Cheung is headed for New York."

Jacob is reading another publication and he tapped his fingers on the page he is reading.

"Well, at least General Syongrui is not in hot water. It seems the army believes the story we concocted for him and he's been cleared of any charges."

Detective Liao sighs loudly:

"Oh, thank goodness for that one victory for us."

"Yeah, he's on page two; a small column buried that reads, in part:

'*Chou Lien Province. General Syongrui, conducting an undercover Armor drill involving some civilian participation, successfully recovered unknown amounts of stolen or missing base weaponry rumored to have been found on the estate of Dr. Cheung. It appears that General Syongrui determined some army weaponry from his drill to be missing, and is immediately given assistance from Police Commander Zhengzhong Zixin, head of Police Headquarters Special Police Operations Task Force who is participating in the army civilian operations drill. Commander Zhengzhong succeeded immediately in determining who is responsible for the missing army weaponry and recovered every missing item. Since all army weaponry has been recovered, and the culprits arrested no further action is to be taken concerning the matter, though the question remains as to how the army weaponry is stolen and by whom and how the weaponry ended up on Dr. Cheung's estate.'* Well, talk about something being convoluted. But ... all's well."*

Chang turned and smiles at Zixin:

"You hero you."

Zixin wanted to protest:

"Sir, I—."

But Chang holds his hand up.

"No, don't bother, commander. We are there. Remember? At least, thanks to the agreement I reached with my boss, Commissioner Kim Jeoling he is able to get Dr. Cheung to drop charges against the department if I am out of here on an extended if not permanent basis immediately. With some of the media describing our operation as, 'A Commando Assault,' my leaving my position is going to be merely a slap on the wrist compared to charges that could be leveled. I'm happy that to keep Jennings name out of it."

Jacob sadly replied:

"I thank you for that, sir."

"It's okay." Chang smiles.

Jacob suddenly perks up:

"Wait a minute!" He looked up at Chang. "Sir, did you say Dr. Cheung is headed for New York? Well, that's where his benefactor and the colony are nesting."

"Nesting? Colony?" Chang asked, "What colony? And what does 'nesting' mean? What are we looking for now—birds? I thought you said they are vampires." Chang wanted to smile but it is just too painful.

Jacob has absolutely no desire to go into all this again, but what did he have left to lose? At this point, the gang probably murdered Ginger by now and he has no intention of letting them get away with that, no matter what.

"Dr. Cheung says there is a colony of vampires in New York, and that is where his benefactor lives, the one who paid him to come up with the synthetic blood. That's why the shipments are all going to New York."

Seeing where this is leading, Zixin interjects:

"Yes, but isn't the doctor being out of China enough for us?"

Jacob shrugs:

"Yes, but now they're again free to continue making their drug in privacy with absolutely no interference from us."

Jacob persists:

"He's with the colony now. I'm sure of it. The vampire colony. We've got to take a chance on believing him. What else can be lost at this point? What difference does it make if they're real vampires or a bunch of escaped psychos drinking fake blood from champagne slippers claiming to be vampires? Isn't it worth looking into after going this far?"

Detective Liao clears her throat.

"Inspector Chang, I just want to remind you that you're running late for your appointment, sir."

Chang looks at his watch and nods.

"Thank you, Detective Liao. I certainly mustn't forget this appointment." He sighed heavily and wearily stood, seemingly unsteady on his feet. "As much as I'd like to, there's no reason to put this matter off. Commander Zixin, I want you to remain here. Make yourselves at home, and Detective Liao will see to your needs. I'm leaving you in charge for now as my successor." He heads for the door. "Well, unless our esteemed Commissioner Jeoling throws me out of his window, I guess I'll be back after our meeting."

Jacob reassures Chang that:

"If you need me in any way, sir, I'll be waiting here to hear from you. And good luck at your meeting."

"Thank you Jennings but you need to go back to your hotel just in case Ginger is still alive and tries to reach you. I think she's still somewhere on Dr. Cheung's compound if she's still alive. I'll contact you later."

Detective Liao is in tears:

"Inspector, I am truly sorry. You have worked so hard on this, and I know that this is devastating to you."

Chang walks over and hugged her.

"Thank you, but I'm not the only one who worked hard on this business with Dr. Cheung. We all have. I'm sorry to have let you all down."

Detective Liao points her finger at Chang:

"You have not let us down at all, sir." Liao's voice is defiant. "Not at all. And I stand ready to do it all again at your order." She hugged Chang and left the office in tears.

A painful silence.

Chang clears his throat:

"I shouldn't be too long, Commander Zixin."

"I'll be here, sir."

On the drive to Jeoling's office, Chang thinks about what is likely to happen in the meeting. Jeoling has too often told him to be careful investigating someone with the political power of Cheung. He also warned him that there might come a point where he is going to be unable to protect him. Chang has a feeling that this is that point.

Inspector Chang parked his car in front of a ten story seemingly all glass building and cut off the motor. He walked inside, presents his credentials to the seated police officer and steps into one of the four elevators.

Stepping off at the third floor at Jeoling's office, Chang took a deep breath at the office door. He knew that Police Division Director Kim Jeoling is a good man, fair, but as is often the case with high rank, he is more of a politician than anything else. When Chang knocked on the door, the coldness of Jeoling's voice tightened his flesh:

"Get in here, Chief Inspector."

A CHANGING OF THE GUARD

Chang returned to his office two hours later. With a quick nod, he acknowledged Commander Zixin who is seated at the round table. Chang sinks into the cushiony chair behind his desk and is followed in by Detective Liao who brought tea, coffee and rolls with her on a tray.

She placed the tray on the table and tries to smile at him but she is unable to accomplish that for the task of holding back her tears at what she knew is going to be bad news from him.

"Thank you, Detective Liao. Why don't you have a seat? I have something to say to you and Commander Zixin here." He looked around. "Where is Mrs. Che?"

"She's still on duty at the hotel, sir. You remember that, like Mrs. Wong, she is required to live in the maid's quarters until it is her day off." Liao said, almost apologetically.

Chang nodded recognition of that fact.

"Yes and I think it's best to leave her there. The gang could be thinking of getting rid of Jennings just for the hell of it. And at this point they would get away with it. He may need backup from her until I can get him out of here."

"Yes, sir."

Chang lit a cigar.

"I've been relieved of duty."

Liao gasped.

"What?"

"Director Jeoling has suggested that I take a year's leave of absence until this entire business blows over and he is able to work something out in my favor. He further suggests that I appoint an interim replacement, temporary of course. And going by the chain of command, that's you, Commander Zixin. Congratulations."

Commander Zixin objected:

"But, sir, that is not fair. Don't get me wrong. It would be an honor to hold down headquarters for you until your return, but everything you've done is in the interest of Chou Lien Province—as I have said before—all of Hong Kong. In fact, you are acting to prevent catastrophes in other countries by trying to end the exportation of this *cherry berry*. How is it cannot he see that?"

"The only way for him to fully understand would be for me to have explained this drug to him and its purpose. But I don't believe vampires is high on his or anyone else's list of believability. So how could I tell him that I've been campaigning against a drug that Dr. Cheung has created for vampires?" He smiled at Detective Liao. "Even you found that amusing, Liao."

"Inspector, I deeply apologize for that silliness that erupted from me earlier. I truly do."

"Don't apologize. I completely understand. How else could anyone expect you or the others to respond to such a statement about vampires being real? Even I know it's just laughable." Chang seemed to shrink even more in his chair. "I wonder, could you pour me a nice, hot coffee, Liao?"

"Of course, sir. I can't believe the director is having you take a year's leave."

"Actually, Director Jeoling could have insisted on my retirement or resignation." He looked at his cigar and grunted:

"… Vampires."

Liao held up a saucer holding a buttered roll:

"May I suggest that you take some nourishment in addition to coffee?"

"Maybe later.

Zixin beat his fist into the palm of his hand.

"Sir, I want you to know that I'm going to be running this department the exact same way you would be running it. I'll be the mirror image of you, and I promise you that. I'm not going to slow down looking for the *cherry berry*, and I'll be keeping a close eye on *The Chinese Blood*. I also would be grateful if you will keep in constant close touch with me, on a weekly basis, sir. I am not replacing you, I am only temporarily covering for you during an extended vacation."

Chang smiled.

"You're a good and capable man, Zixin. But I want you to distance yourself from this *cherry berry* business and I don't care if it's being used by a bunch of damned British werewolves in miniskirts!"

CHAPTER 39

NEVER THE
MOTHERLY TYPE

During the next two days following Inspector Chang's forced leave of absence Jacob has been in constant touch with him, but Chang has had little to say. He is busy tidying up things in his office before turning the temporary reins over to Zixin who is soon to be announced as interim Chief Inspector of Police.

Still Jacob wants to fill him in on the latest information he has concerning the *cherry berry* investigation, so Chang sat at his desk and listened to what Jacob has to say:

"Earlier today I heard from Delilah, she said that her sister has been set free to roam Dr. Cheung's estate. Ginger is alive and fine and the two of them are busy trying to find a means of escaping from the estate, but they are both being watched closely. But there is something really weird happening here. She said that she is sure that *The Chinese Blood* have been given orders to execute them and it wasn't Baofung working a spell on her. She overheard one of the gang members discussing someone's impending assassination but she didn't get the name, only that it's a man. She had also heard that the assassin is going to be a female. Delilah is positive that it's going to be a female gang member they call, 'Pink Girl.'"

Chang knew her.

"Yeah, she is really a very dangerous young woman, almost as bad as Desirlee, just not quite as pretty. We believe that she's murdered two women and a man less than a year ago for the gang but nothing could be proven. A witness says she saw her kill a man during the rain, by pretending to accidentally bump into him on the street; the man dropped dead a second later. It seems she pressed a darning needle into him just beneath his solar plexus and pushed it up into his chest cavity in one deft move the anonymous witness said over the phone."

"Wow."

"And we know that one of the women she killed was poisoned and the other garroted. After that she delivered the bodies of each woman to their homes, leaving one draped over her parents' mailbox, the other hanging from a rope by her breasts in the center of the front door of the mother's home; some kind of superstition of hers to do so. She did a short stint in prison for some minor crime like her brother, Coo Coo, who is also in the gang. I told you about him. It's believed she murdered three of her fellow inmates. Of course nothing could be proved."

The hotel phone is clicking.

"I got another call, sir. I'll be in touch."

Jacob pressed the phone.

"Hello?"

It is Delilah.

"*The Chinese Blood* say they are going to free my sister, but I do not trust them. I am still working on a way for us to leave here on our own." Delilah began giggling.

"What is it, Delilah?"

"I'm laughing because my sister told me before that she misses your voice."

"I miss hers, too. Please tell her that."

"Well" she giggled again, "that's not much for the two of you to miss. Is that all you miss from her? Because I know it is not all she misses from you." She began laughing. "Someone is coming now, and I must go. Good-bye, Jacob The Jew." She disconnected.

The phone rang again and he eagerly picked it up.

"Hello?

"Jacob The Jew"—No, no, make that Jacob the police hookup man." The voice is Chewy's.

"Chewy."

Jacob wonders is Chewy still in Hong Kong or in America with Cheung and Baofung. But if there are any assassinations to be carried out the doctor might not trust anyone in the gang to do it but him; at least to oversee the assassination.

"Who else would it be, fool? This ain't Chang you're talkin' to."

Jacob took a breath. This is the new Chewy. No more jokes, wise cracks, or pretending. THIS IS RAW CHEWY, TIGHTLY COILED, READY TO STRIKE, LIKE THE DEADLY SERPENT JACOB HAS ALWAYS KNOWN HIM TO BE.

"I thought you'd left the country with Dr. Cheung."

"First I've got a little business to take care of."

"You and Jub Jub?"

"Me. Just me. I gotta supervise some garbage removal; see that it ends up in a few garbage cans."

"Sounds like a lot of garbage."

"Don't want nobody to try piecing it back together again. It's just a snake. A really big one, too."

For some obscure reason Jacob's blood chilled a bit. Then he felt himself growing angry and a fury inside him wanted to reach through the phone and snatch Chewy by the throat and for a moment he wished he could be a vampire for just this once to drain Chewy's blood and savor each and every ounce as it is drawn in through his fangs. He wanted to be able to look into Chewy's eyes as the light of life flickered brightly then dim as all that remains of Chewy is a bloodied, despised memory on his Jacob's fangs. He hated Chewy that much for having endangered Ginger.

He balled his fist and spoke to Chewy:

"I guess you're angry, then."

"About what? You're not talkin' about your little jive ambush party you and your police friends pulled off? You don't mean that, do you?"

Jacob's anger is surging again.

"That's exactly what I mean."

Chew snorts out a noise that has the sound of the violent cough of an angry bear who is closing in on his victim.

"Yo', you know how them Indians do to keep a tiger from havin' 'em for breakfast? They tie a mask to the back of their head. But your problem is that you done already used up yours. Happy deathday."

Chewy hung up.

Almost immediately the phone rang again. He snatched the phone and barked:

"What, Chewy? What is it now?"

But Inspector Chang responded:

"Calm down Jennings. It's me."

"Oh, sorry, sir. I just had a nasty call from Chewy. He hung up before I could find if he's here or in New York."

"Jennings, I have some more bad news, well, maybe not really bad. Your unit must have gotten wind of our dilemma here and they sent me a memo for you. You've been reassigned. Let me read it to you:

To: Lieutenant Jacob Jennings,
From: Military Counterintelligence Corp
275 Brigade
Taipei, Taiwan.
Republic of China

I have been in touch with Chief Inspector of Police Owen Chang and I have advised him that I am considering the precarious situation that currently exists in the city of Honk Kong regarding your involvement with his investigation. I have asked him not to speak with you concerning our conversation until I have made a decision one way or another and that I would then advise you and you will inform him of this communication in an expeditious manner. The Inspector assures me that you have acted in the professional manner he expected and have demonstrated superior abilities in assisting him during the entire investigation he has undertaken. I am proud of you and of course this office expected no less from you.

However, your presence there has become tenuous and in the interest of continued good relations between our two countries, and in your best interest, I find it necessary to have you reassigned to temporary duty (tdy) to serve as Military Assistant Advisor to the community affairs department as assistant to Usata Onanoka in Tokyo, Japan.

Enclosed, please find that your orders have been "cut" and let me take this opportunity to thank you for your exemplary service during this rather extraordinary assignment to assist the Chinese government. Due to your lack of remaining time of service in the U.S. Army, I find it necessary to reassign you to return to duty as assisting Senior Investigator, Onanoka in Japan's Community Affairs Department in Tokyo, Japan as Clerical Aide until your enlistment has expired whereupon you will be provided with transportation to return to a discharge station within the United States of America. Mr. Onanoka has expressed his willingness to have you work in some capacity that will not put you at risk until the expiration of your current term of service with the United States Army, approximately five (5) months from this date.

This reassignment will be effective in five (5) days from today's date.

(Signature)
Roger A. Allan
Lieutenant Colonel, G.S.
Chief, Administrative Ref.'

"Well, that's it, Jennings. And look, I'm sorry but I've got some more stuff to clean up here. Give me a call later."

"Yes, sir." He hangs up.

Jacob didn't know which came first: the sound of the person knocking on his hotel room door or his Moor's head vibrating.

He stares blankly at the door for a long moment before going to answer.

"Yes, who is it?"

Someone is answering. It sounds as though it may be a woman's voice, but he did not feel that it belonged to either Ginger or Delilah. He walked to the door, and for some reason, he hesitated this time before speaking again:

"Who is it?"

The response on the other side of his door was almost a whisper. But when he starts to open the door he recalls Chewy's threat and he goes the dresser, takes the gun Chang gave him and slips it into his pocket. Then he goes to opens the door but not before asking again:

"I said, who is it?" Still the voice was speaking lowly but clearly a female speaking.

"Aw, for—! He snatches the door open and is surprised to see Mrs. Che in her maid's uniform smiling at him. He furtively slips the gun back in his pocket. He has forgotten that she is still working at his hotel as a maid.

She is holding a package with a bow around it that she hands to him.

He is very pleased and surprised. He accepts it and bows to her:

"Mrs. Che. Wow, I forgot you're still here. Come on in." He takes the package from her and steps aside to let her in.

A smiling Mrs. Che bows to him and walks in:

"Lieutenant Jennings."

Seeing who it is, Jacob relaxes. He wonders if Chang has told her about him being reassigned back to Japan. At any rate, there is no way she does not know about problems Chang has and about the raid.

"Mrs. Che. I see that Inspector Chang hasn't withdrawn you from duty here yet?"

"He is concerned about a possible aftermath from *The Chinese Blood*. It has been arranged for me to have a room on this floor as a protective measure. I am assigned to continue to work here until you leave, which I have been informed is scheduled to take place soon. Am I correct, sir?"

His decorum and facial expression both become dour, and he nods his head.

"Yes, I'm due to report for temporary duty in Tokyo in five days. He looked at the gift box which is a bit heavy. He knows it is not unusual for Asians to present a gift simply as a token of friendship or of appreciation for having worked together. He is sorry that he has nothing to give her, not having anticipated this.

Mrs. Che points to the package:

`That is a gift for you, sir."

"Thank you, Mrs. Che."

He began slowly, carefully untying the ribbon when the phone rings.

"Excuse me." He picks up the phone. "Yeah, hello."

He is still fumbling with the ribbon on the box.

"Jacob The Jew. It's me, your Ginger."

He froze. His expression is locked somewhere between total amazement and being on the brink of bursting out in tears. Finally, he gasps out a single word:

"Baby!" He turns around and looks at Mrs. Che and gave a thumbs up sign then turns back to the phone.

Ginger's voice is jubilant:

"Is Jacob The Jew happy to hear his Ginger cookie?"

"Yes! Oh, hell yes! Baby, where are you? Are you—?"

"Jacob The Jew must first listen to me! My sister and I have escaped Dr. Cheung's estate! It is most important that you—"

"Ginger, I can't believe it's you! So you and Delilah were able to get away after all!" He turned to Mrs. Che. "Great news, Mrs. Che! Ginger and her sister have escaped!"

"Yes, I know."

He steps over and hugs Mrs. Che and gives her another thumb up then turns back around to continue talking. He is so happy just to hear Ginger's voice that he has not taken notice that Mrs. Che knows Ginger is free; something she should not be aware of. And he is about to undo the ribbon and lift the box top.

But Ginger heard him speaking to Mrs. Che and she asks:

"Wait! Mrs. Che? Is that the woman who works with your Police Inspector Chang?"

"Yeah, she does."

He slips his fingers beneath the ribbon of the box top, lifting the top to reveal its contents. But Jacob is looking away at Mrs. Che when the lid slips off his present and falls to the floor because. But Jacob cannot fathom what the smell is and he is looking around the room. It is a really terribly rancid stink behind him coming from Mrs. Che.

"My God, Mrs. Che what is that smell? Don't you smell that?" But then he is quickly back around to hear what Ginger is hollering to him in the phone. He still has not looked at his "present."

"Ginger, is screaming something but her scream is so desperate that her words are indecipherable to him:

"Ginger, I can't understand a word you're saying." He looks down in his box and, seeing the contents he drops it. "What in—?"

Ginger is still screaming:

"Get away from that woman! Run from the room! She is the one who was doing the spell on me—not Baofung! She is Baofung's *Deschong!* The other one was just to distract us!"

But Jacob hardly can acknowledge her words because they only barely registering in his mind. He is staring down at his "present." The "present' is staring back at him. His body shudders at the sight of the head of the hotel manager, Jun Lao Tzu's severed head and his dead eyes staring up at him.

Even at a glance at Tzu's head it's easy to see it has been ripped from his body not cut off. He slowly turns to look at Mrs. Che who is now only inches away and grinning vacuously sat him. Holds the phone to his ear. Ginger is screaming louder than ever:

"Get away from her! Get out of your room!"

"It was her, your Mrs. Che that killed your maid! She needed to be closer to me to make her spell stronger to save Baofung! So she killed your maid so she could take her place and close to me to work her magic against me. You said you smell a bad smell—that's her! That's her! The smell means she is going to kill you! Please run!"

Mrs. Che's hand locked around Jacob's throat like a vise causing air in his throat to screech to a screaming halt midway up his throat.

Jacob quickly grabbed his Moor's head, but Mrs. Che, with little effort, lifted him high in the air with one hand and with her other she quickly disengaged his fingers from the Moor's head. But Jacob tries to give the command anyway:

"...Corpo Seco rise...be before me."

Nothing happened. He has to figure a way to have the tongue of the Moor's pierce his finger for the conjure to work.

Again he grabbed his pendant and pressed his finger against the face but the moment the tongue pierced his finger, Mrs. Che grabbed his wrist with such an uncanny grip that his entire hand swelled immediately, and he released his pendant, but managed to mutter:

"...Corpo Seco..."

She slams Jacob against the wall with such force that breathing deserted him for a moment and unconsciousness is imminent, but he fought against it desperately. Che reached down and locked her fingers around his throat again, snatching him up from the floor the way a person might do a bag of garbage and she goes back to holding him high into the air. She is holding his pendant between her fingers, looking at it and laughing.

"What strength is there in this Blackamoor?"

A moment before the *darkness* overtook him Che senses that something is amiss and she releases her grip on Jacob letting him drop once more to the floor, finally allowing him to breathe.

Che around slowly and is face to face with a sinisterly grinning Corpo Seco who begins stroking her breasts and the sides of her face tenderly but with obvious lusting.

"So. A *Deschong*, eh?" Corpo Seco's eyes gleamed.

Mrs. Che turns back to look at Jacob and laughs.

"Jacob The Jew has such silly magic."

She turned from Jacob and grabbed Corpo Seco by the neck and squeezed hard as she mumbled words and waved her other hand wildly in the air.

A great wind whipped through Jacob's room, and she laughed and released Corpo Seco who, along with Jacob, is being tossed about the room, caught up in the strong wind. She pointed her finger at Jacob, slowly guiding him to the window and then through it. Once he is outside the window, she released the wind and Jacob began hurtling face downward from his eleventh floor window.

He tries speaking a conjure but the air rushed in is open mouth, gagging him. He managed to turn around, his back to the ground and, finally able to breathe, spoke:

"Ladies of the gales carry me aloft!"

There came a loud whooshing noise along with a sudden gust of air that preceded the appearance of the heads of several women blowing out strong gusts of wind that lifted him upwards until he is level with his hotel room window.

A woman materializes clothed in a flowing bright yellow robe so bright that her features are not quite distinguishable, only the shape of her and most of her face which looks familiar to Jacob.

It is Elizabeth, his grandmother, smiling at him as she guides him through the window with her, both of them seeming to melt as they glide through the glass.

In his room, Mrs. Che and Corpo Seco are in a heated battle, furniture flying about the room, each combatant smashing furniture into the other as they angrily, furiously fly about.

Then he has Che by the throat and runs her head into the wall. No damage to her and so he rips away a great swath of flesh from her face, revealing her facial skeletal structure as she digs her teeth into his chest and rips out a huge chunk of writhing flesh that is spurting wide sprays of blood over her face.

Corpo Seco looks at Jacob, laughing insanely:

"The bitch just won't die!"

Jacob raises both his hands and calls out:

"Deepest cumuli find me!"

Instantly the whirlwind stops and the spinning furniture drops to the floor and it becomes deathly quiet as a wide and thick curtain of black clouds accompanied by loud thunder and multiple lightning flashes rise from the floor, opening a wide black hole. The clouds surrounds Mrs. Che who now looks panicked. She holds out her hand to Jacob, shaking her head and pleading:

"No! Not there!"

Jacob points to the hole and commands her and Seco to:

"Enter that vile place!"

Seco screams a loud laugh:

"Yes, Jacob! Let me have her!"

Mrs. Che glares at Jacob as she and Seco are being sucked down into the black bole. She screams at him:

"Insect! What magic is this nonsense? You interrupter!"

And then the hole seals and is gone.

Someone is knocking desperately at his door. He is hesitant but he opens the door and Ginger and Delilah rush in and survey the damage. Ginger looks around and then demands:

"Where is the bitch?"

"Mrs. Che is gone. You won't see her anymore."

Behind Ginger and Delilah are several inquisitive, frightened maids, the same ones who, days ago, gave Jacob the white candle and Bible. All of them are trying their best to see inside Jacob's room through his open door. He smiles at them.

"Everything is all right now. Don't be worried. But I thank you all." He gently closes the door.

Ginger and Delilah are looking around the room at the disorder. Ginger shook her head.

"My goodness! Ginger slips her arm around Jacob's neck. "Now my Jacob The Jew really does need a maid for sure." The two kiss passionately.

Delilah snickers:

"Why don't you two get a room?|"

Jacob disengages himself from Ginger and reminds her that:

"There's still some unfinished business. I have to call Chang and he is going to have to find a way to explain to Mrs. Che's department in COINTELPRO what happened to her and where she is. Well, no he can't do that, either. But we have to come up with a story explaining why she will never be seen again."

Ginger looks around the room.

"Well, while you call him, me and my sister will try and get this mess to look like a little less of a mess."

Jacob yanked out his cellphone and dialed Inspector Chang's number.

CHAPTER 40

AFTER
THE BATTLE

Jacob, Ginger and Delilah have been sitting in Jacob's hotel room with Chief Inspector of Police, Owen Chang for the past two hours explaining what happened to Mrs. Che and who she is or was.

Chang is sipping at a drink of bourbon that Jacob poured for him and for himself. He is trying to fathom the multitudinous enormity of the impossibly complex series of connective events starting with the *cherry berry*.

He takes a long swallow and then steadily paces the empty Glasson the table and takes a very long inhalation of both air and retrospect:

"Well...let me see if I have this right: first of all, Dr. Cheung and maybe Baofung invent this new kind of blood for vampires that gives them both a great high but also poses certain irrevocable dangers for them and possibly even worse if humans are given the drug; this danger to humans may be intensified if given through a needle. That is yet to be determined by Dr. Cheung. Then Cheung is told that I have heard about his new cherry berry drug so he has his *Deschong*, Mrs. Che who is already infiltrated into COINTELPRO assigned to me. So now he has a direct pipeline to every step of my investigation. Am I right so far?"

His question caught Jacob middrink and he could only nod at first, then swallow followed by his verbal response:

"That's correct, sir."

Delilah pours the inspector another drink but Chang does not notice since he is very likely turning this conundrum of events over in his mind.

"So Jennings, as you always suspected, there was a leak in my department. Mrs. Che."

"Yes, sir." Jacob nodded. "But that leak is sealed now."

"And Baofung loosed the second shadow deschong just to preoccupy us with her and we are misled into thinking she is the problem when all along it was Mrs. Che."

This time Ginger answered him:

"That's right, Inspector Chang. The *shadow deschong* Che has been with Baofung for a very long time. But she needed to be close to me for her aging spell to work well. The closer she is to me the stronger her spell. That is why she killed Mrs. Wong at the hotel. Once she took her place, she is close enough to me to really work her aging spell. All the time I thought my spell against Baofung was not working, but it really was working. But when I was at the clinic I was much better because she didn't know where I was. The aging spell was used to age me and stop me from remembering my spells. Baofung knows I am a student of sorcery. He dared not kill me because he knows my sister would kill him before he could do magic on her."

Owen Chang emptied his glass in another single swallow. He sat the glass down noisily and leaned back in his chair:

"And the last of her was when Jacob used one of the magic conjures you taught him. Okay, but now what about the other one, the *shadow deschong?*"

Ginger and Jacob look at each other. Ginger is the one to speak:

"I think she went rebel. She was in love with my Jacob the Jew and she forced herself off the wall to try and get him but she never seemed able to get enough power to be able to accomplish her goal. She will be sent to the worse part of the lowest area of hell. From there she is frozen in a lewd pose and all kinds of creatures and things, horrible entities do anything to her they want to do. She has to remain in that lewd pose and take it all and that is forever. That's her punishment for betraying her creator, Baofung.

A *shadow deschong* is one of the lowest kind of demon as far as power is concerned and for betraying Baofung, her punishment will be awful."

Chang looks at Jacob.

"Jennings, just where did you send her in that black hole you described? Where did she end up?"

Jacob shook his head.

"She ended up with Seco Corpo who lives, from what I've been able to ascertain, in total blackness somewhere in a really insidious area of hell."

"Well the only remaining problem is how die I explain all this to her department? How can I explain why they're never going to see her again?"

Jacob reassures him that:

"It'll take some time, sir, but we will be able to come up with a believable explanation to her superiors."

Chang gave that some thought and decided:

"Yeah, after all, we did it for General Syongrui and I'll be able to easily squash this Jun Lao-Tzu headless hotel manager thing. What I can't seem to really accomplish is…" he picked up his drink and took a long, long swallow and set on the table briskly, "…to find a way to wrap my head around…" he emptied the rest of his drink, "…all of this damn magic."

Everyone began laughing and Chang held up his hand to say:

"And Ginger you and Jacob keep your hands at your sides, don't be waving them around because I don't wanna disappear in a puff of dog-gone smoke."

Jacob and Ginger laughed heartedly…

IN TIME ALL THINGS

Chang, Zixin, Ginger and Delilah and Jacob are seated at the round table in Chang's office. It seems nothing has changed at Police Headquarters except Chang's name is no longer on his office door. Commander Zixin's name and title have replaced it. Jacob pulls up a chair next to Ginger and Delilah. Detective Liao is serving everyone tea and in the center of the roundtable are bagels and doughnuts. When entering the building, every officer and civilian employee demonstrate that they still regard Chang as their superior; they all bow deeply to him and call him, "Chief Inspector." He is deeply moved by their acknowledgement but manages to maintain his decorum.

Chang sits at the head of the table. The discussion is how to continue their battle against Cheung and Baofung in a subtler and more effective way. The initial difficulty is that the two have fled to New York along with key members of *The Chinese Blood* gang. It's obvious to everyone that the investigation into Cheung's *cherry berry* activities has to be continued in New York; the clear problem is the logistics of location and jurisdictional authority for Chang.

But Jacob has promised that he can obtain that authority by way of his position as a Detective for NYPD for Chang once they get to America. Chang knows it is not only worth the effort but it is also his only avenue to continue the pursuit of Cheung's drug network. He agrees:

"I think maybe you have something there, Jennings. Let's see how it works out."

"Inspector, why don't you come with me back to Tokyo. You know the people that I'm going to be working with: Onanoka and Burney. It'll be for five months and that's when my discharge will come through. Then we can pack up and head for New York. Onanoka and Burney both still think highly of you...Charlie Chan." Jacob snickered. "Please don't let them know that I let that slip out. I should have kept that to myself."

Chang's face lights up and he waves away Jacob's concern:

"Oh, don't even think about it. They never knew that I am well aware that is their nickname for me. Actually, I found it a compliment."

Again, Chang is lost in thought and whatever he is remembering or thinking of is clearly pleasant. Then Chang's face lit up and he slaps his hands together and laughs heartily:

"Well, okay, but you know I 've been to New York and of course you live there, I know, which is why I believe we both realize that looking for Cheung and his people is going to be like trying to find the proverbial needle in a haystack. For instance, if they hid in Chinatown in lower Manhattan, we'd never find them. In fact, that would be one of the best places for them to hide. No one in Chinatown is going to give outsiders information about anyone, not even to other Asians, especially if they are being paid to keep a person's anonymity." Chang throws his hands up. "But, let's give it a go! Man, do I ever know those two! Two of the biggest cutups in class. I was their class instructor for years. Both of them bright as hell, though. Smart students. Burney was Air Force and Onanoka was a civilian. It'll be great to see them again."

He slaps the table smartly with the palm of his hand and reaches out to Jacob and they shook hands. Chang says:

"Yeah, let's get this show on the road.

NOT THE BEST OF NEWS

Jacob feels that Ginger's kisses are only halfhearted and he stops and looks at her. There are tears in her eyes and she sat up on the hotel bed and turned her back to him. He sat up and gently turned her around to face him.

He studies her face trying to understand if she is still ill, but no, the spell Mrs. Che was casting on her is gone and Ginger is young again, her face is fresh and beautifully olive complected; and although the hotel's lamp light is in competition with her flesh's natural sheen, even the weaponry of man's artificial lighting cannot possibly win such a contest.

"What's wrong, Ginger? You're acting kind of sad. This is the part where you and Delilah come back to America with Inspector Chang and me and with you as my bride."

He strokes the side of her smooth face. He loves and relishes touching her just for the sensation of feeling the unparalleled silkiness of her flesh. But now he saw that there is something that is bothering her and he is almost afraid of finding out what it is. But there are, he knows, certain truths and facts that no one and nothing can protect a person from discovering. And he knew that this is one lamentable fact that no matter how much he dreaded it, is going to be revealed to him. And the words felt as though they have rushed from her mouth at a terrible speed, each letter capped with the heads of spears each separately piercing his now stilled heart with a horrible penetration of sadness when Ginger, with her back to him, says:

"I hate having to say this to my Jacob The Jew, but I am sorry, but I must remain behind here in Hong Kong with my sister. I can't go with you to Tokyo and so, I guess, not to America either."

He quickly turns her around, immediately regretting the harshness of his grip on her.

"Ginger, what are you talking about? Why can't you go with us?"

"Delilah and I have gotta stay behind and go back to the mountains where our parents live just in case the gang tries to harm them for what we've done against them. We have to go back home and live there until we know the gang is not looking to harm them."

He knows there is no argument against what she is saying and he does not want to even think of saying anything even remotely hinting that she should not go to protect her parents.

But he is heartbroken and he sees almost all of his plans for the immediate future disintegrating before his eyes due to such an insignificant amount of words that yet carry the force of a nuclear explosion. So he said nothing.

But she speaks:

"When we go back to the mountains, I will study more magic with my shaman. Our parents will be safe as long as we are there. In time we will know if *The Chinese Blood* is seeking revenge against our parents. If they are, then we can deal with them with the help of my shaman and when they see that, there will be no more problem and then perhaps, if my Jacob The Jew is still interested, we will be free to join in America."

Jacob is very disappointed.

"I was hoping you were both coming back with me, but I understand. And you know that I will always be waiting and looking forward to us getting married."

Ginger hugs him and they kiss tenderly. She playfully squeezes the end of his nose and holds him in a tight embrace. He is continually amazed that she does that with his nose just the way his grandmother Elizabeth always did. Jacob unhappily agrees, refusing to blink for fear of his tears escaping

CHAPTER 41

NEW YORK,
BUT JAPAN FIRST

As their plane began its descent at the Tokyo Airport, Jacob feels a sense of calm, and he wondered if perhaps Chang, who is sitting next to him and smiling, felt a similar sensation. He rolled his Moor's head around between his fingers, all the while contemplating what other powers it held for him. He felt an immense spiritual strength stirring within and vows to heed his grandmother's advice to study his powers harder.

His grandmother Elizabeth taught him so many esoteric skills of the powers residing in the *Dark Arts* the powers of the *Darkness*. He is still waiting to discover the powers he is born with. As his abilities stand now, his powers along with the ones Ginger taught him and the others she promised to teach him, all of them combined will give him a marvelous yet fearsome arsenal of *Dark* skills in magic; especially when he uncovers his *veil* powers. In addition to that, he still awaits his lessons in magic from whomever visits him from "The Night People," "The Enchanters."

He and Chang will be dealing with people with occult knowledge and powers but also creatures some of which have always been thought of as not existing; extant in folklore only. They are both going to be in unfamiliar territories, but Chang even more so than he.

Jacob is pretty sure that at times he is going to have to protect him, because although he knows that he now believes in the existence of the supernatural, he is still not quite able to come to terms with it in his reality.

He admires that Chang is a practical man, one who deals with crime in hard, two fisted, of the old school ways of police work; almost hearkening to the era of the old "gumshoe" who is only concerned with the world turning the way he knew it should. He seems the kind of cop who is accustomed to going head to head not head to magic wand, having to face phantoms or things with diaphanous shapes. Jacob knows that will prove dangerous for the two of them.

He also felt that Chang believed in sorcery far more than he is willing to admit to him. He also has the impression that Chang wanted to consider the occult as a kind of science, an esoteric science but still something that has some sort of understandable comprehensive structure to it. That line of thinking will make him more comfortable thinking of magic that way.

Jacob has come to appreciate that there is a distinct difference between the magic of the East and that of the West, and it probably is not a question of which is stronger. But he knew that the effectiveness of the different forms of magic is not as simple as who uses his or hers first, probably it is a bottomless pit of unlearned knowledge on both sides. He would have to deal with that possibility when it presented itself again, but he knew he needs to be prepared for the eventuality of Asian sorcery and magic against American magic.

The cab pulled to a stop in front of Onanoka's building at the rear of Police Headquarters. Watching Chang pay the tab, Jacob felt kind of sorry for him for not having any mystical abilities to draw on, knowing that in the battle they are going to be facing, guns and bullets are often going to be totally useless; but not always.

Japan's Special Investigator for Community Affairs, Usata Onanoka and Colonel Burney are glad to see Jacob, but they are completely overjoyed at the sight of Inspector Chang.

Onanoka, Chang and Burney hug and make loud jokes about each other for the longest time before settling down to drinks of bourbon in Onanoka's office. Looking at Chang, Onanoka could hardly believe his eyes.

"Sir, you look absolutely great! Just how long has it been? Never mind. I don't wanna know how many years have gone by since Burney here and I worked under the great Owen Chang."

Chang has a knowing smirk on his face.

"Don't you two misfits mean Charlie Chan?"

Onanoka and Burney looked at each other in total shock. Onanoka leaned forward.

"You mean you knew what we used to call you?"

"Oh yeah." Chang turned to Jacob. "These two characters almost drove me out of my mind back in the day." Chang smiled at Jacob. "Neither one of them could follow orders. They loved doing things their own way. But most of the time they got results—not always good ones mind you." Chang laughed.

"Yeah," Burney agreed, "and I hate to count the times that we came back to you to get our asses out of hot water. But in those days a man could really fight crime without worrying about the thug's attorney demanding his client be given his rights and color tv."

Burney elbows Onanoka, playfully.

"Well, Inspector Chang actually agreed with the attorneys about their clients having their rights, and more than once we've seen him give them their rights...and lefts, and then a whole lot more rights and lefts. Hell, Burney, you and I weren't too bad ourselves in giving out rights and lefts to thugs!"

The three men burst out in laughter so loud that Jacob could have sworn he saw a picture on the wall actually shake. He liked seeing Chang laugh, and he realized that this is the first time he has ever seen happy. Obviously some relief from an awful pressure came with his suspension from his position in Hong Kong.

Onanoka is gasping for air from laughing:

"Man we really did 'hotdog' it back then."

"Yeah, you guys did."

"Yeah," Burney agreed, "but if not for you, a few times we would have been in jail alongside the very thugs we locked up."

Chang lights a cigar.

"That's sure true enough. Yeah, but now..." his mood changed, "it's all different. It's all about political connections and cash flow and babying cons with libraries and special diets and college courses in prison. Go to prison and get your damn law degree, come out and start practicing law against the same people that jailed you in the first place. There's no more damn law. No, I take that back. There's law, there's just too often minimal justice."

Burney sympathized with Chang.

"Yeah, like that business with Jeoling giving you an indefinite leave of absence. We heard about it. Of course it could have been a helluva lot worse. He could have forced you to retire or even resign your position. But everybody respects you and your record against crime."

Onanoka thought about Cheung.

"Yeah but this Dr. Cheung is really hooked up politically. Even on his way to New York he stops over here in Japan and is interviewed on a television show. Burney and I watched it. The guy's a renowned research scientist. Over the years he's made some pretty good discoveries in the medical research field. I wonder where he went wrong."

Chang is sure that he knows:

"Money is where he went wrong." Chang relit his cigar. "It's where most crooks go wrong. Money. Greed."

Jacob is curious.

"I understand that there's some clandestine teaching going on here in Japan somewhere. I wonder who's ever heard of the *Shadow School*? I understand that Baofung runs it. His students are called, *The Dark Ones*, and from what I've been told, even students of the occult fear them."

Onanoka swallowed his drink.

"Yeah, we've heard about them. Kinda scary people if you ask me. I've even come across some of them. They're weird."

Onanoka became a bit uncomfortable and he got up and peeked outside his open office door. Then he closed it and sat back at the table, locking his hands together.

"Okay, listen everybody…we all know there's not supposed to be any such thing as Vodou or hoodoo magic, black magic, herbal magic, and so on. I never believed in all that hooey." He looked at Jacob with a solemn expression. "Yeah, I've heard whispers about that school for years." He poured himself another drink. "But I have no idea where it's located, I know only that it does exist." Onanoka is clearly becoming even more uncomfortable at this point. "Listen … I've had an experience with three of those students who I learned later are called *The Dark Ones*. Man, they are goddamn scary!"

Chang looks at Jacob then back to Onanoka.

"What do you mean?"

"Okay, look, I think you and Burney here know I am not a person who is easily scared. But let me tell you, some young girls I came across are people you wanna be careful with."

Chang sits up. He is very interested to see a man he has trained and worked with who is genuinely bothered by something that apparently he considers beyond what is thought of as normal. It is starting to look as though he has a brother in arms as far as being inducted into the strangeness of the occult and those who practice it. Chang is eager to hear what Onanoka has to say:

"Yeah, go on. I wanna hear this."

"These people have got what they call 'night walkers,' students who can walk in the air but only during the evening hours. Now I'm not talking about levitation, I mean actually walking through the air—off the ground, I mean. I've seen them do it! I've seen three of those students walk up the side of a house and onto the roof then jump to the next one and then the next until I lost sight of them. And one of the girls, damned if her eyes didn't look to me like they glowed in the dark when she looked at me! Then she did the same thing, except that she ran across the roofs by doing it backwards while watching me with those glowing eyes! It is like some giant vacuum sucked her up the side of the house while she is facing me. Then she kept running backward across the rooftops, running and jumping from rooftop to rooftop while watching me and grinning, jumping through mid-air until she, too, was out of sight!"

Onanoka has to calm himself. He finished his drink in a single swallow.

"I don't like talking about that experience and I don't usually even mention it."

Jacob, Burney, and Chang are all impressed with his candor in talking of how he is affected by what he has seen. Clearly the event traumatized him.

Onanoka has to take another drink before he continued.

"Until I saw those three young girls do those things, I never believed in any of that stuff. And I know how ridiculous it all sounds, and you may want to have me fitted for a straitjacket, but gentlemen, believe me. It happened. And I think this is the time I need to bring it out and you're the people I know I can tell my supernatural story to without ridicule. We have to be ready to face things that maybe we don't want to believe are real. Now if that is only one aspect of what people practicing sorcery can do that concerns me. I mean, some of these gang members study and practice and practically live the occult, especially *The Last Order* gang. I hear they are really steeped in the *Dark Arts*. Now, imagine these gangs combining their numbers and powers to commit some sort of crime, some sort of really huge crime."

Burney suggested another possibility.

"Or maybe just uniting to commit a series of crimes of all sorts in different countries."

Chang cleared his throat and glanced at Jacob. He lit a cigar and spat out the smoke.

"You know, if I had not gone through the mess I've recently gone through, I'd think you are surely losing it talking about all this magic stuff and vampires and the like. But I believe you. I really do. I don't know how this stuff works but I know some weird things are going on and they're real. And like you, Usata, I've been witness to things that no science or reason can explain. He looked at Jacob.

For the next several minutes there is an uneasy quiet in the room. Onanoka is quieting his nerves with bourbon after recounting his encounter with one of the students from *The Shadow School*. Burney is rubbing the chill bumps on his arms and Chang is turning over in his mind what Onanoka has just related to them and how he is aware that sorcery and magic not only exist but that they affect the physical world.

Colonel Burney broke the momentary awkward silence:

"Well, since Usata here has broached the subject of the supernatural, and since we're being real, this is as good a time as any for me to finish telling Jacob about that special department in the NYPD that I promised he'd fit well into. It's a covert operation that's only whispered about among a few police officers in New York. The unit is named 'The Bureau For Special and Unusual Occurrences,' and they deal with strange matters identical to what we're dealing with here: magic, Vodou, the occult, sorcery, Brujeria; you know, that Twilight Zone, or X-Files stuff. That incident you just shared with us would be right down their alley. Anyway, I've already contacted Adelfried Jaegar. He's the one who created and is in charge of that unit. Jennings he's looking forward to meeting you when you get back. You're to report to him directly when you return to the police force in New York. Just wanted to put that out there for you, Jennings."

"Great. I look forward to meeting with him." Jacob turned to Chang. "Chief Inspector Chang is going to be with me. We're going to continue the *cherry berry* investigation in New York."

Burney smiled and shook Chang's hand.

"Good. Welcome aboard, Inspector Chang, I know that Jaeger will more than welcome you along with Jennings. And I don't think it's going to take long before both of you become fast friends. It sure didn't take me long." He looked at Onanoka. "I've seen documented, incontrovertible proof on film of things that would make what you saw with those two girls look like an everyday stroll in a children's park."

Onanoka smiled at his friend Burney. He certainly felt much better now. He poured another round of drinks, took a short sip of his own and then leaned back in his chair with a relieved sigh. But he is still worried about Jacob being in Japan with Desirlee still likely to kill him on sight or use her sorcery on him and anyone with him Someone knocked at the door. Onanoka knew it is his secretary.

"Come in, Miss Yokashira."

A young Asian woman entered the office, bowed to Onanoka, then to everyone else. She handed Onanoka a slip of paper then quickly exited.

Onanoka read the note and abruptly walks over to his window. He stood there a moment frowning. Then he turns around.

"You gentlemen might want to come and take a look at this."

They all group together at the large picture window wondering what Onanoka is looking at below. What they see is an incredible sight: a large group of young men and women, easily over one hundred strong seated on the sidewalk staring up at Onanoka's window.

All of them are sitting with their palms turned upward as though in a yoga position. When they saw Onanoka at the window, one young man who is sitting in the middle of them, clasps his hands together.

When he slowly pulls them apart and holds them skywards, a wide, bright black and white flame erupted from the center of each of his hands; every several seconds, a very wide orange flame jettisoned upward several feet in the air from the center of the constantly flaming palms.

And when the other seated men and women did the same, their palms also erupted in the black and white flames rising upwards from their palms, but none of their palms has an orange flame appear in the center of their palms. He difference in color is, Jacob imagines, a matter of ranking.

A large crowd of curious onlookers who have gathered, gasp loudly, taking care to remain a safe distance from the seated young men and women. Also a large group of uniformed police officers are standing nearby, watching the seated young people. The officers are looking up at Onanoka's window waiting to get a signal from him as to what action they should take. He shook his head at them, waving his hand to indicate that the officers should not get involved at this point.

Onanoka looked at Jacob.

"Jennings, do you see anyone you know down there?"

Jacob immediately recognizes Desirlee, the young woman who imprisoned him in "*The Dream*" her home. He pointed to her.

"That's Desirlee in the middle there."

Onanoka nods.

"It is. And the young man next to her, the only one with orange flames shooting high from his palms, is Etsiow Suyoshi Yuuta, leader of *The Last Order* gang. This business happening here is important in some way, though I have no idea how. But as I think I've mentioned, Desirlee is the gang's war Contessa and very rarely shows herself in public during the day. Usually when you see her during daylight it means trouble. So for someone this business means trouble. And I'm guessing that someone is us."

Chang wonders:

"So are these different gangs we're looking at down there?"

Burney shook his head slowly.

"No, Inspector, these are all from one gang and many of them are not present. These are all members of *The Last Order* gang, and only a small fraction of their membership at that. Their members number over a thousand. How many exactly we don't know yet."

Sometime later, a young female stood. She took a few steps toward Onanoka's building and held her hands up, the fire still burning in her palms. She shoved her hands upward in Onanoka's direction and the flames from her palms jetted upwards and bounced off his window.

After a moment, she claps her hands together smartly and the flames from her palms are extinguished. Then she walks away. Then each seated person, one at a time, stands and repeats the young girl's actions precisely. This process takes almost an hour until there are only two people remaining: Desirlee and Yuuta, both of whom slowly rise in tandem.

For a very long moment, they stood glaring up at Onanoka's window. Yuuta is watching Onanoka but Desirlee's eyes are locked on Jacob; the two remained staring up as the flames in their palms never once flicker or weaken in any manner.

Then they very slowly ball their open palms into fists, and their hands immediately burst into wide torches of red, orange and blue flames. Then, with a quick swipe through the air of their balled up, flaming fists, the flames are suddenly extinguished. They both then point an accusing finger at Onanoka as the two of them screaming in unison:

"And so you have seen and thus have been warned!"

Yuuta and Desirlee walk away but not before she turns back and looks at Jacob, slowly deforming her smile into something cruel and threatening.

In Onanoka's office, everyone is still standing at his window in complete awe of what they have just seen moments before on the sidewalk is bare.

Inspector Chang is the most moved, and he emits a thin, incredulous gasp:

"They just clapped their hands together and their palms burst out in flames—but the flames are white and black fire. But there is no such flame color in fire! And they are all just sitting there with their palms afire at least a foot or so high!" He turns to Onanoka. "What the hell are we dealing with here?"

Chang still found it difficult to come to grips with what they had all just witnessed; he even found it difficult to form a question:

"But, how…" He could not find the words. "I mean, I know about sorcery, but—! And did you see that expression on her face? I've never seen such a beautiful young woman's face turn into such an evil thing—thing is how I have to describe what her face became down there for a moment when she was looking up here! And unless I'm wrong, she seemed to be looking at—."

Chang did not want to finish his sentence. But Onanoka finished it for him in case Jacob has, somehow, not seen Desirlee's intent.

"Yes. She was fixated on Jennings. We know why. That's why it was dangerous for him to remain in Japan before and possibly even more now. That's why we sent him back to his unit and asked them to consider allowing him to join you in Hong Kong. But now he is back. And the worse of it is Desirlee is aware that he is back. Now we must decide what is best for his safety."

Onanoka turned away from the window and took a deep breath.

Burney lights his pipe:

"So it seems it is going to happen after all, this business with these gangs converging." Jacob is studying Onanoka's concerned expression.:

Onanoka nods:

"It certainly looks like it. If that business down there wasn't an out and out threat, then I don't know what it was. They're ready for some kind of move, otherwise, they would never have thrown down the gauntlet the way they just did. Earlier my secretary informed me that according to some reliable sources, many gangs have recently arrived here in Tokyo from the other countries for this big meeting." He turns to Jacob. "Including your gang, *The Chinese Blood*. These gangs are all set to convene their summit."

But Onanoka and Burney have their suspicions about the gangs merging but nothing concrete. But they have grown aware of the gangs' prerequisite of having to be involved in the occult to be properly recruited.

Onanoka says:

"I guess what our informants tell us is true that the big meeting is for the purpose of uniting as many gangs as is possible to do some kind of work with Dr. Cheung's new product, distribution or something. Inspector Chang and I enjoyed a long discussion before you guys left to get here. It appears that the good Dr. Cheung is somehow financially involved with these gangs; he has, according to our sources, provided them with living quarters somewhere in Tokyo. Jacob I want you to know that Colonel Burney, Inspector Chang and I have had a long and rather unusual conversation about your revelation I guess is a good enough term for what you say you discovered in Hong Kong with Dr. Cheung; at least what he told you about the purpose of *cherry berry* being a synthetic blood designed for vampires."

Onanoka rearranges himself in his chair and says:

"That is one reason why I came forward about those young girls walking the rooftops. Even then it was a most difficult thing for me to recount much less admit to being real and telling anyone about it. Now, that together with what we have all just witnessed, well to me the idea of vampires is not quite so ridiculous; and maybe not quite as scary as those gang members we're going to be doing some kind of battle with."

Chang looks out the window and lights a cigar, shaking his head slowly from side to side as he considers what he has just witnessed and trying to tie it all together. He is no longer surprised at the magic but he is impressed by the suggested power of those who use it.

Onanoka knows the situation is growing dire and so he says:

"It looks as though we are going to be facing quite a battle here. I don't know how effective guns are going to be. Lieutenant Jennings, I'm going to need you to give me every bit of information you have on this *cherry berry* before you leave for the States. Yes, I'm going to request that your unit, due to safety concerns, reassign you immediately to the States. Of course, at this moment, our battle is not going to be with the *cherry berry* or its creator, Dr. Cheung." Onanoka looked out the window and seemed to become lost in his thoughts. "Our fight is going to be against gangs who are consolidating not simply their numbers but also their magic. But we have to get Jennings out of the country first. Desirlee's first order of business might be killing him. So our first order of business has to be getting him to America immediately before she can formulate a strategy to do that."

Chang and Jacob looked at each other. Chang feels it is up to him to let Onanoka and Burney know the full story about Jacob. There could be no more perfect time than this moment to do that. Chang stood, cleared his throat and looked at his cigar.

"Gentlemen we can't let Jennings leave the country now. Well, the fact is we need to ask him to stay and help us with this battle. You don't know everything you need to know about Jennings here. We need him more than any other person—more than anybody in this room or in this country. He's our only source for magic. He's the only one here who can wield magic and use it against the gangs."

Now Onanoka and Burney looked at each other neither having any idea what Chang could possibly mean. They are wondering just what Chang is referring to and they are paying rapt attention to his every word.

"I'm going to explain to you what was explained to me, guys. The story is not too long but it is intriguing." He smiled at Jacob. "And it's the story of a man and his magic. *The Chinese Blood* members call him Jacob The Jew. I think a more appropriate name would be Jacob the Sorcerer. Have a seat and I'll regale you with some amazing facts about our Lieutenant Jacob Jennings here.

BRIEFING ONANOKA

An hour later Onanoka, Burney, Chang and Jacob are still seated at Onanoka's office table having just finished listening to Chang explain the events about Ginger using her magic against Baofung and subsequently Jacob using his in his hotel room including the demise of Mrs. Che.

Jacob takes the opportunity to fill in everyone, including Chang, on his years of instruction from his grandmother and his magic and other occult associations. After Jacob's revelations about his upbringing, even Chang is awe struck. After all is said, the men sit at the table in quiet contemplation.

Now Onanoka realizes that he does, indeed, need Jacob's magic; and maybe that he can uses his magic to protect himself from Desirlee and the gangs. He no longer has to worry about Jacob's safety, instead he is glad to have him aboard able to use his magic in the coming battle between them and the gangs.

The discussion at the table turned to what they all needed to do concerning the gangs in Tokyo. It is clear that they must find out where the gangs are staying and the most important thing to determine is what the gangs are actually here for.

Although no one has voiced it, they all seem more relaxed knowing that they have some magic on their side to do battle with the gangs. Onanoka knew the tremendous task set before them. Ideally, he knew that they needed to find a means of locking up the leaders of the gangs on charges that would imprison them for lengthy terms, hoping that would disrupt all present matters and maybe lead to the gangs returning to simpler gang activities.

Onanoka cleared his throat:

"This is all so hard to come to grips with. Think about it. Here we are trying to figure out a way to stop ruthless gangs from increasing their membership to numbers that may possibly be unmanageable by any local police authority and that's just for openers. Secondly these gangs are going to be comprised of thugs from different countries so none of them are on our watch list so we have no idea what they look like, we know only that they are organizing here in Japan. And I believe that they're already here. And just how did they get here? I'd say they're being sponsored by Dr. Cheung. That's a moot point now."

Jacob wondered:

"But what use would gangs to be to a person as sophisticated as Cheung?"

Onanoka shook his head:

"Maybe distribution I've heard."

Burney was not sure about the gangs being used for anything covertly illegal:

"I dunno about that. Usually anybody doing illegal activities wants to remain hidden or incognito. They prefer concealment, certainly not publicity."

Jacob has another point

"They usually don't want to be known unless they know that there is nothing that anyone can do to stop them. They could be in such a powerful position that no one can touch them."

Chang sums it up:

"The fact is that we can sit here and conjecture all day and into the night and the next day and we still will be at first base with this thing. We are not going to know what they are going to do until it's done. But… and I can't believe I'm saying this…I think the thing to do to find out is to have someone infiltrate their ranks. Unfortunately we don't have anyone in my small department that can accomplish that; the gangs already know my people."

Onanoka shook his head and takes out a bottle of brandy from a cabinet and places it and several glasses on the round table.

"You're right, sir. Now, in the meantime, help yourself gentlemen. Pour your own troubles and let's relax here and give this entire problem another reconsideration."

Jacob offers his opinion:

"I'm pretty sure that was meant to put a scare into everyone. Sir, I don't mean to be a wise guy or anything like that but maybe it wouldn't hurt to include classes on things like certain religions that use supernatural or at least unnatural means as part of their practice."

Burney agrees:

"That makes sense to me. That way, when something like this comes up, it doesn't seem like something that comes out of Hollywood or comic books. After all, police Departments as far as I am aware, don't teach about sorcerers or witches and do not take either subject very seriously."

Onanoka thought about it.

"Well...maybe. But on that same line of thought, just how do I explain to my superiors the reason we want to get these gangs is because they are likely going to form part of a blood delivery service of synthetic blood to some vampires in New York. That is not going to be an easy sell to my superiors. I can't go with the vampire thing—that's not an option, but I can say this tainted blood can possibly be integrated into any country's blood supply system and cause a pandemic. I'll argue that they just might start here in Japan. Then my superiors will say, 'We hope you're not talking about that cherry berry business that Dr. Cheung was being persecuted for by that Inspector Chang in Hong Kong, are you? We hope you're not talking about that particular synthetic blood.' No, this whole business is a problem no matter which angle we look at it from."

CHAPTER 42

OUT OF
NOWHERE

And so, with his fists clenched and his brow furrowed, he concentrated with every ounce of his ability to find a way to create intense anger; this causes his inner focus to become so astonishingly intense that it changed the sweat dripping from his forehead causing it to cascade in a torrential manner.

Then the wall of Onanoka's office began trembling violently, possibly on the verge of reducing itself to powder; and the floor suddenly warped and became unsteady, shifting back and forth underfoot seemingly only seconds from disassembling itself.

Jacob closed his eyes and immediately his mind created an eclectic panorama of strange, and peculiar symbols and images rushing about madly, all the while displaying oddly shaped letters, uncovering areas of his thoughts he has never known to exist; he is fascinated by the parade of such strange, unusual symbols totally foreign to him that he has never seen and could not begin to understand and yet for some reason he felt a vague familiarity with everything he is seeing.

He senses that the *veil* is divulging itself to him, revealing that it existed within his body and releasing all its secrets. The feeling of acquiring this knowledge is a sensation he has never felt before; he sensed, somehow, that the *veil* understood his desperate need for it at this moment, and he wondered if what he is experiencing is a prelude to the veil assaulting his present adversary and he hopes that he is petitioning it in the proper manner.

Onanoka, Burney and Chang, all on tenterhooks, are staring, aghast, at him, while trying to fathom Jacob's unusual behavior. They all imagined that in some way all this has something to do with magic; but, since they are unable to see the impending danger in the room, they are totally confused as to the reason he is using magic or preparing to do so.

Jacob opens his eyes when he feels a sudden freezing cold tense his body and cause him to shudder. Seconds later his body locks as an icy, bitterness starts to network through his body. Now, feeling great strength beginning to surge, he feels sure that he has successfully summoned a *veil* power.

But then Jacob's eyes involuntarily slam shut, startling him as he beheld the vision of a red, mushroomed cloud and slowly from within this crimson image, what appears to be death masks floating towards him; slowly, one by one, the red cloud releases thirteen death masks of men Jacob did not recognize, but each mask the cloud issued, hovered horizontally before him.

He tries to open his eyes but they remain closed as did the eyes of each mask. Next came more symbols flashing now at quantum speeds, but this time not beyond his vision's ability to grasp each symbol, leaving cerebral imprints somewhere in his thoughts as to the means of using and summoning this *veil* magic. Full knowledge of the mechanics of all of his *veil* powers and how to use them to full advantage are now his.

And now, as he is again able to open his eyes, he begins to quickly formulate a means to end the present threat that has begun hissing loudly as it nears accomplishing its goal of escaping from the wall. Jacob raises his hand in the direction of the rejected *shadow deschong* whose unrequited love for him has transformed her once tentative beauty into an unnervingly horrific mask of contorted evil.

But then, with a final, furious and obviously agonizing twist, she manages to rip herself free from the wall imprisonment; however, in the process of doing so, she left behind her on the wall, a wide swath of her flesh still pulsing, bloodied and trembling on the wall's surface and then this move causes her to become suddenly visible to everyone in the room.

Then, before Jacob can speak or act, the *shadow deschong*, energized by what must have been all of hell's fury she can command in her throat— screams a shriek of such uncanny horror and power that the stunning noise shatters the office windows and momentarily stuns the breathing of Onanoka, Burney and Chang.

In the blur of an instant the *shadow deschong* pounces on Jacob. Her thickly taloned fingers dig deeply into his chest. Her bleeding torso seems to be undergoing a wretched ecstasy of pain as her black, pointed teeth ripped at his neck with horribly fierce dedication, instantly causing his flesh to wither and decay until he is reduced to a pile of ashes at the *shadow deschong's* feet.

She glances down at the ashes not affording Jacob's remains not evidencing even a nanosecond of any possible remorse, she turns to Onanoka, Burney and Chang who remain petrified by the horrific scene they have just witnessed.

The *shadow deschong's* features display what each man thought to be a kind of pleasurable anticipation of the horrific death she planned for each of them. The office door begins to slowly open as Onanoka's secretary's face peeks in from around the door as she inquires:

"Sir, is everything—!"

The *shadow deschong* grabs a thick mahogany table as though it is weightless and slams it against the door which in turn crunched into the secretary and her body thuds loudly from the collision that leaves her lifeless and she collapses to the floor outside the office.

Onanoka pulls his weapon and fires four rounds into the *shadow deschong*. She freezes in place, her back with its separated flesh still attached to the wall came alive, its muscles and an intricate networking of fibrous nerves torn veins began a macabre "dance" as the blood of her exposed back seems almost to be percolating as it rushed up and around her deformed spinal cord sputtering out bursts of sprayed blood during the course of its terrible convoluted journey to her front to seal the bullet wounds, bullets that that now energize her as her head snaps around to glare at Onanoka.

She spins about and angrily begins ambling towards them all, glaring at Onanoka. Her features have become even more hideous, more horrendously distorted and she utters some indistinct sound of angst as she struggles with each step.

Hissing noises come from between her slightly parted lips, and she appears to be writhing in what Onanoka judged must be unfathomable pain from the flesh that is ripped from her back.

Then when she is within reach of him, her mouth stretches open in a wretched, grotesque yawn, her rancid breath flush against his face, producing a putrid odor that Onanoka feels may be capable of stealing the very air from his lungs.

She moves still closer to Onanoka as her open mouth reveals three rows of yellowish, pointed teeth. Her gurgling becomes louder and a slimy, reddish brown froth rises in her mouth and spills over her three rows of teeth and her black mouth; then a thick, undulating tongue languidly accompanying the froth, slides up from the depths of some horribly hidden place inside her throat as though not to be left out of this diabolical visual assault. |The shadow deschong's throat begins throbbing as it spreads terribly wide with throbbing, bleeding sores that slowly pierce her flesh there and open to become eyes that busily blink while scanning the faces of Onanoka, Burney and Chang.

Onanoka releases a gasp of surprise as a thick, green tongue now rises from the rear of her throat, insinuating itself over her teeth, sliding across the slime that now overflows from her mouth, coating her thick, bulbous lips. Then, like a huge snake waiting for the first victim to move before it strikes, the shadow deschong begins to sway from side to side as her tongue whips about, lashing to within inches of each man's face.

It is then the men see there is a tiny human head dangling from the tip of the *shadow deschong's* tongue; the gaunt features of the Lilliputian's head is frozen in terror but its mouth is open and moving but soundlessly, obviously begging the men for rescue. And though no words are being issued through the head's trembling lips, its eyes leave no doubt as to its state of desperation and together they frantically continue their indecipherable pleas soliciting deliverance.

A leaden lament weighs heavily into the hearts of each man, all of them fearing that the head doubtlessly is that of Jacob's and so there passes a communal second of sorrow for him. And finally, the *shadow deschong*, allowing that each man's focus is on her tongue, languidly withdraws it into her mouth, and hovering over the desperate, animated human head, her pointed teeth—abruptly crunch down exploding the pleading head into a spray of blood.

Onanoka, Burney and Chang are frozen in awe by the horror of it all, gasp in tandem. No one in the room, not even the *shadow deschong* takes notice that ...

... Jacob's ashes have burst into bright red flames...and something is rising from them.

EXIT...